THE LAST TELEGRAM OF MRS HUDSON

A LADY HOLMES AND HUDSON INVESTIGATION

THE LAST TELEGRAM OF MRS HUDSON

MATTEA ORR

HEAD of ZEUS

An Aries Book

First published in the UK in 2026 by Head of Zeus,
part of Bloomsbury Publishing Plc

9 7 5 3 1 2 4 6 8

A catalogue record for this book is available from the British Library.

ISBN (PB): 9781035926510
ISBN (eBook): 9781035926527

Cover design: Gemma Gorton | Head of Zeus

Typeset by Lumina Datamatics Ltd
Printed and bound in Great Britain by Clays Ltd, Elcograf S.p.A.

MIX
Paper | Supporting responsible forestry
FSC® C018072

Bloomsbury Publishing Plc
50 Bedford Square, London, WC1B 3DP, UK
Bloomsbury Publishing Ireland Limited,
29 Earlsfort Terrace, Dublin 2, D02 AY28, Ireland

HEAD OF ZEUS LTD
5–8 Hardwick Street
London, EC1R 4RG

To find out more about our authors and books
visit www.headofzeus.com
For product safety related questions contact productsafety@bloomsbury.com

*To my parents, for having the best bookshelf,
and to my husband and his vasectomy, for giving me
the inspiration to write this book*

Historical Note

Some sharp-eyed and dedicated readers will notice a discrepancy between the most widely presumed birthdate of Sherlock Holmes (1854) and the age of young Sherlock in this series. First, well done! The game is afoot! If you spied that, then you're in for a delightful time of spotting all sorts of nods and winks hidden in here toward the ever-expanding Sherlock canon.

Second, though these stories are a reimagining, I'm hardly the first author to alter Sherlock's birthdate or the facts of his life in the pursuit of telling a good story (I'd assert even Dr. Watson indulged in that from time to time). Interestingly, the one original Arthur Conan Doyle story that mentions Sherlock's age, *His Last Bow*, only does so in reference to Sherlock undercover as an Irish American mechanic, "...a tall, gaunt man of sixty." But we all know how skilled Sherlock was with a disguise. Thus, it seemed more correct to play with Sherlock's age than the real historical events around which my stories are based.

If you decide to keep reading, and I sincerely hope you do, then you'll discover the origins of Sherlock's famous disguise skills and so much more. I can only offer to make up for any discrepancies from the original stories by being as scrupulously attentive to the facts of the era as faithfully as I can.*

* Except in the matter of the solar eclipse. Did you know there were no total solar eclipses visible in the United Kingdom from 1724–1925? *Because I did not.* A fact as inconvenient to astronomers of the time as it is to novelists who had a clever plan to include one. Sorry, I made that one up. But it was worth it.

It linked all perplexéd meanings
Into one perfect peace,
And trembled away into silence
As if it were loth to cease.

"A Lost Chord"—Adelaide Anne Proctor

Chapter One

FOR THE LAST SIX MONTHS, I WAS THE GHOST THAT haunted the small town of Sherrinford. Sweeping around corners in my black dress and veil, even the bustle of a market day amid the sun-soaked blossoms of spring couldn't chase me out. At least not before I accomplished what I came here to do.

As if to illustrate the point, a woman with a cart of bouquets trundled by the carpenter's stall where we stood waiting. Was it my imagination or did she hold her breath until she was past?

"Katy, is *H* four dots or is *V* four dots? I can never remember," my brother Oliver asked in the reedy voice he'd used ever since his sickness this winter. We were at the bottom of his last bottle of medicine and had no money to pay for more.

At the hem of my skirts, seven-year-old Oliver, his twin sister Louise, and our youngest sibling, Rosie, translated the Morse Code I'd scratched onto the cobblestones. Georgie and Ralph, the eldest of my younger brothers, were both at work today, while Ma and my sister Elizabeth shopped for food.

"Four dots for *H*, Ollie," Louise said. Since Oliver's illness, she'd taken to filling in for her twin whenever she could, completing his chores or finishing his sentences. "Because it looks like a hare hopping."

"I saw a rabbit yesterday. He went like this," Rosie said as she leaped up to demonstrate the mnemonic. She promptly tripped and tumbled into Louise with a squeal of protest. This was only differentiated from her usual shrieks because it was muffled by Louise's skirts. Rosie was five and, as such, believed the world belonged to her. And with nearly twenty years between us, I was inclined to give the littlest what she wanted.

I disentangled the girls and ran a fond hand over their dark curls, childish copies of my own. "Yes, Louise. And *V* is three dots and a dash because it gets *very* long at the end."

The carpenter, Mr. Monroe, looked up from applying glue to the frame of my slate and smiled at us. Ordinarily, I would've given them their lessons on becoming first-rate telegraph operators at home, because at least there, no one judged me for the odd fit of tears. I even snuck in lessons for Ralph when I could convince him to listen to me. So, rarely.

However, the frame was loose on the slate John had given me as a present when he taught me Morse Code, and it needed to be glued back together, lest the stone slip out and break. That was the first task I'd come to market to accomplish, the work of a few moments and pennies. I had plenty of the first and never enough of the latter.

That was the object of my second task—to scour the town's grapevine for news of anyone desperate enough to offer me employment.

I pretended to study Mr. Monroe's handiwork. "You've been doing a brisk business this morning. It must be hard to attend to your books and your carpentry projects all at once. If you need a bookkeeper, I have extremely legible handwriting."

He gave me another smile, this one apologetic as he'd no doubt heard me ask the costermonger in the stall next to him if he needed a bookkeeper. "Ah, I'm lucky there. My missus is a dab hand at the books."

"Have you perhaps heard of anyone else looking for accounting help?" I asked with hope I didn't feel.

"Sorry, ma'am. Nothing. But I'll keep an ear out."

I swallowed the familiar taste of failure, sending it to lie heavy and hot in my stomach. There. At least I'd tried again. The problem with living like a ghost was that, of the positions available to women in the town, no one wanted me scaring away their customers. I cast a pall over all except the most somber transactions. Even if I'd arrived attired in a shimmering party dress, my grief was written across my face and my heart, clear for all to see.

Perhaps the local undertakers needed a model?

The job I truly wanted sat just out of my reach. My eyes once again found the swoops of the telegraph lines running parallel to the railway tracks along the eastern edge of the town. In the six months since John's death, I'd inquired no less than seven times for employment in the small telegraph office attached to the rear of the railway station. Once every thirty days, and an extra time when Eli Yardley, their young clerk, tripped over his dog and broke his wrist. However, they would rather have a man with a broken wrist sending five words a minute than a person who could send three times that but do so wearing a skirt.

I located a scrap of wood from Mr. Monroe's work and pulled out John's pocket watch, one of his few possessions I didn't have to sell in London before returning to Sussex. Sherrinford had exactly zero pawn shops. Watching the second hand, I fluttered my wrist against the side of the carpenter's stall. Each strike of my imaginary telegraph key was perfectly timed. No clips. No drags. The precision of my dots flawless, wings of the damselfly. The halt of my dashes a mere hitch in the breath. Just as John had instructed me.

Today, it only took me thirteen seconds to tell John I loved him.

If I closed my eyes, I could believe he stood just behind me, encouraging hands on my shoulders—warm, alive, and forever reliable.

I never closed my eyes.

Thirteen seconds exactly. Before I left London and the Post Office, I'd worked my way up to fifteen words a minute. A solid second-class telegraph operator, I'd been near the top of the women in the office. John was first-class, the quickest in his row. At a blinding thirty-five words a minute, he could nearly spell *lightning* faster than the bolt that killed him.

I turned my back on the telegraph lines and cast away the scrap of wood with a sigh. There was one establishment near Sherrinford where I could find a job, where I would fit in perfectly because I was born there. But I wasn't that desperate. Not yet. However, after yesterday's letter from the local building society reminding us we were several months late on our mortgage and in danger of losing our cottage, I would soon be desperate enough.

"Here you are, Mrs. Hudson," Mr. Monroe said as he handed me the slate, once again secure in its frame.

I reached for my reticule, but he waved a hand at me and shook his head. "No charge, ma'am."

"Oh, but I thought—"

"It's a fine morning to be doing my work out of doors, and t'was nothing but a bit of glue. You take care of the young ones, now. The lad's looking peaky."

With six months of practice, five years in truth, my cheeks barely flushed when one of our neighbors offered us such charity. As though it were made up of dots and dashes, I translated his pity into something everyone else wanted to see: my gratitude.

I gathered up the children and headed to the other side of the market. "Come on, you three, let's go help Ma and Elizabeth," I said, tugging Rosie's hand away from the ears of an ancient stray sheepdog that, much like us, often lived off the charity of Sherrinford.

Ma rose earlier and earlier these days, taking care of the chores, stuffing me with food, trying to avoid speaking about John. About my loss. One she knew all too well. Today I'd risen before dawn, determined she shouldn't have to shoulder my portion of the household any longer, but she was already awake. At least as we worked, side by side to save on fuel, we both stole a moment of peace. Eight people living in a cottage no bigger than four market stalls jammed together competed with the clatter of the telegraph offices of the London Post Office at the stroke of noon. With its whitewashed walls and low ceiling, it could never be more than humble, but it would soon belong to us outright. At least it would if I secured a job so we could continue the mortgage payments. It was a wonder we'd even been able to afford our own cottage in the first place except for a generous gift from Ma and Da's former employer. Blood money.

I scooted the children across the street, but Oliver's breathing grew a little too loud. He would've forged ahead, but I stopped with a hand raised. "Oh, I almost forgot. First one to tell me what the message said earns themself my bread at tea today."

Louise and Rosie hid smiles as they pretended to whisper to each other. Children loved a secret. They were old hands at this game now, tricking Oliver into eating portions of our food he wouldn't touch otherwise. The dear thing would cry, saying he didn't want us to go hungry for his sake. He had a great streak of fairness in him that I could only hope the world wouldn't snuff out. One he displayed now.

"Katy, they're cheating." Oliver's wan cheeks reddened unevenly.

"Then you'd best hurry," I said.

He bit his lip and looked up, squinting. "Um, I think it's: 'Katherine Hudson loves every Bunting. Even when Ralph is obnoxious.'"

The girls giggled, and Oliver smiled, but then he piped up, "Did you know Ralph cut off work—"

"Star pupil!" I cried. The last thing Ralph and I needed was another wedge between us. I'd ask Georgie if Ralph had trouble at work and let him handle it. "Double bread for Oliver. And an extra story tonight for all my—" The children were too busy cheering to notice, but my words clicked off as though someone had thrown a switch. I could see what they couldn't.

Behind them, Inspector Goodwin marched Ralph down the street, one giant hand clamped onto his thin shoulder.

CHAPTER TWO

INSPECTOR GOODWIN'S CHESTNUT WHISKERS wagged as he spoke to Ralph, but the noise from the market's crowd ate up their words. I stepped in front of Oliver, Louise, and Rosie, who must have caught the seriousness of the situation, because even she quieted. Or perhaps she was just impressed by Inspector Goodwin's impeccable blue uniform and polished silver buttons. I was hardly immune to them myself.

By contrast, Ralph's dirty collar and scuffed boots were accompanied by the distinct reek of horse dung. He'd left in clean clothes this morning, so he must have already been to The Four Hounds where he worked odd jobs, mostly in the stables. Unsurprisingly, Ralph wouldn't meet my eye. Even if he hadn't been escorted by the highest-ranking police officer for miles, he would have pretended at being a man twice his fifteen years. One who needed advice from no one, least of all his sister. Ma had been so ill after Ralph was born that much of his care fell to Georgie and me, so the three of us grew up as a close trio. Since I'd left with

John for London three years ago, though, Ralph barely spoke to me.

Next to the towering inspector, Ralph looked even younger than fifteen. "You look like you need saving," I said, trying to keep the irritation from my voice. Three brothers deep, I was an expert on how often boys needed help out of one scrape or another.

"Mrs. Hudson?" Inspector Goodwin asked, his wide mouth firm but his tone kind.

It wasn't a question of whether he recognized me. Reggie Goodwin had been my fourth kiss, and several kisses after that. His sister Annabelle had been my first three. He harbored a fond memory of our past acquaintance, and I'd been avoiding his offers of courtship since I returned to Sherrinford. Now, his question was clear: was I finally ready to be something more than Mrs. Hudson to him?

"Is something wrong, Inspector?" I asked.

"Not at all." His voice remained normal, but his grip on Ralph's shoulder had drained the color from my brother's face. "Can we speak privately?"

My cheeks flushed. Inspector Goodwin's dark gray eyes, though still serious, sparkled under the shadow cast by the narrow brim of his hat.

"Of course," I said, but glanced down at Oliver, Louise, and Rosie.

Inspector Goodwin held up the twist of paper in his free hand. "I've just visited the baker, and the children can have a bun while we talk."

We made our way to the edge of the green not far from a group of children laughing and shouting as they evaded the grasp of a tall girl wearing a blindfold. Inspector Goodwin and I settled in the dappled grass and handed out buns as I tucked the repaired slate in beside me. Yeasty and warm, I salivated as soon as the bun landed in my palm. I'd hidden most of my eggs and sausages on Oliver's plate at breakfast this morning, and so my stomach pinched now.

"Ralph, why don't the four of you take your buns onto the green to watch the children play blind man's buff?" Inspector Goodwin instructed.

Ralph, still avoiding my eyes, shepherded the young ones away.

I watched them go. If only George were here right now, he could talk sense into Ralph. "Thank you for the buns," I said after they were out of earshot.

Inspector Goodwin handed me his own bun as well. "For Oliver," he murmured. "And you can thank Ralph." He pressed his lips together at my inquisitive look and sighed. "I hate to be the one to do this, but I caught Ralph stealing these from the baker's stall."

The bun's floury surface left a fine grit on my black gloves, and I also tucked mine back into the twist of paper. "Ralph wouldn't steal. Surely there's a mistake."

"He walked away without paying. There's no mistake. I'm sorry, Katy."

The use of my first name squeezed an uneasy breath from my lungs. The inspector held power in this town, so he could speak to me like I was a child or a prospect. I stuffed the paper twist with its purloined buns into my reticule. Oliver desperately needed to put on weight, and we were all hungry.

Still, I had to ask. "How much do I owe you for the buns, Inspector?"

He frowned, pulling the bottoms of his long ears below his whiskers. "I'd give much more than the price of a few buns to hear you call me by my name."

My heart fluttered into my throat. This was why I was here. Sure, I tutored my siblings in telegraphy so they could find work and rise above merely surviving. But that wouldn't last forever. This moment right now was why I left the job I loved and all the memories of my life with John far away in London. This was what awaited me. It was the best I could hope for.

I breathed deep enough to cleanse the heated words from my tongue and soothe the ache in my chest. Then I gripped the frame of the slate beside me and put on a smile.

"Thank you, Reggie. For the buns and for what you did for Ralph. He's a good lad, but I don't know what's in his head lately. He took it hard when I moved to London."

"I can't say I blame him." Reggie removed his tall cap and placed it between us on the grass. The heavy scent of his soap lingered in my nose.

I hadn't meant to admit so much to him, but more often than not my feelings came boiling out of my mouth.

"The boy needs a man's influence in his life. And I'm sure you need someone to talk to about everything," Reggie added. His gaze took in my dress—a neat ensemble without embellishment, it had been dyed black like the rest of my wardrobe following John's death.

I couldn't help but see we looked like a family out picnicking on market day. So would anyone else who noticed us. Shortly after, small towns being what they were, everyone in Sherrinford would have heard.

Not trusting myself to speak again yet, I nodded.

"Annabelle's in town visiting my mother. We would love to have you over for tea. I could pick you up tomorrow afternoon?"

Louise and Rosie had joined the other children at their game, but Ralph sat beside Oliver whose breathing problems prevented him from running. How would I ever keep them all safe?

I tapped out the word *courage* against my thigh to settle the last of my nerves, turned to Reggie, and smiled. "I haven't seen Annabelle in years. That would be lovely."

"Excellent. I'll tell Mother to expect us." Reggie stood and held out his hand to help me up. I took it.

He brushed off his uniform, bade me farewell, then sauntered across the green, stopping for a quick word with Ralph. I simmered in place, but as soon as Reggie was out of sight, I strode over to my brothers and snagged Ralph by the collar.

"Ralph Bunting, what on earth were you thinking?"

He scrambled to his feet, but then so did Oliver, staring up at us with eyes as big as empty bowls. Ralph's brow pinched. He glanced at Oliver then back at me and shook his head. Damn everything. He was right. Oliver didn't need to hear his brother had turned into a thief. And none of us needed him reporting it back to Ma. I cursed my loose tongue and fumbled for some excuse.

"It's not even noon and look at you. The state of your collar." I swiped at a long streak of something brown there.

"Leave the bossing to the Queen, Katy." He knocked my hand away, but not before giving me a grateful look. "Billy's scarpered, so we're short a hand at the inn."

Furious as I was with Ralph, his statement snagged my attention. Billy was the only surviving son of Ma's cousin Frances, and she kept a tight rein on him. "Billy's left for where?"

"Only to his da's in Eastbourne. He's fifteen now, same as me—we can do as we like."

I'd backed away from Ralph, but Oliver inserted himself between us as though sensing the fight we weren't quite having. "Frances says he's run away and broke her heart," Oliver said.

"Enough of your fancy tales!" Ralph said with a scowl.

"I heard her tell Ma!"

Ralph grabbed for Oliver's ear, and I reached out my arms to stop him. "Boys!"

His sleeve hooked on the slate clutched in my hand. It flew across the green and smashed into the trunk of a tree. The fragile inner surface cracked from top to bottom with the *snap* of breaking bone. The boys froze, eyes all whites and mouths matching rounds.

I caught my breath and hurried to pick up the broken slate.

Footsteps rushed in behind me. "Honest, Katy, I didn't mean … I'll pay for it," Ralph said after a long moment. Oliver still stood several feet away, his face the awful color of doctored bread.

Despair, a battle I fought every day, made my eyes burn. I swallowed against the knot in my throat and rounded on him. "Take the children and leave them with Ma. Then do something useful for a change and get back to work." Ralph blanched as though I'd struck him. "Oh, and Ralph?" I lowered my voice until I bit out the words. "If Inspector

Goodwin catches you stealing again, I'll tell him to toss you in jail and bury the key."

I stayed long enough to make sure Ralph followed my orders, and then I fled.

Behind a costermonger's stall was a nice, private spot to have an emotional collapse. I could recommend it as a place where one might weep in peace for upwards of a quarter hour. Nestled at the rear of the last row of market stalls, I'd squeezed myself between crates of cabbages and lettuces, their sharp scent dulled by my swollen nose. Every time I thought I'd spent all my tears, I lifted the broken pieces of slate in my hands, and when I still didn't know how to fix them, a fresh fit overtook me.

Even if we had the extra shillings to replace it, they wouldn't be enough. The slate had been a gift from John when he started tutoring me. We'd spent months of long nights and Sundays with our heads bent over it so I could earn a position at the Post Office and send my wages home to Ma. Newly married, cozy in our London flat—the world had felt full of such treasures. I ran a finger over the wooden frame where John had carved my maidenly initials in Morse Code next to a small heart.

KTB. Using my initials gave me some anonymity on the telegraph wires. Who would suspect Mrs. John Hudson was little Katy Bee all grown up? Nobody had called me that except Da, and he hadn't called me anything for five years.

I hadn't cried for Da in nearly as long, but now I allowed myself the luxury. After all, what was a rainstorm to a river?

Just then, a man's voice broke through my grief. "Is Mrs. Hudson about the place? I saw her brothers and sisters out with their Ma, and I thought to myself, well, she can't be far away."

Could I not even have this? Anger choked my tears, and I twisted on my low barrel, scowling through the slats of the crates.

There stood Philip Beale, a prosperous local farmer twice my age. He swiped a hand over his head to smooth down all four of his hairs before jamming his cap back on. There was no Mrs. Beale. At least not outside the graveyard. That shady spot held no fewer than three in eternal slumber. There were, however, a judicious number of little Beales, and the tittle-tattle of Sherrinford speculated on who Mr. Beale would convince to become the fourth. If he failed, it wouldn't be through lack of trying. He'd asked nearly every available woman in the town and, once, caused a lamentable stir when he mistook the vicar's wife for her unmarried sister and proposed.

I crouched before he could notice me. In my current mood, fending off a proposal from the likes of Philip Beale would be easy enough, a pleasant release of my feelings even, but making a spectacle of myself at the market would dissuade anyone from ever hiring me.

Mr. Beale straightened his thin shoulders like a pigeon masquerading as a peacock and raised his cap to a pair of twin sisters, Mary and Sarah Whitmore, who'd just approached the vegetable stall, their baskets laden with groceries. "Miss. Miss. I suppose you're wondering why I'm in town so late this morning."

The women only nodded at him and set about choosing their produce at great speed.

The costermonger himself, James Severin, probably

sensed the damage unwanted marriage proposals might have on his morning's business. "Did you ever get the matter of your marrow plants sorted out?" he asked as he took the Whitmore sisters' coin.

After the first few minutes of Mr. Beale's response, I saw why Mr. Severin had chosen this topic of distraction. Mr. Beale told the saga of his marrow plants with epic fervor. Unfortunately for me, if I didn't want to be spotted, I was stuck listening to it until Mr. Beale moved on. Fortunately for Mr. Severin and his customers, the tale required only a few sparse questions to keep Mr. Beale wound up like the family clock.

"Did you say an entire row of marrow seedlings was destroyed?"

"The third time this season?"

"Have you consulted Inspector Goodwin?"

"And he dismissed you?"

"What a shame. Now, this is all planted on that strip across from the Hudson land along the river, aye?"

I'd settled with my back to the stall, grateful for the numbness overtaking my senses as the heat of the spring day grew, but perked up again at the mention of my last name.

When John's cousin gave up his tenancy on their family farm here in Sherrinford and moved to Scotland, Mr. Beale took on the rent as he'd long coveted that land's position near the river. Perhaps his interest in my whereabouts was akin to the notion that marriage to me wasn't that different from acquiring the former Hudson property. Fertile land was fertile land, after all.

"Aye, the edges of the Hudson land down by that old

barn get too marshy for planting." As if to prove my supposition, Mr. Beale went on, "So, you haven't seen Mrs. Hudson about then?"

"No, not today. I was sorry to hear about her husband, though. John was a good one."

My chest ached as though I had touched a loose wire on the telegraph. Hearing John's name on the lips of a near stranger, it was as if he'd died yesterday. As though only last night I'd suffered that long, torturous watch. Sharp tears gathered hot and fast along my already swollen eyelids.

"Aye, good," Mr. Beale replied. "But an odd one. Mucking about with all that electrical business shouldn't be allowed. That's the Lord's purview. Now I'm not saying he deserved what he got, but allowing his wife to get within sight of such a contraption, let alone take up a public position in the city—it's as unnatural as a frog with teeth."

Mr. Severin's chuckle found me on my feet, ready for battle, gripping the remains of the slate in each hand, wishing they were blades. My own heartbeat sounded the drums of war. How dare they? How *dare*—

"Bit like your landlord, isn't it?" Mr. Severin asked. "Talk about unnatural. Imagine, a lady running an estate all by herself, engaging in scientific experiments? Monroe went out there to fit a new door after the old one got blown clean off its hinges. How do the servants stand it?"

Mr. Beale huffed. "Why do you think I'm late? Musgrave Hall was in such an uproar this morning, deliveries were backed up six carts deep. Lady Holmes' maid quit before breakfast. Third one this year. And it's only April. The Hall's been bleeding staff since Lord Holmes' death."

An opening as a lady's maid? Lady Holmes hadn't been

here many years before I left for London with John, but all I'd heard was a whisper about her being eccentric. Nothing about scientific experiments. Three maids in four months, though? Bleeding staff? What was she asking them to do?

The uncertainty left my stomach in a mash, and my palms grew sweaty around the pieces of slate. Working in service had been my last resort, and the thought of it soured my throat. Still, if I was to have any hope of keeping the eight of us safe, fed, and in ownership of our four market stalls jammed together, I needed employment. Just like I needed the slates or a date for tea with Reggie Goodwin. They were tools to secure my siblings' futures and a glimpse at my own.

Though I'd grown up on the largest estate in the county, I wouldn't have called myself outstandingly, or even technically, qualified to be a lady's maid. I wouldn't even have called it a position I desired, those who owned the necessary funds to engage a lady's maid being what they were. But the position was one that I needed.

Quite.

Well, I could only hope Lady Holmes' desperation would be a match for my own.

CHAPTER THREE

THE BLACK GATES OF MUSGRAVE HALL LOOMED about twenty yards ahead. Now, I slowed my pace and caught my breath. Woodlarks, their reedy calls flooding the morning air, flitted through the thick hedges lining the walls of the estate. Somewhere behind this blockade, the main house waited, but I could no more glimpse it over the walls than I could take wing with the woodlarks.

I took a last deep breath and grasped one of the cool wrought-iron bars. "Hello? Is anybody there?"

At my call, something scrabbled in the bushes just inside the gate, and a boy of about seven or eight appeared. All wrists and ankles, his knobby shoulders poked through the thin fabric of his shirt.

"Hello, there. Are you stuck out here minding the gate all by yourself?" I asked.

He cast a quick look behind him down the drive. "We don't donate to charity collectors."

"I'm not collecting for a— Wait, what do you mean?"

The boy jerked his chin at my dress, inky and plain as a

chimney sweeper's face. "Widows and orphans."

I managed to laugh off his assumption, but it came out sharper than I meant. "No, I'm seeking an interview as a lady's maid."

He shook his head. "Mistress says she's fed up with lady's maids. They're already fixed in their ways and opinions. She wants someone with no experience so she can train them up herself." His wide eyes narrowed. "She's *very* particular. Very harsh. You should just go."

An imposing mistress whose scientific experiments drove more experienced maids to quit? I gulped. "Well, I've never been a lady's maid before, so perhaps I'll be the one to please your mistress."

The boy scowled over his shoulder then back at me. "Is Mrs. Greaves expecting you?"

"Is that the housekeeper?"

His answering sigh made him seem much older. "I guess you don't have an appointment, then. She won't like that."

The lad's rough accent and dusty cap claimed him as a gardener's apprentice. A bit young for it, but if Musgrave Hall was bleeding staff, perhaps they had no choice but to engage in the distasteful practice of employing children.

"I need this job. Surely you know what that's like." My smile felt like an empty beggar's cup. "If it goes poorly, I'll say I sneaked onto the estate with a delivery, so you won't get in trouble."

"I won't get in trouble." His assertion was undermined as he threw yet another glance over his shoulder down the lane.

Guilt sunk a claw into me, but I shook it off. No one in their right mind would expect a seven-year-old to guard the gates, and anyway, it wasn't as though the gates were locked, just fastened with a latch.

I curled my hands around the bars and pressed my face between. "As a lady's maid, I could help you. Sneak you extra food or—"

"How do you feel about frogs?" He tipped his head to the side like a formal inquisitor.

"Frogs?"

He nodded.

"They're fine." I shrugged. "So long as I'm not being compared to one."

This startled a half smile out of him. Rather than angles and shadows, his cheeks rounded, reminding me of Oliver before his sickness. I couldn't help but return his happy expression.

Just then, a resounding crash echoed through the morning, shattering its peace. As it shook the air, I gasped and ducked while the woodlarks flew off in a huff. "What on earth? Did that come from Musgrave Hall?"

Instead of answering, the lad started counting out loud. Once he'd reached sixty, he braced his feet against the drive, swung the gates wide, and waved me through. "Just watch out for the horses on your way to the house. The kitchen door's around the back."

My thoughts were so scattered I was several feet down the drive before I stopped and turned. "What horses?"

Behind me, the gates stood open, but the gardener's apprentice had disappeared.

Hopefully he hadn't thought better of letting me inside and run off to avoid reprisal.

Armed with inside knowledge of how to impress Mrs. Greaves with my lack of experience as a lady's maid,

I strode past the ornamental hedges obscuring the main house. Beyond these were delicate formal gardens as well as a pond with a tiered fountain at the center, though its waters were still.

The front of the hall was reflected in the placid surface, and I faltered to a stop. Not grand, it was nevertheless a dignified building of sandy stones, all a little worn at the edges. Much like the society of Britain herself. Three levels high, a massive gable dominated the facade, while two smaller ones gave the impression that the building receded to join the wing marching along the back of the structure. Its rows of windows, dominated by diamond lattices, caught the morning light the way the sun spilled over the Thames, almost tricking one into believing it hid nothing ugly underneath.

It was beautiful.

I hated it.

I'd just choked down enough of my ire to proceed when I heard the horses.

A few seconds later, two men on enormous bay mounts trotted around the lane leading behind the hall. One was tall, with wide shoulders, and the other stocky, his balding head thick with whiskers.

They shouldn't be here.

Phantoms on horseback, these men had haunted my memory since Da's death.

There was plenty of room on the wide lane, but I nevertheless sprang behind some bushes, pressing my skirts against them and going still, as though the men had been dressed for hunting and I was a fox. I kept my head down as they passed so I wouldn't have to see them again, but even imagining those two here felt like a grim omen. A bubble of fear pressed up my throat, and I stood there, shaking as they rode away, growing ever smaller.

Five years might have altered all three of us, but my fear alone told me what I needed to know about Lord Wallace Sterling and his son Clarence. I needed to do whatever it took to gain employment at Musgrave Hall, otherwise Lord Sterling, as well as the manor house he owned, would be the landlord of my last hope. Hopefully, they weren't frequent visitors here, but even if they were, it was better than living with them.

Head down, I hurried along the footpath as if I could outrun the dread coursing over my skin, only stopping when I reached the kitchen garden. Tendrils of sugar peas waved in the breeze, and the scent of ham and toast perfumed the air. The door to the kitchen stood propped open with a cast iron pan as the low ceiling kept much of the light from spilling through the squat windows. The polished slate of the floor caught up what little there was and splashed it over the long counters and cupboards lining two walls.

"I will not calm down!" a woman shouted, her deep voice rough as an old leather strop. "If Sherlock has used my best tureen this time, then you'll need to find a new cook as well."

"You've been at Musgrave Hall since before me; you saw Lord Arthur born. I know you don't mean it, Mrs. Kelley," a second woman spoke, her voice firm and smooth.

"I do mean it!" the first woman shouted. "We're already down two housemaids, a footman, a butler and, another lady's maid. Now, just look at Daisy's hand."

Here, I couldn't help but peek around the doorframe deeper into the kitchen where three women stood in front of an enormous cook stove. One, a bent-shouldered woman holding a spoon, stirred something on the stove even as she spoke. The second, a strong-jawed woman with steely hair, wore a black dress whose expanse was covered in several jagged burn spots, one of which still smoked. The third, a much younger woman, clutched her hand in a white towel against her black and white maid's uniform. An identically attired fourth woman perched on a stool in front of a worktable, shelling peas as though the other women weren't arguing mere feet away.

The woman with the spoon, Mrs. Kelley most likely, waved it at the woman in the black dress. "Daisy scalded her hand when that infernal explosion went off, and now she won't be able to work for a week. We've been scrambling to do the work of twice our number, but this can't go on." Mrs. Kelley slammed open an oven and thrust a loaf of bread dough inside. "Two years and two hundred and sixty-four days until he leaves for Winchester. Seeing the backside of Sherlock Holmes will be the best day of my life."

Who was this Sherlock? I'd assumed Lady Holmes caused the thunderous noise with her experiments, and that she'd done it so often it no longer rattled the remaining staff. That was why the gardener's boy hadn't flinched.

I must have made some small noise as the maid shelling peas spied me hesitating in the doorway. "You expecting someone, Mrs. Greaves?" she asked the woman with the smoking hole in her dress.

All three women by the stove stared at me. Mrs. Greaves brushed at her skirts, but before she could deny me entry, I stepped inside.

"I'm here to interview for the lady's maid position."

A ridge formed between her graying brows.

Curse my unbridled tongue. Perhaps I shouldn't have been so forward.

But then she gave Mrs. Kelley and the injured Daisy a quick glance, and her expression became calculating. "Yes, I'm so glad you're here. Follow me."

The three other women gave me shocked looks as I passed. Likely Mrs. Greaves was using me as an excuse to escape the argument and to make herself look competent, but I would gladly play along.

She led me down a short hallway into her sitting room, leaving a whiff of sulfur in her wake. A polished desk and workbench held rows of glass jars and stacks of bound ledgers, all labeled in a neat hand. The only thing amiss in the room was a pile of untidy papers on the desk.

One piece sat askew from its fellows, revealing most of its contents. As I squeezed past the desk, I caught my breath. I'd filled out dozens of identical forms each day for the last three years, seen them passed from hand to hand or clasped to the chest of a relieved recipient. I dreamed of them most nights. My gaze slipped down the page, the neat script of the telegraph operator as clear to me as any sequence of dots and dashes. The bulk of the stack blocked the bottom third of the telegram, but I didn't need to read the rest to take its meaning.

My heart hammered with all the speed of a first-class telegraph operator. Scientific experiments, disappearing boys, explosions, a mysterious Sherlock, the Sterlings, and now a telegram like this? Perhaps the worst of it all, Mrs. Greaves, gatekeeper of my future prospects, was a gullible fool.

Chapter Four

FOOL OR NO, MRS. GREAVES CAUGHT MY GAZE lingering on the stack of papers and swept them into a desk drawer as we both sat.

"So, Mrs. …?" she asked.

"Hudson," I supplied. "I heard about the opening today at market …" My voice trailed off as her face darkened.

"Gossiping at market?"

I would have snipped my tongue out and hidden it in my reticule if I could. Of course she wouldn't like being the talk of market day. "Mr. Beale's a family friend. I spoke of it only to him. He knows I've been looking for employment since my husband's death."

Mrs. Greaves made a noise—part sympathy, part acceptance—as she ran her gaze from my undecorated bonnet to my dusty shoes. "Perhaps you'd best recount your experience and qualifications."

Recalling the advice of the boy at the gate, I shook my head, sliding the letter of reference from my former supervisor across the desk. Here I was on firm footing at least. "As you can see, I've spent the last three years employed as a telegraph clerk and operator for the Post Office in London."

"No doubt you must have been diligent and sober to be employed by the Post Office, though I'm not sure it's a position one would expect of a woman." She set the letter aside, a confused expression on her face. "So, you've not worked as a maid at all?"

I smiled primly. "Exactly. I've no experience in the position, and as such, Lady Holmes may train me up to be whatever sort of maid she requires."

Instead of rejoicing, Mrs. Greaves frowned.

My nerves chattered. "I'm a quick learner," I added and bit my lip. "With a great deal of discernment. As it says in my letter."

"I saw." She slid my letter of reference back across the desk to me without looking at it again, and my heart slithered to the polished floorboards. "Mrs. Hudson, this isn't a school for training lady's maids. Lady Holmes requires a maid of … distinction. I wish you the best, but I'm afraid your employment here will not be—"

"I served six years at Sterling Place." My words tumbled out as though they might save me from drowning.

Mrs. Greaves rocked in her seat. "I don't understand."

My cheeks blazed. "My parents both worked at Sterling Place, and when I was old enough, I worked in the laundry and the scullery."

"So your story of being a telegraph clerk was a fabrication?"

"No, of course not."

"Then why hide your past? Mrs. Hudson, I won't stand

for liars, exaggerators, or those trying to rise above their station. We here are dedicated to Musgrave Hall and to the Holmes family. We're proud to serve this great house."

"Please, Mrs. Greaves—"

She held up a narrow hand. "Now, I do believe in second chances, so I will ask you one more time. Why did you hide your past employment at Sterling Place?"

"I—" Words fled. My unruly tongue just lay there, cowed by an impossible weight.

"Yes, Mrs. Hudson? You what?"

I couldn't blame the lad at the gate. Da always told us we make ourselves useful in the world only through lightening the burdens of others, and I'd promised the lad I would lie about how I'd got onto the estate if he'd let me through. He'd upheld his part of the bargain. Not that he asked for such a promise, but I'd offered it all the same. Just as the information he gave me might not be a secret, but it was gossip. Something Mrs. Greaves clearly hated. If I exposed him for gossiping, who knew what might become of him. He was just a little thing and would have no idea what he'd been doing in repeating mistaken information. I was the fool who'd assumed it was accurate.

"I don't have all day," Mrs. Greaves said sharply.

My heart pounded at my temples. "Please! I need this position. If not here, then I'll have to go back to Sterling Place, where my father—"

"This is a place of employment." Her eyes flickered with genuine sympathy. "We aren't running a charity."

"Roses!" I blurted out.

"We're not looking for gardeners, either," she said, leaning away as though I might start barking next.

I held out my hands. "Investigators call those sorts of telegrams 'Roses'." I pointed a clammy finger toward the drawer where she'd shoved the stack of papers from her desk. "Your telegram's a fake. The Royal Orphans Society and School doesn't exist."

If I'd been less desperate, or if I'd had more time to consider Mrs. Greaves and her position, I might have kept my peace. After all, no one likes to have a mirror held up to their folly, least of all by someone they view as beneath them.

Still, last resorts were seldom the true bottom, and I dug myself deeper. "It's a fraudulent charity set up by hucksters to prey upon the soft-hearted. You aren't ... I mean, I can see from the type of reply you've had that you've already donated to them. My husband ..."

The explanation died upon my lips as Mrs. Greaves thrust to her feet, hands planted on the desk. She wasn't a tall woman, but nevertheless, she loomed. "That sort of nosiness might be tolerated in telegraph offices"—her stormy face soured—"but the finest lesson a servant learns is discretion. See that you practice this essential skill before applying to Sterling Place. Someone will escort you to the gates."

Flames of panic licked the walls of my chest, setting them ablaze. All my hopes, all my dreams clutched close, all my plans to keep my family safe and educate my brothers and sisters into safer professions lay mangled at my feet.

Mrs. Greaves returned me to the kitchen door, where a footman collected me. I trudged after him, escorted off the estate as if I were the swindler. All along, I kept my eyes fixed on the ground. Too embarrassed to accept anyone's pitying looks, too sorry to leave behind the promise of this place. Defeat coated my tongue like the bitterest medicine, and I didn't look up again until I exited the gates. But there was no lad about.

I gave Musgrave Hall one last look through the iron scrollwork. The chimneys peeked over the tops of the trees, six disapproving sentinels. The longing for safety and freedom choked me. A shabby sob forced its way out of my mouth, and I clamped a hand over it. How was this the way of things? That some should have so much while others scraped together a meager existence, sorry even on the best of days. Was the problem with me, that I should expect something different?

"Maybe Mr. Beale was right," I said to myself, "unnatural as a frog with teeth."

Hatred snapped along my bones. The ease of the few built on the suffering of many. I wasn't asking for their charity or pity. I was asking for a chance to prove myself. That was all I needed: employment. I dearly missed my friend Eleanor who hated the wealthy even more than I did. She would have stood here with me and reminded me that every inch of this place was built on the labor and suffering of another.

Dejected, I spun away from the cursed gates, almost slamming into a woman behind me.

"My goodness!" My hand pressed against my galloping heart.

"You're very easily startled," the woman said and stepped back, her sharp eyes watching me.

Though taller and fairer, we might have been twins in our black frocks, except hers already had a white apron covering most of it, and she wore a white ruffled cap like Mrs. Greaves and the kitchen maid.

"You must be one of Musgrave Hall's victims," I said.

The woman's bright green eyes flew wide, and she peered past me through the gate. "You interviewed to be the lady's maid."

I winced. "Yes, briefly. May you have better luck. Perhaps they'll promote you." I waved an angry hand back at the hall, determined to take what I could. "A word of advice: don't expect to be treated fairly by Mrs. Greaves. The woman is dim enough to fork over her hard-earned money to the likes of the Royal Orphans Society and School and their twaddle by telegram. That's the thanks I get for trying to save her from losing her money to fraudsters. Lady Holmes must be a ripe idiot to put her trust in the likes of Mrs. Greaves."

"I don't understand. What telegram?" the woman asked, hefting the basket she carried over her arm a little higher between us, as though it might shield her from me.

That checked my unbridled anger. What a sight I must present—cheeks aflame, dusty widow's weeds, wild words flying from my mouth.

I sighed and turned to leave, exhausted. "Just feed the lad who watches the gates a bit of extra, please. He needs it."

CHAPTER FIVE

THE ACHE IN MY BACK TIGHTENED INTO A KNOT, AND I massaged the muscles with my fists. Raw after a morning in and out of water, my knuckles snagged on the seams of my dress. Ma and I, along with Oliver and Louise, had been in our backyard processing laundry orders all morning. Usually, I fetched laundry to and from the back doors of our neighbors who couldn't, or wouldn't, wash it themselves, but Ma had recently let me take on the harder jobs, like lugging water and wet sheets to the line.

"I was thinking, tonight for supper I could make—"

"Don't bother yourself, Katy. Your brothers will be home tonight, and we've only liver in the pantry. I know how to make it stretch."

George, who did chores and errands for Dr. McNulty, was often stocking the dispensary late, and Ralph kept to The Four Hounds as long as he could. Since our argument on the green two days ago, he'd been staying even later than usual. We'd barely spoken ten words to each other. Oliver and Louise folded dry sheets from the line, and Elizabeth kept Rosie out of mischief indoors.

"Have you heard back from Sterling Place yet?" Ma asked, thick arms scrubbing a pair of sheets against the board.

"No, not yet, though I've had another letter from Eleanor. She and Samuel are well and thinking of getting a small dog."

Eleanor and Samuel were the dearest friends John and I had in the world. We'd all started at the Post Office near the same time and spent most of our free time together in London, at parks, cafes, or one another's homes. She'd written to me faithfully every month since John died, had held my hand all through his funeral, and later held me while I wept.

"Are you planning to finally write back this time?" Ma asked, gently scolding.

"Of course," I lied. I had no new job or prospects, nothing but a heavy grief I could barely speak of. My heart was broken. What would I say to her that she didn't already know?

I shrugged off my dark thoughts. "Anyway, it's only been two days. I hardly know what to hope for—that they don't have any openings for maids, or that they do. I hate the idea of service and everything it stands for. Especially there."

Ma shook her head. "Now, Lord Sterling runs his estate with a steady hand. After all, he treated your da and me fair for thirty years." Her words fell flat, as she'd repeated them several times a year since Da died.

Nevertheless, I swallowed hard and pressed away the memory she'd called up, the specter of Lord Wallace Sterling and his son Clarence leaving Musgrave Hall two days ago. "Musgrave Hall, Sterling Place. There's no difference. The work's endless. Never mind spare pennies, you've not even two minutes of your own time to rub together. At least when you work for a business, your hours are set and so is your leisure. Besides, thirty years of loyal service, and then what? Kicked out of our home when—"

"Katherine Theodosia Bunting"—Ma stood straight—"don't you lecture me. My knees remind me of exactly what it takes to be a maid." She raised her arms and flicked the sheet she'd been scrubbing wide, her hands and forearms a deep, angry red. Faint brown stains still marred one side of the fabric, and she bent to continue scrubbing.

Ashamed, I hunched over my own sheet and board again. "I'm sorry, Ma. I know you want what's best for all of us."

"It's me who's sorry." Her face softened, and she gave me a guilty look. "If your father and John were still with us, you wouldn't be trapped serving as a helpmeet to me and teacher to your siblings all while trying to take on a new job yourself."

I couldn't listen to that song again. "Am I supposed to leave things up to the town's schoolteacher? The old codger who sends the girls outside during science or arithmetic lessons, claiming he can't think with such chatter going on, only the girls aren't talking. Ridiculous. Not that sticking around for his lessons is much better. He doesn't even have a certificate. It took John a full year of tutoring me in the evenings to fill in enough gaps to get me hired at the Post Office."

Ma winked as she nudged me. "Maybe you'll be getting a different kind of support soon."

A laugh clapped my chest. "Ma! It was only tea."

"But it went well?" she asked yet again.

"Yes, it did." I fought off a sigh. "Mrs. Goodwin is just as I remembered her—cheerful and wholesome as porridge."

Ma finally wrung out the sheet and set it in the rinse basin. "That tidy cottage where Reggie set her up after her husband died sits on one of the largest lots in town, so he must be doing quite well for himself."

"Not that he lets anyone forget it," I murmured.

Ma *tsked* and tapped my knuckles. "Katy, mind your tongue."

I set my teeth into the offending organ. Even talking about this left me feeling like a faithless traitor to John, though all three Goodwins had spoken carefully of him at tea. Annabelle even broke into tears several times, but she had an excuse. "Annabelle was in fine form—sallow cheeks, dull hair, vomiting at irregular intervals."

As I knew she would, Ma snatched up the bait. "That was quick. She's been married just four months." The distraction didn't last. "So, when Reggie walked you home—"

"It went fine," I said, taking out my desire to snap on wringing my own sheet.

"The two of you lingered under our oak tree for much longer than just 'fine.'"

I tossed the sheet among its soggy fellows. "Ma, enough. It may all still come to naught."

"And then you walked out with him to The Four Hounds yesterday evening? Georgie was there with Amelia and said you were sitting close as leaves in a pile. How was it? Do tell."

"Fine."

Ma threw her hands up. "Ah! *Fine*, again. Is that all you can say about the man?"

I'd been asking myself the same question for days now. I considered it yet again as a few stray soap bubbles floated through the air, set free from the big tub, fragile things tugged this way and that by a slight breeze. Oliver and Louise dropped the sheet they'd been folding into a basket and raced to clap the bubbles out of the air, Oliver lagging behind as his face grew red.

I was about to remind him to slow down, when the screech of a wild Rosie Bunting spilled from the house. We all froze, staring at the kitchen door. Another scream followed on its heels, and I wiped my hands on my heavy apron. Somebody needed saving.

But before I reached the door, it burst open, and Rosie scrambled out, Elizabeth a few steps behind.

"Give it!" she shouted, swiping for Rosie's chestnut braids.

"It's not for you!" Rosie replied, running flat out in my direction.

"Girls!" Ma said, limping to my side. "Elizabeth, you were supposed to be minding your sister."

Elizabeth gave Rosie a look ripe with poison. "I had to answer the door—"

"Katy, Katy, you have a *letter*!" Rosie shrieked again as Elizabeth made another grab for her, but she danced out of reach, then thrust a piece of paper up at me.

My heart shuddered, and the ground seemed to shift beneath me. This was it, then. The evil bargain I'd come to make was calling in the debt. Serving and scraping. *Yes, my lord. Right away, my lady*. No right to sleep. No right to rest. No right to my own thoughts, even, because if I didn't swallow them down well enough, they'd come spewing out and cost me my place as sure as Mrs. Greaves had warned. Of course, there was always Reggie Goodwin instead.

I worked a finger under the crisp seal but couldn't bring myself to remove the letter from the envelope. I wanted one more moment before my future arrived.

A future I hated, begging for a job from the very people to blame for Da's death, who threw us out of our home like a sheet past mending when we were no longer of use to them. That was the cost of being here for Ma, to teach my siblings, and to add my salary to the meager savings my parents had somehow scraped together before Da's death. If only there were another choice.

I sank onto the stool Ma sat on for sorting the laundry when her knees bothered her, the envelope already wrinkled against my damp palm. I wiped my shaking hands again and eased the letter free.

A moment later I shot to my feet and started pacing, reading the missive again and again.

"What is it? What does it say?" Ma plucked at my arm as I passed. "Katy! Stop."

As though her words were a magic spell, my feet froze, and I thrust the letter at her.

When Ma looked up, her chestnut eyes found mine. "You're wanted at Musgrave Hall? But why? How? Are you sure you should—"

"I don't know, but I mean to find out." I pawed at my apron strings, hands shaking so that Ma had to pull the knots free.

"But, Katy—"

I waved off Ma's flurry of objections as I made myself

presentable and hurried down the road. But my thoughts scattered like dandelion seeds in a strong wind, and I slowed. Had Mrs. Greaves reported me to her mistress or, worse yet, the police? To Reggie? Perhaps she'd implicated me as revenge for calling out her gullibility. But if so, why Musgrave Hall and not the local police station?

Ma's doubts caught up with me, and I almost turned back. If I started now, I might make it all the way to London before anyone noticed I was missing. But London wasn't an escape anymore, just a different sort of reckoning. No, if there was even a chance to escape working at Sterling Place, I would take it.

Chapter Six

THE MILES PASSED BY IN A BREATHLESS BLUR. THIS time a thickset gardener let me through the gates, and before I knew it, I set my hand on the kitchen door of Musgrave Hall, closed this time. I tapped out the word *luck* and knocked.

A kitchen boy opened the door. Behind him, the room bustled with activity. Mrs. Kelley, a short woman possessed of a tall voice, boomed orders at a young man and woman, none of whom seemed inclined to notice me.

Scrawny as a wet kitten, all dark eyes in a pale face, the boy had a red birthmark along his cheek. "We're not hiring any laundresses," he said in a thick Yorkshire accent.

"I'm not—"

"Your knuckles are red, you stink of lye, and you've a patch of white where the soap dried on the side of your skirt."

I glanced down and brushed at the offending spot. "I'm not … that is, I *was* washing clothes this morning, but I'm not here to apply to be a laundress."

The same maid who'd been shelling peas before staggered by with a crate of dishes. "Who do you think you are, the sleuth of Musgrave Hall? That's enough of that sort of thing, lad. Show the lady up to the study and then come help me with these."

Study? Not Mrs. Greaves' office? What on earth had I got myself into now?

The kitchen boy snuck several looks at me over his shoulder as we wound our way through Musgrave Hall. At first, I tried to memorize our route, but I was too anxious to hold it, and I soon lost the way, surrounded by dark wood and polished windows that wove themselves into the walls of a maze. Several long hallways, two sets of stairs, and an enormous great room later, we stood outside a thick wooden door in the upstairs of Musgrave Hall. Here, the lad gave me one last measured look, then knocked on the door and dashed away.

A woman's clear voice spoke from inside. "Come in."

The room was a library of sorts. That was, there were shelves, and those shelves were stacked with books, among a great many other things. Skulls, plants, a collection of irregular clear glassware, and racks of metal gears stood side by side with hefty tomes and intricate pieces of brass equipment I couldn't imagine the use of. One of which gave off a steady ticking sound.

Standing in front of a large desk was the tall woman I'd met outside the gates of Musgrave Hall. Dressed again in maid's black, though of finer material, today she'd foregone the white cap to reveal a striking head of light blonde hair. Even without the cap, I recognized her serious green eyes and sculpted nose. I gave her a rough smile.

"I hope your work here has been happier than mine. Do you know what this is about?" I withdrew the letter from my reticule and showed it to her.

She ignored the letter. "During your interview with Mrs. Greaves, did you observe a telegram from the Royal Orphans Society and School?"

My heart's running patter stumbled. "I didn't ... I mean ... am I to be arrested?" I gripped my reticule as though it held my last penny. It nearly did.

The woman motioned to the pair of chairs beside me. "No one is getting arrested today. What you do with tomorrow is up to you. Please have a seat."

I did as she asked, more confused than ever. This woman spoke with a striking amount of confidence for a maid. Mr. Beale's gossip about odd goings-on at Musgrave Hall piped up in my thoughts, and I studied the shelves again, my eyes settling on a stack of neat wooden boxes on a low shelf and a set of scales. Were those some sort of experiment? Was I? Why was I speaking to the lady's maid instead of Mrs. Greaves? Did that mean ... Only one thing mattered.

"Is there a job for me?" I asked, trying and failing to hide my eagerness.

The woman settled into the chair beside me. "How did you know the telegram's sender?"

"Roses," I said, rewarded with the first change in expression I'd seen on her face. A flicker of surprise. For some reason, the sight warmed my chest.

"Explain, please."

Here, at last, I was on firm footing, and if I explained myself well, perhaps word would trickle up to the scientifically minded Lady Holmes herself. "When I worked as a telegraph operator, we had trouble with confidence men sending telegrams to people, pretending to represent a fake cause. The more complicated schemes had an official charity, only the money didn't go to retired nurses or injured soldiers, just to line pockets."

Off in the house, someone began playing the violin, the notes straining into the mournful tones of "The Unquiet Grave".

The woman gestured for me to continue.

"I saw messages like that several times a month. We all did, though I didn't know they were fakes until John, my husband," I added, faltering a little, "started assisting Scotland Yard in their investigations. Sometimes he'd talk about the case in the evenings, show me their catalog of messages, and explain how they reeled in the unsuspecting."

She curled a finger under her lips. "But, 'roses'?"

"Investigators referred to the Royal Orphans Society and School by taking the first letter of each word, a shorthand to protect their work. Baps, Gussys, Sobs, Roses—that sort of thing."

"Roses." The woman turned her unsettling eyes to me with a gaze that locked me to my chair. "You also deduced the telegram wasn't the first Mrs. Greaves received from the swindlers? That she'd already sent them money?"

I leaned forward. This was my favorite part. "Certain types of messages were bait to get people to send them money; others were news about the residents, pleas for further donations—all sorts of piteous drivel meant to prey upon unguarded hearts."

"And Mrs. Greaves' message?"

"The investigators called that type 'poor Annie'. News

about a fictional person who the mark has supposedly been supporting with their donations, but who suffered a setback and now needs additional funds. Medical emergencies or deaths in the family were very popular."

She kept her face still but tightened her grip on the arms of the chair. I'd guessed correctly, though that part of the telegram had been hidden by the stack on Mrs. Greaves' desk.

"Mrs. Hudson, are you employed?"

I frowned. "Not currently."

"Are you familiar with Philip Beale?"

I narrowed my eyes, and my pulse raced. What was she implying? "In Sherrinford, you might stand on one side of the town and spit on the other. Everyone knows Mr. Beale."

The violin scratched out a sour note in the middle of the song, then took up the beginning once again.

"Do you know how to make tea?" the woman asked, running her hands over the wrinkles in her skirt.

"Of course."

"Do you wear strong perfumes?"

I didn't know whether to laugh or scream. This string of nonsense questions set my heart pounding again. "Perfumes? No, I'd rather put food on the table."

She tapped her chin. "What about horses?"

Da had been one of Lord Sterling's grooms and taught us most of what he knew. I adored horses more than most people, but what would Lady Holmes want to hear? "What about them?" I asked carefully.

The woman raised her fair brows. "Do you favor them?"

The urge to pull a face tugged at my cheeks and lips, but I resisted. Just. "What sort of interview is this?"

"I don't believe I ever said it was an interview." She stared at me, eyebrows still high on her tall forehead.

A wave of truth hit me. If this woman was a maid, I would propose to Mr. Beale myself. I stood up. "Not an interview and not an interrogation. Well, that only leaves an experiment. I'll be damned if I'm going to waste my time playing into the manipulations of a woman with too much time and money on her soft little hands, who employs the likes of Mrs. Greaves. And … and … children!" I turned and strode toward the door. "This entire place is a madhouse."

The woman, whoever she was, frowned but didn't try to stop me. Her voice, however, caught me as I exited the study. "Mrs. Greaves is no longer employed at Musgrave Hall."

The violin successfully reached the end of the song and laid "The Unquiet Grave" to its own sort of rest.

In the silence, her words rolled over me, and I threw her a dark look. "How lucky for Mrs. Greaves." I pivoted toward the main staircase.

Today would be the last day I set foot in the incomprehensible Musgrave Hall.

To my surprise, quick footsteps followed me. "At this speed, we'll soon be on the road," the woman said.

I tried to outpace her, striding for the staircase, but I was no match for her longer legs. "Are you escaping as well?" I asked over my shoulder.

"As frequently as I can. I just hope Mr. Beale is at home this afternoon," she said as we reached the bottom of a wide staircase.

I ignored her comment about Mr. Beale and maneuvered

down an interminable hallway hung with six tapestries done in rusty reds and blues. In all of them, a noblewoman stood draped next to a lion and a unicorn. My eyes snagged on the final one in which the noblewoman held a necklace, the expression on her face one of utter loneliness.

"What on earth do you want with Mr. Beale?" I asked, no longer able to stave off my curiosity.

"It's not what I want, but what Mr. Beale does that concerns me." The woman pointed to the door at the end of the hall. "That's the quickest exit."

"What Mr. Beale wants is another biddable wife he can plow into the earth, just like the first three." I flung open the door at the end of the hallway and paused just inside the great room. Cut with Jacobean crossbeams across the walls, their lines drew my eyes to a stern chandelier that brought to mind interlocking manacles. I swung my head from side to side, wishing I'd paid more attention to my surroundings as the kitchen boy led me through the hall.

I flung out my arm and huffed. "You said this was an exit. How do I get out of this cursed place?"

"You agree to accompany me to Mr. Beale's farm." She circled in front of me.

Now that the woman no longer stood in the dim light of the study, I realized what I should have seen right away. When I first met her, she wore black wool like most maids. But whereas two days ago her sleeves had been thin and her gown many years out of fashion, today a sheen rippled off the stylish black moiré folds of the fabric, a thick gold ring sparkling on her finger. In my excitement and confusion, I'd overlooked the obvious, or perhaps I'd just been unwilling to believe my instincts. Everything about this woman's ensemble was well out of a maid's reach because clearly, not only was this not a maid, this was the elusive mistress of Musgrave Hall.

My throat squeezed closed, and the air whistled with each breath.

"I propose an experiment," she said, features kindling as though reading my mind.

Blood roared in my ears. Damn everything.

"Of course you do, Lady Holmes." I clenched my shaking hands into fists.

I'd fallen into her trap and thanked her for it. She certainly wasn't going to offer me a job after I'd called her home a madhouse.

In for a penny I couldn't spare, I lifted my chin and shook my head, determined to at least walk away with some pride. "You'll have to find another subject. I'm not interested in being anyone's experiment."

I made my way across the great room on weak legs to a pair of doors at the far end. There could only be so many exits even in a house this large. I'd reached the other side of the room before she spoke again.

"What about for thirty pounds?"

My mouth actually watered. It was more than I could hope to make in a year's wages working as a lady's maid unless I took up thieving the family silver. Even as a telegraph operator, it would take me over a month to earn that much, and the cost of living on my own in London would have eaten it right up again. But here? The mortgage would be secure, we could afford a new doctor and medicine for Oliver, a slate for each of my siblings, and have enough left over to buy more than liver for dinner. Perhaps most importantly, Reggie Goodwin could remain just that and nothing more.

I hated the woman for ferreting out my soft spot, for having the money to tempt me with and knowing I couldn't refuse. I was no stranger to hate. The aristocracy, and Lord Wallace Sterling in particular, frigid nights without enough coal, hunger, the fear of losing those I loved. Sometimes I even hated John for abandoning me, never answering my Morse Code devotions with a single tap.

But I saved a special kind of hatred for my own weakness. As a telegraph clerk, I'd fancied myself a part of the technological uprising lifting the plight of working-class women. Now, I writhed against my place in this world, powerless to lift myself out of it. Though, I could easily fall lower. That was always the great dark pit yawning under each of us because, should we slip through, nobody would be there to catch us.

Certainly not Lady Holmes. I'd insulted this woman to her face, repeatedly, and somehow cost her a housekeeper. No wonder she'd called me back for this humiliating "experiment." Of course, I would stay. Of course, I would accompany her to the Beale farm. If she wanted to see how far she could manipulate me, how far I'd bend before I could break, what choice did I have? How could I refuse thirty pounds for a single day's work?

My only question: was that all Lady Holmes hoped to prove?

CHAPTER SEVEN

I WOULD HAVE LIKED TO SAY I PASSED EVERY INCH OF the two-mile ride to the Beale farm in stony silence. After all, I was there against my better judgment, if not my will. But since Lady Holmes held the power—reins, funds, and knowledge—I grabbed another currency: answers.

And the way she drove her phaeton, as if time and gravity did not exist, meant I had only a few minutes to pepper her with my questions.

We flew over a rise, and I clamped my hand to my head to keep my bonnet in place. "An investigative matter? Why would you need my help?"

Lady Holmes sheared back with one hand to urge her horse into the turn. A spry Hackney whose mane echoed her mistress's long black veil, both whipping to the side like a raven's wing.

"You said Mr. Beale's name when you were considering burning Musgrave Hall to the ground. A thing like that tends to stick in the mind."

"Burn down … excuse me?"

Her amusement at my shock was clear even through her veil. "Of course. That's why I was keeping a close eye on you. I remembered the connection after Inspector Goodwin complained about Mr. Beale while I was at the police station yesterday."

My feet went numb. "Inspector Goodwin?"

"Mrs. Greaves skimmed from the household accounts to fund her donations, and so I dismissed her."

I bit the inside of my cheek. I didn't like Mrs. Greaves, but I hadn't wanted her to lose her position. The two of us ought to have raised our swords against a common enemy, but because we were disposable, we had to fight everyone for what we wanted, even each other. A plight Lady Holmes could never understand. I swallowed down my sharp words with that bitter truth.

Thirty pounds. Thirty pounds. Thirty pounds. The refrain beat through my mind steady as the racing hooves of the horse. However, it wasn't the only refrain. Curiosity had nipped at my heels since she first mentioned Mr. Beale.

I angled myself to see Lady Holmes better. "What is it you require from me?"

"Finally, the right question. Mr. Beale has suffered a series of destructive incidents the last two weeks that, while financially modest, are nonetheless troubling."

"We're here because of three rows of *marrow* plants?"

Her eyebrows raised. "So, you're familiar. Excellent. Tell me what you know."

Confused, but more curious than ever, I searched the dregs of my memory for the threads of Mr. Beale's tale. "Thrice now, Mr. Beale has sown marrow plants along the southern edge of his field. When they begin to sprout, something comes along and destroys them."

"I have a theory about the cause of this destruction, so I need you to ask Mr. Beale a few questions." Without slowing, Lady Holmes reeled them off; only some of them seemed to have any direct bearing on marrow seedlings.

Questions. I could survive doing this once, even for a stuck up, high-handed manipulator. If she was going to make me do it, though, she could at least have the decency to be honest about why. And it wasn't as though I needed to worry about offending her since I'd already dug that grave.

"So, I'm to act as your proxy because it wouldn't be fitting for a lady in mourning to be doing this sort of work?" I gestured at my black skirts, then at hers.

"No, what I need is someone less conspicuous to ask the questions." She tipped both fists back, and we slowed to the approximate pace of a charging bull.

That Lady Holmes considered my looks and station plain enough to fit the bill stung more than I liked to admit. Still, something didn't add up. If I thought she cared about my feelings at all, I'd assume she was trying to put me off. Luckily, this was a temporary arrangement, and though I needed to keep my tongue on a leash, no one said it had to be a short one.

"I admit to some confusion," I said.

"Were my instructions not clear?"

"They were."

"Are you unable to remember them long enough to go about your task, then? Shall I write them down?" She frowned. "Since you read Mrs. Greaves' correspondence, I knew you could read, but I admit, I don't know how well."

I huffed. "Of course I can read. I worked in a telegraph

office. And no, I've a hold of the questions."

The road rose, and she clucked to the horse to urge speed. "Then I admit myself confused as to your confusion."

I tapped my thigh, spelling out *courage*. "A lady in mourning, out at her tenant's farm, skirts in the muck and mind on the marrows? It's a trifling matter. It's not even a scientific experiment. Why not leave it to the police?"

If Lady Holmes was upset by my questions, she didn't show it. But then, she rarely seemed to show anything. "The police deem the matter to be beneath their notice."

"Then why is it not also beneath yours?"

We'd reached the turning for the Beale farm, and she pulled the horse to a dead stop, feet braced and slim arms straining. Then she faced me.

"Since my husband's death, I have become an understudy thrust onto stage overnight and asked to play every role. Though most of my tenants don't seem to agree. They used to come to Musgrave Hall, bringing my husband matters of all sizes. They trusted Arthur, and he did right by them. Now, I am their landlord, but it has been seven solid months since any of them knocked on my back door." Her eyes skidded to the side. "If they can't trust me, then I can't help them. And if that happens, where will any of us be? When I make rounds to their farms, I find them polite, but they won't talk to me openly. Hence, this experiment."

I climbed down from the phaeton, which was older but well kept, and put out a hand to the warm cheek of the horse. "What if Mr. Beale interprets my visit as ... an interest?"

"I've faith in your ability to dissuade him of any such notions." A dull flush rose in her pale cheeks. She reached into a carpet bag at her feet and withdrew a small amber jar. "Mrs. Greaves' finest salve. One of the young Beales is suffering from a rash."

After giving the horse a farewell pat, I made my way down the well-worn drive, jar of salve clutched tight. A squat cottage formed from rounded stones, their colors worn down to gray, gave the impression that the building had been thrust up from the earth. The various outbuildings and barns leaned toward it like a group of old women at the tea table.

Once I reached the yard, flustered chickens squawked in a soft frenzy. My knock at the weathered door brought a narrow-faced boy out on the steps, but instead of greeting me, he sprinted back inside. I stood there, jar in hand, the chickens circling my skirts.

Then Mr. Beale appeared in the entryway.

"Good afternoon, I've brought you a rash salve from the mistress of Musgrave Hall, for your little one." Here I held up the jar like an official talisman. "It's always one thing or the other with them, isn't it?"

He chewed his mustache with his bottom lip, then gestured back toward the kitchen. "Aye, thanks to you both."

A girl of about twelve stood at the counter kneading dough, the scent of laundry soap and vegetable peelings heavy in the air.

"Elizabeth, put the kettle on and see about some tea," Mr. Beale said to her as we entered the large room. Breakfast dishes were still piled in the sink, and the windows could have used a good washing six months ago. Their cloudy surfaces pilfered the strength of the spring sunshine.

The girl hurried to the stove, and a sad smile crept onto

my face, thinking of my own Elizabeth at home helping Ma when all of them ought to have had fewer cares weighing them down. "I've a sister of the same name about her age."

He cleared his throat. "T'was her mother's name. My second wife."

"My condolences on your loss." I sensed he was about to launch into the full tale, and wanting to stay far away from any talk of wives, I dove into Lady Holmes' questions. "Speaking of your children, which one has the rash?"

A tousled head of red hair peeked around the corner of a door leading deeper into the cottage.

Mr. Beale pointed at the boy. "That'll be Eddie. Come here, lad, and show Mrs. Hudson your ankles."

Eddie, my brother Ralph, and Billy Mudd used to be inseparable when they were in school, but they were so busy working these days that I hadn't seen Eddie since returning to Sherrinford. Eddie was only fifteen, but nearly twice Ralph's size. He hobbled into the kitchen shoeless, his lower limbs bound in linen wraps.

"My goodness." I knelt next to him and patted the chair.

Once he settled, I peeled back the outer bandages. The inner layers were stained with yellow blossoms from his weeping skin. A flat red rash spread over his feet, ankles, and calves, blisters dotted here and there in oozing stripes. I had no idea what caused it. The closest I could come was when my brother George had a sunburn so severe it raised blisters. But Eddie's cheeks and hands, though ruddy from working outside, showed no signs of burning or peeling.

"What have you got yourself into?" I asked.

Eddie winced as the air hit his skin and threw a glance at his father, but Mr. Beale was greeting Elizabeth's return with the tea things. "I don't know, ma'am."

Being the eldest of seven didn't come without a few perks. He was definitely lying.

I uncapped the jar, and the sweet scent of chamomile filled the air. I leaned closer, dotting the salve on the red islands around the blisters. "When did the rash begin?"

"Started burning three days ago," he said, a line between his brows.

"Did you—"

"So, you've taken up work at Musgrave Hall?" Mr. Beale interrupted from his perch in a nearby chair.

My jaw clenched. I neither wanted to explain the circumstances nor lie. "Lady Holmes is not what I expected."

He grunted. "Head in the clouds, that one." After a long, noisy slurp of his tea, Mr. Beale waved a hand at my ministrations. "Seems like you're a natural with children."

Well, that had progressed quickly.

"Just doing as Lady Holmes directed." I capped the jar and handed it to Eddie. "Keep the area clean and dry and reapply the salve at least twice a day. Can you help your brother with his wrappings?" I asked Elizabeth.

"Yes, ma'am." She handed me a napkin.

Mr. Beale frowned. "Your mistress hasn't driven you to quit yet? It won't be long. That one's as unnatural—"

"I quite like her experiments. They remind me of working in the telegraph office." I wiped my hands then joined Mr. Beale at the kitchen table. "Speaking of something that's actually unnatural," I smiled sweetly, "what's been disturbing your marrows? It was the talk of the market." I managed to say the words and keep a serious face, which was a feat worth thirty pounds alone. "Green marrows, weren't they? When were the plants disturbed?"

"Aye, green-striped autumn squash. I don't grow too many, but some like to stuff them with chopped up meats and vegetables, so I always sow a few 'round the edges of things. As to the sowing, let me think." He stared at the ceiling. "We had an early break in the weather, and I set out the first seedlings four weeks ago. Tried again a week later, and then just this last week."

"No, Da, it was right before my pies went missing," Elizabeth said. She'd been so quiet with Eddie behind me I'd forgotten she was there.

"Your pies?" I asked.

"A week and a half ago, then," Mr. Beale said. "Like I told Inspector Goodwin—"

"Three pies, poof! Gone like that and with them all my hard work," Elizabeth said, wringing her apron through her hands.

"Enough of that talk," Mr. Beale said. "That'll be owed to Hal Dunham's mischievous lot, mark my words. Had to chase them out of my woods twice last week."

"Is Mr. Dunham causing you trouble?" I asked.

"Aye, he's convinced my back fencing's on his land, but as I told him, don't take me for a fool. My line's always begun at the great oak tree and run northerly from there." Mr. Beale arced a hand through the air. "Gone soft in the head, he has. No call to bother you with it, nothing but a matter between neighbors, ma'am."

Elizabeth vibrated with indignation behind me.

"You don't suppose Mr. Dunham's to blame for your marrows?"

Mr. Beale ran a finger over his mustache. "Possible, but

why bother going after such a meager crop? Haven't even bothered to grow anything there in years."

I'd exhausted Lady Holmes' list of questions, but somehow, I couldn't help myself from asking, "Well, maybe Mr. Dunham isn't the only one with confusion on your property lines. Could someone else object to your use of the land, thinking it wasn't owned because it wasn't farmed until now? Are there strange tracks down there?"

"Just ours." He shrugged. "Nobody's down beyond that way. After my field, it's naught but large trees and rocky hummocks." His tone implied I ought to know better. "If it was the other side of the farm, now that I could understand. People are always climbing over the stile and traipsing through there as a shortcut between the south end of town and the bend in the river. Great fishing down there."

"And you don't mind that?"

He sighed and glanced at Elizabeth as though seeing someone who wasn't there. "Those fish are mine for but a passing moment, so I don't begrudge anyone their evening meal."

"Even Mr. Dunham?"

Mr. Beale let out a quick laugh. "Especially Dunham. He's a poor enough farmer that I'd hate to see his little scamps with empty bellies."

Eddie and Elizabeth giggled behind me, and even I smiled into the bottom of my teacup. When I set it down, Elizabeth jumped up, grabbed the teapot, and poured me another.

Mr. Beale smiled. "Seems the children have taken a liking to you, missus."

He pointed to where four more little faces peered at me from through the doorway where Eddie first appeared.

The walls of the kitchen, snug but cheery, now felt all too close and warm. "There certainly are plenty of them," I said, trying to wrest the conversation back onto the tracks.

He cleared his throat. "Always room for more."

The rumble of hooves and wheels on stone came from outside, and Mr. Beale went to the kitchen window. "Looks like your mistress has come to fetch you. Best get back to it; after all, your time is hers now."

I sprang to my feet, but even through my relief, his innocent comment set the tea in my stomach swimming. Her time, indeed. I departed to a chorus of thanks and farewells, then went to claim my fee.

Chapter Eight

"You failed to mention a time limit," I said, more angry than surprised at Lady Holmes' unexpected arrival. "Or was that part of the experiment as well?"

She eased the horse onto the road. "That's because there wasn't one. I was saving you from becoming a biddable wife."

I frowned at her stiff profile muted by her black veil, her dress a smudge of inky blankness against our lush surroundings. Much like my own. "How could you be sure I'd finished the questions?"

"Social interactions are easy to map. They follow a predictable pattern, with little variation. The walk down the lane, introductions, seeing to the rash, one cup of tea, and five questions comes out to about an hour."

I just stared at her.

"With ten extra minutes to account for Mr. Beale's desire to monopolize the conversation," Lady Holmes added with exaggerated patience.

I squinted and shook my head. "Is that all we are to you? Numbers?" I asked.

Her look was so keen it raked across my skin. "Did you or did you not manage to ask all of the questions?"

I opened my mouth to demand an actual answer, but the weight of thirty pounds stoppered my sharp words. Instead, I reported what I'd learned of the farm, the marrow plants, and when they'd been planted, throwing in a report of the stolen pies and the discord between Beale and Dunham for free. After all of that, Lady Holmes made a dismissive noise and asked about Eddie's rash.

My eyes narrowed. I tapped my fingers against my thigh and spelled out *thirty pounds*. I could almost feel John smiling at me.

"Redness on the skin and blisters in lines from the knees down."

"Swelling?"

"He can barely walk."

"Curious." She pulled an envelope from her pocket, holding the reins in one hand as she handed me my payment absentmindedly with the other. "But why would he? No, we don't need to know why. It is only our job to know who."

"Who are you talking about?" I asked as I secured the banknotes in my reticule. It was more money than I'd ever held at one time, and my fingers itched to count them, but I contented myself with wrapping my shaking hands over their bulk instead.

As if in answer, Lady Holmes only waggled the reins, and we picked up speed. The sheep in the field along the road bleated as we passed, safe behind their fences.

Other than being in close quarters with Lady Holmes, this experiment had been surprisingly easy. Apparently, Lady Holmes was satisfied as well.

"Have you solved the mystery then?" I asked when it was clear she wasn't going to answer my earlier question.

"Of course. The nights in question were all clear, with a high moon," she said as though that explained everything.

I tried to keep silent, I really did, but despite my resolve, I'd become invested. "How did you know that, about the moon?"

"Contrary to your feelings about them, numbers mean a great deal to me. I study them." A small smile lit her eyes. "My older son Mycroft and I used to memorize the astronomical tables together after dinner. The moon's cycles, eclipses, planetary conjunctions. He's away at school now, but Sherlock and I have kept up the habit."

"Oh, Sherlock is your son," I said before I could think better of it.

She whipped me a look. "Yes, why?"

A flush rose up my neck. "I'd heard the name mentioned in passing and noted it as unusual."

Neither of us appeared to believe the lie, but she didn't remark on it.

"May I offer you a ride back into town?" she asked instead. "I can drop you at your home on my way to see Inspector Goodwin."

"Inspector Goodwin?" I was about to ask her who she planned to report to the police, when she sighed.

"Though I doubt he'll be glad to see me again."

"Again?" I bit my lip. Why could I not keep my mouth shut in her presence?

"After my investigation of Mrs. Greaves, Inspector Goodwin accused me of 'being devilishly persistent.'" She made an indelicate sound. "As though that were an insult. Not that he would assist me. I had to make my inquiries with my late husband's cousin at Scotland Yard, the ambitious Sergeant Forrester."

"You turned Mrs. Greaves over to Scotland Yard?" We hit a hole in the road, and the strings of my reticule jingled accusingly.

"No. Why would I do that?"

"Most of your sort would." I almost regretted my words when Lady Holmes flinched.

"My sort." She took a deep breath. "I couldn't knowingly employ a dishonest housekeeper, but she didn't steal anything from me that I couldn't afford to give. I went to Scotland Yard to report The Royal Orphans Society and School." Lady Holmes frowned at the road. "Did you think I'd dismissed Mrs. Greaves without a fair investigation?"

"I didn't think you'd have dismissed her at all." We both fell silent a beat. "It would ease my conscience a great deal to know what happened to Mrs. Greaves," I said.

Lady Holmes' face went oddly blank. "She's gone to live with her sisters in Eastbourne. With an excellent reference and a letter of introduction to a woman who runs a charity for orphans there. No police necessary, much to Inspector Goodwin's relief, I'm sure."

We took the turn toward the town at a reasonable pace, the road ahead crowded with foot traffic. My time with Lady Holmes, disagreeable and confusing as it had been, was almost at a close. A pleasant thought, followed by one decidedly less so. Why hadn't she answered my question?

"Reggie Goodwin never took a job he could get someone else to do for him," I said because I could. Lady Holmes had no idea of my relationship with the inspector. "He'll be pleased you're bringing him the solution to Mr. Beale's problem." I brushed invisible lint from my dress, as though I didn't care about the answer to my next question. "So, who destroyed the marrow plants?"

"Eddie Beale, of course."

"Oh—Oh, no." I rounded on her. "Wait. You can't mean—"

"Mr. Beale's son is responsible for the destruction of property on his farm. I'm afraid so."

"How can you know that? You've never even spoken to him. He has no discernable motive."

"Precisely. The crime isn't costly, and therefore, it must be personal. Who else but someone close to the Beales would know the destruction of these plants would cost him time, but not money? That narrows things down. No one flew to the marrow plants—they must have left tracks. But Mr. Beale reported only their own footprints were found in the area. So, the perpetrator must be someone whose tracks would go unnoticed."

"But—"

"If someone traipsed through the fields with a lantern, they would've been noticed, so they knew the land well enough to navigate by moonlight alone. However, even on the brightest of nights, it would be difficult to decipher wild parsnip from wild angelica. A distinction that becomes vital the following day when the sap on the skin is exposed to sunlight and results in a flat painful rash and blistered skin." Despite the brilliance of her reveal, she sighed like an old magician, tired of even his own tricks. "Mr. Beale has battled patches of wild parsnips on his farm for years now, but there are none between the borders of the farm and the location of the marrows. However, there are several between the house and the site of the destroyed seedlings."

Bludgeoned by the facts, I held my knees, dizzy. "But Eddie would never do that."

"It may sound improbable, but it's the only solution that fits all the circumstances, and therefore, it is the truth."

Sweat broke out under my arms as I recalled my certainty that Eddie had lied about where he got the rash. Still, lying wasn't against the law. Eddie was only a child, one of Ralph's best friends. "Why not go and speak to Mr. Beale discreetly?"

"I doubt Mr. Beale would be glad if his landlord brought him these tidings. Better that the news comes from a neutral party like the inspector," she said as we neared the High Street. "Which way is your house?"

Stones in my stomach, I gestured to the large trees before the bridge. "You may drop me here. It's easier on foot the rest of the way."

She pulled to a stop, and I climbed down. "Goodbye, Lady Holmes. I wish you luck with the inspector."

"Goodbye, Mrs. Hudson. What a singular experience it's been." She gave me a long look then sped away.

Traffic had to circle the town square to reach the High Street, so I hadn't lied. The shortcut to the police station was faster on foot. I hurried down the side path behind the store fronts and, from there, cut behind the doctor's office where George worked.

Of course, my brother chose this moment to pop his head

out of the doctor's back door. I almost collided with his slight frame.

"Katy?" he asked, catching me by the arms. "Where are you running to?"

I just shook my head at him as I pulled away. "I've no time, Georgie," I said, then paused. "Ralph or Eddie, are they in trouble? Have they said anything to you?"

George frowned, the dimple in his chin identical to Da's. "No, the boys have been quiet lately, if anything. Why, did something happen?"

"Not if I can help," I said, tearing off down the path, Georgie staring after me in confusion.

For as large as Eddie was now, I couldn't help but imagine him as a little boy, his shock of red hair as cheery as his smile. Eddie, Ralph, and Billy had gone everywhere together. School, the woods, fishing at the river, and since Ralph and I sparred more often than we made peace, I'd sometimes been fonder of Billy and Eddie than my own brother. Even if Eddie had been a stranger, though, I wouldn't let Lady Holmes turn him in without a fight. I thought, as I so often did, of how Da always told us we make ourselves useful in the world only through lightening the burdens of others. It was how he lived his life. I had so little left of him that I couldn't afford to abandon a single item, let alone one that had shaped me utterly.

My breath came in short bursts, and my forehead was damp when I popped out in front of the police station. No Lady Holmes in sight. I entered the two-story brick building with a feeling of grim satisfaction, finally one step ahead.

Inside, there was no sign of Reggie. A hunched figure wearing mismatched shawls banged her fist on the constable's desk. "You'll show me my husband, or you'll regret it, young man!"

Clean-shaven and stout, Constable Marks shook his head. "Mrs. Logan, as I've told you before, you can have your husband back when he's sober and you pay his fine."

The woman threw her hands up. "What am I meant to do till then, eh? He hid all our drink!"

To Constable Marks' credit, he didn't laugh. "You'll have to take your coin to the pub today, Mrs. Logan." He rose and led the woman past me and out onto the street, a fug of alcohol in her wake.

When he returned, he stepped inside and held the door open. "Come right in, Lady Holmes."

My heart sank. With no way to hide either my person or my intentions, I stood my ground, and still, when our eyes met a rush passed over my skin.

"I'm here to see Inspector Goodwin," we said in unison.

The constable's gaze bounced between us. "If you'll wait here, Lady Holmes, I'll get the inspector."

"Coward," I muttered to his retreating back.

"If you wished to see the end of our case, you could have asked to accompany me," Lady Holmes said, coming to stand beside me.

"If I wished to— No! Eddie's just a boy."

"Precisely. He should learn the consequences of his actions before they become much harsher. Perhaps the boy needs a mother's guiding hand," she said, her clear green eyes unwavering.

"And perhaps you should direct *your* attention toward home."

"Ladies!" a deep voice cut in, and we turned to where

Reggie stood in the arched hallway. His familiar dark hair, studded with a few threads of gray, curled over his long ears. When he saw me, his eyes widened and he tugged at his cuffs. "How can I help?"

Lady Holmes stepped in front of me. "I am here to inform you of Eddie Beale's guilt in the destruction of his father's marrow plants."

Reggie threw me a wondering look, his message clear. Did I know what I was doing, picking a public fight with our local gentry? I did know. It was a terrible decision. The problem was I didn't care.

I edged closer to him. "What Lady Holmes is trying to say is that Mr. Beale's complaint has been resolved. It's a family matter, and you may strike it from your books."

Lady Holmes stepped in front of me again. "The problem with Mrs. Hudson's suggestion is Mr. Beale has no knowledge of Eddie's involvement. I thought they might hear it better if the news were to come from you, Inspector."

He made a face as though he'd swallowed his brass buttons then covered it with a polite smile.

"Have you ever had any trouble with Eddie Beale, Inspector?" I asked, putting a soft emphasis on his title.

"Not a bit," he admitted.

"A good lad, that's always been my impression of him as well. After all, *I* was the one to question him. Lady Holmes has never met Eddie."

Reggie threw me a surprised look. "I've heard enough," he said. "Constable, why don't you take a written statement from Lady Holmes, and I will deal with Mrs. Hudson."

CHAPTER NINE

I'VE ALWAYS HAD A STRONG IMAGINATION.

When I was seven, my brother George and I spun ghost tales in the apple tree outside our old cottage. Deep in one particularly chilling tale—a ghoul with a single jagged tooth it scraped along the wall on its way to devour you—I terrified my brother. He tumbled to the grass, screaming, and went to hide in Ma's skirts. However, I couldn't move.

Afternoon tea, supper, came and went. I clung to the branches and pressed my cheek to the rough bark, certain the ghost, the one I'd raised out of nothing, waited for me by the front door.

We lived close to Sterling Place then, in the cottage that was my first home, so Da made it back from the stables before bedtime. His strong arms fished me out of the tree with a chuckle and a kiss on the head for my troubles. He set me free from myself.

As Reggie led me into his office, I allowed a fleeting wish that Da were here to save me from my own foolishness now. I might be innocent, Eddie might be blameless, but facts bent along lines of wealth and power like a red-hot nail under the smith's hammer.

Reggie shut the door after me. "Have a seat," he said, circling behind one of the heavy wooden chairs in front of his desk.

His office held more papers and fewer instruments of torture than I'd pictured. I thought of the shabby building a few streets over where the previous constable and his watchmen had resided all my childhood—when they weren't at the pub or coaxing rent from poor farmers with their fists.

All-white walls and gleaming woodwork, this building seemed to promise more, and the inspector's uniform was nothing but a cloth and brass version of the same. New tools constructed to attend to the needs of the new policeman, surfaces clean and intentions noble.

Somehow, I preferred the dirt on the outside.

Reggie sat next to me and reached for my hand. His dark gray eyes full of the same expression he'd worn the other day at market when he'd presented my brother as a thief. "Katy, picking a fight with Lady Holmes? Really?"

As Reggie walked me home from The Four Hounds last night, we lingered in one of the darker lanes for a moment. We hadn't kissed, not exactly, but it had been a near thing. Now I was glad we hadn't as it kept things a little cleaner.

Best that we stuck to the business at hand. "Eddie Beale—"

"I heard you the first time. You don't think the boy's guilty." Reggie squeezed my hand.

My face twisted. I wanted to be *right*. "Oh, Reggie, she has no proof."

He ran a large hand over his whiskers and sighed. "But you think Lady Holmes is right."

"Of course not," I said.

"But you—"

"I may agree with Lady Holmes in fact, but not in principle. She sees Eddie as a solution to a riddle she's taken a fancy to solving, the result of an experiment." I threw a hand into the air. "But he's a boy, and whatever his reasons for destroying those marrow plants, should we let something so trivial cast him down in the eyes of his family and his neighbors?"

Reggie rubbed his thumb over my knuckles and said softly, "I know you like the boy, and he's Ralph's mate, but—"

My voice rose as I cut him off. "Maybe if Eddie's innocent, then Ralph ..." I trailed off. I didn't want him thinking of Ralph in connection with this. "You and I grew up here. We know. Small-town gossip is like building with pine; it'll be weeping pitch through paint or polish for the next fifty years."

A door slammed somewhere in the building.

When he leaned forward, the rich scent of his soap hit me, and I was back in that dim lane from last night, my heart stammering as though caught in a fist. "Mr. Beale is Lady Holmes' tenant and Eddie is his son. They've the right to determine how to deal with his actions. You can't dispute that?"

"I don't. But are you ready to condemn him over a few dead plants?" No lads were going to come clattering into Reggie's office the way they had down the lane last night and prevent our lips from touching. I sat back but left my hand in Reggie's. "I could speak with Eddie, warn him. I'm sure that would be the end of it."

Reggie frowned, pale skin showing through his dark brown whiskers. "How did you get mixed up in this matter, anyway? I don't like it."

I opened my mouth to retort that it wasn't his business to like it or not but reminded myself I'd invited him in. So, instead, I stuck to the facts.

"Following her husband's death, Lady Holmes found her tenants were keeping their distance from her. Though I can't say I blame them. Anyway, when I applied for a position at Musgrave Hall, she employed me to investigate the matter, hoping Mr. Beale would be more frank to a neighbor than a landlord."

"Listen, Katy." His eyes flicked from my face to my black dress, and I knew what he was going to say next as though the words were written on his forehead. I was finally going to have to endure the speech I'd avoided during tea and dinner at The Four Hounds. "Mourning is a difficult time. Grief can do strange things to people. You and Lady Holmes are doing your best, I'm sure, but is this fitting behavior for two respectable women? What would John think of you out here, acting like this?"

Grief. An interloper who lay next to me in the dark and dogged my every step, one with nothing but terrible questions in its mouth. Who was I now? How much of me was left? Was it enough?

But the awful and wonderful truth was that only I held the answers. I was sick to my very bones of everyone from my family right up to the Queen herself telling me the shape my mourning should take. Draped in black cloth, poured into good deeds, and whispered as prayers. That it should sap all color from my life and force me to be nothing but a shade in my own town, wandering my home but no longer a vital part. What *could* John think of any of it? If he was listening, if he was anywhere, he was beyond even the reach of Mr. Field's cable, the one that stretched from Ireland to Newfoundland, crossing unfathomable miles of frigid ocean.

John wasn't answering my words of devotion, so he was hardly going to show up to scold me. For better or for worse, he'd lost a say in the matter, and bloody Reggie Goodwin had done little enough to earn one. Even his sister, Annabelle, had always been the better kisser.

"Reggie, I don't think—" He squeezed my hand, and I was no longer sure how I wanted to finish my sentence.

Then he smiled. "I'll speak to the lad privately if you promise that you and Lady Holmes will keep your distance from each other until you're thinking more clearly." He shook his head. "What your poor Ma would feel, hearing of this. I hate to think about it."

As much as I wanted to argue with Reggie, he was right. Ma would be upset if she knew I'd challenged Lady Holmes in this way, putting my new relationship with Reggie at risk. I had his word he would take care of Eddie, and that was enough for now. I patted his hand before standing. He rose with me. "Thank you. I promise to leave Lady Holmes far behind."

As Reggie walked me to the front door of the station, he whispered into my ear. "Come and see me when you're feeling down instead of making a spectacle of yourself, aye?"

His eyes were kind, but I needed some time alone to sort out my feelings—about Reggie, John, and myself.

The door to the room where Constable Marks had led Lady Holmes was still closed. At least I wouldn't have to face her again, a relief in light of my recent promise.

At the heavy front doors, Reggie gave me an encouraging smile, which I managed to return. I'd only made it a few steps down the street when a woman shouted.

"Reginald Goodwin!"

His smile slid into an angry stare directed over my shoulder. "Now before you start—"

"*Start?*" The stout woman who had spoken marched up the steps, face hidden by her bonnet except for the firm set of her jaw. "My boy's been missing for over a week, gone without a word, and I've been worrying myself into the ground with every passing minute. You're the one who needs to *start*! Do your job! Find Billy!" She jabbed a long finger toward Reggie's immaculate uniform.

"Mrs. Mudd, calm yourself."

I caught my breath as the woman raised her face. If he hadn't said her name, I wouldn't have recognized Frances Mudd, even though she was Ma's cousin, and she and Billy were often over at our house. Her wide, happy face had been rewritten with swollen eyes and wrinkles deep as gills lining her pale lips.

Despair. The face Ma had worn after Da was killed, the face that had stared back at me from the mirror in those first broken days after John's death.

"Billy's fifteen," Reggie said. "He's gone to live with his father to further his prospects, as any man might. You've a telegram saying exactly that."

Frances gave a sickly laugh. "A caring telegram from Tom Mudd! Not likely. What will you believe next? That I'm to take tea with the Queen? You've got to find Billy." Her voice cracked so that it made my skin ache for her.

"Her Majesty's police force has more important things to do than act as nursemaids." Reggie pointed down the road. "Get a train to Eastbourne if you're not satisfied."

I gasped. I'd never heard Reggie speak harshly before.

Frances hissed. "Your Da always said you were useless, Reggie Goodwin, but I never knew you were cruel as well. Are you offering to pay for my ticket, lodgings, and lost wages while I take a holiday?"

A rush of blood climbed his cheeks.

"Billy's a good lad. He wouldn't have left without saying goodbye. Not to me. If you won't help, I'll find him myself, and when I do, I'll make sure everyone hears how you turned me away!" Frances spun on her heel, careening into me as she plowed down the street but giving no sign of recognition.

I turned to ask Reggie about Billy but was met with a bang as he disappeared into the police station.

"A good lad?" A familiar voice spoke from just behind me. "Isn't that your call to ride to the rescue?"

Chapter Ten

"ARE YOU AWARE THERE ARE MORE PLACES TO STAND in Sherrinford than in the three feet directly behind me?" I asked, my smile full of sharp edges. At least I'd kept my startled yelp inside this time.

My barb entirely escaped Lady Holmes' notice. She gazed in the direction Frances disappeared. "What did she mean by 'a caring telegram from Tom Mudd'?"

"They had a troubled marriage before he left, so I suppose she was surprised to hear from him at all."

"Curious." Her wide eyes found mine.

I wished I hadn't spoken. Seeing Frances like that left me worried for Billy, but it wasn't Lady Holmes' business.

"I've been assured Inspector Goodwin will see to the issue of Eddie Beale, so we're free to look into the disappearance of Billy Mudd," she said.

Shock wore my face like a new shoe, stiff and bright. "You no longer have a right to promise me and my time."

Lady Holmes shrugged. "But we've already had one success where Inspector Goodwin failed."

A wagon stacked with crates rumbled by the grocer's at the far end of the street, and three young boys raced toward the opposite end, a terrier at their heels. They looked so much like younger versions of Ralph, Billy, and Eddie that it knocked a chip out of my newly polished resolve.

"There is no *we*," I said, stepping away.

Her much longer stride easily outpaced mine. Again.

"Are you telling me you would withhold your help from Mrs. Mudd?" Her voice was neutral even if her words were a well-executed salvo.

"Billy isn't missing. He's gone to his father's in Eastbourne. My brother works with the lad, and he heard it himself." We were approaching the turning to the shortcut, and I slowed. No need to give her any ideas of how to sneak up on me the next time by walking her to my door.

"Even more curious, then." She tipped her head in the direction Frances took. "Because if that's true, why doesn't his mother accept it?"

Two days ago, when Ralph mentioned Billy was gone, I'd been too busy with my own worries, but now my oversized imagination worked to make up the deficit.

Had Billy gone to live with his father? Tom Mudd was a rough man soured by drink and the belief that life owed him an easier road than the one he'd been given. And Billy was devoted to his mother. Her last living child, the only reason she let him get a job was because he'd be working alongside Ralph. Frances was right. If he were to leave, he would at least say goodbye. But if Billy was missing, what had happened to him? Was he running away from someone? Had he been kidnapped? Or worse?

And if so, why couldn't Reggie see it? He wasn't

particularly clever, but he was dogged. Anyway, it wasn't as though our town was overrun with other cases, so he should have time. I would speak to him about it, and clear things up. Maybe even help him to find Billy.

I leaned forward until I could see Lady Holmes clearly through her veil. "The Mudds don't need you putting your high-handed ways into their private business. You're far too comfortable handing out judgments and calling them justice. If you truly want to help people, sell your land to the tenant farmers rather than lining your pockets with their profits, and work for your bread like the rest of us." I gobbled down the hurt in her eyes and reached for more. "At the very least, see to your precious Mycroft and Sherlock. Look after your estate. They're your responsibility to manage."

The pain in her eyes flickered out. Lady Holmes was gone. A closed door, a distant whisper, a worrisome riddle—she had been all these things and more—but now she was a frozen island far out to sea. There, yet unreachable.

She blinked twice, quickly. "I've misjudged your interest in the matter. It won't happen again."

The edge in her voice severed whatever inexplicable tie was between us. After a very long day, I was free. Finally. Free from experiments, free from what I would sell for thirty pounds, free from questions of innocence and guilt.

Although my cruel words left a sour taste in my mouth as I turned and walked away, I felt lighter than I had in months. Even Sterling Place didn't sound awful. Perhaps marriage to Reggie. At least I understood what each of those would ask of me. If I was lucky, they would cost me nothing extra. Perhaps seeing Lord Wallace Sterling and his son Clarence outside Musgrave Hall had been a sign and not an omen, a symbol of the future.

I almost floated behind the doctor's office, retracing the shortcut to our lane. Either way, my family would be well-fed and educated, my siblings able to find work in telegraph offices, and our mother retired from the body-breaking work of taking in washing. When was the last time I'd made such a choice for myself? Even if the rest of my steps were already written, at least in this moment my decision belonged to me.

By the time I reached our cottage, I was so sure a letter from Sterling Place would be waiting for me, that my heart barely fluttered when I found it on the table inside the door.

Dear Mrs. Hudson,

I was pleased to receive your letter inquiring after employment. We would be happy to see your return. Please present yourself to the housekeeper, Mrs. Nash, tomorrow, and she will decide where your skills would best fit at Sterling Place.

I ran the thick paper through my fingers and traced the signature of Lord Sterling's butler, my blood humming with possibility.

Drawn by loud voices, I headed for the kitchen to inform my family of the glad tidings. It sounded like half the town was assembled behind it, which meant at least three Buntings.

Inside, I stopped short, the letter raised in victory. At our kitchen table, Frances Mudd sat weeping into a cup of tea, surrounded by Ma, Georgie, Elizabeth, Oliver, Louise, and little Rosie, who patted Frances' arm. Even Ralph was there, squeezed into the far corner of the kitchen by the cook stove, looking just wretched. I plunged the letter into my pocket.

"Again! That useless sack of potatoes trussed up in a policeman's uniform won't listen to me." Frances buried her face in her handkerchief, and her shoulders shook.

If I admitted I'd overheard the altercation between Frances and Reggie, then I'd have to explain what I'd been doing at the police station. And even if I swore my family to secrecy about Eddie's guilt, word would spread. A Bunting hadn't been born yet who could keep quiet. Bless us.

"Is it Billy?" I asked Ralph, who shoved his hands in his pockets miserably. George put his hand on Ralph's shoulder. I sat at the table and tugged Rosie onto my lap, the warm weight a comfort. "What do the police say?"

Frances lifted her face, freshly etched by her tears, and shoved a small envelope at me. "That *this* is all the proof they need."

A telegram. I couldn't help myself. I tugged it free and scanned the neat writing at speed.

```
Billy wants to live with me STOP Letter
to explain STOP Tom
```

I read it again, thinking I must have missed something. "But this says Billy's with his father?"

"Aye, there's no problem with the words; it's the date that's wrong." She pointed to the upper corner. "The third of May! I'd just put a letter in the postbox that afternoon, asking Tom if he'd seen Billy. It hadn't even been collected when the telegram came."

Ma made an angry noise. "I wish my Bernard were here; he wouldn't stop till he'd found a way to help." She rubbed her palm over Frances' knuckles, worn down to similar shades of red.

"Maybe Billy asked him to send it or sent it himself and signed Tom's name so you wouldn't worry," I said. "That could account for the wrong date. Did you receive the letter it talks about?"

This brought on a fresh round of weeping, and I looked at Ma in alarm. "The letter came alright, with nothing inside but a five-pound note."

"It's like what happened with Bernard." Frances dashed the tears from her eyes. "It isn't right! Why's Billy suddenly worth five pounds to a man who didn't give two pence for him in all his years?"

Georgie and I locked eyes, his confusion a mirror for my own. Bernard? Did she mean Da? Nothing made sense, not why Frances would bring Da into this, or why Tom would take such an interest in Billy. Instead, I studied the one thing I knew: the telegram form and envelope.

"Who delivered this?" I asked.

Frances gave a great sniff. "I found it shoved under my door."

"A messenger boy ought to have delivered it and asked you to sign for it. Wait, when I visited our local telegraph office looking for a job, I overheard the clerk complaining about having to take the messages to the Post Office."

"They don't have enough staff for home delivery," Ma said.

"Has Tom ever—" A ghost leaped from the page and stole my words, my lips growing numb.

Scrawled across the line where the counter clerk always signed was a familiar signature. That of a man who didn't exist anymore. There, at the upper left corner of the telegram form—John Hudson.

Chapter Eleven

After a long night and even longer morning, I once again found myself in the bustling kitchen of Musgrave Hall. The air was thick with the scent of roasting meat and onions, but I was too exhausted to be hungry. Out of patience, I handed the kitchen maid, Daisy, a note for Lady Holmes containing a single word. If that wasn't enough, an entire book wouldn't win her over.

"Wait here, ma'am, and I'll see if m'lady is available," Daisy said before hurrying off.

The kitchen boy, elbow-deep in potato peelings, threw me a curious look but showed me to a low stool by a bowl of rising bread. I ground my teeth at the thought of facing Lady Holmes. My jaw ached from where I'd spent the last twenty-four hours doing much the same. I swore I'd never see her again, and yet here I was ready to beg for an audience. Neither my first choice, nor my second or third—indeed, I had no choice.

Grief was such a noxious weed. Beat it down in one corner of the garden, only to find it budding in another.

When I'd recognized John's signature, the cruelest part had been the whisper of hope. Given the date of the telegram, it was impossible he'd signed it, and yet, my first thought had been—*What if?*

All night, tears flooded my dreams in a way they hadn't since the first days following his death, and I faced the dawn with a heavy heart and eyes. In the unforgiving light of day, however, my pitiful hope had transferred itself to Billy Mudd. He couldn't afford for me to spend my time grasping at phantoms.

The kitchen boy stalked by, carrying a basket of greens, and Mrs. Kelley dumped the rising bread onto the counter with a flurry of flour speckling the sunlight. But even in that familiar rhythm, I found no comfort.

Where was Billy?

Not safe and well, living with his father in Eastbourne. Even if Tom was clever enough to forge a telegram, which I doubted, why do so when he could send one through the usual channels? Luckily, Frances and the rest of my family were too caught up in the telegram's contents to bother examining the clerk's name, so even if they'd been familiar with John's signature nobody else noticed the forgery. Only George had questioned me last night, but he had the foolishly admirable quality of jumping first and asking questions later, and the last thing I needed was two brothers in trouble. So I'd lied and said I was only worried about Billy. Which meant at least I didn't have to explain the theories and worries spiraling through my mind to my loved ones.

What I needed right now was a more neutral confidant with a sharp mind, because someone had forged that telegram. Of that, I had no doubt.

The question nagged me no matter which way I turned the puzzle: why go to the trouble of forging a telegram? All one needed to do was pretend to be Mr. Mudd, write their message, hand over the postage, and sign the receipt. Fairly anonymous.

The kitchen boy passed me with another basket of greens, his chin tipping up in a way I'd seen somewhere before.

Just as though someone had whispered in my ear, a thought arrived. What if the sender of the telegram couldn't risk being recognized or having a record of the telegram?

That left me terrified for poor Billy because, right now, I was the only one who knew what was amiss. Our local telegraph manager didn't care. He'd made that abundantly clear when I spoke to him first thing this morning. And Reggie, well, his face had soured as soon as I'd mentioned Billy's disappearance. He ranted about how I couldn't keep pressing on our connection to use the police force like my servants. Then he'd made an awful accusation against me before suggesting I see a doctor for my hysteria. However, none of that stopped him from suggesting we stroll on the green after supper tonight as he deposited me back on the front steps of the station.

So here I sat wearing my cold resolve like a knight before battle, trying to think of anything except for the two different letters I'd drafted to the butler of Sterling Place and how much I didn't want to send either of them. My mouth grew dry, and I scraped my cold palms over my skirts. The kitchen boy wandered past me with yet another in a seemingly endless supply of identical baskets of greens. His spindly limbs and dark curls pained me the way Oliver's did. If Musgrave Hall insisted on employing children, they could at least feed them.

"Don't you eat anything except spinach?" I asked.

He flushed at my words but didn't back away. "Your hair's not fancy 'nuf to be a lady's maid. Your dress is too fine to be a housemaid or a laundress. Are you a governess?"

His challenge made me feel braver, and I lifted my shoulders. "My goodness, the maid was right. You really are the sleuth of Musgrave Hall. I'm almost sorry to say I'm not a governess. I am the oldest of seven, though. Does that count?"

He didn't laugh, only shook his head before saying, "Lady Holmes will see you in the study." He set down his greens and waited for me to follow.

I was more collected than on my last visit, but I had less opportunity to study Musgrave Hall as this time we took a direct path, following a long corridor to a narrow set of back stairs. These spit us out at the opposite end of a hallway, studded with thick paneled doors that I recognized. As before, the boy knocked before scampering away when Lady Holmes bid me enter.

When I did, she waved me into one of the chairs opposite the desk. There was a large ledger spread before her; my note lay on top. She tapped it. "Kidnapping? I thought you were sure the lad had gone to live with his father."

The same regular ticking came from a shelf to my left along with a whiff of ammonia.

"Yes. Well, that's what I thought until I heard the facts from Mrs. Mudd herself." Lady Holmes raised a delicate brow, and I explained my connection along with what Frances had said about the date of the telegram. "It's a forgery. A very good one. I suspect the stamp is fake as well. The perforations at the corners are odd and the printing blurry. Even the franking is smeared over the stamp rather than clear, which obscures the location and date the telegram supposedly passed through a telegraph office."

I didn't mention John, only tapped his name against my thigh.

"For all that telegraphy is a marvelous technology, it is still one operated by humans. And humans make mistakes, clerks as well as printing offices," Lady Holmes said in the same patronizing tone as Reggie and the manager of our local telegraph office.

I bit my lip. Revealing my suspicions to them had only left me with regrets. Would Lady Holmes react any differently? I should be on my way to secure a position at Sterling Place, but I was here instead. If I couldn't walk away from Eddie Beale, how could I leave Billy and Frances alone? Da would have been broken-hearted if I did that. They needed my help.

I steeled my nerves. "It isn't a mistake."

"Mrs. Hudson, you can't—"

"I *can*. They forged John's signature on the telegram."

Whatever Lady Holmes had been about to say evaporated on her parted lips, and all that came out was a startled hiss. Her large green eyes, like a pair of puddles on the river road after the rain, locked onto mine. "Your husband?"

I nodded. "Done with an expert hand."

"Forgive me for asking an indelicate question, but you're sure—"

"I sat with his body through the night until the undertaker came the next morning." My jaw clenched, but I kept my voice steady. Barely.

"I see." A clock somewhere in the house began chiming the hour. "And the stamp?"

"John's best friend, Samuel Scott, who works in the

telegraph office at the stock exchange, had what he thought was a forgery and asked John's opinion on it at our home one night over supper. It had those same angled edges and smeared franking. Samuel's wife Eleanor is a telegraph clerk as well, and we went round and round on whether the printing on the stamp itself appeared blurry or how such a thing might happen—as you say, humans make errors."

She waved a hand in the air. "Leaving aside the matter of the stamp, which cannot be proved at the moment, what did the local telegraph office and Inspector Goodwin say?"

My skin rippled in surprise. "How did you know I'd spoken to them?"

"If you hadn't spoken to others first, you'd have been here hours ago. And you wouldn't be here at all if I wasn't your last resort."

I couldn't deny the charge. "The telegraph manager claimed if the message was forged and the stamp fraudulent, the blame couldn't fall on his office. Reg—that is, Inspector Goodwin insinuated *I* had forged the telegram myself in an attempt to aid Frances' case."

"Which, of course, you didn't," she said. "I saw your face yesterday when she accosted the inspector, and you were as shocked as I."

My anger, which had been boiling just under my chin, evaporated. How had she been watching me on an empty street without my knowledge? And why had she been making a study of my expressions? I flushed at the thought of being scrutinized like the subject of yet another experiment, but Lady Holmes seemed untroubled by her admission.

She cupped her chin and stared over my shoulder. "Even if Mr. Mudd would or could go to such lengths to disguise

Billy's disappearance, the question would still be 'why?' What reason would he have to lie? Equally, why would anyone else?" Her gaze settled on mine again, familiar if not comforting. "Hence, your charge of kidnapping."

This was the opening I'd come begging for, and Billy needed me to sacrifice my pride, to be brave enough to force a change. I swallowed hard.

"Precisely. We should interview Frances first, then ask around at the inn where Billy worked. Contact the authorities in Eastbourne ourselves. Or perhaps your late husband's ambitious cousin in Scotland Yard, Sergeant Forrester? Someone must have seen Billy at his father's place, if he's there." The ticking from the shelf ceased, and my breath sounded loud in the sudden silence.

"I find only one fault with your plan," Lady Holmes said.

"Yes?"

"As I was recently informed, there is no 'we.'" She folded my note in half and slid it to me across the polished expanse of her desk.

I pushed it back, willing my riotous heart to still. "There could be."

"In what capacity?"

"While we investigate, I act as your lady's maid. I know I'm not qualified, but I'm a fast learner."

Lady Holmes studied me, but I couldn't read her expression. "Mrs. Hudson, the truth is I've little need for a lady's maid." She gestured at her inky gown. "My clothes are plain, I favor simple hairstyles, and I dislike scents or cosmetics. Even if it were otherwise, I'm eight months into my mourning period and not out in society again. I agreed to engage a lady's maid again at Mrs. Greaves' insistence, and now that she's gone, I'm left to please only myself."

As much as the Mudds needed help, my circumstances hadn't changed. I could no more volunteer my services to Frances than I could to Lady Holmes. And though I disliked the idea of working at Sterling Place or marrying Reggie, could I live with myself if I took a job with Lady Holmes, suffering her unpredictable ways and hidden motivations?

The problem, the pricking thorn in all my minutes, was that I wasn't left to please only myself. What childish terrors my imagination had conjured once upon a time were nothing compared to the reality my family would face. The workhouse, homelessness, death. I no longer had my father's arms to fetch me from danger and carry me to safety. I should have to swallow my pride and rescue myself.

"A lady's maid in name only then," I offered. "What you need, if you want to continue local investigations, is a partner. I've already proven myself capable." Lady Holmes frowned, and I jumped in. "Please. They stole my husband's good name. It's one of the few things I have left of him."

Lady Holmes stood. "I'm not concerned about John Hudson's name, good or otherwise. If we are to work together, you can't undermine the investigation because you feel sorry for the culprit."

"Well"—I thrust myself to my feet and squared my shoulders—"I can't have you making decisions for both of us. These are real people, not experiments."

A smile softened the sharp planes of her face. "I'm sure we'll both do our best. Now, to settle terms—how about thirty pounds to engage your services and another thirty when we solve the case?"

CHAPTER TWELVE

FRANCES CAST YET ANOTHER GLANCE IN LADY Holmes' direction and fidgeted with the already straight plate of biscuits and the tea things. Having a lady dressed as a maid sitting in her kitchen seemed to be too much for Frances' nerves.

She had my sympathy. I rarely knew what to make of Lady Holmes either. Following my brief introductions, Lady Holmes had remained unnervingly silent, sipping her tea and studying the room while Frances and I talked. Since Lady Holmes had accompanied me, I thought she would be asking her own questions, but instead she'd rattled off another list to memorize on the drive into town. I'd almost reached the end of them, and we'd learned little more than what we already knew about Billy's disappearance.

"Was Billy acting strangely before he disappeared?" I asked.

Frances shook her head. "I've dragged my mind over it again and again, but there was nothing out of the ordinary."

I chewed another stale biscuit and washed it down with

a sip of tea. I'd taken a handful of them to offset the single untouched biscuit on Lady Holmes' saucer.

"Ralph once hid a festering toe for a month, and we only found out when Oliver stepped on his foot and Ralph burst into tears," I said, and we smiled weakly at each other. "Was Billy the sort to keep things bottled up?"

"Oh, aye, little things. That he'd torn his new trousers or nipped down to the river to fish with his mates instead of coming straight home after work. Once, he hid a stray kitten in the coal chute for a few hours before the poor mite gave itself away mewling. Tom made him give it to my mother."

Frances plucked at the sleeve of her dress where it had frayed, and my heart twisted. She earned her living as a seamstress, and I'd never seen her less than turned out.

"When was the last time you saw Tom?" I asked.

"Had to be about four Christmases ago, when he came around begging for another 'loan.'" Her face clouded. "He was living with some woman, and she was … caught. Or so he said. I can never be sure with Tom."

My cheeks burned, and I took another bite of biscuit to cover my discomfiture.

Lady Holmes, however, spoke for the first time since we'd arrived. "Caught? As in with child?"

I choked, soggy crumbs spraying down the bodice of my dress and the kitchen table. While I coughed, Frances jumped up to fetch a cleaning rag, and I glared at Lady Holmes.

"*Now* you find your voice?" I whispered, then coughed again. "You can't just ask something like that. And you ought to eat your biscuit."

She blinked at her plate, then at me. "How else was I to know?"

Frances returned and brushed at my dress. "I'm not ashamed of Tom's faults. He owns 'em. Don't fuss at m'lady, Katy. She's trying to help, even though it's no obligation of hers."

In fact, Lady Holmes' motives remained a mystery to me as well. I was too worried that if I pressed her on them, she might abandon the investigation altogether, and though I'd argued she needed me, the reverse was even more true.

I cleared my throat. "Speaking of Tom, could you give us his address?"

"It's written down in my bureau. I'll have to fetch it."

"While you do, could we examine whatever Billy left behind?" Lady Holmes asked, rising.

Frances pressed the rag to her chest and looked at the ceiling. "Left behind?"

It was all I could do not to grab Lady Holmes by her perfectly formed ear, drag her outside, and let my tongue give her a lesson in not insinuating that someone's beloved son had run away. I stood as well, putting a hand on Frances' arm. "I'm sure you've already looked for a note or clues, but you never know what fresh eyes might notice."

Tears swam down her cheeks. "His room's the small one on the left. Around Christmas, I tried to give him the bigger one, a boy should have space to grow, but he wouldn't hear of it. Said that I deserved—" She clapped a hand over her mouth and bent double, but when I wrapped my arms around her, she waved me off, sniffing. "No, Katy, don't waste your time on me. Go search and I'll find that address."

How did she put one foot in front of the other, let

alone manage tea for us? When she couldn't hold her son, couldn't see him safe or speak to him? As often as Ralph and I sparked like a negative wire touching a positive lead, I would be frantic if he were missing. I'd be taking the world apart to bring him home. With no other way to help Frances and Billy, I rubbed my hand over my aching heart and followed Lady Holmes.

The Mudds rented a newer home in the town, one of a connected modern block built to house the workers when the railway came through and converted after the tracks were complete. The house had windows at the front and back, leaving the central hallway dark until we reached the rear of the house where light spilled in. There, two low casements overlooked the small garden plot.

Frances disappeared through the opposite door, and we entered Billy's bedroom. Small but relatively neat, it held a single bed pushed against the far wall. This left enough room for a makeshift desk under the window, cobbled together from what looked like spare boards and boxes. In their former life, they'd held wine bottles, but now the wooden dividers were stuffed with rolled-up papers, writing implements, and small tools. A long roll of butcher paper lay along the back of the desk, held in place by a T-shaped wooden ruler.

"What are we looking for?" I asked as Lady Holmes lifted the bedclothes and shook them. Specks of dust and small feathers danced through the sunlight from the window.

"Everything in and out of the ordinary, Hudson. You take the trunk at the foot of the bed."

Hudson. I gritted my teeth but knelt before the trunk. After all, referring to one's lady's maid by their last name was common practice, and I had begged my way into this bargain with eyes wide open.

Less a trunk and more of a wooden chest, when I lifted the loose lid, the scent of old mud soured the air. I wrinkled my nose, searching the folded pile of trousers, shirts, underthings, and at the bottom, a winter coat. After checking the pockets—a coil of thick string, four receipts dated last year, two nubs of pencils, and a moldy eraser—I felt into the corners of the chest and even tipped it up to examine the back and underside.

Lady Holmes had moved to the desk, and I joined her there with my motley collection. "Any luck with the bed?"

She made a low noise and shook her head, peering at the receipts I handed her. "Not illuminating, are they? These are all from The Four Hounds but are at least a year outdated. I'd guess he was saving them for sketching on the back."

Laid out on the desk and held down by smooth river stones in each corner was a section of butcher paper covered in the detailed sketch of a tree. I pulled it toward the light. "Billy's always had a knack for drawing, but I had no idea he'd got so good."

"Untrained, I assume?" she said.

"Did you think he had the money for drawing lessons?"

She gave me an arch look. "Asking questions is sometimes the most efficient way to gather facts. And facts are how we solve the case."

"In another life, in another world, Billy would be an artist—not unloading deliveries at the local inn and sketching on the back of receipts in stolen moments."

"Do you want to debate the lad's artistic talent, or do you want to find him?"

I puffed out my cheeks and nursed my ire while she emptied the rolled-up drawings from their cubbyholes. Sketches of birds, flowers, and Frances were sandwiched in between detailed drawings of the High Street and The Four Hounds. Snakes, an abandoned boot, a close-up of a horse's eye, and even portraits of the other young men who worked at the inn appeared as Lady Holmes unfurled them. Some appeared as the work of minutes to him, mere foolery, not something he'd labored over. And yet, they had a life about them, finer details that left me feeling like I might squint my eyes and step into the picture.

"That's my brother Ralph!" I tapped the likeness of him sitting beside some dilapidated barn. But she didn't pause to look, only piled the next sketch on top, a landscape divided by a river and dotted with a cluster of trees and scrub bushes.

When she reached the end of the drawings, she pulled two free, then pinned the rest in place with a spare river rock.

"His animal sketches quite rival those I've seen in texts on the subject. For example, *Vipera berus*." Lady Holmes handed me the first sketch.

In it, a thick serpent lay on a rock with a neat zigzag of gray and black striping its coils. I stroked the page, almost expecting to feel the nubs of overlapping diamond scales that mirrored the tuft of meadowgrass beside it.

I swallowed down a shudder of disgust. The last, and thankfully only, time I'd touched such a creature had been when George found a grass snake in the compost heap and hid it in my school bag. At first, I'd mistaken its cool body for one of the leather straps. Until it moved, shifting under my fingers like a fist in a glove. After that, the lovely baker's daughter somehow found out Georgie still sucked his thumb while he slept.

"What manner of snake is it?" I asked.

"The adder. One of only three native to England, and the single venomous species. Common enough, though not populous as they're often killed when spotted."

I glanced about the room and fought off the urge to check under my skirts.

"Don't worry." She smiled wryly. "They favor wooded glades and grassy heaths, not dimly lit bedrooms."

She offered me the second sketch, and I swallowed hard. This was a different beast altogether. Thick as a man's arm, it curled over an angled branch, its coils drooping almost to the floor. The markings on its pebbled skin resembled pools of lichen on a blackened log.

"What on earth is that?"

"*Boa constrictor occidentalis.* Native to the Argentine and Paraguayan rainforests, they are much maligned because they feed on live animals. The more sensitive members of the public cast them as minor devils for it, and I had to write a letter to *The Times* in their defense. Their methods of feeding are natural and not calculated to excite painful human emotions. This one appears to be female, judging by its larger size."

"Why would—"

"Ideas abound." She waved a hand. "Female reptiles are often larger than the males, perhaps because they carry clutches of eggs. Or it may be a signal males are becoming less necessary to the continuation of the species. After all, parthenogenesis has been observed in isolated female snakes in captivity." She must have read the growing confusion in my face because she added, "So-called 'virgin births.'"

The air in the small room evaporated, my breath quickening. I thrust the sketches at Lady Holmes. "No. I meant why would Billy sketch a serpent like this? Where could he have observed it?"

"Possibly in a volume of ..." Lady Holmes trailed off even as she gestured at the room. There were no books here. "A borrowed text, then. Or, I first observed a boa constrictor at the Reptile Gardens in London, and Billy could have done the same."

"London?" Frances said as she walked through the bedroom door. "Billy's never been."

Lady Holmes tipped the sketch toward Frances, who *tsked*. "I never liked that one. He said he copied it from a postcard Alfie gave him." She handed me a scrap of paper where she'd printed Tom's address.

"Alfie Stewart who runs The Four Hounds?" I asked.

"Yes, why? Do you think it's important?"

The pleading hope in Frances' thin voice reminded me of our serious purpose here, and all I couldn't promise her. My throat twisted so I couldn't speak.

"Very likely not," Lady Holmes said lightly. "We are just getting started here. Thank you for your time, Mrs. Mudd. Come along, Hudson." She turned for the door and stepped into the hallway.

Frances' face crumpled, and she plopped onto Billy's bed—the mess we'd left of his tidy room all around her. I stepped closer, but she waved me away again. "Go find Billy. Please."

I backed up to the bedroom door. "Lady Holmes and I will see ourselves out," I muttered before following my employer outside, where I planned to cheerfully drown her in the river.

CHAPTER THIRTEEN

OUR ROUTE TO THE FOUR HOUNDS DIDN'T BRING US close to the river—unfortunately for my hot-headed plans to tie a rock to her ankles and toss Lady Holmes into the deepest part. Nevertheless, the long walk gave me plenty of time to address my grievances.

"The next time someone brings up a tender subject, such as their wayward husband's family entanglements, keep your fingers out of the wound," I said as we rounded the corner beside the greengrocer's.

Lady Holmes squinted as though confused. "I was clarifying the facts of the case."

Two tall men in suits walked by, barely lifting their caps in our direction, and I couldn't help but speculate how they might have acted were Lady Holmes dressed as herself instead of a maid. She, however, didn't seem to notice the slight.

"This again. How are we to secure your precious facts if no one will speak to us?"

"I'm not doing this to make friends, Hudson," Lady

Holmes said more loudly than necessary.

"Clearly."

She threw me an unreadable look through her short veil.

"Why are you here, then?" I asked before my better judgment could stop me.

"A boy is missing."

"You're not the police. The Mudds aren't your tenants. You've no responsibility to them." I pressed my lips together.

Her wide eyes slid to mine, catching there on whatever she found in my expression. "Careful or I shall mistake you for Inspector Goodwin." When I didn't laugh, she shook her head. "My mother was a woman who had the good sense to pass away shortly after I was born. I couldn't seem to manage the same trick. So here I am. With an abundance of time and resources. Some problems simply merit solving."

Her unexpected honesty cooled my molten temper. "I see. Well, it's kind of you."

"On the contrary, it's entirely selfish. I should like to prove I can help someone using my own abilities instead of through my husband's name or fortune. Our business arrangement came along at precisely the right moment."

"Our business arrangement. Of course." Precise and damning, as usual it was impossible to parse my feelings around her words. This business arrangement was mutually beneficial, and I didn't need or want anything more from her except sixty pounds. So why was I suddenly walking as though I had a thorn in my shoe? I pointed down the street. "I need to call into the Post Office."

We turned together, the sour reek of the gutter rising up to meet us on the arms of the afternoon sun.

"Hudson, so long as we find the truth, our clients can't

fault our methods. Most people prefer plain speaking, anyway," Lady Holmes said.

"That's obviously what you prefer, but I assure you, the opposite is true with 'most people.' Aren't these social graces second nature for Lady Holmes of Musgrave Hall? Trained from the cradle knowing the correct spoon to use, who to snub, and with an army of polite conversation—"

"What is so important that you need to visit the Post Office while we should be looking for Billy?" she asked, her voice rising again. Were it possible, I could have sworn Lady Holmes stood straighter and her stride lengthened.

The dual letters I carried seemed to tug on my reticule. "I must send word to Sterling Place that I've found … employment."

Her steps slowed. "Oh. I see. You've been offered a position there?"

"I had."

"Why didn't you take it?"

Sterling Place might be my haven of last resort, but she didn't need to know why. I'd hoped she would hire me, and in doing so, save me from the soul-splitting work of being in service, yes, but that I needed saving at all, let alone by Lady Holmes, left a bitter poison on my spirit. One made worse by being referred to as a "business arrangement." However, I wasn't about to expose my vulnerabilities to her sharp tongue and even sharper discernment.

"I found word from Sterling Place waiting for me along with Frances when I returned from the police station. But after speaking with her, the situation had changed."

We walked down the street in silence, and I thought we were safely past the topic when Lady Holmes spoke again.

"We should settle the terms of your employment."

My heart galloped out of my throat and made a loop around the town square, only to collapse, panting, at my feet. "Settle? I thought we agreed—"

"We did. But as you say, circumstances have changed." Lady Holmes brought her hands together as though she meant to wring them—something I'd never seen her do—then dropped them back to her sides. "What would you say to coming to live with me at Musgrave Hall?"

Three days ago, I'd been eager for a place at the hall, which would have meant lodging there, taking some of the strain off our crowded household while staying close enough to help. That was before I met Lady Holmes and her attendant army of complications.

Now, the thought of living under the same roof, no matter how expansive that roof might be, left me wary, as though I were wading barefoot through tall grass. Perhaps I just had snakes on the brain.

Reggie's warning to keep my distance from Lady Holmes, which he had kindly repeated this morning after he accused me of forgery and claimed a kiss on the cheek, reared its patronizing head. As though that unwelcome specter had conjured him, the man himself appeared, exiting the solicitor's office several doors ahead with none other than Clarence Sterling, Lord Sterling's lone child. One half of the phantoms on horseback I'd encountered outside Musgrave Hall before my disastrous interview—the last thing I needed was another ill omen. Luckily, he donned his cap and walked away from us, but Reggie headed in our direction.

Lady Holmes' stride quickened as though she planned to intercept him, probably because he hadn't recently accused her of hysteria. I lunged forward and hooked my arm through her elbow, dragging her to a standstill in front of the draper's window. The shock of touching her echoed through my body and, finding no place to settle, left my nerves jangling like a runaway telegraph key.

"Hudson?" she murmured, our faces inches apart. She smelled of soap and starch, and something clean like broken rock.

My senses overwhelmed, stalling, I stared at a vivid blue hat in the window.

"Hudson?" Lady Holmes asked again, the question in her voice flipped from uncertainty to concern.

Reggie's footsteps drew closer, his bulk crowding the corner of my eye.

"What was your favorite color before all of this?" I asked, running a hand down my skirt, my eyes drifting to the rainbow of colors in the millinery display. Reggie walked past, bringing the reek of cigars with him, but failing to take notice of us.

Lady Holmes turned her face to mine, the web of her veil sapping her eyes of something vital. "I was never—"

"Katy?" Reggie said from several feet behind me.

Damn everything. I gritted my teeth and turned, dropping Lady Holmes' arm in the process. "Inspector."

He frowned as I used his title and crossed to where I stood, suddenly too close. "After we spoke this morning, I dropped into your house to check on you, but nobody seemed to know where you'd run off to."

Did he think I'd be happy to see him so soon after accusing me of forgery? Could a man be so gorged on his own importance? No wonder he was still a bachelor.

"I'm right here. No running, just ..." I flapped a hand at the window of the shop.

"If you've finished your shopping, perhaps we could walk together? I've a matter to discuss with you. That is if your companion can see herself—" His speech cut off as though someone had thrown the switch and dropped the current.

As Reggie and Lady Holmes stared at each other, I considered bursting through the door of the draper's shop to hide among the bolts of cloth until it was safe to come out. Namely, never.

Lady Holmes' smile didn't spill into her eyes. "Hudson is otherwise engaged, Inspector. We've just been to offer our sympathies to Billy Mudd's poor mother."

A storm gathered on Reggie's brow, but didn't break, though his lips made a noise that could best be described as wet. "You can't be ... are you seriously getting involved in this matter again?"

I tipped my chin up in an attempt at bravery I didn't feel. "Frances is beside herself with worry. We're just doing what we can."

He gripped my arm and jerked me to the side, voice low. "What's the meaning of this, Katy? After you promised me ..." His eyes flicked to Lady Holmes, and I knew exactly what he meant. "After that telegram business this morning? I could've put you in a cell to think things over. Is that what you want?"

Until now, shock bore the brunt of the fire in my arm; however, the threat to freedom wasn't as easy to weather. I tried to twist away, but he held fast.

"Answer me."

"I'll tell you the same thing I said this morning, I had

nothing to do with that telegram except for discovering clues left in plain sight." My voice teetered on unshed tears.

A single hand, gloved in neat black, snaked out and wound around my other arm. The trail of heat it left was a different sort of fire altogether. "Unhand my lady's maid, Inspector," Lady Holmes said, as though asking him to pass the sugar, but drawing an uncrossable line nonetheless. "If you wish to be sure of contacting her, you can write. Care of Musgrave Hall."

He dropped my arm; however, the strips where his fingers had gripped would be a bouquet of bruises by tomorrow.

Reggie wiped his hand down the front of his jacket, eyes heavy on mine with an unmistakable warning, something like a promise. "Good day, ladies." His mouth popped open, and for a moment, I thought he was about to say more, but instead he spun on one polished boot and strode away.

CHAPTER FOURTEEN

THANKFULLY, LADY HOLMES DIDN'T SPEAK UNTIL after we turned away from the long counter inside the Post Office. Once outside, she launched into the list of questions she wished me to memorize for our visit to The Four Hounds, specifically for the owner, Alfie Stewart. Listening to her with one ear, I was grateful for the time to collect my thoughts; I just wasn't successful in doing so.

The pain in my arm lingered, and I massaged it yet again. I never believed Reggie would hurt me—I'd once found him crying behind the schoolhouse after some younger boys teased him for his atrocious spelling. He hadn't laid a hand on them. Of course, training for the police may have done for his fists what it failed to do for his spelling. When I visited this morning, his paperwork had been spread over his desk, and he'd spelled *enforcement* differently on three separate documents.

Without the proof burning my arm, I would have said he had more in common with a pedantic tree branch. Whether or not he would make good on his threat to arrest me, would he retaliate against Eddie or Ralph for my missteps? Reggie's expression had hinted at that desire, among others. It didn't take much imagination to understand his intent in visiting my house, or what matter he wished to discuss. No way Lady Holmes would have missed that. I'd yet to see her miss anything.

As we approached The Four Hounds, I scrabbled together a thimbleful of courage. "Before we go inside, I wanted to say that Inspector Goodwin isn't, he's not, his presumption that I—"

"Hudson, the nature of your relationship with the inspector is not my business." Lady Holmes held my gaze. "How you spend your free time, and who you spend it with, is your own concern."

Heat roared in my cheeks. "That's what I was trying to say. The inspector and I—"

"Clearly have a history together. No need to explain, especially when every moment we waste is another one in which we aren't finding Billy." She gestured toward the inn, its deep-set windows shielded from the afternoon sun. A swinging sign hung over the entry of The Four Hounds, its four canine silhouettes freshly coated in black paint. "I've never been inside this establishment, but your brother works here, correct?"

I bit my cheek. She was right. Reggie, Inspector Goodwin—for safety, that's how I should think of him—didn't matter, and what Lady Holmes thought of us mattered even less. "Yes, Ralph. The Four Hounds hosts travelers, folks celebrating, or just people out for a drink and a meal after work ..." I trailed off as movement caught my eye.

A young man exited the side of the gray stone building and walked to the rear. His movements drew my eyes to the fenced-in yard, surrounded by a stable and outbuildings. Now that I was paying attention, I couldn't believe I'd missed the three boys clustered there. Ralph's dark curls only came up to the shoulders of the inn's other workers, who were all older than him, but his laugh rang out.

Why were they all outside? I angled myself behind the fence post, fumbling in my reticule for John's pocket watch.

"Your late husband's?" Lady Holmes asked, peering at the initials engraved on the cover.

"I had to sell most of John's things before I left London, but I couldn't bear to part with this. It belonged to his grandfather," I said while scraping my memory for what Ralph had told me of the delivery schedule at The Four Hounds.

"It's a fine piece of silverwork. Almost everything in Musgrave Hall belonged to Arthur or one of his ancestors. I've had to work hard to put any mark on the place at all. However, I do often carry Arthur's pistol with me."

I couldn't parse her meaning. "To remember him by?"

"No, Hudson, I'm not in the habit of forgetting. It's for protection." Lady Holmes leaned back so as to see around me. "Who are you hiding from, and why does the time matter?"

I jerked my chin at the workers. "Fifteen minutes until the beer wagon arrives. After that, the boys will be too busy transferring stock to talk. If we want to question them as well as Alfie today, we'll need to divide our efforts."

"Divide?"

"I have the questions for Alfie memorized, but I've no

time to memorize more for the boys, let alone ask them. You take them, and I'll take Alfie."

"Me?" She shifted to stand next to me behind the fence post's meager cover.

"You're dressed like a maid, so they won't know who you are. All you have to do is catch their interest and trust, find some common ground. You know, charm them."

Lady Holmes frowned, a soft wrinkle between her fair brows.

"Listen, my brother is the short one with dark hair, and if he sees me, he'll question what I say and fight me on every point before he gives a single answer. Just ... go. It'll be fine. Remember, charming."

Perhaps I was trying to convince myself as well. What little I'd seen of Lady Holmes in the wild didn't inspire even a fledgling confidence, but how bad could it be? It would be good practice for her, that was, if she wanted to pursue investigations on her own someday. The thought lit a small hot wire in my chest, and I rubbed it as I entered the inn.

Inside, the scent of roasted meat, pipe smoke, and wood polish lingered in the air. A narrow set of stairs led to the inn's rooms, and the hallway ahead wound to the dining and sitting rooms. I followed the warm buzz of voices and footsteps to the doorway of the pub on my left.

Even with all the heavy beams and stone walls, the row of mullioned windows caught the fine May morning and left the low-ceilinged room bright.

A young man with red hair sat writing something with a pint of dark ale at the ready, and though it was well past the middle of the day, men in work clothes lingered at the bar and scattered about the tables. Behind the bar, its panels of polished oak striped in brass, stood Alfie Stewart.

He hadn't been working last night when I was here with Inspector Goodwin, so the last time I'd seen Alfie we'd both been in our teens. He'd been soaked to the skin with every knob and joint of his wiry limbs sticking out through his clothes like kittens in a sack. John had been in much the same state, the two of them having taken their quarrel into the shallows of the river. With me—the object of their disagreement—looking on from the safety of our picnic blanket, feasting on worry and excitement. John had been the victor that day, but time, lifting barrels of beer, and a steady diet of meals at the inn had transformed Alfie into the approximate size and shape of the beer wagon itself.

He handed a short old man a pint and then looked up, his light brows getting lost in his shaggy hair when he noticed me. "Katy? As I live and breathe. Ralph said you were back." His deep voice matched his gargantuan stature.

If you'd once helped a person fill the teacher's desk drawers with live frogs before he was even out of short pants, you could hardly go back to formal address.

I smiled. "Alfie, nice to see you looking well."

He dusted his wide hands down his straining shirt then gestured around him. "Aye, The Four Hounds has been running high. Can I get you something to drink?"

If he wasn't going to mention John, then neither was I. Not yet, anyway. My emotions fizzed and prickled in my chest, half sweet and half pain. I hadn't considered how seeing Alfie again would make me feel, hadn't considered much at all before returning to Sherrinford a few months ago. Each memory—both old and fresh—sliced at still healing wounds.

I'd given no thought to what was waiting here for me. My own past. And for now, my future. At the time, I'd told myself Sherrinford was a temporary retreat, a regrouping of my feelings and finances. Like a hare in her den for the winter, snug and safe until spring came and I could build something new.

Grief was wilier than any plan. John might be the one who died, but I was the one living in the past.

How was it possible I should have new memories—of Alfie, of Sherrinford, of *me*—that John would never have? Loneliness washed over me, thick and cold. He was gone, along with the life we'd built, and I didn't fit anywhere. Not anymore.

"No, thank you, Alfie. I'm here to ask you a few questions."

His grin faltered. "Listen, Katy, I don't know what you heard, but Ralph's a good lad—"

"No, no, I'm here on behalf of Frances Mudd. About Billy's disappearance," I added, and Alfie's eyes cleared.

"But Billy's not disappeared. He's gone to live in Eastbourne with Tom. I was sorry to see him go. He was a good worker, and everyone here liked him. Fit right in."

"Wait, what about Ralph?"

Alfie's broad face flushed, but he shook his head. "Nothing at all. You know how the lads talk. More than half of it's gammon, and the other half belongs on a pig's backside." He grabbed a rag and began polishing the already spotless bar.

I squinted at Alfie's thick torso, whose size rivaled the

British Empire. Just the lads talking indeed. They could be a bit of a handful once they got going, but hopefully Lady Holmes was managing well on her own.

"That's what I heard about Billy too, but ..." I paused. For some reason, saying it to Alfie felt different, like stepping out into the rain without an umbrella. "Why doesn't Frances believe he's with Tom?"

Alfie tossed his rag onto a shelf and started racking mugs. "The poor woman's beside herself, but I don't know what else to tell her. Billy told me himself he was going away with his da."

"He did?"

"Aye, Billy was a good worker and wouldn't have left without a word. I offered to pay for Frances' ticket down there to check on the lad, but the shopkeeper won't give her the time off to make the journey. Says they're all booked up with orders, and if she leaves him in the lurch, he'll find another seamstress." He shook his head. "It's all a lot of fuss over nothing in the end. She's had a letter and telegram from Tom saying that Billy's with him. I know Tom's not always been the best husband to her, and maybe that's affected her mind on this."

I pursed my lips. Alfie seemed so sure of himself. "That's why I'm here. The telegram has come under suspicion, and the 'letter' was no more than a five-pound note wrapped in blank paper."

Worry beetled his furry brows as he crossed his arms. "You think something happened to the lad?"

"I'm trying to find out. So, Billy told you he was leaving?"

A loud clatter came from the open door leading to the kitchens as though someone had dropped a box of cutlery.

Alfie waited until the sound of voices resumed before he answered. "Nearly two weeks ago now."

I leaned an arm on the gleaming bar. "When did you see Billy last?"

"At the same time. He cleared out the odds and ends he kept here, mostly things for drawing, and left the next day." Alfie ran a rag over an already sparkling glass.

"Did he take the train?"

Alfie shrugged his thick shoulders. "He didn't say, but I assumed as much."

Lady Holmes' questions were turning up dud after dud. Out of sight, I tapped the number seven against my wrist. "Would he have mentioned his plans to anyone else? The other lads?"

"Not likely."

I raised my eyebrows. "And you didn't try to talk him out of it?"

Alfie tipped his head back and forth. "Not for long. I saw the boy's determination, mind you. He knew what he was about. Said he had plans for his drawings and such. Big ideas like that aren't easily turned aside."

"Isn't it strange that he'd think to tell you of his leaving, yet give no word to his friends or to Frances?"

To my surprise, Alfie shrugged. "And save himself being nagged, worried, and harped on half to death before being guilted into staying in Sherrinford? Not strange at all in my books." The church bell clanged the hour, and Alfie lifted a board to come around the bar. "The beer wagon's due any minute, Katy, but if you want to talk more maybe stop by after the dinner rush? We'll have a few drinks together. On me."

He draped his long arm over the bar, and my thoughts flashed to the boa constrictor.

"Of course. By the way, Ralph told me about the postcard with the giant snake. Where'd you get something like that?"

He frowned. "Giant snake? I don't know what Ralph's on about. Maybe something the other lads showed him?"

"Oh, those lads," I said with a grin, but after I said goodbye, I tucked my smile back in my reticule and made my way out of the inn, mind flying.

Alfie had given me a plausible explanation for Billy leaving, and it was the first time I'd considered it from his perspective. If he wanted to escape Sherrinford, a clean break would be his best chance of success. Frances would've done all that Alfie suggested and more to keep Billy with her.

For a moment, I wavered.

What if Ralph wanted to run away? I pictured my brother—jostling with the other boys in the inn yard, pinched in the kitchen corner while the rest of us fussed over Frances, nodding above his supper after a long day making up for Billy's absence at work. A shiver tugged at my stomach, but I pressed on the idea. How would Ralph do it?

He wouldn't get far with all of us Buntings dragging at his feet, sinking our hooks into his dream. The how of it finally made sense to me, Billy leaving. I could pick it up and feel its edges, but the why of it was still a mystery.

I'd known both boys since they were born, though I'd been in London for most of the last three and a half years. Time enough to make yourself anew over and over again. My heart could attest to that much. Perhaps Billy had grown into his dream of being an artist, and I'd missed it.

But if that were true, Tom Mudd seemed like the last place to pin his hopes.

As far as I knew, neither Ralph nor Billy had anything to run toward, but I could imagine a hundred mishaps or specters they might be running from. When I laid that thought next to my concerns over the telegram's forgery, they moved in rhythm like two telegraphs receiving the same message. Billy had been hiding something. Of that much I was certain. Why else would he lie about Alfie showing him the postcard?

I was so focused on trying to piece things together that I didn't think of Lady Holmes again until a shout from the inn yard startled me. I bounded forward, then stopped short at the corner. If I showed up, I'd give away her identity to the boys and lose any chance of her questioning Ralph without connecting back to me.

With quiet steps, I eased toward the lane leading to the inn yard, but I needn't have bothered. Another shout and *whoop* filled the air, then a chorus of excited laughter.

"That's the way, missus! Get him!"

"Better not flinch, Bunting!"

What on earth was going on?

Around the corner, Ralph stood frowning in the middle of the enclosure. Alone. Perhaps twenty feet away on the far side of the inn yard, the rest of the lads clustered behind Lady Holmes. Compared to the jostling boys, her rigid posture made her seem even taller. But the lines of her long body were still fluid as she lifted her veil, raised her arm to shoulder level, and pointed a revolver at my brother.

CHAPTER FIFTEEN

RALPH, BLOODIED AND PALE, HIS RANGY LIMBS FAR too still, flooded across my vision. And once it was all I saw, I couldn't stop myself. I picked up my skirts and ran.

"Don't shoot!" I flung the words out like a shield, that they might wrap themselves around my little brother and keep him safe.

My boots skidded across the cobblestones as I dragged myself to a stop in front of Ralph, arms spread wide. One arm protected his face, and the other extended where his arm jutted from his shoulder like a signpost. Time drew long and lean. My skin zapped as though I'd been dunked in an icy river. I was sure I'd never breathe again.

A *crack* echoed across the inn yard, and the board Ralph held flew from his hand. It clattered to the stones behind us, followed by a ragged cheer from the lads.

"Hudson!" someone shouted.

I spun and grabbed Ralph's shoulders, his cheeks, his hands. Was he all there? Was he bleeding? "Ralphie, Ralphie, oh, Ralphie. What were you *thinking*?" I muttered as I searched.

"Katy? What are you doing here?" Ralph glanced between me and his fellow workers.

I clasped him tight to my chest. "Ralphie, I just—"

A crowd of footsteps thundered across the inn yard, and suddenly we were caught up in a storm.

"What a cracking shot, missus!"

"Oh, is poor Ralphie hurt?"

"*Ralphie?*"

"Missus! Missus! You hit the X dead on."

"Is your sister here to give you a bottle before your nap?"

Ralph thrust me away. "Leave off, Katy, you chatterpie. I'm fine!"

I reeled back and locked eyes with him, angry and hurt. My heart ached as though the bullet had struck me there.

"Hudson! I said, are you injured? Answer me." Lady Holmes said, veil thrust back and green eyes pinched. "What were you thinking? You jumped in front of a bullet. You must never do that again."

I glared at Ralph, but he backed away until he stood in the middle of the lads, untouchable.

Lady Holmes reached for my hand, but I jerked free. "You were just supposed to talk to them!" I yelled.

"I'll take your excessive volume as an indication of your robust health." She settled her veil back over her face. "Though shouting hardly seems necessary since I was simply following your advice."

I thumped my chest. "*My* advice? At what point did I suggest you point a *revolver* at my baby brother?"

"Wee baby Ralphie," a lad squealed, and the others broke into fits, slapping Ralph on the back. His cheeks afire, he shoved the squealing lad and skulked to the back of the group, the other lads in his wake. Some still jostled him, and the others marveled over the board he'd been holding where a neat hole pierced the heart of a crude bullseye.

She tipped her head. "Ralph doesn't seem to appreciate your concern. What was that colorful term he called you, again? A 'chatterpie'? I will have to make a note of it as I've only heard it used to refer to magpies before."

"While you're at it, make a note of this: if you *ever* act in such a cavalier manner with any member of my family again, I quit."

"Need you be so dramatic?" She sighed but looked at least mildly chagrined. "How about a nice brisk drive to Musgrave Hall to get it out of your system? Then we'll take tea."

"I don't need a *drive*. I need you to listen to me. You can't honestly expect me to go back to Musgrave Hall with you. Not after—" I waved my arms at the scrum of boys staring at us from by the gate.

"I don't know why you're so upset anyway, I was charming the lads, as you instructed. 'Common ground,' you said. In my experience, Hudson, males are inordinately fascinated with firearms. Well, those and horses. Occasionally kissing. Anything deadly, really. We'd already exhausted their interest in racing and snakes. When they showed no interest in the upcoming solar eclipse, I grew desperate, so I resorted to a small lesson in firearms and a demonstration of my skill as a revolveress." She patted her reticule with a small smile.

"Perhaps you had trouble charming them because they sensed you'd throw them to a wolf like Inspector Goodwin at the first whiff of troublemaking just like you did Eddie."

"I can't think your inspector would appreciate you referring to him thus."

With nothing breakable to hand, I clawed the air. "He is not *my* inspector."

"Though I can see why you've dragged Eddie Beale into this, Hudson."

The beer wagon rumbled around the corner of the inn, its approach vibrating the soles of my feet. None of the boys moved to intercept it, however, their eyes were glued on us.

"What'd she say about Eddie?" asked a tall lad with eyes barely set wider than his nose.

Damn everything. I'd worked so hard to keep Eddie's transgressions a secret, and now I'd almost allowed them to be spilled underfoot like flat ale.

"Fine! Fine." I grabbed Lady Holmes by the arm and steered her around the approaching beer wagon. "We'll return to Musgrave Hall. After all, we have much to discuss. Just ... don't talk about Eddie until we're in the carriage. In fact, perhaps it would be best if you didn't speak at all."

But Lady Holmes didn't stay silent for long enough. Once we reached the stables where we left her carriage, she shook her head. "I still don't understand why we argued."

"Because you used my brother for target practice!"

She huffed as we both climbed in her phaeton. "Ralph was acting as a means to hold aloft the bullseye I'd marked on a stray board. He was never in any danger as the board was one and a half feet long, and my aim has a standard deviation of less than one eighth of an inch when I'm firing Arthur's revolver. It's very well made, and I do not miss."

Fury strangled my words, and I made a series of short

noises in the back of my throat. "He's my *brother*. Accidents happen!"

She shook her head as though I were a tiresome child. "Hudson, I want you to know that as your employer, I'm listening to your concerns. I was not and will not ever use a member of your family for target practice." The thick leather reins across her gloves reminded me of Da so suddenly that I had to look away. "I hadn't considered how my activities might look to someone in your position, with so little familiarity with quality firearms. I apologize for not considering that their use is uncommon for someone in your position. It won't happen again."

If Lady Holmes mentioned my "position" one more time, I would scream. No, actually, I was going to scream anyway. Just the thought of Ralph, injured or worse, and because of my involvement—it coated my stomach with fear. Not even Lady Holmes offering an apology could stem my feelings.

"Just drive," I muttered, tapping the word *safe* against my thigh.

Once she'd maneuvered us back onto the main road, I'd calmed down enough to say, "Whatever you found out about Billy had better be worth it."

She clicked to the horse and slowed our speed from catastrophic to simply troubling. "Billy was shy about his talent, but upon encouragement showed his drawings to the other boys quite often. They even described several memorable sketches we didn't find in his room."

"Of what?"

"A waitress at the inn whose proportions they all admire, a stray dog who they bed down in the inn's stables without telling Mr. Stewart, a dead bird Billy found in the rain barrel, and some men who'd come to eat at The Four Hounds a few months ago. One of whom I'm certain Ralph recognized as Tom Mudd, though he wouldn't say it aloud."

My jaw dropped, but before I could ask for more details, she went on.

"Did you know Billy never spoke of his father to the other boys?"

I shook my head. It felt significant, but none of it meant much. "That's all? I'm glad you endangered my brother for such pearls."

"On the contrary, it is notable, Hudson."

We passed the hilly section of the road, which meant once we hit the straightaway we'd be going too fast to speak soon.

"Notable how?" I asked quickly.

"The absence of information can sometimes tell us more than its presence. Our words, in their tenor and subject, so often betray our thoughts that choosing not to speak can be the wisest counsel. And since Billy isn't here to speak for himself, we must also read his silences."

Chapter Sixteen

After that, we flew. Like two ravens winging over the fields and lanes, nothing stopped us until we reached the now familiar gates of Musgrave Hall. A groom met us out front to collect the carriage, and the older maid I'd seen twice before appeared before us in the foyer.

"Tea, m'lady?" she asked. Her light eyes flicked to me with curiosity. "Mrs. Kelley has fresh seedcake today."

I'd only been a lady's maid for a few hours, but even I knew any changes in the hierarchy of servants was valuable information.

"Thank you, Helen. Why don't you introduce Hudson to the way things are run here at Musgrave Hall. She can bring the tea up to the study with her."

Grateful for a respite from trying to argue sense and heart to a woman who often appeared to have neither, it still grated to have to leave on her orders. For all that I was here by choice, the idea of serving another person left me feeling like I'd stood behind a team of horses as they sped down a dusty track—all grit in my teeth and burning eyes.

Thick silence muffled our footsteps as I trailed Helen through the labyrinth of the hall to the kitchen. Compared to the four market stalls all jammed together that I was used to, Musgrave Hall unrolled around me like a tomb. On top of a mountain. In the middle of a lake. A very fancy one. Money bought more than security—silence, beauty, and space enough to think.

Angry as I was, I couldn't deny the late afternoon light slanting through the polished windows, the rich hues of the curtains, and the fine landscapes in gilt frames were pleasant to look at. I hated myself for thinking it, and I hated them even more. Not only for what they'd cost in coin, but in time parceled out in someone else's labor, their life's minutes, so that Lady Holmes shouldn't have to squint around a smudge on glass, or heaven forbid, have to wipe it away herself.

By comparison, once we reached the undecorated simplicity of the servants' corridors, our shoes tapped the bare boards as though spelling out how difficult my new position was here at Musgrave Hall.

I was about to take tea with the mistress, but I wasn't her guest.

My intent had been to question Helen, to ask her for advice on the best way to handle her—our—mistress, but the wild swing of my emotions tamped down my questions until we'd made it to the kitchen.

The room was a riot of smells—the rich scent of roasting pork and fresh bread underlaid with the sweet perfume of baking apples. Mrs. Kelley stood at a wide table chopping wild garlic and carrots, while two women in smart black uniforms worked something in large bowls across the room. There was no sign of the kitchen boy.

"Tea preparation happens over there, Mrs Hudson." Helen swept an arm toward the other side of the kitchen where a wheeled trolley stood next to a counter with a china tea service and tools. Her eyes crinkled as she smiled. "The name's Helen Reddyman, and before you ask, no, there's not a jest I haven't heard about it. Not that you seem the type. I just like to get it out there." She nodded at the counter. "The seedcake is under that cover. Of course, Lady Holmes never takes sweets, but Mrs. Kelley keeps some on hand for Master Sherlock, and you're welcome to it."

"That reminds me, I've yet to see the elusive Sherlock. Where in Musgrave Hall does he hide?"

Helen raised her flat eyebrows as Mrs. Kelley directed a strange look at us. "Here and there. A real hard worker, that boy," Helen said quickly. "Would you like me to show you how strong the mistress takes her tea?"

Feeling like I was missing something, I shook my head. I didn't care what Lady Holmes thought of my tea making skills or whether she liked sweets, and in fact, aiming for less than perfection offered a quiet sort of revenge.

"Thank you for the kind offer, but I'm sure you have so many other duties. I'll just muddle through," I said.

She hesitated but left me to my own sins. A few minutes later, I headed upstairs with a pot of weak tea and two generous plates of seedcake nestled beside the dishes on a gleaming silver tray engraved with what I assumed was the Holmes family crest. A wizened fox among shields and curved icons, as unimpressive as it was impenetrable.

The study door stood open, but the room was empty. I paused in the doorway.

"Hello?"

Her voice came from behind a large cabinet. "Put the tea things on the table. I'm collecting data."

The service rattled as I balanced it next to a brass tube fixed onto a three-legged stand. The stand took up most of the tabletop, the wide end of which pointed out the bank of windows overlooking the western grounds of Musgrave Hall. I cast about for a place to either move the delicate instrument or a better spot for the tea things.

On a nearby wall, the portrait of a gentleman with a sweep of dark hair and a long face looked as though he expected little from me and was surprised at how correct he'd been in that assessment. There was something familiar about him. Probably some Holmes or other. I'd seen plenty of portraits on my walks through Musgrave Hall.

"The table is meant to support the tray, not you," Lady Holmes said, appearing just off my shoulder.

Though I was getting used to her knack for catching me unawares, I still started. "There is a … this in the way."

"Telescope, Hudson. A tool for magnifying astronomical features in order to study them." She placed it between the table and the wall, then sat while I slid the tray into place. "I was eighteen years old in 1859 during the Carrington Event, and if I'd had access to the proper equipment, I can only imagine the data I might have been able to collect. I won't be caught unawares again."

I sat stiffly, unsure whether I was meant to serve or to let her preside as hostess. "John taught me about the Carrington Event when he was training me to be a telegraphist because of the effects it had on telegraph equipment. At the peak, operators could transmit messages on the lines even while disconnected from their power sources, such was the electrical charge in the air. I was ten when it happened, and I still remember the moving rainbows in the night sky."

A wistful look softened Lady Holmes' precise features. "The auroras were unparalleled. It was as though someone sliced open the sky and heaven poured through. I shall never forget it."

Her description thrilled me, both in substance and in this unexpected side of her on display. "Will another event like that ever happen again?"

"With our current methods of measurement, no one can say." Her eyes sparkled. "However, remember there is a total solar eclipse in four days. Have you made any plans?"

"Plans for an eclipse?"

My lackluster response seemed to confuse her. She frowned. "I'm surprised you haven't read the notices in the papers. After all, no other total eclipses have been visible in the British Isles for 148 years, and there won't be another here until 1925. This will be many people's only chance to see one, myself included. My heart is set on seeing it, and I have plans to travel if the weather refuses to cooperate. Scientific observers from all over England as well as the Continent have been preparing for years now and are gathering even as we speak."

Grief, work, lack of time to read and funds to procure the newspapers—any of these excuses might sour this fragile peace between us, and I wanted to hear her say more. So instead, I smiled and lied. "I've seen it mentioned, of course, but didn't make a note of the date. Four days from now? What will it be like?"

She poured herself some tea into a cup she snagged

from her desk, then gestured for me to do the same with the fresh one on the tray. I hardly knew what to make of it. We weren't equals. Equals didn't bring up a tray of tea through the servants' corridor or fling around thirty pounds to force the other's hand. But neither did mistresses take tea with their servants and offer them astronomical lessons.

"During a total solar eclipse, nature plays a magic trick." Lady Holmes leaned closer as she warmed to her topic. "No matter if it's high noon, seeming twilight overtakes the sky, and the earth appears to wind down for bed. Even the crickets and night birds will begin their dusk chorus, mistakenly of course. It will be quite dark for mere minutes, during which it may be difficult to see much of your surroundings, but you may view the passage of the moon across the surface of the sun through a specially constructed box or pinprick camera."

I sipped my tea, considering. "Surely looking at it in the sky is more impressive?"

"Yes, but also ruinous to the eye. Some use a smoked lens for brief glimpses of the corona, but you take your sight into your hands with this method."

"Goodness." I spluttered and set down my cup. I needed to warn the children very firmly on this point.

"After that, the process reverses itself." Her expression settled into its carefully neutral lines once again, and the room felt a little colder without her enthusiasm. "What's this?" she asked, pointing at the second plate of cake.

"Caraway seedcake?" I'd almost forgotten my culinary mutiny.

"I don't take sweets." She pushed the plate to the center

of the tray. "Don't worry, you'll learn. Speaking of which, I meant to ask, how many of you are there?"

"I beg your pardon?"

"If I am to be on guard against brandishing weapons at Hudsons in a cavalier manner, I need to know the quantity."

At the reminder, I wanted to be angry again but found a sort of buzzing in my chest instead. "Oh. Well, John's remaining family was a cousin who moved to Scotland, so you only have seven Buntings to avoid threatening with death. An eminently manageable number even for you."

A smile cracked open her calm expression, and a happy bubbling sound filled the room as her hand floated to her chest. It wasn't the first time I'd made her laugh, but it was the first where I could see her face as she did so. Her eyes tilted from almost hazel to a sparkling green, and roses bloomed in her slim cheeks, lending them a fullness and life that made me catch my breath. I was so busy watching her I almost forgot to smile myself.

"Still, best to take precautions," she said after a moment. "What are their names?"

I took a deep breath. "My mother is Molly, and you know Ralph. The others are George, Elizabeth, the twins Oliver and Louise, and little Rosie."

I expected some comment on the number, but she just nodded distantly.

"And you?" I asked after a bracing sip of tea. "You mentioned your elder son, Mycroft, being away at school, but the younger one still lives here?"

"Yes. Sherlock. He's ..." Her mouth snapped shut.

It was the first time I'd seen her lost for words. "How old is he?"

"Nearly eight. This time of day he should be deep in his Latin exercises." Shadows appeared on her face, weaving long lines around her eyes. "So, have you formed any theories on Billy's whereabouts?"

Clearly, she didn't wish to discuss Sherlock. Instead, I took a bite of cake and let the taste of butter and spice bloom across my tongue. I immediately took a larger bite. It'd been ages since I had cake.

"No real theories, just questions," I said. "Why would Billy have drawn Tom in Sherrinford? And if he did, where is it now? For that matter, where are the other drawings the boys recall, but that we didn't see in the collection in his room? Do you think he took them with him or has some sort of hiding place?"

She leaned forward. "Precisely. However, Hudson, the more important question might be, what did Billy have to hide?"

Chapter Seventeen

It sounded dramatic when she put it that way, but it didn't mean I would let her label Billy as some secret miscreant.

"Children hide things," I said. "That's what they do. Well, except my sister Louise who's overtaken by guilt and confesses her wrongdoings immediately after she commits them. Pity we aren't Catholic, she'd have made a perfect nun." A pinched smile sprang up on Lady Holmes' face as I continued. "A finger in the cake, a kiss from their sweetheart, ditching school to meet friends by the river—everyone dares such things and then buries them deep until they're adults and free from punishment. I'm sure you and I both have stories of our own colorful youths."

She hummed noncommittally, no past misdeeds flaring to life in her eyes. Had she really never put a toe out of line? Even so, with two sons she must have realized what they were capable of by now.

As I finished my cake, I let Lady Holmes speculate on what flavor of mistakes Billy might be hiding. Truly, the woman had a prodigious imagination. She made it as far as piracy when I started clearing the tea things. I left her staring out the window, no doubt casting Billy as a spy for the crown. Perhaps I wasn't supposed to return them to the kitchen, but Lady Holmes didn't act surprised, so she must have been expecting it. I didn't mind the work, only the expectation that it was mine. I wore my grudge all the way to the servants' stairwell, where I found I wasn't alone.

The kitchen boy tromped up the stairs, his swath of dark brown curls glinting in the poor light. A dusting of snowy powder trailed behind him, marked with neat footprints distributed over each stair tread. The imprints not only ran below him but also ascended the stairs, as though an army of bakers or angels had been marching four abreast through the corridors.

He jolted at my gasp and looked behind him, then back at me.

The poor lad. What would his punishment be? Laboring late into the night, knees and back screaming, as he washed each tread? I glanced at the open door of the study. Lady Holmes had far too keen an interest in justice as a blunt instrument. Would she take it out of his wages? Dismiss him? Perhaps he knew better than I what fate awaited him because his already pale face blanched until it matched the flour coating the steps.

I set the tray on the landing and smiled. "Hello, you look like you need saving. I'll fetch some brooms, and we can clean it."

The kitchen boy narrowed his wide green eyes and glared at me. "I've spent the last month collecting shoes from a gardener, a surgeon, a gentleman, and a chimney sweep, so

I can see the different footprints they leave. And I haven't finished taking measurements yet."

I blinked. He looked the same—a worn jacket and short pants—but with shoes many sizes too large for his feet, his skinny legs resembled butter churns. However, his rough northern accent had disappeared. In its place was a clear, if squeaky, Oxfordian. I'd assumed he worked in the kitchen, but if so, what was all this about measurements? Had Lady Holmes heard of his nickname as the sleuth of Musgrave Hall and recruited him for an experiment? If that were the case, he wouldn't need saving.

I retrieved the tray, preparing to make my way down the stairs. "I'll let you get to it."

He threw out a little arm. "Stop. You'll mar the footprints."

I sighed. "How would you suggest I reach the kitchen, then?"

"Aren't you the new lady's maid?"

"After a fashion. Don't you work in the kitchen?"

His expression remained impassive as a little emperor. "Are you always this familiar with your betters?"

My earlier sympathy for him didn't just flee; it evaporated. Damn everything.

No wonder the portrait in Lady Holmes' study looked familiar. This boy took after his father, except for his eyes, which were purely those of his mother. Proud and sad, but clear as glass. They were windows to nowhere, more like mirrors, before which we all stood as witness to our own actions.

And mine were reprehensible. If I'd known who the boy was at first, I wouldn't have offered to help. The ghost of

Da's frown haunted me, reminding me. He was a child and not responsible for the sins of his illustrious forebears.

I grabbed my polite smile by the ankles and dragged it back kicking and screaming. "I was informed you were deep in your Latin lesson, but I see I've disturbed you. I shall take my leave, then, *Master* Sherlock, Sleuth of Musgrave Hall."

For a second, something twitched at the side of his hard mouth.

"Hudson, were you speaking to someone? I thought I heard voices," Lady Holmes said, emerging from the study.

Sherlock winced and drew back. He was still so small, and whatever advantages of birth he might have, the world was very big.

"Just trying to decide which way to go," I said. That was close enough to the truth.

"That's the quickest route to the kitchen." She stepped closer. "I'll accompany you, and we can discuss the unresolved matter of your current living arrangements."

Sherlock's narrow shoulders slumped, whether in defeat over the prospect of his lost work or despair over a punishment, I couldn't say. I knew how he felt.

Three days ago, I'd shown up for my interview with Mrs. Greaves ready to beg for a live-in position, but now that I faced the opportunity, I saw the cost.

Leave home and live at Musgrave Hall? In silence and servitude, always putting my foot wrong until I learned to bend my ways to her rhythm and whims, wasting the seconds of my existence to smooth the jagged edges of living for another. With no Rosie to curl beside at night, her warmth soothing my sore heart when an empty bed proved too much for me. Who would make sure Oliver got something extra to eat and Louise became her own person? That Ralph stayed out of trouble and Elizabeth didn't try to solve everyone's problems except her own? That Ma didn't work herself to the bone?

Grief was a trickster. Just when I thought I caught the shape of it, the beast shifted its skin and cast a shadow, wielding novel ways to make me bleed. I feared I would never feel ready to leave the past behind. But the future was here, now, bearing down on me with a simple black dress, impossibly long limbs, and sparkling green eyes.

Half an orphan, a wife, a telegraphist, I hadn't felt ready to become any of those. So why not something like a lady's maid for someone who was something like a lady?

A few more long strides from the lady in question and she would be able to see Sherlock along with the state of the stairwell.

I shut the door, my leaden legs miles away from the dizzy lightness in my head. As though I were preparing to throw myself from the carriage while Lady Holmes drove at breakneck speed. "Actually, I've already considered your proposal to live here while we're working together"—I swallowed hard—"and I accept."

"You will? You do?" Lady Holmes clasped her hands together, then slid them down her skirt as though attempting to hide her first movement. "Excellent. That's quite … convenient. For the case."

A finger of disappointment curled up my spine, though I couldn't say why. "Yes. Convenient." I tried to shake it off. "If we left now, we could retrieve my things before dark. If you would drive me?"

She smiled. "Leave the tea things in the study, and Helen

will be up to gather them. The stables are most easily reached this way, however."

As I'd guessed, she gestured toward the other side of Musgrave Hall, leading us far away from Sherlock. On the way, I once again felt like I was walking one step ahead.

CHAPTER EIGHTEEN

I NESTLED *THE VICTORIA REGIA*, THE SLIM VOLUME OF poetry John had given me on our second anniversary, into my trunk, the deep green of its cover like an island in a sea of black. However, it wasn't the only spot of color.

When I lived in London, I'd sent the first paycheck I ever earned back home to Ma, but with the second, I bought a dress. Its rich blue—of butterfly wings and bachelor's buttons and late summer skies just before the sun goes down—left me breathless when I saw it in the shop window. My friend Eleanor had urged me to buy it, but longing wasn't an emotion I was used to, and I felt guilty and feverish afterwards. When John died, Eleanor helped me take my things to the dyer to have all their hues erased, and that felt right, muted, like covering our beloved flat with a fine layer of dust and closing the door. However, I'd been unable to bring myself to alter that dress. It lay, untouched, nestled in tissue under a forest of black garments at the bottom of my trunk, its perfect vibrant blue hidden like a closed eye.

The sniffling of my siblings brought me back to the

present moment. I double-checked that *The Victoria Regia* wouldn't be crushed by the clever little shelves John had built into the top of my trunk and then, with a sad smile, Elizabeth helped me snap the trunk shut.

"You're sure about this?" Ma asked from the bedroom doorway, one hand twisted in her pinny and the other around Oliver whose breaths whistled again. "Things have been so back and forth with her. What if you move out there and she dismisses you tomorrow?"

Rosie wailed from her perch on our bed. "You just came home. You can't go! I won't let you!"

Louise, who sat with one arm around her, swabbed first her own wet cheeks and then Rosie's with her apron. Oliver ducked under Ma's arm and scrambled onto the bed next to his twin, their dark brown eyes shimmering with tears.

We'd been having some version of this argument for nearly an hour, but still sharp tears pricked my eyes, and I took a deep breath. "It's the only way I can help Frances and Billy and make enough money at the same time." *It's also the best way I can help myself*. The thought rose to the surface, but was it truth or a pretty lie? Was this an awful mistake, a disaster not just for me but for my family?

"What if Billy shows up tomorrow, sorry as a wet dog, and it's all over? What then? Will you turn around and beg for another chance at Sterling Place?" A flicker of terror sparked in Ma's eyes. "You were lucky to get an interview after ... after everything."

I narrowed my eyes. "After everything what?"

Ma flapped a hand at me. "Don't change the subject, Katy."

A sigh squeezed out before I could catch it. "I don't know

the answers to the questions, Ma, no matter how many times you ask them." Her face crumpled. "I'm sorry. I know you're only worried about me."

She dried her eyes yet again. I secured the straps on my trunk. The last time I'd stood in this room and packed the objects that spelled out my life, I'd been a giddy newlywed ready to embark on the adventure that was supposed to last a lifetime. Now, I wished I could pack the messy tumble of emotions and memories into the trunk with my things.

Rosie gulped down a sob, and so did I, embracing her, Louise, and Oliver as tightly as I could. "All this fuss. I'm only three miles down the road, more like two the way Lady Holmes drives." Ma made a strangled noise, and I rushed on. "I'll be back on Sundays to set your lessons for the week and visit for a few hours. Now, I must be off."

After several more rounds of embracing, Elizabeth and Louise carried my trunk to the front door, and I bent to whisper to Oliver, slipping a packet from my pocket to his. If Lady Holmes wouldn't eat her seedcake, someone ought to enjoy it. "Keep it a secret, promise?"

"Thank you, Katy. I'll miss you." He kissed me on the cheek, then we joined everyone in the front room.

Ma wrapped her broad arms around me so that I lost my breath. "My little Katy Bee," she whispered, "all grown up."

My tears spilled, and I pressed my face into her shoulder. All laundry soap and sunshine, and something warm that was just Ma. Four soft *thumps* hit us, and soon I was wrapped in a hot tangle of arms, the six of us sobbing.

"You be careful. The last time you left ..." Ma squeezed even harder. I couldn't speak around the ball in my throat.

She pulled away and cupped my face. "Every. Sunday."

I sniffed and mopped my tears with a fresh handkerchief. "I will. I promise. Give Georgie my love. And Ralph … tell him I'm … don't let him …" My lips wobbled. Ralph wasn't even speaking to me at present. At least there might be one Bunting who was happy to see me go.

"I'll set him straight. But, Katy, you're sure?" Ma asked, for what must be the hundredth time.

Before I could answer, someone rapped on the door.

Trading tears for a delighted squeal, Rosie sprang away.

"You're not supposed to answer the door anymore!" Elizabeth shouted, just missing her grab for the little scamp's arm.

She whipped open the door with a roar of triumph. There, on the scrubbed front step, stood Lady Holmes. She blinked as she took in the crowded room, red eyes, and meager surroundings. Her cool mask slipped a little. Something hollow flitted across her face.

"Ma, there's a lady here!"

Lady Holmes jerked and, for the first time, looked down far enough to see Rosie, whose brown curls reached to the bottom of Lady Holmes' bodice. What she thought of Rosie's face—covered in various liquids and crowned with a grin of victory that would have made Queen Boudicca proud—I couldn't even guess. Possibly, she was regretting her promise not to point weapons at any more Buntings.

Ma scooted Rosie back. "Can I help you, Miss …?"

"I'm just looking for Hudson." She stepped into our main room.

Part sitting room, dining room, and parlor, it was where we'd gathered, fought, loved, and wept ever since we'd been evicted from our cottage at Sterling Place after Da's death.

Now, I viewed these dear surroundings through Lady Holmes' eyes. Late-day sunlight dripped through windows that revealed the low ceiling, smudged by years of smoke from the open fireplaces, the tatty sofa we all left open for Ma to relax on, and the mismatched chairs at the dining table. At least we could spread a clean cloth over its scarred surface, but we could do nothing about the worn polish on the wood floors except keep them clean and place the rag rug over the worst scratch.

John and I sent home everything we could afford to help Ma pay down the mortgage. Now we were *this* close to owning a home, one from where we couldn't be tossed like kitchen scraps. It wasn't fancy, but it was ours.

I stood frozen, partly in horror and partly in shame, waiting to see judgment wash over Lady Holmes' face.

Instead, she checked her slim gold wristwatch. "Fifteen minutes for packing and two minutes for leave-taking per Bunting. You're thirty-six minutes overdue. Musgrave Hall is nearly twenty minutes away, so we need to hurry if we are to arrive before dinner."

Ma staggered back. "I ... you're ... Katy didn't say you were waiting for her, m'lady." She swept an expert curtsy, a little muddled now with her bad knee.

Lady Holmes' eyebrows rose in an expression mirroring Ma's, and I almost burst out laughing. Apparently, they'd both just recognized there was a lady standing in our doorway.

"Mrs. Bunting, it's a pleasure to make your acquaintance." She surveyed my siblings as though memorizing their faces. "Elizabeth, Oliver, Louise, and Rosie. Hopefully, I'll get to meet George before I mistakenly aim—"

"Sorry to keep you waiting," I said, hustling toward the door.

Just then, a hatless Frances burst through it, breathing hard. A streak of scarlet streamed down one cheek. Before she could say a word, her eyes rolled up in her head and her knees buckled as she fell.

CHAPTER NINETEEN

THE QUIET WAS BROKEN BY THE SNIFFLES OF MY siblings. Even in the warm room, Frances' hands were freezing, and I rubbed them harder. Lady Holmes frowned where she sat near Frances' head on our short sofa, pressing a cloth to the wound above her eye.

Ma waved a smoking feather under Frances' nose.

Almost instantly, she spluttered and pushed the feather away. Her gray eyes flew open.

"Frannie, *Frannie*"—Ma touched her face—"what on earth happened to you?"

Tears rolled down her thin cheeks, and her voice was so low I had to bend to hear. "They robbed me. First someone took my boy, and now they've come back for more."

"Robbed?" said Lady Holmes. She half rose as though she meant to dash out to catch the thief, but subsided, pressing the cloth back to the jagged cut.

Frances winced. "I went to tell Mr. Hooper I was leaving. Alfie lent me the money for a train ticket, and job or no job, I was going to Eastbourne to look for Billy myself."

Ma clucked her tongue. "Oh, Frannie."

"I know. I wasn't thinking straight. By the time I got there, he'd already gone home for the night."

"Was the store being robbed?" I asked.

"No, it was shut up tight. I wandered home in such a state I didn't think anything when my front door was unlocked." Her lips wobbled. "That's not true. I hoped ... with the door open ..."

Ma gasped. "You thought it was Billy."

At this, Frances turned her head against Lady Holmes' skirts and wept.

After an awkward pause, Lady Holmes plopped a weak hand to Frances' shoulder. "Hope is a dangerous thing, Mrs. Mudd." She sighed. "You surprised the thieves at their dark work. Did you see them? How many were there? Was anything missing?"

"All I remember is waking up in the hallway, our things strewn about in a devilish mess. After that, I ran like a coward. That's my home, and I should have stayed to protect it. Billy won't even have anything to come back to." She tried to sit up.

With a firm hand, Lady Holmes pressed Frances onto the pillow. "On the contrary, you have a nasty cut and have lost consciousness twice. I believe you may have a concussion. The doctor can attend you here while Hudson and I make our investigations at your home."

I squeezed Frances' hand. "We promised to help. Please, let us."

When she finally nodded, Ma shifted to take Frances' head into her lap, and we ran for the carriage.

A tense few minutes' drive found us in front of the

Mudds' home, its bright red front door hanging open like a mouth agape.

One in a row of adjoining houses, it shared walls with the neighbors on either side, so accessing the rear of the house could only be accomplished by circling the entire structure. This was a quiet neighborhood, filled with clerks, day laborers, and young families, and it was often busy, but this late in the day, its inhabitants were at their suppers. An advantageous time of day for a thief to go unnoticed if they knew Frances wasn't at home—unless they'd planned all along to do her harm.

The darkness beyond the doorway ate at me. What if the thief stayed behind to finish their nefarious work? I took a deep breath and followed Lady Holmes down the walk.

"At least you're armed," I whispered as we paused outside the open front door.

She gave me an odd look. "I would never bring a firearm to the very source of the Buntings."

"Oh." That she'd immediately been so respectful of my wishes left my cheeks flushed, but I tried to cover it with a frown. "You might have mentioned that before we hared off to confront a violent thief. At sunset. Alone."

The sun had dipped beyond the distant hills, casting the windowless hallway before us into deep shadows pierced by a single bright rectangle at the far end. Lady Holmes had foregone her usual black veil in favor of being able to see any incoming threats, and it left me feeling exposed with her face close enough to mine for low speech.

Lady Holmes leaned in, her breath brushing my cheek. "Hudson, I'm not going to let anyone hurt you. Besides," she smiled at me, and my earlier flush spread to my chest.

I willed my wildly beating heart to still. "The rear door is open, and the attacker probably ran out that way."

A rattle came from inside, and the silhouette of a man passed before the backlit rectangle of the far door.

I grabbed her arm, but Lady Holmes, tall and immovable as a birch tree, called out, "Thief! Stop where you are!"

The man whipped around and strode toward us. "Who's there?" His deep voice striped my arms in gooseflesh.

"Have you lost your wits? He's a thief, not a *servant*." I bent, hefting the clay pot filled with violets beside the front door.

That last part seemed to get Lady Holmes' attention, and she scooped a stout stick from the ground.

A few seconds later, we jointly clobbered the man when he sprang from the front door.

"Ow, bloody hell!" Inspector Goodwin shouted. One hand clutched his head and the other held his knee, the remains of a clay pot and dirt at his feet. "Katy? I should arrest you for assaulting a police officer." He pulled himself upright and pressed a handkerchief to the growing lump on his forehead. "Where's Mrs. Mudd?"

"On our sofa with a much worse wound than yours." My fear gave teeth to my anger. "Why do we have police officers if you can't keep us safe in our own homes?"

Lady Holmes, now stickless, put a quelling hand on my arm. "Hudson, I'm sure the inspector is doing the best he can with his limited resources."

He scowled. "I say—"

"Though that does raise the question"—Lady Holmes stepped in front of me—"what *are* you doing here, Inspector?"

For a moment, I didn't think he was going to answer.

"I was on my way to deliver some news to Mrs. Mudd, and found the door ajar, the place turned over. What the devil are you two doing here?"

"Frances arrived at our house, injured. We're investigating on her behalf."

Inspector Goodwin reached up as though to grab me by the shoulders, but glanced at Lady Holmes, then dropped his hands at his sides in clenched fists. "On your own? Why wouldn't you stop at the police station first?"

"What? So you could accuse me of staging the break-in? You've never taken our investigation seriously," I said.

Inspector Goodwin's cheeks wore an unbecoming red. "Your investigation? Now see here, even if we weren't ..." It must have seeped through even his thickened skull just who he was addressing. "It's not a scene for ladies."

"Nonsense, Inspector. Mrs. Mudd is a lady, and though she experienced the cruelest aspect of this crime, she isn't howling in hysteria." Lady Holmes gestured at the open door. "It will do us no great harm to view the aftermath, and in fact, it may do Mrs. Mudd a great deal of good. Of course, I would never broach the scene of a crime you are investigating, so you will have to lead the way."

This last bit soothed the inspector's ego enough to stem his grumblings, and he gave me a proud look. He put away his handkerchief and straightened his jacket. "I believe the thief entered by the garden door."

"Fascinating, Inspector. Could you please show me," said Lady Holmes. Then, as he stepped into the house, she pressed her lips to my ear. "I will distract him, and you see what you may uncover."

A thrill traveled over my skin, though whether at her

breath on the small hairs of my neck or the idea of running a second investigation under the inspector's nose, I couldn't determine.

The two of them pulled away toward the garden door while I crept down the long hall. To my left, the kitchen was a mess of broken crockery and mounds of dry goods, the cupboards empty above. A long pool of brown broth spread across the floor where it had lain long enough to grow a skin.

Directly across the hall, the door to the sitting room was also wide open. The back portion, closest to the little coal stove, held two chairs and a table. Their meager collection of books, a Bible and a few volumes of Dickens, lay on the floor, pages standing proud from their binding like a grandmother's starched skirts. Frances had turned the front half of the room, near the single window, into a sewing area. Her projects were tangled together on the floor in a sad heap with the tools of Frances' trade—a rainbow of spools, measuring tape, and needles glittered from the floor.

Kitchen goods, books, sewing things, what on earth had the thief been looking for?

The voices of Lady Holmes and the inspector grew distant, and I hurried to the rear of the house, where her skirt was visible through the door outside.

"The scratches on the wood are indeed suspicious, but you mentioned crushed plants in the garden. Which ones?" Lady Holmes asked.

I pressed myself into the door of Frances' bedroom to avoid being seen by the inspector. In contrast to the other rooms, her room was as neat as if she'd just made the bed. Had the thief run before they could take apart her things?

Unsure how long Lady Holmes could keep Inspector Goodwin distracted, I waited until his back was turned and dashed across the hall to Billy's room. It was a disaster. So much paper littered the floor that it looked like a snowstorm had passed through. My skirts stirred the air, thin strips sweeping away from me in an alarmed whisper. I covered my mouth.

"No, no, no."

All of Billy's beautiful drawings, the sketches that pulled life onto the page and pinned it there for all to see, had been shredded. I circled the room to his makeshift desk, not wanting to step on the remains. There, I bent to the deepest pile and ran my fingers over them. Eyes, leaves, a corner of a window—the ghosts of his work were everywhere, his unique view of Sherrinford and the people it held—even the remaining scraps were beautiful.

I flipped the pieces over, trying to make sense of it. At the bottom, half-hidden under the bottom crate of the desk, was a mostly intact sketch of a horse's collar hanging on a wall. I wanted to give Frances one thing from her home that was still hers, so I picked it up to smooth the crumpled corner. However, the thing slipped from my shaking hands and floated to the floor where it landed upside down.

Across the back of the sketch, was the perfect outline of a dusty footprint.

There was a line where the heel met the sole, but another irregular line angled near the toes. For a moment, I recalled Sherlock's experiment on the stairs. Could something as simple as a footprint truly offer clues to the identity of the owner?

As I crouched to study the print, Lady Holmes's voice

came from the open window above my head. “I agree with you, Inspector. Billy must be involved, but even if Mrs. Mudd saw him here, she would never admit it without striking evidence.”

“I haven’t found anything like that,” Inspector Goodwin said a little too quickly.

Lady Holmes didn’t speak for a long moment, heavy with the weight of iron. “Of course. But if you keep me apprised of what you do find, I can use it to apply pressure to Mrs. Mudd and find out if there’s something she’s not telling us.”

Us. The word rang in my chest like a distant bell. One I’d heard countless times before, one whose song wasn’t for me.

CHAPTER TWENTY

ALONE IN A STRANGE BED, IN A STRANGE HOUSE—IN a strange life, frankly—I'd lain awake until the wee hours, despite a day as long and muddy as the Thames, finally subsiding into sleep near dawn. Now, awakening, alone and confused, my eyes fluttered closed again, and I began tapping my lips.

When I learned Morse Code, the hardest letter for me to master was *v*. Telegraphing *dit dit dit dah*, your wrist tapped out the first three marks faster than a blink, and if you didn't catch yourself, the movement carried you forward until a *v* became an *h*. Once, I'd transmitted the word *how* when I meant *vow* and almost cost a young man his inheritance. A quirk of mine ever since had been an extra pause before that final *dah*, a tiny mental check to make sure. John said he recognized me whenever that stutter came down the line. At first, I resented his teasing, that my fist should be so plain, but no matter how hard I tried, I couldn't train myself out of it.

Now, I was grateful for such a signature. I couldn't spell

my love on John's shoulder as I'd done every morning of our marriage, but if he could still hear me tapping out my love to him when I woke—on the bed frame, on my lips, over my heart—he would know it was me. Even if I had to say it from a maid's bedroom in Musgrave Hall.

The scent of cedar and starch wafted from the mattress beneath me as my wrist flicked up, poised over my lips for a breath, then struck the final *dah*. I finished the rest of my morning message to John in a flash and opened my eyes to face my new life.

Besides my bed and the trunk I'd brought with me, a table and chair clustered on one side of the room. Along the opposite wall spread broad wardrobes and a table filled with clothes irons, sewing tools, and a hatmaker's dummy. All dark wood and whitewashed walls, the room spoke of life in service of another. Sleep here, sew there. Read here, press clothes there. Dress here, brush dresses there.

I pinned my night braid back into its usual low twist and sighed.

Like an old pair of shoes I'd handed down to Elizabeth, the thoughts didn't fit me anymore. Lady Holmes had proven herself to be more than my unkind assumptions of her. Without a word, she'd paid Dr. McNulty's fee for treating Frances, unerringly recalled the names of my family, protected me. She listened to me, and if I challenged her, she met me word for word without pulling rank. No doubt our primary attachment was through her purse strings, but instead of chains, they might be a sturdy rope. One I could cling to as I stood on the edge of the unknown and peered into the crevasse below.

Despite all of that, her words to Inspector Goodwin about

Billy being involved in the break-in at his home, that final *us*, left me unsure. What if she cast Billy onto the pyre of justice as casually as she had Eddie Beale? Those thoughts had sealed my lips as we checked on Frances, returned to Musgrave Hall, and all through the night, the footprint I'd found, hidden in my trunk. I needed to bring her proof of Billy's innocence before I revealed my discovery.

Set aside for the lady's maid at Musgrave Hall, my room wasn't on the third floor with many of the other servants' rooms. Instead, I slept a few doors down from the mistress of the house, at the end of a wide corridor.

I encountered Helen at the kitchen door with a stack of linens in her arms, graying hair pulled back under her cap. "Morning, Mrs Hudson."

"Good morning. Do you know where I might find Sherlock at this time of day?"

A patch of vertical lines appeared in her forehead. "Master Sherlock is a great favorite of mine. His mornings are taken up with studying writing and 'rithmatic in the nursery."

"I've certainly enjoyed the few times I've met Master Sherlock, both here in the kitchen and on the servants' stairs yesterday," I said. Then inspiration clicked into place. "As well as at the gates the other morning."

Something flickered in the back of Helen's eyes. I had guessed correctly.

"I'll be sure not to interrupt his studies," I pressed. Gardener's lad indeed. "I just have a little puzzle I think he might like."

She considered this. "Speaking of, we've a fine set of beehives, beyond the gardens. A pet project of Master

Mycroft's. Before he left for his schooling, those two were inseparable."

"The boys?"

Helen went on as though I hadn't said anything. "Nearly six years apart, but alike enough to be twins. Master Mycroft loves the honey, but Master Sherlock watches the bees." She spoke the last three words in a sing song.

"Watches the bees?"

She stared at me so hard I expected her to break into prophecy and pronounce the moment of my death, then she laid a finger aside her nose before disappearing with her armful of linens.

After clues as broad as Piccadilly itself, I grabbed two sweet rolls from the kitchen and swaddled one in my handkerchief. Outside, spice and sugar mingled with the taste of the fresh morning air as I wandered past the neat rows in the kitchen garden.

The landscape of Musgrave Hall wrapped around the front grounds like a series of outdoor rooms, just beginning to burst with the raw and tender growth of springtime. Separated by wide avenues constructed from the same sand-colored brick as the main buildings, the focal point was the reflecting pool nestled at its heart. Each crenelation of the fountain at the center mirrored some aspect of the main structure—here the diamond windows, there the insouciant pitch of the roof or the march of the chimneys. And where stone embraced water for many years, green lingered in the crystal depths just as it did in the eyes of its mistress.

Was a worker bee eager to spend the day with her queen? Despite my confused feelings about this job, about failing

Frances and bringing danger to my family, I was looking forward to investigating with Lady Holmes today.

But all of that had to wait until we found Billy. And he was far from safe.

Inspector Goodwin had come to Frances' home to inform her he'd finally sent inquiries to his colleagues in Eastbourne. None of Tom's neighbors noticed Billy at his father's boarding house, and what's more, Tom himself hadn't been seen in weeks. However, even after recounting what Lady Holmes had learned from the inspector, she didn't tell me of her suspicions regarding Billy, an oversight that left me more worried than if she'd shared them.

Because Billy was out there somewhere, alive or dead, but either way, gone. The possibilities, each one more terrifying than the last, had stolen any hope of sleep, but left me with nightmares aplenty. Ralph lying in the inn yard with a dark hole spreading in his chest. Frances collapsing on our doorstep, bleeding, but never waking up. Lady Holmes and I meeting a shadowy man in Frances' wrecked home, a stranger this time, one who meant to do us harm. All of it leading to Billy somehow.

Thus, why I needed to find Sherlock.

My search led me to the rear of the home, where order and geometry splintered into something wilder, more humble. The tidy crunch of my footsteps released the slick scent of mud on rock. Beyond an allée of pear trees, whose bouquets bustled with the drowsy conversation of the bees in question, spread a short field with a path running along the two edges, which greeted each other at the toes of a hedgerow of yews.

Beyond those unfolded a meadow topped with a series of

white structures like dolls' houses. Sherlock's dark brown hair poked above the meadow's wavering grass, his chin resting on his knees.

He didn't turn as I approached. "Father wanted to bring in bees from Northern Italy, but Mycroft said a native species would be more adapted to Sussex. Really, he just thought the honey tasted sweeter."

The warm scent of it perfumed the breeze as I held out the second sticky roll and knelt beside Sherlock in the grass. "I promised when you let me through the gates I would sneak you extra food."

He eyed me and then the roll, but after a moment he scooped it up and tore an enormous bite from the side.

Around us, the insects were busy darting in and out of their homes. Formed of two or three wooden boxes in a stack, each had a semi-circular handle cut into the sides as though they were drawers of a cabinet freed from their frame. A decorative roof topped the stacks, and since the entire assemblages had been painted white, they looked like narrow cottages lining a country road.

"I thought bees were kept in those round baskets," I said.

"With skeps, you can't get at the honey without destroying the hive," Sherlock said around his mouthful of roll. "An American vicar designed a method with removable trays so the keeper can extract the honey without harming the hive. But Mycroft went to stay with a friend between Hilary and Easter terms, so I'm watching things until he gets back."

Sherlock spoke of his elder brother in the hungry tone Ralph and Oliver used when they bragged about George to their mates. I nodded seriously. "They're fantastic, the way the bees use that slot at the bottom for a door. How did you convince them to move into their new homes?"

"Mycroft made them a ramp to the door and put the queen inside. After a big change, they know to find somewhere tiny and dark where they can rebuild a new hive." He nudged a curious bee from the sugary crust on his roll and shoved the last of it into his mouth.

A sympathetic buzzing began in my chest. "How do they know what the others are doing if they can't speak?"

Again, those eyes, so like his mother's, seemed to strip away some outer part of myself. "Humans don't need to speak to communicate either. Haven't you ever heard of Morse Code?"

A smile popped the tips of my mouth up, but I dragged them back down lest Sherlock think I was laughing at him. "Perhaps I read something about it in the papers."

"It turns the alphabet into groups of dots and dashes. Mycroft made me memorize it so we could talk across the nursery at night by tapping on the bed frames. I think the bees must use something like that to tell each other things, like where all the good flowers are or when they need to grow a new queen."

An ache tugged at the bottom of my heart like a stone sinking in a still pool. Like me, Sherlock had lain awake and alone, reaching out for some connection in the dark. I'd thought Sherlock serious and proud, much as I had his mother. However, he might be wearing those aspects like armor, might have learned to do so by watching those dearest to him. His father had died less than a year ago. And in the midst of such loss, his only brother, his idol, had been sent away to school. Poor soul.

When John died, at least I had people who loved me and a place that knew the shape of my bones. Our home might be small, but the walls kept us together like a pair of arms in a tight embrace. Musgrave Hall was a place where you could cry out and no one would hear you or come scrambling across the room when you wept into your tea and smothered your sadness in the company of others like a wet cloth over a fire. It was a place where you could lose yourself.

I turned to pull out the rolled-up drawing I'd taken from Billy's room yesterday and used the moment to press my sleeve to my tears. I bit my lip and took a silent breath.

Then I handed the drawing to Sherlock. "When I'm feeling sad, I like to find a way to help others. It makes my own problems seem lighter."

"I'm not sad."

"Oh, I know, but I am, and I was hoping you could help me with something."

He unrolled it like a treasure map, his little hands making even the half sheet of paper seem large. "The missing boy drew this?"

Now I did laugh. "How did you know?"

Cheeks flushed with pleasure, he pointed at the lower right corner where a piece of Billy's neat signature was visible despite the rip.

Avoiding the topic of how he knew a boy was missing, let alone Billy's name, I pointed at the drawing. "Very clever. Now, I found this—"

"Master Sherlock. Master Sherlock!" A young man's voice rippled across the meadow where he stood on the edge. "She's looking for you! You'd better hurry."

With a surprised grunt, Sherlock sprang to his feet and dashed toward the house, Billy's sketch waving from his hand like a flag.

CHAPTER TWENTY-ONE

I HURRIED ACROSS THE GROUNDS IN SHERLOCK'S WAKE. I couldn't let Lady Holmes catch him with a drawing from Billy's house, one I hadn't shown her.

Helen, white cap flapping, met me at the kitchen door. "The mistress wants you to meet her in the study 'at your convenience,' but time's a funny thing to her. She either means right this minute or forgets she ever asked. 'Course, you never know which until the bell tinkles again thirty seconds later and you feel her scowling at you through the floors."

I gathered my skirts. "I'm going to err on the side of 'right this minute' and dash upstairs."

"I put together the tea things for you." She shoved a laden tray into my hands.

There were two sweet buns on separate plates, and I threw her my thanks along with a conspiratorial smile before I headed up the servants' stairs. I paused outside the study, balanced the tray with one hand, and smoothed my hair, but before I could knock, footsteps came from the direction of the main stairwell.

Lady Holmes rounded the corner. "I apologize for my tardiness, Hudson. Sometimes Sherlock needs assistance settling into his studies."

"No apologies are necessary, I've just arrived." I lifted the tray like a shield.

As she drew near, her face lightened. My heartbeat turned from a steady rain to a downpour. What would she do if she found out I'd abetted Sherlock in avoiding his studies and brought him into the periphery of a criminal investigation? One that grew more dangerous by the day? My palms slipped against the tray as I pictured the judgment in her eyes directed at me.

Her demeanor seemed at ease, however, so my secrets must be in Sherlock's hands, safely deep in his schoolwork by now. I would collect the sketch later and find out if he had any insight into the footprint or who might have made it.

I made quick work of setting out the tea, and Lady Holmes poured herself a cup. She frowned at the second sweet bun as I took an innocent bite of mine.

After she finished half her cup, she shifted the books and a set of scales from a nearby worktable where morning sunshine picked out the gold lettering on the covers and called forth fire from the bronze instruments. "Could you fetch the roll of paper from the window seat?"

Deep and wide, the ruby velvet cushions were already stacked on the floor beside the window seat. Though the lid was heavy, the hinges lifted smoothly. Inside lay several squat wooden boxes, a collection of long rolled-up papers, and finally, clutching one of the scrolls in his lap, Sherlock.

Before my mouth could pop open, whether in shock or

to decry his position, he thrust the rolled-up paper into my hand.

"It's the top one," Lady Holmes said, stepping closer.

I glared at Sherlock, who appeared perfectly calm, and slammed the heavy lid shut. My heart flailed against my ribs as I returned to the table and handed the roll to Lady Holmes, staring into her unnerving eyes.

"Is everything alright, Hudson?"

"Sherlock," I said, my thoughts on the boy in the window seat.

She raised an eyebrow as she secured the edges of the now unrolled paper. "Yes?"

"You mentioned his schooling. What is he studying?" I said, snatching the first excuse that floated close enough and slapping it down with as much grace as a fishmonger presenting his wares.

She gave me an unreadable look. "He and I are at odds about that. I counsel balance, and he insists on galloping after his own interests, giving little notice to anything he deems uninteresting. Unfortunately, that includes little things like the entirety of the Latin language and much of human history."

"What are his interests?"

"The natural sciences. Chemistry mostly, though his abilities have far outstripped his good sense in that area, resulting in the loss of endless clothes, no less than three workbenches, and one door this year, along with a pervasive stink in the hallway outside the workshop. You narrowly escaped the latest explosion on the day you first interviewed here. Mrs. Greaves' dress wasn't so lucky."

So Sherlock had been behind that explosion. My lips

curled in a smile as ripe as a plum as I pictured Sherlock waiting by the gates for the result. "He likes experiments, then?"

Her answering frown could have stripped London of its damp. "Yes, yes, we all reap that which we sow. If he is like this at seven, I despair over his future."

A muffled sound came from the window seat, and I spoke over it. "So, what did you want to show me?"

She tapped the unfurled paper. "I've created a way to organize our investigation."

In the center were Billy's name and details. Age: Fifteen. Occupation: Day Laborer at The Four Hounds. Hobbies: Fishing and drawing. A list of his family and acquaintances. His parents, Alfie, and the boys at the inn, even Ralph, had been cordoned off into their own sections. A timeline of events, dated from Billy's last known sighting two weeks ago, crept along the bottom of the long page. To the left—a forged telegram, the suspicious stamp, five pounds instead of a letter, a violent thief.

Lady Holmes must have read the shock on my face. "What is it, Hudson?"

"Violent thief?" I slapped the case map, and Lady Holmes flinched. "I heard what you said to Inspector Goodwin. But you're wrong. Billy would never steal—" The specter of Ralph at the market extinguished my certainty, and I bit my lip. What did I truly know of him or Billy? Of anyone? "You saw how neat he kept his room, how he gave Frances the larger one, let her have the chair by the fire. How can you think he would wreck his home, destroy his drawings, and strike his mother unconscious? Why, she might have been killed." By the time I finished speaking, I no longer looked at Lady Holmes but stared at my reflection in the polished surface of the table as though trying to convince myself. I might as well have been. "Nothing but facts will ever convince you that Billy isn't guilty."

"You think I suspect Billy?" I glanced at her just in time to see her mouth part and eyelids flutter. She drew a deep breath and backed away. "I've been trying to save him. How could you ... We can't keep secrets from each other, Hudson. Why didn't you say anything?"

"Because I wanted to prove you wrong." I'd hurt her feelings, but what was that to a lost boy? Anyway, I wasn't the only one hiding things. "You don't want to keep secrets? Then why didn't you tell me you and Goodwin were making a case against him?"

She twisted the pencil in her hands. "The inspector went on and on about Billy committing the break-in, but Goodwin was clearly hiding something. So I pretended to agree with him to try to pry the information from his lips. My ruse failed. However, I didn't tell you about it because by the time I finished considering the idea, I had to admit it might be true. Billy could have committed the break-in at his house and the assault against Frances. We can't turn a blind eye to those clues simply because they hurt us."

With the pencil, she began underlining the words *violent thief*.

I snatched it from her hand, snapped it in two, and clutched half in each fist like daggers. "He isn't. You're wrong, and I'll prove it to you. I'll show you that there isn't a single clue against him." I tossed the pencil pieces onto the table. "Take us to the Mudd house."

CHAPTER TWENTY-TWO

WE DIDN'T SPEAK ON THE DRIVE TO TOWN, AND from the moment we turned onto the Mudds' street, things grew even more strained as my heart sank into my stomach where it promptly turned both to stone. The pointed hat of Constable Marks was outlined against their door.

He wore a bored expression on his face, but his eyes widened as we approached. Lady Holmes was dressed as herself today, her long mourning veil dancing in the light breeze.

"My lady. Ma'am." He didn't bow, but it was a near thing as his police training battled with his upbringing.

"Constable Marks, how nice to see you again," I lied with a smile stamped on my face. After what had happened at the police station the other day, he either thought I belonged in a cell or on Inspector Goodwin's arm. I couldn't decide which was more terrifying. Either way, I doubted he was going to just let us waltz inside. "Your presence will make us feel safer during our investigation."

Was it still *our* investigation? I glanced at Lady Holmes, but her expression had gone blank again.

"Actually, my lady, Inspector Goodwin gave strict orders that no one enter the premises," Marks said.

"Surely he wasn't referring to us." She reached for the handle of the Mudds' front door.

After just the slightest hesitation, he put out a hand to block her. A fine line of sweat decorated his upper lip. "In fact, he named you especially, my lady."

Lady Holmes drew herself up and took a deep breath, clearly about to unleash the full force of her title on the young constable. While it would have been holy to witness, I couldn't prove Billy's innocence from a jail cell. I needed to figure out a way inside so she could see for herself that the facts cleared Billy of any wrongdoing.

I stepped in front of her. "Do you at least have any leads for us to report back to Mrs. Mudd?"

When Constable Marks nodded, the strap of his helmet dug into his chin's soft belly. "Yes, ma'am, but I'm not at liberty to disclose them. This is an active investigation."

"I wouldn't call it active," Lady Holmes mumbled, drawing me back down the walk when I hesitated.

My chest hollowed out. How could I prove Lady Holmes wrong about Billy if I couldn't even get us into the Mudds' home? Frances was too injured to let us in herself, and Marks would block everyone else from entering—everyone except one person perhaps. I tapped out a quick *Sorry, John* against my thigh and rounded on the constable.

"Mrs. Mudd sent me here to pick up clothes and personal items. I don't think Inspector Goodwin would be happy to know you denied his fiancée entry into her cousin's house," I said.

Lady Holmes stiffened behind me and let out a soft breath.

"Ah, no, missus. He was quite clear about that. Named you both." The constable leaned forward from the waist. "But congratulations on the wedding, ma'am. I hadn't heard."

"Congratulations, indeed, Hudson," Lady Holmes said as she slipped an arm through my own and led me back down the lane. "Any more secrets you're keeping from me?"

I jerked away. "You can't honestly think—"

"You'd marry Inspector Goodwin? I wouldn't have this morning, but then I wouldn't have thought my investigative partner would keep secrets about our case."

Investigative partner. The world held little room for women who declared themselves as such, and the idea was both a thrill and a terror. My heart spun in a circle, and my words abandoned me. It wasn't as though people with a Debrett's entry referred to me as their investigative partner every day.

Lady Holmes' expression grew scuffed and dim. "I abhor secrets. My entire life, I've felt as if I'm always pretending at what comes naturally to others."

Guilt scraped me raw. She was right. If we were partners, we could have differences of opinion, but no secrets. We should be proving Billy's innocence together.

"In fact, Hudson, one of the things I noted when I first spoke to you—"

Metal struck rock behind us with a wicked *clang*.

"Are you two finished?" A grizzled woman had planted

herself outside the door of the house next to the Mudds'. Still tall despite the hunch of her shoulders, she clutched a metal-tipped cane in one hand and jabbed the other at us like the arm of a pillory. "My son bought me this house, so I'd have a safe place to live. And what's the result of all his hard-earned money? First a strange man creeping around my garden last night, disturbing both Admiral Whiskers and my supper, and now you two. Standing in the street like common women with no brains and loose morals."

"I beg your pardon?" I said, but I might have been a rhododendron for all the attention she paid to me.

"As if it wasn't already bad enough that Billy was sneaking out night after night, crossing *my* garden, and bringing ruin to my apple tree." She hit the pavement with the metal tip of her cane.

"Wait, Billy Mudd?"

She nodded with satisfaction.

My fingers spasmed as though I'd accidentally touched the wrong switch. Maybe I could gather enough evidence to convince Lady Holmes after all. "Sneaking out? For how long?"

"All last month!" She gesticulated with her stick, just missing my bonnet. "Meeting some slattern or the other. Probably someone you know."

"An upstanding woman such as yourself did nothing about such a state of affairs?" Lady Holmes asked.

I made a choked sound. "Do not provoke her," I whispered.

"I've never been accused of having loose morals before. I find it quite diverting." She fairly vibrated with mirth.

The old woman glowered at us, clearly adding

impertinence to the evidence of our having morals like an undone corset. “Mrs. Mudd wouldn’t hear a word against her golden boy. And look where he’s ended up. I didn’t spare my David a switch when he stepped out of line, and now he’s the manager of a bank in London.”

“Far away from his beloved mother,” Lady Holmes murmured.

“Do you know where Billy might have gone, Mrs. …?”

“I’m not introducing myself to the likes of you, and I don’t have all day to answer your questions. If Mrs. Mudd can’t be bothered to look after her own, then she got exactly as much as she deserves. As will the two of you, if you don’t leave this street. I’ll sic that weak-chinned bobby on you. Now, shoo!”

She flicked a hand at us as though we were neighborhood strays. Lady Holmes and I didn’t speak until we reached the end of the street, out of sight of both Constable Marks and the old harpy watching us leave.

“Inspector Goodwin made a show of alerting me to crushed weeds in the back corner, but they looked as though they’d been dug up by an animal rather than stepped on,” Lady Holmes said.

“If we hurry, that harridan might stand guard long enough for us to view her garden as well.” I quickened our pace.

Behind the terrace of houses, a high brick wall ran along the entire length. A peek over revealed a lower version separated the gardens themselves. We counted off plots until we stood behind the home of the old woman. The branches of her apple tree stood well above the top bricks, and it was easy to see why Billy had used them to cross from his garden into his neighbor's and, from there, over the wall.

Lady Holmes and I made use of the same entrance, and after a brief scramble, we found ourselves at the foot of the tree. Its "ruinous" state was too subtle to see with human eyes, though we searched the bark and branches for clues. Possibly the old woman had been referring to the tree's mental state.

The base of the trunk was protected from the rear of the house by a large gooseberry bush, thick with barbs. I was about to move closer to the wall separating this garden from the Mudds' when Lady Holmes held out an arm.

"Stop. You'll mar the footprints."

Sure enough, in the strip of sparse grass between tree and bush, was a clear set of footprints. We both lifted our skirts and squatted for a closer look.

A tide of dread pulled on my nerves. They appeared identical to the print I'd found on the back of Billy's drawing. Would this be the clue she needed to turn her blade of justice on him?

"I should've known," she said.

My stomach spiraled into a knot as she put a hand to the earth and canted to the side to view the prints better.

Lady Holmes grinned. "The spare boots in Billy's room were several sizes smaller, so these aren't his."

I wanted to pant in relief, but these prints were a match for the one currently in Sherlock's hands. One more secret I hadn't shared with my investigative partner.

Innocent of my deceit, Lady Holmes hummed. "I wrote an experiment but haven't performed it yet. In it, I propose amassing a collection of shoes worn by those from different professions and lifestyles, then using them to make footprints in different mediums. Not only loose dirt, for example, but ash, mud, snow, dust."

"Flour?" I asked, my throat thick with sudden understanding. Oh, *Sherlock*. Entering his mother's study while she was out, reading her work, enacting it. If so, why not tell her of his accomplishments? Perhaps he only wished to feel closer to her. Perhaps he hadn't been escaping the fallout from his explosion by the gates, but he'd been waiting for his mother. After all, she'd arrived outside them not too long afterwards. My heart squeezed tight, my breath a wisp in my throat.

"How clever of you, Hudson. I had proposed flour as the most ready substance." She pulled a folding ruler from her reticule. "The print is especially deep here, as though the person raised themselves onto their toes to peer over the wall." She quickly did the same. "You can see into the back windows of the Mudds' home. Near the toes of the left foot there is a distinctive scrape or a crack of approximately two and one-quarter inches. Did you see any footprints during your examination at the Mudds' last night?"

My nerves wobbled like a boat struggling against the tide. "If I had, I would've brought it to the attention of an expert." Lies, even without the gall, could still taste bitter. I should just admit my guilt. "In fact, I wanted to tell you—"

"Did you see them scurry away, Admiral Whiskers?" Though the old woman spoke in more honeyed tones, her voice was clear. "Now's your turn to do the same with those pesky voles in the garden."

The snick of a door opening and the squeak of hinges came from nearby. My confession cut short, I tapped Lady

Holmes on the arm, motioning for us to move deeper into the bushes. Careful to keep the gooseberry bush between us and the house, we crept into the narrow gap behind a row of forsythia bushes and the brick wall separating the old woman's garden from the Mudds'. It was a tight fit, and the bell of my skirt stood out almost a foot beyond the bush.

"You little rascal," the old woman said before making kissing noises toward, presumably, Admiral Whiskers. "Where did you run off to this time? Behind the forsythia again?"

Her voice grew closer as she spoke, the tapping of her cane like the seconds of a clock as I tried in vain to gather my skirt with one hand. The fabric slipped and bulged, tumbling over itself again and back into view. Before I could try once more, Lady Holmes slipped a long arm around my waist and pulled me against her. The black fabric of our dresses and veils mingled with the rapid puffs of our breaths.

"*Meow*." Admiral Whiskers gave a plaintive cry from the other side of the garden.

"Don't you be digging up my mums." The tapping of the woman's cane receded, and after a moment, the squeak of hinges came from the house again. "Don't come back without a vole and expect any of this chop for dinner."

We waited in silence, as though we were the voles, until the door clicked shut. Lady Holmes still grasped my waist, the warmth from her arm spreading to my chest despite the layers of fabric separating us. This close, I could see through her veil—the sharp plane of her nose, each fair lash now distinct, the pleasing fullness of her lower lip when she worried. My mouth grew dry, and I ran my tongue into the corners. The beat of my heart grew tangled with hers like the wings of river birds taking off, churning and splashing, until they finally broke free.

I had to tell her about the footprint. It would be best to come clean now, when only a brief time had passed. Perhaps she would be touched by Sherlock's interest in her work. "Lady Holmes—"

"Shh," she almost breathed the sound.

I was so distracted by her proximity and the snarl of my own feelings it took me a long moment to realize she'd heard what I hadn't, men's voices approaching from behind the garden wall.

"But you kept them out?"

Reggie Bloody Goodwin. My hands bunched fistfuls of my skirt until the fabric squeaked.

"I did, though they weren't happy about it. I stayed firm, just as you said." Constable Marks only needed a wagging tail to complete his role as guard dog.

Goodwin chuckled. "Good man. I shall mention you to his lordship tonight."

"My inspector rubbing elbows with the likes of a lord, how about that? Hopefully he rubs our palms with a few extra pounds. Perhaps for the wedding, eh?"

Wedding? My blood chilled. Oh, God, had Marks told him?

I couldn't see the inspector, but I was certain he'd just brushed invisible dust from his pristine uniform. "Perhaps, Marks."

I wanted to bang my head against the bricks behind me.

"Now, tonight is an intimate gathering, and I have hours to impress his lordship with tales of our police work,"

Inspector Goodwin said. "If I play my cards right, we should expect more than a few pounds."

Constable Marks made an ingratiating noise. "Funny how it all worked out. Billy leaving was the best thing for all of us," he said.

Beside me, Lady Holmes stiffened, and I shot her a wide-eyed look. Billy leaving was for the best? What could he mean?

"In this profession, Marks, you have to follow where the clues lead, even if it's directly to the door of a lord, of a king, or of the Almighty himself. Yes, I could've taken Tom's word for it, but if I'd been too cowed to question his lordship, I wouldn't have earned myself the opportunity to gain his trust and, dare I say"—here Goodwin oozed into the silence—"his admiration."

Lady Holmes' arm tightened once more, her hold so painful I gasped. She frowned an apology at me and dropped her arm. Though I could breathe again, I found myself sorry for the sudden absence. The space between us, no more than a few inches, had grown vast.

"Admiration, respect—I don't see how his lordship could help but be impressed by you, sir. Solving Billy's disappearance in a matter of days and managing the mother as you've done. It's a marvel, if you don't mind my saying."

"Not at all, Marks. If you know where to set your sights and who to follow, it'll take you all the way to the top. Tomorrow, I'll show you my maneuvers in my case notes at the station so you can use that as a lesson in best practices. But first, I have a few things to attend to before tonight. Best not to keep his lordship waiting."

CHAPTER TWENTY-THREE

WE'D STOPPED TO SEE FRANCES AT THE COTTAGE ON our way out of town, but our questions were stymied when we found her being examined by Dr. McNulty. Still bursting with them, the drive back to Musgrave Hall seemed to go faster than usual. As we sped along, we tossed answerless questions between us as though we shared a mind.

"Was Billy sneaking out at night?"

"Where was he going?"

"Did Tom know of it?"

"Should I call Arthur's cousin at Scotland Yard, Sergeant Forrester, and make Goodwin and Marks weep into their infant mustaches?"

"Do you still believe Billy's guilty?"

"I didn't say he was guilty, just that he *might* be. I can only work with facts, Hudson. Everything else has always failed me. As to facts, which lord is the inspector going to see tonight? There are several within driving distance."

"Speaking of the inspector, if he knew any of this, why keep information from a heartbroken Frances?"

"No, if we are speaking of the inspector, how can we transfer Eddie Beale's terrifying rash to Goodwin before the wedding?"

Wedding. The thought filled me with dread. The inspector couldn't believe I would marry him after he accused me of forgery? I rubbed the bruises on my arm.

But then I dropped my hand to my waist where the wiry loop of Lady Holmes' arm still lingered along with the memory of her breath and heartbeat mingled with mine. For those moments, it felt like no secrets separated us. I'd wanted to admit my secret, almost had several times, but thank God I hadn't. Because then I would have to admit Sherlock's as well. I couldn't do that without speaking to him first.

My arm around my midsection was a pale comparison. What I wanted was a reason to do it all again. A reason to sit closer to her as we took the turns at great speed. A reason for her hands to grip mine the way she did the reins, with a precise care that spoke of years of practice and pleasure in performing a skill you were built to undertake.

What I wanted was to ask her the question that crowned the dizzying circle of my thoughts. *"In fact, Hudson, one of the things I noted when I first spoke to you—"* Her unfinished sentiment echoed and danced in my memory, first meaning something that left my spirits collapsing, then taking on a shine that made me grateful for the wind whipping past my scarlet cheeks.

Did she feel she could speak freely in my presence? If so, why? Or did she think so little of me it hardly mattered what she said?

Questions inside questions. Like a box of paper dolls,

I held pieces of Lady Holmes. Different costumes that allowed her to pass as a maid, a widow of middling income, or a lady—depending on what best suited her needs—masks and shields she'd grown so used to holding that she seemed unable to lay them down.

Or so I hoped. To feel otherwise meant the air of equality she took pains to maintain—my role as her investigative partner, rather than her lady's maid—were nothing but the paper cutouts she'd constructed to adorn me. No substance, only a series of useful charades.

That uncertainty sealed my lips. Lady Holmes didn't appear to be the type of woman who would be offended by such questions. It was the answers I feared. Yet another secret, and it made me sad.

We slowed to turn into the estate's long drive. When Lady Holmes finally spoke, her words churned the whipping winds of my emotions into nothing short of a tempest.

"I can read your thoughts as though they were pressed upon the page, Hudson."

My nerves and stomach somersaulted from the carriage and writhed in the dust behind our wheels.

"Inspector Goodwin is a liar even under the most generous interpretation and a patronizing traitorous insult to his profession at worst. I would advise you not to marry him."

I huffed. "We are quite agreed on that point."

"If he meant to reveal the developments in the case, he would have done so already. Therefore, we must find a way to steal into the inspector's office and read his notes."

Grateful she hadn't understood the actual subject of my thoughts, I agreed instantly and regretted it even more quickly. "Yes, yes, of course. Well, no, I ... what? Break into the police station?"

Lady Holmes urged the horse toward the stables rather than the front door. "Precisely, Hudson. It's remarkable how alike our thoughts run. I've been testing possible plans as we rode, and I arrived at the same conclusion. Our safest course with the greatest chance of success is to wait until nightfall, make our way across the countryside to the station, and let ourselves inside to peruse the inspector's notes."

"Safest? There are a thousand dangers. Even if it were proper for us to be out at night unaccompanied, we'd be recognized. If we were lucky enough to sneak past the town, what about the night policeman on duty at the station? He won't just let us into the inspector's office. Anyway, what if the notes aren't even in there?"

The creak of the carriage and the jangle of the harness grew as we pulled to a stop in front of the stables, so I raised my voice. "Your carriage alone is so well known the townsfolk can feel their forelocks tingle while we're still a mile away."

"We aren't taking the carriage." Her eyes grew stormy as she raised her chin to the stables. "My late husband was something of a horse enthusiast, and I've yet to decide what to do with his collection. The entire stable is full of under-exercised and overpriced horseflesh, so we shall have our pick. Don't worry, we've the rest of the day to teach you to ride."

"I can ride." My voice came out stiff as cold leather. "My father was a groom."

There was plenty more I could have said. How Da had worked for the most renowned horse breeder in England,

Lord Wallace Sterling. And how Da rehabilitated an enormous thoroughbred that pulled up lame near the end of a race. That Lord Sterling had been so grateful he gifted my father a driving mare, Lily, who ate grass from our hands with lips as gentle as a kiss. I made the pilgrimage to her stall after school every day for a solid month, until Da finally taught me to ride. At first, I could barely get my legs over her broad back. Then, we moved. And it felt like climbing a tree, jumping from the hayloft, and laughing all at once. I never wanted to stop.

Usually more tired than Lily, Da would stand, arms draped over the fence, smiling, stopping me every so often to pass along his deep knowledge of riding, breeding, and grooming. Ma was afraid of horses, George and Ralph too little, and at work, horses were serious business. But Da and I, we could just love horses together, and it didn't have to be anything more than that.

When Da died and we had to sell Lily to a local farmer, it felt like another death. One more piece of my life that could only live on in memory now. One more tally in the debtor's column against Lord Wallace Sterling and what he'd cost us.

"I can ride well," I added, then cleared my throat, "but I shall need slacks."

Blood flowed into her high cheeks, the blossoming pupils of her eyes deep and shiny as fresh coal. I waited for her judgment, her incredulity at the very least. Women didn't wear slacks for a reason, at least ladies didn't. My entire legs and behind would be on display. As the silence between us grew, I wanted to fall back, but I forced myself to meet her gaze as best I could, without explanation, my feet solid roots.

The corner of her tongue darted out and wet her lips. "I have only ever ridden sidesaddle."

Cool lead filled my chest. I had expected as much and was a fool to hope for more. "Perhaps this is a bad idea." I turned away. "We can arrange—"

"Teach me." Her hand shot forward, hovering over my arm. "I shall need you to teach me."

My thoughts collected on the front of my tongue with the buzz of a thousand messages coming down the telegraph line at once. In truth, it wasn't the complexity of the problem that made me pause; it was how my palms grew damp at the thought of what it involved. A skirt served as a sort of cage, but also armor. With a fortifying bustle, an army of buttons, and a skeleton of boning, it kept the world at a distance a little less than the span of one's arms.

Perhaps it was unwise to proceed without those layers between us.

As we'd been behind the forsythia, the way Lady Holmes pressed me close, and how I hadn't wanted her to let go.

I flogged my retiring tongue into action. "Let's start."

CHAPTER TWENTY-FOUR

THE EFFICIENT MACHINE OF MUSGRAVE HALL supplied us with the necessary garments, and I had no time to speak to Sherlock before I found myself in an empty tack room, changing into my borrowed things.

It had been over a decade since I'd last worn slacks, aside from the few times Eleanor and I donned men's clothes around our flats as a joke to amuse each other. The ability to move was intoxicating. Too large through the shoulders and a little tight across the chest, the shirt still offered freedom of movement like nothing else. I flapped my hands at my sides, unsure of what to do with them without the folds of my skirts as support.

Outside the tack room, Lady Holmes sat on a crate, bridle in hand. Her legs stretched out before her, even leaner and taller without the padding and tailoring of a dress.

I shifted from boot to boot. "Which horse?" I asked.

Lady Holmes rose and strode down the double row of stalls running the length of the barn. "Arthur gave me Rhadamanthus as a wedding gift." She unlatched the stall of a beautiful chestnut Hackney, and he lifted the curve of his neck, his coat sparkling even in the dim light.

I scratched the white star emblazoned between his eyes, and Lady Holmes started to say something, but stopped when he let out a nicker, nuzzling his nose into the palm of my other hand. "Hello there, Rhadamanthus," I said. "How goes it with you, ducky?"

The sweet name Da used for any horse he ever encountered slipped from my mouth, snagging my heart in the process. I hadn't cried over Da in years. What was wrong with me? Stripped of my usual clothing, I had no handkerchief, and so I pressed my stinging eyes into Rhadamanthus' broad nose. The scent of his soap stung my nostrils, identical to the one Da used to bathe Lily, and for a moment, I let time and longing flow over me.

"Remarkable," Lady Holmes said.

I lifted my head, cheeks flushed but dry. "What is?"

She slipped the reins over his head, tugged the bridle into place, and secured the throatlatch. "It usually takes two grooms to saddle Rhadamanthus." She grinned at me. "He bites."

I gazed at my unmarked palm. Da would have had my head for shoving myself at a strange horse.

"And kicks," she added. "He seems to like you, though."

"And your husband thought he was a fit wedding present?"

"My brother Lewis, an even greater horse lover than Arthur, if such a thing were possible, convinced him having a dangerous horse would keep me from riding as often, and thus, I would be more likely to follow womanly pursuits. As he put it."

I gripped the bars of the stall. "But that's ... that's *awful*."

She gave Rhadamanthus an affectionate pat on his neck. "Don't worry, it didn't work. An outcome Lewis and Arthur could have predicted had they stopped to consult with me on the matter. Hand me that saddlecloth, please."

Once Rhadamanthus was saddled, the other horses watched as we led him toward the mounting block in the stable yard. Lady Holmes clambered to the top of it and turned her head to me.

I lined up Rhadamanthus and handed her the reins. After a false start, she took a deep breath and shifted her weight, sliding into place. "There," she said, "a task much easier to accomplish without the limitations of one's skirts."

"Indeed." At this height, her thighs were inches away from my lips, and I dragged my eyes back to the reins still clutched in my fist. Breathing hard, I patted Rhadamanthus. "There's a good lad." He shifted his four white socks as though eager to proceed. Too late, I noticed the stiff angle of Lady Holmes' calves. "No, no, lean back."

She overcorrected and leaned too far, bracing herself in the stirrups and rising out of the saddle. Rhadamanthus objected to the unfamiliar movement and reared up his front feet. I swung around and grabbed the reins where they met the bit. A gentle tug brought the horse back down, but Lady Holmes glared at me, stricken.

"Don't worry, Rhadamanthus and I won't let you fall." I gave her a smile of encouragement.

Her breath came in short angry bursts, and red dots crowned her cheeks. "You could have been injured. Trampled. Crushed! I order you never to do something like that again."

Da had trained us how to move around horses almost as

soon as we could walk, but the fear in her voice touched me. "I won't do it again," I said. "As your employee, I want you to know I'm listening to your concerns."

Lady Holmes speared me with a look. "Just show me the next part."

"Point your toes up and lean back a little." I placed my hands on her ankle and thigh, angling them in.

Her leg stiffened, muscles freezing into rocks under my fingers. She bent her legs, but her wide eyes flicked to mine, unreadable.

I snapped my hands back and plunged them into my pockets, heat climbing my chest. "Now let him know it's time to go. Squeeze gently from your bottom to your leg and then your foot."

With the movement, Rhadamanthus eased into a walk. "That's excellent," I called as they approached the far wall of the stable yard. "Just move your outside leg to close and turn back."

"Outside of what? Hudson, Hudson, how do I—" She cast a frantic glance at me and said something else, but it was lost in the jingle of tack and hooves.

"Close the outside leg!" I shouted, my thoughts scrambling.

Rhadamanthus made the decision for them and stopped, stiff-legged before they crashed into the brick wall. I dashed along in their wake. "This is your outside leg," I said, gasping for breath and gesturing at her far leg.

"Hudson, I am astride a *horse*. All of me is outside."

"No, to turn. You bend your leg and bring your calf against his side to push his hindquarters into the turn. At the same time, you open up your opposite hand."

Following a final dark look, Lady Holmes slowly did as I instructed. Then, while she and Rhadamanthus worked, I watched from the doorway as though I'd slipped into Da's shoes. He would be proud of me. My eyes grew warm and tight, exposed, standing here with all my heart as newly visible as my limbs. If only I had the protection of my usual clothes.

But I couldn't take my eyes off Lady Holmes. She was a good student, and her experience riding, though sidesaddle, served her well. Before long, the pair moved together, making loop after loop in the stable yard.

Staving off a flutter of regret, I waved her down on the next pass.

Her eyes shone as I helped her out of the saddle, but her breath stuttered when I grasped her arm. Had it been my touch or the riding that drew her shrouded emotions to the surface? But then Lady Holmes pulled away as soon as her feet touched the ground, and she brushed at her clothes, making the answer clear.

I tried to keep the hurt off my face. "We shouldn't tire Rhadamanthus if you plan to ride him tonight during our doomed excursion."

She grinned, the color still high in her cheeks. "Even your dour pronouncements won't bring down my spirits. I cannot believe I wasted my life twisted onto a sidesaddle, that any of us do, when there is such freedom to be had, such control. Mounted thus, I feel solid as the hills and as powerful as a general surveying the battlefield. I do not think I could be unseated."

Rhadamanthus tossed his head as though in agreement. Far from being tired, he seemed disappointed to see the inside of the barn again, nipping at a curious bay who stuck its head over the door to its stall. I kept my hands clear of his mouth as I coaxed him back into his own box and unbuckled his saddle, using this time to calm my heart. Why could I not keep such foolish hopes out of my head? We were temporary investigative partners and nothing more. And it was for the best. Truly.

Lady Holmes stood just outside, stretching her limbs. "Let's go. There's much we need to add to our case map."

I heaved the saddle onto the rack outside the stall. "Fetch me a brush while I get the rest of his tack off, please."

She paused before speaking, clearly unused to taking orders. "That isn't necessary."

Something hardened in my chest. "On the contrary, it's how you build a relationship." I bit my lip. "If you knew someone who only came around when they wanted you to work for them, how would that make you feel?"

"I'm not proposing we leave him alone. The stablehands will take care of the horse," she said.

"*Rhadamanthus*." I took a deep breath. "He has a name, as, I suspect, do the stablehands. Now, bring me a brush." I unfastened the bridle and rubbed the bridge of his nose where the leather had flattened his coat. "There, ducky, is that better?"

Lady Holmes could take offense to the facts or my imperious tone if she liked, but the ghost of my father and my own disappointed hopes lingered at the moment.

She handed me a brush. "You neglected to mention your father was a groom for Lord Wallace Sterling." Her voice was drawn to a keen edge.

My heart took a sudden dip. "I didn't realize it was

relevant." I plucked the brush from her hands and stroked the horse's back while he drank. "Da worked at Sterling Place all of his life."

"Sterling is the largest landowner in the county. Arthur, Lewis, and Sterling's son Clarence were at school together and came away as best friends. We were often guests at Sterling Place, and I met your father there." She ran a hand over the now empty bridle.

She'd met Da? I knew Lady Holmes was older than me, but I'd never pictured her as a young bride. Trying to do it now reminded me how little I knew about her.

Lady Holmes picked up a spare brush and joined me in running it over Rhadamanthus' opposite flank. We worked in silence for a few minutes, and then she spoke again. "He used to say the same thing about horses, that we only come around when we want them to work for us. A lovely man. I can see why you detest Sterling Place since your father gave his life to protect Sterling from horse thieves."

What? Blood roared in my ears, and my face grew hot. Lady Holmes had to be mistaken. "No. No. A horse kicked him in the chest. That's what my mother told us." My own sternum ached as though I'd been the one to receive the blow. Ma's tearful announcement of Da's death had been the worst day of my life, until John died. I would have known if something was off. Ma would have told me.

Lady Holmes stopped combing. "There was an investigation by the coroner. Arthur and Lewis discussed it over the course of several dinners. Perhaps your mother sought to spare you the details?"

I bit my lip. Ma lying was one thing, but in a town this

size, and one filled with various connections to Sterling Place—how could I have missed something so important?

Lady Holmes laid a hand over mine. "I'm sorry I upset you."

All I could do was shake my head, ears ringing.

"Take your time and meet me in the study when you're ready." She put a long-fingered hand on Rhadamanthus' velvety nose. "Thank you for the ride, Rhadamanthus. I shall see you later this evening."

CHAPTER TWENTY-FIVE

AFTER I FINISHED COMBING OUT RHADAMANTHUS, i scrubbed off in the servants' baths next to the kitchen. Helen found me when I exited and handed me another stack of borrowed male clothing from the laundry.

"M'lady said you'll be needing these for later." Helen's inquisitive expression begged for more details.

It was a servant's job to keep their eyes down and their lips shut, but secrets and gossip were valuable currency below stairs, so long as the butler or the housekeeper didn't catch you at it.

"You know m'lady's fondness for astronomy. We're preparing for the upcoming solar eclipse," I said. This lie even had the added benefit of being the truth. "Thank you for the clothes."

I retreated upstairs to my new bedroom with a sigh of relief, placed the clothes on the bedcovers, and plopped down next to them.

Ever since Lady Holmes mentioned Da, my thoughts looped like a horse on the track, reaching the same conclusion every time. Her understanding of his death must be a mistake. She possessed a remarkable memory, yes, and she didn't seem as bad as most of her rich brethren, but she was still an aristocrat. So why would she pay attention to the death of another person's groom? It had nothing to do with her.

On the contrary, Da's death changed everything about my life, and the details of it—the scent of stew cooking that day, the long green dress I wore, Rosie's baby babble in the background—were the language of grief written upon my heart, indelible.

I examined my flushed cheeks in the mirror above the dresser. Between the bath and the riding lessons, my hair had sprung a forest of loose tendrils, so I pulled the pins and took my time fixing the low knot.

It didn't make sense to blame Lady Holmes for her remarks. She'd been trying to be kind. We could consider the matter closed.

The final pin slid into place as a whisper came from behind me. In the mirror, a piece of paper appeared through the crack under my door, coming to rest near the rag rug at the center of the room.

I flung the door open to discover the sender, but the hall outside was empty. Returning to the paper, I recognized it as Billy's drawing. Sherlock. I still needed to talk to him about admitting our secret to Lady Holmes, but I would have to find him later. I studied the drawing where a series of dots and dashes now decorated the bottom.

`Horse driving collar on a tack room wall STOP Approx fifteen inches STOP Patch`

```
repair to the lower left quadrant STOP
Location unknown STOP
```

I smiled at Sherlock's care in deciphering the less important side and in attempting to keep his communication secret by rendering it in Morse Code. How had he determined I knew it? With rising excitement, I turned the paper over. Here, the details were thick.

```
Size twelve shoe STOP Likely a man's STOP
Not laborer by trade STOP Professional
who is active STOP Shopkeeper, police
officer, or innkeeper STOP Crack approx two
and one quarter inches near toes of left
foot STOP
```

My knees grew weak, and I sat down hard in the chair. Shopkeeper, police officer, or innkeeper. Frances' boss at the dressmaking shop? Inspector Goodwin or Constable Marks? Alfie? What did Tom do for a living? Billy's life was full of possible suspects, it turned out, but none with a discernible motive.

Of course, it needn't be any of them. And a thief might borrow another's shoes. Whatever the case, one thing was certain: the print on the paper matched the one we found in the garden next door to the Mudds' home. That long crack under the toes was quite distinctive.

As soon as I discussed the matter with Sherlock, I would go with him to admit our secret to Lady Holmes and show her his impressive work. For now, I opened my trunk, rolled up the drawing, and hid it in the longest compartment next to Eleanor's letters. There was plenty of room in the little cabinets John had built into the lid specially for me since I had so few possessions. Then I went in search of either Holmes. When I couldn't locate Sherlock, I made my way to Lady Holmes' study, but the sounds of clanking metal from inside stopped me at the door. I raised my hand to knock, but a heavy thud came from inside, followed by the high tinkle of breaking glass.

Had Frances' attacker found Lady Holmes alone in her study? I thrust the door open, ready to spring forward.

The culprit stood at the center of the room. Surrounded by expensive scientific equipment dismantled into their brass viscera was a red-faced Sherlock. Not panicked, just resigned and hopeful.

"Is Mother with you?"

His question overcame my shock, and I shot a glance down the hallway before easing the door shut. "No, thank goodness. What on earth are you doing? And how did you manage to do it so quickly? You were at my door moments ago."

A questioning scowl crossed his face, but instead of answering, he tilted his pointy chin even higher. "Aren't you going to ask me?"

"Ask you what?"

He blinked. "If I need saving."

I stared at the wreck of the study. The gaping holes on the shelves where there should have been a shining instrument stood out like missing teeth. Brass fittings, lenses, and fine leather straps lay jumbled on every horizontal surface, especially the floor. Luckily, the things weren't smashed, only broken down into their component parts. Near the window lay the scattered parts of the telescope Lady Holmes had moved earlier. Otherwise, the groups were a hotchpotch of components from different instruments and machines, as though he'd taken apart one, and finding himself unsatisfied, attacked each one faster and faster until he ended up at the center of a maelstrom.

What could I do for him other than give him a package of sweet buns and a head start? He was a bright lad. Surely the circus could find a job for him. Any fate seemed better than facing Lady Holmes' judgment, her fine features and mossy eyes hardened into agate.

My heart shrank several sizes at the thought, but if I felt so, what must Sherlock be experiencing? I'd felt so close to Da today that his voice was right at the surface. *We make ourselves useful in the world only through lightening the burdens of others.* I took a step forward. "Do you need saving, Master Sherlock?"

After a moment's hesitation, he spoke. "Yes."

A bushel of impractical solutions rushed through my mind, wasting precious seconds. We could remove the pieces and claim they'd been stolen. We could lie down among the remains and say we'd been attacked like Frances. Perhaps the circus would have room for two. Even if Sherlock could put the instruments back together, it wouldn't be fast enough. But I refused to have another secret from Lady Holmes, not when the one I already had was so heavy.

I could help Sherlock put them all back together, but not before his mother noticed them dismantled. She noticed everything. Except for Sherlock's various shenanigans.

Of course. Oh, the poor thing. How had I missed it?

I pictured him as I'd first met him, keeping a lonely watch by the gates of his home, waiting for his mother. Pretending to be a member of the kitchen staff, enfolded into their warm bustle. Alone on the back stairs, traipsing up and down, pressing heavy shoes into the flour he'd painstakingly spread on each step. How he must have hidden in his mother's study and read her notes, searching for whatever pieces of her he could have, searching for a way to force her to see him, to really *see* him. The way he'd hidden himself in the long grass beside the beehives, chin to his knobbly knees, standing guard on a mission for his beloved brother. This scrap of a boy, with his father's face and his mother's mind, he was surrounded by staff day in and day out, but he was utterly and completely alone.

When Da died, even when John died, my world broke apart, but at least I was never alone. Except for once. The interminable night when I sat vigil with John's body. In the dark, when it was just me, and John, and death. Even now, I never, *never* wanted to think about that night. How the pit yawned beneath me. How it called. How I began to form the words to call back.

I couldn't give Sherlock what he actually needed, but I couldn't stand by and do nothing.

"Here's what we'll do. You hurry back to the nursery, and I'll wait here to explain the situation." I smiled reassuringly, though I had no idea what I would say when Lady Holmes arrived. I opened the door.

Despite the gesture, Sherlock didn't move. "You're different from Marie." He fixed me with his piercing gaze.

"Who's Marie?"

"Mother's last maid. When she found me scraping the

family portraits to test the paint for arsenic, she pinched me by the ear and dragged me in front of Mother."

I frowned at the casual cruelty but knew enough of Sherlock by way of Lady Holmes to keep the pity out of my voice. "And was there?"

"I beg your pardon?"

"Was there arsenic?" I asked.

"Oh, yes. In the whitish-yellow parts. Don't lick the dog's fur in the portrait of my great-great Uncle Mortimer," he said, picking his way through the mess strewn across the floor.

"I'll take that advice to heart." I gestured toward the open door. "Whatever happened to Marie?"

He gave me a sly look as he passed. "She had a great terror of frogs. There might still be one in your room. Some of them got away."

No wonder the lad wanted to know how I felt about the creatures before he let me on the estate. I winked at him. "It sounds like Marie received exactly what she deserved. Now, straight back to the nursery with you. Promise?"

He nodded solemnly. "What will you tell Mother?"

I knew what she needed to hear. The truth. All of it. The problem was how she might receive it. I ran a hand over his curls, so like Oliver's, then set it on his shoulder as we stepped into the hallway. "I'll think of something."

"Think of what, Hudson?" Lady Holmes asked from a few feet down the hallway. Her eyes landed on her son in the doorway, my hand still on his shoulder, and they grew as dark as the bed of a lake. "So, you've met Sherlock. What are you doing in ..."

Her words trailed off, lost among the bits of brass and

glass littering her study. For a moment, no more than a breath, I thought she might scream. A creeping horror pulled her mouth down and her cheeks high, but then it was gone again.

She reached past me and yanked the door shut. Her one concession to her feelings over the dismantled scientific instruments. "Sherlock, you are to return to the nursery and wait there."

He threw a glance between us, then marched down the hall toward the main stairs.

When he was out of earshot, Lady Holmes sighed. "I'm sorry this was your introduction to him."

I wanted to explain about my dealings with Sherlock, but I despaired of adding such tinder to the fire. "I'm sure he didn't mean to break your things. He was probably trying to figure out how they work. He's clearly a clever lad."

"Far too clever, I fear. Sometimes Sherlock is … difficult."

She couldn't have handed me a better opening. I took a deep breath and plunged in. "Of course, he's so young. After all, he's been through a great deal this past year. It makes perfect sense he'd go to great lengths to gain your attention."

She pulled back. "My attention? He sees me each day when I set his lessons, and half the time, he can't sit still to listen to those."

I touched her arm. "He's so desperate for you it breaks my heart. Don't you see it?"

The angles of her face softened into the bland lines Lady Holmes wore when she wanted to hide. An island shrouded in fog, all lights doused. Even her voice took on a bored tone. "He is not some lost boy you need to save. That will be all, Hudson."

"So much for being an investigative partner and not a maid." I dropped her arm, but she didn't flinch. "On the contrary, he may be the most lost boy I've ever met. Don't let him go. You can still reach him. He wants—"

"Enough. Meet me at the stables at nine o'clock, dressed to ride. How you spend your time between now and then is your own decision." She stopped as that toneless facade wavered again.

I should have left. However, I promised Sherlock I would explain, and instead I'd made it worse. "Please, neither of you needs to do this alone. You have each other."

I'd hoped to crack the walls she kept tugging into place, but I feared I'd broken something else instead. Us.

"Get out, Hudson. Another word and you'll find yourself outside the front gates yet again." With that, she turned, let herself into the ruins of her study, and shut the door in my face.

CHAPTER TWENTY-SIX

WE TOLD THE SERVANTS WE WERE TAKING OFF INTO the night to make observations of the stars ahead of the eclipse. That and several boxes of astronomical equipment, packed tight with straw so the newly disassembled pieces wouldn't clink, were our cover story. Lady Holmes didn't speak a word to me until we hid the astronomical equipment inside a shed on the outskirts of the estate.

"Be mindful of that case, it's full of the *pieces* of my favorite telescope." After that, more silence.

I'd traveled silently beside Lady Holmes before, mired under the heft of my own thoughts. But this trip to the town felt like I was alone in the wilderness instead of weaving across the familiar countryside with a companion. If I couldn't even trust her to answer me when I spoke, how would I trust her to keep us from being discovered as we broke into the Sherrinford Police Station?

Despite her refusal to at least divulge her plan for tonight, as well as the almost certain imprisonment awaiting us at our destination, it was a thrilling ride. We avoided the road, opting instead to cut across the hills and river bottom. A wash of stars unfurled across the night sky like the skirts of a dancer.

In the distance, silent flickers of lightning blinked. Since John's death at the crack of a bolt, I'd been uneasy during storms, and each time one flashed now, my pulse gave a small jolt in response. Thankfully, just being in the saddle again was its own sort of balm. My borrowed mount, a lovely bay named Belianis, danced underneath me, each step kissing the earth before he transferred his weight to the next. A grin crept across my face with every breath, only to be washed away as my thoughts swung again to the silent companion a few feet ahead of me.

I was grateful for the dark that hid the endless sunrise and sunset of my face from Lady Holmes' scrutiny.

With our hair tucked under soft caps and our limbs outlined again in men's clothing, my feelings also vacillated between power and vulnerability. I wasn't quite myself, but neither was I someone else. It left me with an itch just under my skin that no amount of adjusting my collar or my belt seemed to ease.

When we finally approached a dense copse of trees on the outskirts of town, I was already exhausted from fighting off terror and clamping down on joy. The burnt-out buildings had been a bustling goat farm, but a fire ravaged the main house while I lived in London, leaving the remaining structures empty, the edges soft and wild.

We stashed the horses in the ramshackle barn and made our way into town on foot. At least now I could pretend our silence was as much about stealth as it was about Lady Holmes' quiet fury.

The bell rang for ten o'clock as we entered Sherrinford, and we wound around buildings and down alleys without encountering any townsfolk. The High Street, however, contained a couple walking arm in arm, a group of four hatless men, and Mr. Betts, a town staple who wandered the lanes at all hours to ease the pain in his joints.

Instead of avoiding them by sticking to the alley, Lady Holmes strolled from the shadows and into the spill of lights from the oil lamps outside the grocer's and the little town church.

I made a noise of protest and tried to catch her arm. "La—" Good sense snagged the reins on my tongue just as Mr. Betts passed us.

"Evening, sirs." He touched his cap and toddled away.

An electric buzz gripped my abdomen, and I hurried to catch up with the madwoman outpacing me. "You could've warned me we'd be boldly masquerading as men in public. In fact, you could have told me one damned thing about this little outing."

Her voice came out deeper, as unhurried and relaxed as her stride. "Oh? Are we through keeping secrets from each other now?"

We weren't, and I knew it. I had yet to tell her of the footprint. But, tonight, we needed to be on the same team. "It wasn't a secret. Not exactly. I wanted—"

"Stop mincing, Hudson, you'll give us away." She waved a hand at my hips.

I bit my cheek and forced myself to lengthen my steps, rolling the soles of my borrowed boots over the cobblestones, walking as though I'd invented it—and everything else besides.

"Think what you like of things, but I had everyone's best interests in mind," I said.

"I've no doubt you believed you knew best. That is, after all, what you do."

"What on earth does that mean?" I longed to grab her arm again, but I stuffed my hands into my pockets. "This is senseless, plunging in when only one of us knows the plan. Just tell me your strategy and hate me tomorrow. Don't let your ire— *Will* you slow down?"

"I do not require a chaperone, Hudson. I told you I would secure us entry to the police station, and I will. Your expertise comes after."

"Fine." I huffed out a ragged breath, and though she didn't answer, her pace eased.

She stopped diagonally opposite the police station, just outside twin circles of light from oil lamps mounted on the front. Built a few years ago, it looked like two identical narrow brick buildings that had started life as separate edifices only to be joined into a single structure. The beige stepped brickwork along the corners and in the gables pulled the eye skyward, making the building appear much taller than its two stories.

Lady Holmes checked a pocket watch just as the distant lightning gave way to a soft rumble of thunder.

"Are we late for our appointment?" I blurted. The thunder set me on edge, and I'd left my patience behind with my skirts.

"At this moment, Mr. Logan, a man whose love of drink often outstrips his good sense as well as his funds, is making a fool of himself at The Four Hounds. Not only will he be serenading passersby, but he will shortly decide he no longer has need of his trousers." She leaned against the doorway of the barbershop.

The idea of leveraging the town drunk as a distraction was rather brilliant, but I refused to give her the satisfaction of my jaw dropping. "How can you possibly know that?"

"I've hired a trio of passing farm laborers to fund Mr. Logan's entertainments this evening."

"That's not a terrible idea," I admitted though it made my teeth ache, "but how is the night constable supposed to know any of this? Did you also hire a circus to perform in the middle of town to alert him?"

Lady Holmes gave me a bland look. "I'm about to go tell him."

By the time I figured out she was serious, I could only splutter an objection at her back as she crossed the street. Awe and horror and shock made their own riotous party in my chest while I watched Lady Holmes enter the well-lit station and present herself—all borrowed slacks and attitude—to Constable Sloane.

She had little need to bind her chest, and her hips were slim enough that, in trousers, she had almost the correct silhouette to be a tall, lean man. With the application of soot on her jaw and brows, the transformation was startling. But would that be enough to hold up under such a test?

I held my breath. If she were caught, she wouldn't face real punishment. Dressing up like a man? Wandering the town at night unaccompanied? Just another eccentric aristocrat. A lark, nothing more. I, on the other hand, had neither Lady Holmes' fortune nor title to gird my reputation.

Two men with thick beards turned onto the High Street and walked my way. Though I'd bound my chest, I was far softer and curvier than I should appear, shadows or no shadows. The police station was my only chance at salvation. I took off across the street.

I'd made it halfway when Lady Holmes emerged, this time followed by the towering Constable Sloane.

"We should have the postmistress direct Mr. Logan's mail to the lockup," he said in a resigned voice as he closed the door to the station and turned the key before dropping it into his pocket.

Lady Holmes let out a deep chuckle and touched a finger to her cap. "I just hope you reach the inn before everyone gets an eyeful," she said in a perfect copy of the local accent.

The constable hurried off in the direction of the inn while Lady Holmes wandered the other way as though even her worries had no cares, with me in her wake.

"Constable Sloane is no longer in the station. Full marks for that. However, neither are we." I gestured at the now distant front door.

"How observant." She turned down the lane perpendicular to the High Street, lined with smaller shops and homes. From there, we slipped into the empty alley behind the High Street.

Lady Holmes rooted among the boxes and slop cans at the back of the police station and shifted them in front of the rear door, securing a broken broom handle between. She then led me a few feet down the lane and pulled out her watch again, tipping it to catch what little light came from the upper windows of the station. "We aren't inside, but Mrs. Wakefield is. And she should be finishing her work right about … now."

Like an actress late for her cue, Mrs. Wakefield, my neighbor from two lanes over, bustled through the door with a pail in one arm and a basket of laundry tucked under the other. Before the door shut, Mrs. Wakefield caught her foot against the broom handle across the threshold. Pail, laundry, boxes, and her familiar starched cap all tumbled to the ground with Mrs. Wakefield sprawled across them. A clatter echoed from the bricks.

In a flash, Lady Holmes knelt beside Mrs. Wakefield, grabbed the broken broom handle, and used it to catch the lip of the door before it could shut behind the prone woman. "My goodness, ma'am, are you alright? George, get the spilled laundry, man."

This last was directed at me, and I staggered into action. George? How did she know that among my brothers, I resembled George the most?

"Oh, thank you, lads," Mrs. Wakefield said shakily. "Those dratted water buckets always make the hallway so tight if Constable Sloane doesn't empty them for me before I leave. Still, I think I'm all in one piece, just a few bruises to my pride."

Lady Holmes levered the stout woman to her feet, and I handed her the lost cap, then the pail and laundry she'd been carrying.

"Thank you, Georgie. Working late for Dr. McNulty tonight?"

I nodded and backed up a few steps before Mrs. Wakefield saw through my disguise, even with her nearsightedness.

However, she only waved a hand at Lady Holmes' declaration that we should walk her home. "Nonsense, my son'll be waiting for me out front. You lads get back to work before this storm bursts." With that, she made her way down the alley, muttering to herself as she went.

Once she was out of sight, Lady Holmes opened the door with an irritating flourish. "After you, George."

"I hope my brother has an excellent alibi," I grumbled.

Undiluted by her veil, Lady Holmes' eyes sparkled in the dim light. "If we do our jobs right, he won't need one."

The door creaked closed behind us, and I held my breath in the silence, my heartbeat rushing in my ears. Constable Sloane might not be here, but that didn't mean we were alone in the building. The three holding cells might be occupied, other staff might be there, or the inspector's plans could have changed.

Lady Holmes, however, walked down the corridor to Inspector Goodwin's office as though it were yet another polished corner of Musgrave Hall, and I had no choice but to follow. There, she pulled out a leather pouch and unfolded it to reveal a set of picklocks. After a few moments' work, she stood. The door clicked open under her hand.

We hurried through and shut ourselves inside, the darkness swallowing us.

Lady Holmes, who apparently had thought of everything, made a rustling noise, followed by a match striking. A round lantern, shielded by her body, flared to life. She narrowed the panel to a slim finger that wouldn't be noticed on the street below.

"First you pick a lock, and now you just happen to have a thief's lantern?" I asked, imagining a second life for her, one full of jewelry heists and bank robberies.

"They're useful in astronomical work to take notes in the field without ruining your eyes' adjustment to the dark."

A frown stilled her features, then she sighed. "The picklocks are a surprise for Sherlock. He's been begging for them for years."

Knowing what I did of the two of them, that made perfect sense.

"Now"—she approached the bank of filing cabinets—"let's get to work."

The record-keeping of Her Majesty's police force was commendable. Billy's file, unfortunately, filled just a few pages. A handful of interviews, a telegram from an inspector in Eastbourne, and a single page of notes written in Inspector Goodwin's looping script.

A creeping dread began in my stomach and clambered up my chest. If they'd solved Billy's disappearance, then where were the notes on his whereabouts? The interview with Tom? The unnamed lord? I flipped to the beginning again and threw Lady Holmes a disbelieving look.

She laid a hand over the pages, stony faced. "Put the file back."

"But maybe—"

"Goodwin's case notes aren't there. You know him well. Where would he keep his secret files?"

As much as I wanted to disavow myself from Reggie Goodwin, or worse, I swallowed my disgust and made a slow circuit of the room, running my hands under the furniture and pulling out drawers to peer behind them.

Twin chairs sat opposite the expanse of his gleaming behemoth of a desk, his own high-backed chair tucked underneath. Three framed official documents and a print of sailing boats hung on the off-white walls opposite the bank of filing cabinets, but there was nothing hidden behind them.

The desk's drawers held little of interest—tobacco, writing implements, a handful of lemon drops. In the bottom drawer, weighted down by a Bible of all things, was a manual concerning the nine principles of policing as laid out under Sir Robert Peel.

I slammed the drawer shut and sat down in the inspector's chair. Elbows on his blotter, I steepled my fingers. While I studied the room, Lady Holmes had skimmed through the rest of the files in the cabinet.

"It's not hidden in one of the other folders," she said.

A flash of lightning lit the office as though it were daylight. I startled just as a rumble of thunder slammed into the building, vibrating underfoot. My heart raced as though borrowing some of the terror from John's final moments. There was no time to panic. We needed to hurry and locate the rest of Billy's file, and then we could wait out the storm somewhere safe.

Lady Holmes had held up her end of things magnificently, and here I was failing at mine. I growled, unable to meet her eyes.

Deciphering the office felt like trying to put my foot through a brick wall. Everything was so new. There was hardly a personal mark on the place, and in truth, it'd been years since I knew much of the inspector's life. There was nothing of the young man I'd once kissed, the farm where he grew up, or the wild outskirts of the town we used to frequent. Everything here was bought elsewhere, probably London, made by strange hands in a factory or shop.

What if he kept the notes in another part of the station or at home? "No," I murmured, "he'd want to keep them close so he could work with them."

I thrust to my feet and prowled the office again. A coat rack, a cabinet with a set of glasses and a decanter of whiskey, a train timetable, a bookshelf with several law books, and—

"It has to be," I said.

Mixed in with the others was a volume bound in black leather, *The British Almanac of the Society for the Diffusion of Useful Knowledge*, remarkable because it was the single personal item from Inspector Goodwin's past. His father, a prominent farmer, had displayed a full set of these books in the front room of their home. Goodwin had kept the volume from the year he was born, 1844. A fitting repository for his private notes since it seemed he would rather keep his humble origins a secret as well.

As I riffled through it, the ghost of beef stew and stolen kisses rose on the whisper of the pages. There, folded between sections detailing prisons in Ireland and soap duties, was a sheaf of papers.

With a hiss of triumph, Lady Holmes met me at the desk with her lantern. At first, we both scanned the notes, but she read at a furious pace, hopping from page to page. I ceded the notes to her and crossed to the window, gauging the approaching storm and on the lookout for Constable Sloane returning with Mr. Logan.

I'd already seen enough to know Inspector Goodwin kept vital details of Billy's whereabouts from Frances for well over a week. How dare he? Deny a mother her child, her rights as a parent, her human decency?

A white-hot fury forked through my chest, more vicious than the lightning splitting the sky again. Seconds later, rain crashed to the ground, wicked and thick. I bit my lip and wiped my damp palms on my borrowed slacks. We should be soaked on our way back to the horses, but at least we could wait out the storm there. If we ran, it would be no more than a few minutes. I could last a few minutes with lightning if—

Three men emerged from the gloom and entered the flickering circles of the oil lamps. I caught my breath and eased to the side in case they spotted me even in the weak light of the thief's lantern. Two of the men held the third between them, clearly Constable Sloane leading Mr. Logan to his cell for the night. But the third man, dressed in a dark suit and tall hat, was a mystery.

Suddenly, the wind whipped the hat off the third man. As he spun to retrieve it from the street, he faced the lights, cheeks twisted against the storm and slick with rain. It was Inspector Goodwin.

Chapter Twenty-Seven

Terror snapped along my limbs, sharp and hot. "We have to go. Now."

Lady Holmes didn't even look up. "I require another minute. Distract them."

I sprinted into the hallway. The front door and reception area lay to my left, but even if the policemen weren't about to enter, it held little that might help my plight. I dashed to the right. A conference room and the bank of three cells along the back of the station flew past. Empty, the doors stood ajar, as though any of those cells might be where I was about to spend the night.

A gaslight sconce flickered across the hallway from them. Could I rip it from the wall and spark an explosion? Before I tried, an easier, and safer, target presented itself. Three buckets brimming with dingy water clustered just inside the door where we'd entered. A film of grime coated the surface, broken by a few halfhearted bubbles. The buckets of wastewater Mrs. Wakefield mentioned. If she was blamed for what I was about to do, Lady Holmes would just have to hire her on as another maid.

I kicked all three buckets over and gagged at the stink. Gray water coursed over the polished wooden floors, ricocheted off the skirting boards, and seeped under the locked door. I squeezed by, careful to avoid leaving any wet footprints, and hurried back to Inspector Goodwin's office.

Inside, Lady Holmes waved me through the doorframe. "Watch at the window while I relock the door."

The men were climbing the steps of the station, hauling a reluctant Mr. Logan up with them. Mr. Logan pulled an arm free and whipped it through the rain as though gesturing to an audience. A wild note of his song, a bit off-key, bounced off the bricks and reached me even through the storm.

All too soon, the officers subdued him and pulled him in through the front door. Their boots and voices echoed through the empty halls.

"Hurry, hurry, please hurry," I said, half encouragement to Lady Holmes and half prayer to any god willing to listen.

Giving no sign she'd heard me, Lady Holmes worked her tools in the lock. I flung open the window and hovered like a bird ready to spring into the air.

Footsteps marched down the hallway, and Mr. Logan's song grew louder.

"Enough, Mr. Logan, you'll need to … What the devil is all of this?" Inspector Goodwin said from just outside his office door.

I froze as Lady Holmes turned her long metal instrument.

"T'wasn't like this when I left. Maybe Mrs. Wakefield had an accident on her way out, sir? Is Mr. Logan … should I—?"

"Get the bloody mop, man! I've enough of a mess on my

hands now the Mudd boy has run off for real. He's ruined an important evening for me."

As the men argued, Lady Holmes pocketed her picklocks and joined me at the window. I had thrown my leg over the ledge, but I stopped as the import of the inspector's words sank in like the rain soaking my trousers. Where was Billy now?

"Out, Hudson. Before the rain comes in and leaves a trail."

I set both hands on the sill and jumped. Ground floor or not, the windows were a good seven feet off ground level, and the rain lashing my eyes made it impossible to see beneath me. As I hit the pavement, the impact echoed through my bones. My teeth clacked together and fire seemed to arc up my right leg.

Pain wrapped heavy hands from my ankle to my knee, and I let out a sob as I collapsed. A clap of thunder covered my cry. For a blinding second, I was certain the lightning had struck me just as it had John. The flash of light, the searing pain, my breath gone—I imagined them countless times, and now finally, I had lived John's last moments with him.

A second later, long arms wound under my own and hoisted me to my feet.

"Can you walk?" Lady Holmes asked.

I scrabbled against the wool of her jacket, desperate for something to hold onto. "No. No. I ... leave me here."

"Out of the question." She grunted as she lifted me from the pavement and onto one foot. "We just have to get back to the horses."

The pain of my injured ankle rocketed me back into life.

I hissed as we started forward, but she didn't slow. "I'm so sorry, Hudson," Lady Holmes said, "but we need to get out of sight."

The firm patience in her voice anchored me. I staggered along, trying to look less like a thief and more like a man who'd seen the bottom of a regiment of pint glasses. We were both panting before we'd gone a hundred feet. Sherrinford felt miles across, like two Londons set back-to-back. The scent of horse dung and wet rocks filled the night as we stumbled through the lanes and into the jaws of the storm. My stomach roiled in pain, competing with my whipping heart. Somehow, she knew the exact distraction I needed.

"If you'd taken a job at Sterling Place, not only would you be uninjured and safely abed, but you'd also have solved Billy's disappearance alongside our cretinous inspector."

"Billy's been at Sterling Place?" I bit my lip.

"Yes."

In the distance, men's voices grew louder and someone shouted.

"This entire time? How?"

"You'll have to cross this fence," she said. With both hands around my waist, she steadied me from the far side. When I was over, she answered. "Tom worked there when he was a lad, as a houseboy."

I winced as another cannonade of thunder volleyed across the hills, the rain cutting sideways.

I cracked the seal on my memories of Sterling Place, and the storm, my pain and peril, it all grew distant. Instead, before me unfolded the wide sweep of the avenues, the buildings and gardens as crisp as they must have appeared under the architect's pen—it all came rushing back. If Lady

Holmes hadn't been holding me, I would've fallen.

With her free arm, she wiped her face. "Tom claimed he wanted to secure Billy a job as a houseboy to make up for his years of financial neglect."

I scoffed. "It might pay more than working at the inn, but it's hardly a goldmine. I'm sure your houseboys wouldn't refuse a pay rise."

Her chuckle drowned in the next round of thunder. "I shall take that under consideration. The inspector knows Billy was at Sterling Place because he talked to Tom, went there, saw Billy happily working, and met with Lord Sterling."

"Of all the damnable, underhanded bastards." My foot came down too hard, and I yelped as a fresh burst of pain exploded in my ankle.

Another distant shout came from the town. We hadn't left a trail. They couldn't be after us. But then, what was the commotion?

"Careful, Hudson." She threw a quick glance over her shoulder and gripped me tighter before forcing me to pick up the pace. "The men decided it was best for Billy to get established in his position and not to tell Frances, who would demand he come home. I will quote Tom's words if you promise not to injure yourself in outrage."

"Fine," I ground out.

"Tom said, 'He needs to be out from under her thumb, cut the apron strings, better for both of them.' I've never met Mr. Mudd, but he doesn't sound like a credit to humanity."

We made for the rectangle of weeds and scrub separating us from where Rhadamanthus and Belianis waited.

"Well, this explains why Inspector Goodwin was so

unwilling to investigate. But tonight, he seemed shaken. Did you hear what he said?" I asked.

"That Billy's run off in truth this time? That accounts for the inspector's unexpected return to the station." Lady Holmes propped me up against the wall of the barn and opened the door. I missed her warmth immediately. My wet clothes clung to my skin, and I shuddered.

The damp air, carrying the gluttonous reek of goats and old hay, rushed out to meet us as we stumbled inside. We were safe. I sheltered by the door while she checked on the horses. To my surprise, she drew Belianis even with a stack of old boards.

Surely she didn't mean for me to mount him right now? "But the storm? Shouldn't we wait here?" My panic bled into my words, voice quaking.

"We need to get back while you can still ride. It's also possible they're pursuing us." She waved me forward.

I wanted to argue with her, but my words fled. Instead, my nostrils filled with the reek of burnt hair and wool and charred skin. I couldn't move. The lightning that had killed John was right here. Was it ready to take me too? A wicked crack of thunder shook the ground, and Lady Holmes reached for me.

She wrapped her long arms around my own, then spoke low and soft as though I were Belianis. "Courage, Hudson. You can do this."

I breathed in her clean sharp scent, as she steadied my hips while I heaved myself into the saddle.

Once we flung ourselves into the storm, we couldn't have talked even if I'd wanted to. I hunkered over Belianis, freezing and terrified. Pain lit up my ankle with each jounce of the horse's hooves, but there was nothing I could do except to set my teeth and ride.

The complicated safety of Musgrave Hall drew me forward until only my chest bindings kept me upright. A sharp crack of thunder split the sky and left my ears ringing. I shouted my fear into the muffled din as Belianis rippled under me, skating to the side. Lady Holmes shouted something in response, but the storm chopped the meaning from her words. A cacophony of sound barreled toward me, thunder and churning hooves. The jagged noise cut through the din.

Seconds later, Lady Holmes was upon me. She turned her soaked face and shouted, "Gunfire! We are discovered! Ride, Hudson!"

CHAPTER TWENTY-EIGHT

IT WAS TOO MUCH FOR BELIANIS. HE SHIED, STRIKING the gravel underfoot with a shower of sparks. All of my attention narrowed to my exposed back, the muscles bunching as though to brace themselves against a bullet or a lightning strike. After that, I rode in the grip of a thousand deaths, sure my end was rising up to meet me. The tattoo of nervous hooves ate up the miles, churning mud and rocks in our wake.

As we mounted the last hill before the estate, the storm relented to a steady drizzle. I slumped over my saddle, weak and buzzing. My teeth clattered together and didn't stop. I lowered my arms, giving Belianis his head, trusting him to get us back safe. This day had stretched long and mean, like the skin of a starving animal. Even Lady Holmes' tall back had taken on a curve as we headed for the stables.

A groom met us at the door, the light from his lantern picking out the few drops that still fell and setting them ablaze.

"Thank you, Eliot, but no." Lady Holmes waved away

his offer to rouse more servants to help us. "We got caught in the storm and left our instruments in the outhouse of the hunting lodge. Send someone to collect them in the morning, please."

He yawned. "Yes, m'lady."

The long ride and cold soak in rainwater had numbed the piercing ache in my ankle enough for me to hobble to the door with Lady Holmes' arm for assistance. The solid warmth of her beside me helped a little, but a hard shiver gripped my back and my teeth clacked.

"I need to get you warm," she said as we made our way to the back door. "Do you think you can make it upstairs?"

A warm puff of air met us at the kitchen door, but the room itself was empty, fires banked, tools cleaned and tucked away for the night.

"Yes, if you'll help me," I said.

Her answer, simple as it was, moved me like another clap of thunder. "Don't worry, Hudson. I won't let go."

Her promise couldn't mean what I wanted it to, and yet, hope eclipsed my wisdom again. I clung to her as we navigated the stairs, both of us shaking by the time we reached the second floor, though whether from fatigue or emotion, I couldn't judge.

At the door to my room, I paused, but Lady Holmes shook her head and pressed my waist. "Not there. We need supplies."

I reasoned we were headed for a washing room of some sort, but when Lady Holmes threw open a door, we entered a spacious room holding an enormous bed.

More castle than sleeping spot, it was unlike anything I'd ever seen. Four thick posts bracketed the sweep of delicate yellow bed curtains, and a tangle of carved leaves and flowers nestled along the elaborate wooden canopy crowning the entire structure. The room possessed other furniture, though most of it lay outside the light from the fireplace.

Lady Holmes helped me to one of the mossy velvet armchairs beside the fire, and I dropped gratefully onto the edge, not wanting to soak the upholstery. I bent to loosen my laces but growled in pain as my hands picked at the sodden knots.

"We'll need to cut those." She turned up the lamp and rummaged in the wardrobe before thrusting a glass of amber liquid at me. "You drink, and I'll cut."

"No, I think I can manage."

Lady Holmes knelt on the carpet before me and my protests ran out of steam. She'd removed her cap, revealing her blonde hair. The rain had left it more honey than hay, rising free from its surface like a field of ripe wheat—damp, sweet, and muddy.

She set my foot in her lap, rucked up the leg of my trousers, and produced a pair of silver scissors, then glanced up at me. "Who do you think was shooting at us?"

"Are you trying to distract me with attempted murder?"

Though her head was tipped down, the corners of her curled lips appeared. "Would it work?"

"Probably." I sipped whatever liquor was in the glass. Whiskey. Warmth spread across my chest, adding to the drowsy heat of the fire. My chill subsided as I sipped again. "Someone was chasing us? But who? Inspector Goodwin seemed quite preoccupied. If it was someone trying to scare us off the case, how would they know who or where we were?"

Lady Holmes made quick work of my laces and eased my boot off. I caught my bottom lip between my teeth but didn't make a sound even as the fire bit into my ankle again. Somehow, she still knew.

"I'm so sorry. This is the worst part," she said, sliding my foot free from my stocking.

As soon as the warm air struck my skin, the throbbing grew into a piercing ache. A wicked bruise bloomed over my swollen ankle and foot. I gasped when her fingers brushed the arch of my foot, but not from pain. "Ow," I said to cover my reaction.

She prodded it. "I don't believe it's broken, but we'll have the doctor check tomorrow. I'll bind it for tonight."

I sipped my whiskey and stretched my foot into her lap.

A blush climbed to the tips of her ears. "So. Your insights regarding the gunshots were correct. Pursuers, someone connected with Billy, or an unfortunate coincidence. Though I don't believe in coincidences. We continually have more questions than answers. Was Billy sneaking out? If so, he was probably meeting his father, but what were his motives in keeping this all a secret? And most importantly, where is Billy now?"

"I'm so scared for him." My drink sloshed like amber waves in my glass.

"Me too," Lady Holmes murmured. Her fingers moved in a mesmerizing pattern, transferring my heel from palm to palm, winding a linen strip around my foot and ankle.

"I'm sorry you have to do this," I said. "I know … I know you don't like me much, especially right now."

Her hands stilled, but she didn't look up. "Not like you? When have I ever given you that idea?"

"Oh, not often, just throughout the entirety of our acquaintance." I scoffed when she frowned up at me. "Perhaps I shouldn't have mentioned it or expected any differently. I should just be grateful you're speaking to me now."

"What do you mean?" Her fingers flexed around my ankle.

I leaned my head against the top of the chair, too hot and cold all at once, my limbs loosened by warmth and spirits, by narrowly escaping death. "I wasn't built for this sort of danger, I don't think. Only I don't know what I was built for. Boring things, probably. No matter where I go, I never fit in. The world doesn't think I'm womanly enough to know my place or manly enough for proper employment. My family thinks I'm too broken by grief to be in control of my own life or to be of much help to them. And maybe I am. But I don't want to be. I want to be more. To you—" I took a large mouthful of whiskey and tapped the word *trust* against my leg. "You, well, everyone here, thinks I'm neither clever enough to speak my piece nor maid enough to be of use. What even *is* an investigative partner? Especially one in a skirt."

The expression on her face was one I'd never seen before, part tenderness, part something unreadable. Driven by fear, pain, and whiskey, my tongue had lost all control, and I'd said too much. This tentative peace we'd forged, this connection, would snap under the weight of it. I had cast the pieces of my heart upon the tide, but I couldn't snatch them back from its inexorable pull.

She took a slow breath, reached for my glass, and drained the rest of the whiskey in one gulp. "Hudson, don't you understand? When I saw you lying on the cobblestones, injured, I was more scared than I've ever been in my life. That you were hurt, and it was my fault."

She knelt before me, and I grew dizzy at the sight.

"I do like you. Very much. Spending time with you is many things, but it is never boring." Her voice had gone rough around the edges. "I apologize for not speaking to you earlier, for making you feel as though you aren't enough for me, that is, for implying you aren't wonderful at your job. Clever and brave and relentless. Those might not be traits of a lady's maid, but I don't expect you to be such. I have plenty of servants, Hudson. If I'd wanted another, I would have hired one."

My skin felt too tight for my body, and I didn't know where to place my hands. "No one has ever called me clever before. All my life, cleverness was never rewarded as much as an extra farthing brought home."

She looked sad. "You should hear it every day."

I shook my head. Hearing it even once from someone as brilliant as Lady Holmes felt like someone had turned the pages of my heart and discovered a new chapter.

"Thank you," I said a bit soggily, heat building behind my eyes. I sniffed and pressed my wobbling lips together. When John died, I'd thought I would be carrying the pieces of myself alone, but now someone had come along and scooped them from the surf, handing them back to me as though they weren't flotsam but something precious. I wanted to give her something in return. "You, you're brilliant. I know I was dismissive earlier, but your plan? It was amazing. You thought of everything. We've uncovered so much more about this case, and it's all because of you."

The green of her eyes took on warmth, like the sun through the trees. "Thank you, Hudson. Though it would've been more satisfying to witness dismay on Inspector Goodwin's traitorous face when his evening with Lord Sterling was ruined."

I giggled. "Hopefully, I'll see it when I break our fake engagement."

Even Lady Holmes chuckled as she tied the ends of the bandage, then she looked up at me with the air of having decided something. "I wasn't upset that you and Sherlock kept secrets from me. I was hurt because I believed you were critical of my parenting. You've had a hand in raising six younger siblings and I … well, it's always been difficult to know what Mycroft and Sherlock need from me. What anyone needs from me, really, other than my status or my fortune. But especially the boys. They have their father's name already, and I cannot give them anything like its equal. And now, with Sherlock … ever since Arthur died and Mycroft went away, most days it feels as though Sherlock and I are at war."

My heart, already brimming, couldn't hold anymore. "I'm so sorry. I only saw how much Sherlock wanted to be close to you, and as usual I stuck my nose in all the way down to my toes. Of course you're a good mother. I can see it in Sherlock, in the way he looks at you. He adores you."

The shutters almost came down over her expression again, but I reached for her hand and squeezed. She allowed me to hold it for a moment, then pressed them both to her face and looked up again as though to throw the shutters wide. "That means more to me than you can know. However, no apology is necessary. Your actions weren't a critique of me.

You would've done it for anyone. Saving people, finding what connects us, helping those in need. *That* is what you are built for. And it is noble. It is commendable. That righteous core at the center of you, driving you toward justice even when it costs you, that's part of what drew me to you." She blinked and dropped my hands. "I cannot think of any finer asset in an investigative partner, in or out of a skirt."

My hands chilled again immediately, though the ghost of her soft cheek lingered against my palm. I wanted to weave her words into a fine shawl and lay them across my shoulders like a mantle, one to stand between me and the world. But the warp and weft were twisted because the truth was, when I realized Sherlock was a Holmes scion instead of a kitchen boy, my instinct had been to leave him to the consequences of his actions. I loathed the striations of society that put the worth of some above others, but I too was guilty of shoving people into categories, seeing not who they were but what. That was the misery of the world, and the stain of it was writ across my soul as well. It was a lesson I would carry with me from now on.

She rose and plucked at her sodden jacket in distaste. "Now, to get both of us out of these wet clothes. I'll help you change first so I can assist you back to your room without soaking you all over again."

Gone far past blush, my blood surged in my ears. It was one thing to have her be so close to me, even touching me, with the barrier of clothes to guard against the feelings she stirred. But to be without such armor? My unruly thoughts would lie as exposed as my skin. The desire to refuse clung to me like my wet clothes. However, exhausted, injured, and bound in soaked corsets as well as a complicated linen wrap, I couldn't say no. I needed her help out of this labyrinth.

In a series of jerky movements, I managed my own jacket and trousers, using the armchair for balance. Once free of those, however, Lady Holmes stepped closer, sandwiching me between the warmth of the fire and of her body. We didn't speak. I wasn't even sure I could. I leaned forward against the chair's high back. My head swam with the brush of her fingers against the tender skin at the center of my back. Each accidental touch no more than the tap of the hammer against anvil on the telegraph key, but just as electric.

She eased off the men's shirt I'd donned, the material made all the rougher for being wet through. I fought the urge to sigh as the fire's warmth hit the chilled chemise covering my torso, digging my fingers deep into the chair's upholstery. But when she turned to add the shirt to the growing heap of wet clothing, I half-turned with her as though my body's rhythm were attuned to her own.

The vulnerable hollow between her jaw and throat were cast in deep shadows, and my eyes lingered there, wondering at its mysteries. When she turned toward me once again, I lowered my gaze to the carpet before our eyes met, but her movements stuttered nonetheless.

After a long pause, she reached for the sodden knot on my chest binding just under my breasts and loosened it with several short jerks. Only a few translucent layers of linen guarded me from my desires.

She grasped the loose end of the binding and brought it around my torso again and again, her arms a whisper touch on my ribs with each rotation. By the end, I was breathless and acutely aware of my own near nakedness. What would it feel like if she put her arms around me and left them there? What would I do? Certainly not what I ought, because then—

Lady Holmes let out a vicious hiss. "I will destroy him. When I am through, he will be inspecting nothing other than the inside of a prison cell."

Her vitriol cleared the fog from my vision, and I turned to glance around us. "What? Who?"

"That regrettable man." Her hand covered the ring of bruises Inspector Goodwin had left on my upper arm yesterday as though she longed to erase them from my skin. "Do they hurt?"

With my neck bent, I shook my head. I couldn't look away from where our bodies connected. She brought her other hand to my neck and traced the bones there, taking their measure. Then she wound a delicate finger into one of my curls that had escaped its pins, and I tipped my head back until it rested, cradled, in the palm of her hand. Under her touch, every hair on my body drew to attention, and I shivered.

"You're still cold," Lady Holmes whispered.

On the contrary, my body blazed, but I could hardly say so.

She withdrew to fetch a nightgown and robe from her dresser. "Here." Her eyes lingered for a moment on the pink skin of my exposed chest. "Dress by the fire. I'll be behind the screen."

It was the work of seconds, and when it was done, I slumped against the back of the green armchair, more aware of my body than ever before. I would tell Lady Holmes about Sherlock and the drawing as soon as she was settled next to me by the fire, and we would work it all out. At first, the small sounds of Lady Holmes changing out of her own wet things came from the far side of the room where she had lit a low lamp, and my imagination stalked her. But soon, my eyelids drooped, and everything grew muffled by the crackle of the fire, the susurrus of my breath.

After that, I must have dozed off because I had to fight to open my eyes as a gentle weight settled around me. The blanket pressed me deeper into the chair, and I fell without falling as sleep claimed me again.

Behind me someone whispered, perhaps in a dream, "You were built for love."

CHAPTER TWENTY-NINE

I'D FINALLY FOUND THE WORDS TO WRITE BACK TO Eleanor and had made it to the third page of apologies and news and questions about our friends in London when Rosie snuggled beside me on the sofa and tipped her little round face up to mine. "What is it like to work for a lady?"

It felt so good to have an outlet for my complicated feelings that I spoke my first thoughts. "Lady Holmes? Infuriating, mostly. She's proud, private, and sensitive. Eccentric. But also confusing. She's either engaging in an uncanny ability to think a dozen steps ahead of everyone else, or she can't see what's right in front of her face."

Frances, who was staying with us until she recovered, glanced up from her sewing with a concerned look. Even Elizabeth, who sat beside us making a shirt under Frances' expert tutelage, frowned.

Rosie's nose crinkled like corduroy. "But does she have fine dresses and lots of jewels? Are there big parties every night? Oh, oh! Does she have an evil stepmother?"

I put down my writing things and drew Rosie close.

"You're confusing ladies with princesses, you goose." She giggled. "And no, Lady Holmes dresses plainly. Not a crown or jewel in sight. Guess what? She's not thrown a single ball in the three days since I've worked for her. I don't know anything about her parents, however, so she may have a very wicked stepmother indeed."

Though I have slept in her bedroom under the duvet from her very own bed.

Waking up this morning was like opening my eyes in a fairy tale. Golden light spilling through enormous windows overlooking the sculpted gardens of Musgrave Hall, a fire crackling on the hearth, and a pot of steaming tea waiting for me alongside a generous slice of seedcake. My mysterious benefactor was nowhere to be found. Just a note listing questions to ask Frances when I visited home today. The luxury overwhelmed me after all I'd endured the night before, not least of which was the dream vision of Lady Holmes tucking me under a blanket, and her final words. *You were built for love.*

Had she spoken them? Or were they nothing more than the product of my longing for a world where I could keep those I loved close to me, safe and alive? A world where there was more to existence than surviving, where my heart wasn't buried on a narrow shelf in the Brompton Catacombs.

The scent of roast pork and baking bread, a Sunday meal Ma could make again thanks to my sudden income from Lady Holmes, crept into even the darkest corners of the cottage and filled me in a way nothing else could. For the first time, it felt like maybe there was a future that held more.

Elizabeth pinned two pieces of fabric together. "But do

you *like* Lady Holmes, Katy?"

In truth, I was quite afraid that I did. Too much. "I've only known her for four days."

"Leave more material on that seam, so the shirt can grow with Ralph," Frances said from the sofa beside me. "Lady Holmes seems kind, but odd if you ask me," she added.

"She is kind, smart, and generous, too. I don't know about odd, though I would've used that word myself when I met her." The image of Lady Holmes dressed in a shabby maid's uniform and standing outside the gates of Musgrave Hall rose up in my memory. What had she been doing? Did Sherlock ever find her? "She just has no time for fools or what society thinks of her. If she's interested in something, she's driven to pursue it."

"Lucky for me," Frances said softly.

"Elizabeth, take Rosie to the kitchen and see if Ma needs any help with the potatoes." Once the girls had left, I faced Frances. "I apologize, but I have some private questions to ask you. Frances, Billy has worked the last fortnight as a houseboy at Sterling Place."

Her quick fingers had been hard at work whether her mind and eyes were on her sewing or not, even directing Elizabeth simultaneously, but now, her hands fell still in her lap. The fabric there, a bright yellow cambric meant to be a lady's bodice, lay wrinkled like a knife run over butter.

"Sterling Place? But how? Why?" A sob ruined her voice on the last word, and my heart clenched in sympathy.

I ran through the details of our discoveries without mentioning police stations, picking locks, or desperate rides through the night. Still, Frances was no fool.

She raised an eyebrow at my ankle where it lay on a low

stool and a pile of pillows. "Is that the price you paid to find him?"

I smiled. "It's nothing, really. Just don't tell Ma. Please?" Dr. McNulty had examined me this morning, and I could walk, though every step was a fiery reminder of how close I'd come to something dangerous last night, from alley to meadow to bedroom.

Frances pursed her lips and picked up her sewing. "She'll put it together the same as I did. It's a pity you're hurt, but I'm not sorry. Not if it means getting Billy back." She plucked out a pin and stored it in her pincushion. "He's a dear lad for wanting to set us up with more. Still, he's better off with me at least for a few more years. It's that inspector who needs to pay for keeping me in the dark. The most important thing is getting Billy home."

Rosie let out a screech of laughter from the kitchen, and Elizabeth's voice grew louder, joined by Georgie's. Dinner would be served soon.

"Frances, you don't understand," I said, my heart throbbing in my ankle.

"I know you're injured, but you and m'lady can go and collect him." She looked up from her sewing again. "What is it? Your face is miserable."

My nerves hacked at my skin. "There's no soft way to say this. He's missing. Again. Or rather, he's missing for real now."

This time, she didn't drop her sewing, but she placed each stitch as though it were the next inch of rope keeping her afloat. "You'd better tell me everything."

When I finished, I added, "We'll visit Sterling Place as soon as we figure out a reason that won't tip our hand to the inspector." The idea of returning to Sterling Place made me want to crawl under the covers and never come out again.

"You're right, and I know you're right, but it isn't *fair*," Frances said, her long face flushed against the white bandage on her forehead. "How dare they keep my own son from me? They had no right!"

I offered her my handkerchief, but she seemed unaware of the tears coursing down her cheeks.

"Tom's still your husband, and even if he weren't, he's Billy's father. The law *is* his right. Fairness doesn't enter into such things."

Her tears, sometimes the only way to rage against the injustice of the world, were fierce but brief.

"It's unwelcome news, but we're closer than we've ever been." I patted her hand. "Also, if Inspector Goodwin interviewed Tom, then perhaps we'll stumble across him in the course of our investigation. He probably knows more than he told the inspector."

Frances snorted and dabbed at her face. "Tom Mudd would wear a smile while he lied to the Devil himself. He'll never talk to you. You'll have to drag every answer out of him."

My memories of Tom were few and unpleasant. That she trusted us to get answers at all, to act as her proxies, filled me with a black dread so deep that if I thought about it for too long, I really would take to my bed.

"Listen, Frances, when we spoke to one of your neighbors, she raised some questions." I explained what the old woman had said about Billy.

Frances slammed a fist into the sofa. "If my son was

sneaking out to meet a girl, don't you think I'd have known? He's always drawing whatever he's up to or on his … oh. Oh my." She turned watery eyes on me. "I saw him drawing pictures of Tom! Standing around with other men. I just thought they were people Billy met at The Four Hounds, and he'd put Tom among them as a sort of daydream. But they were true. I can see that now. Tom even looked older in them."

I sighed. "We think Billy must've been sneaking out to meet his father."

Frances choked back a strangled sob. "And here I believed him when he said he wanted me to keep the bigger bedroom because I worked so hard for us. Instead, he wanted the window with the tree below it."

Tears of sympathy flooded my eyes. "When did you see the drawings? Where?"

"Perhaps three weeks ago? Just at home, they should've been in with his other drawings, unless of course he took them with him."

"We found nothing of the sort." Not sure if Frances had seen the destruction before she was struck, I didn't mention that Billy's collection of drawings currently lay in ruins drifting across his bedroom floor. "Where were Tom and the men in the pictures? Was there a background you recognized?"

Worry drew the lines of her face even deeper. "Billy slid them under other drawings when he realized I was there."

I pressed my lips together. "If there's anything else you can tell us about Tom, it could be vital, even a small detail. Lady Holmes can make miracles out of small details."

Frances shook her head and grasped my hand. "I'm

grateful for her skills, but you're the one who noticed the forged telegram, the injured one, the one who's spending her morning off hard at work. You're a marvel, Katy Bee, and don't you forget it."

A few hours later saw me trundled into Lady Holmes' carriage with Eliot driving. The weight of Frances' trust rode beside me, usurping the pleasant memories of the meal I'd shared with my family. Where had Billy's drawing gone? Shredded, missing, or stolen?

The thief believed something incriminating would be found among the sketches. I dragged a net through my memory of Lady Holmes stacking one after the other on Billy's desk, but there was nothing he wouldn't want Frances to see in them. Knowing what I did of adolescent boys, more than I wanted to frankly, that seemed like proof enough. He was hiding them. But where?

My pulse thudded in my injured ankle.

The clock had been reset when we discovered Billy had been at Sterling Place, but now it raced ahead again. We needed to find him, and soon. Each tick of that clock echoed like another bullet in the dark.

The crack of last night's gunshots roared in my memory. No one knew we were there. But what if someone wasn't shooting at us? What if they were shooting at what they thought were two males sneaking across country on horseback?

"Eliot, turn here." I grabbed his arm and gestured down the High Street. "We have an errand to run."

Thankfully, the Mudds' doorstep was empty when we arrived. I could only hope Goodwin and Marks were hard at work on Billy's disappearance. Since Frances had given me a key, Eliot helped me in through the front door, and after a brief glance through the rooms for any possible intruders, he waited for me there.

The Mudds' rooms were much as I remembered. Someone had sluiced the pool of broth from the kitchen floor, though a sour scent still lingered, a grim reminder of a once happy home now cracked and spoiled. With one hand on the wall, I hobbled to the back of the house and into Billy's room. Mounds of paper scraps trembled as I entered as though my arrival had breathed life into them. I knelt and sifted the nearest through my fingers, the scent of rubber erasers and mud wafting up to greet me.

"Where are your secrets, Billy?"

What did we miss? Since we searched this room the first time, nothing had changed.

Changed.

If his hiding place was in a piece of furniture, he could've changed rooms with Frances as she offered and brought his secrets with him. The room itself was important—more than a bed, more than a trunk, more than a desk.

I crawled forward and peered under his bed. His pillow and a heap of torn sketches greeted me, but no dust. Beneath the trunk, no dust. The wardrobe, no dust. However, under Billy's makeshift art desk, a fine gray film marked the crates' position on the floor.

I wedged my fingers into the crack between crates and wall, dragging the structure several feet forward. The dust underneath stopped where the final floorboard met the narrow skirting. A jagged strip of paper stuck in the crack there, and I tugged it free, my hands and heart vibrating in a wild dance. The section of sketch revealed the wrinkled brow and light hair of a man. I whirled and sifted through Billy's drawing tools for his penknife. It squeaked against the wood as I wedged it between the boards, but after a little wiggling, the plank came away.

The cool scent of muddy earth tickled my nostrils. I stared into the shallow space below at yet another slew of ravaged paper and ran my finger over one tantalizing curl.

"Eliot," I called, "we're going to need some boxes!"

CHAPTER THIRTY

SHERLOCK SLID FOUR PIECES OF TORN DRAWINGS into place on a sheet of foolscap in rapid succession. "A close-up of a man's hand with a scar across the first two knuckles," he said and pushed the reconstructed drawing across the table to me.

When I'd arrived with my purloined boxes of scraps, Sherlock was reading in the study with Lady Holmes, and he grabbed one of the smaller boxes, tagging along when we needed to move outdoors. Soon he was putting together ripped sketches at an impressive speed.

"Are you sure all the pieces are correct?" Lady Holmes asked without looking up from the half-completed jigsaw in front of her.

There'd been no mistakes in his work so far, and when he scowled at his mother, I smiled. Too alike for their own good. "It's a wonder I can even keep up with the two of you." I pulled his completed sketch closer and picked up my pasting brush.

It was a fine afternoon, and we'd spread our work on

the rambling rear lawn of Musgrave Hall. Luckily, most of the staff were on their Sunday holiday, so there were fewer to watch them wander among the pieces, pouncing on any matches. I sat at a little table armed with a pot of paste, a selection of brushes, and a stack of squares of foolscap to glue down any completed sketches the they placed before me.

Drying in the dappled shade of gnarled yew trees, we had a modest collection of reassembled sketches, glued at the edges so as not to smudge the drawings. Among them, horses in what appeared to be the east meadow of Sterling Place; Tom Mudd, looking as though life had knocked him around and then down; and two strange men reaching out to shake hands. As well as a tall Arabian horse, the gates of Sterling Place, and young women wading in the river with their dresses tucked up. Lady Holmes had confiscated that as soon as I'd glued it down.

However, that was her one concession to censorship around Sherlock. I'd been careful not to discuss the case in front of him until Lady Holmes asked me about it openly. While we worked, I filled them in, but nonetheless, there were three things I wanted to tell her in private. One about Sherlock.

When he turned his back, I raised my eyebrows. Locking onto Lady Holmes' wide green eyes still unsettled me, and I had to fight back a smile. "Sherlock," I said, "I'm going to need another pot of paste and more rocks for the finished sketches."

"But we have to finish before Unc—"

"You have my permission to bring out the new glue you developed," Lady Holmes said.

"Really?" he asked in an excited squeak.

"Yes, it has a superior drying time."

His tiny face opened up under her words, and he dropped the scraps he'd been collecting onto the table before sprinting off to the house. She settled next to me and began assembling her pieces as well as his at the same time.

"What did you wish to discuss, Hudson?"

Her hand around my bare arm, her finger wound around my curl, the way her hair blossomed when it was damp, what she may or may not have admitted when she believed me asleep last night. I settled for the least dangerous topic.

"What if those gunshots weren't meant for us?" I pasted down the pinky finger on the scarred hand.

"I have not often been shot at, but the angle of the bullets suggests we were the intended targets. It's tempting to want to—"

"We're going to have a long talk about any other times you've been shot at, but what I meant was, what if the shooter thought we were two males sneaking through the countryside on horseback at night?"

The rare fruit of a smile had crossed her face, but now she frowned. "Tom and Billy. We'll have to check the timing, but I shall add it to the case map."

The acrid scent of paste fought with the blossoms of the garden. I swallowed my reluctance over the idea of returning to the scene of Da's death, the people who had cast us aside, smashing flat my years of happy memories there. "Following your remarkable showing in getting us into the police station last night, we'll no doubt be investigating at Sterling Place within the day. How to disguise ourselves this time? As traveling artists? Horse farriers? I'm not the most experienced cook, but I could fake it briefly."

"My dear Hudson, there's no need for dissembling. We will attack Sterling Place as ourselves."

I laughed then noticed her patient expression. "Wait, you're serious?"

"I am. As much as I hate being a lady, it does throw wide many doors." She pushed another reassembled sketch in my direction. "Glue that down before the pieces shift, please."

My hands moved automatically, but my thoughts snagged on her words. "You can't mean that. Being a lady—"

"Is a burdensome gift that gets in the way of all I try to do. I am a lady first, and all else second." She shifted another pile of pieces in front of her. "I don't believe these are from the same sketch. Does this look like the same man to you?"

She offered me two jagged strips of paper, but I ignored them in favor of a look that communicated more than even the fastest telegraph operator.

"You're displeased with me, Hudson."

I waved a hand. My pleasure was not the issue here. "You're lucky. You're *so* lucky and you don't even appreciate it. Your husband left you more than a name. He left you power. It's up to you to seize it. Stop waiting for someone to give you freedom. You're already free. You may do as you like and damn the rest."

She tipped the contrary piece into another pile with a soft whisper of paper. "Do you know how Arthur and Lewis met?"

"Did your families know each other?"

She shook her head. "At Cambridge. Neither the school matters, nor what they studied. What matters is they were brought together. Raised to see their power writ large, to seize it en masse, at one of the many temples built for its worship. I had read every book in our library by the time I was Sherlock's age, but there was no institution welcoming me. My education was left to the indifferent clutches of a sleepy governess who was a gentlewoman herself, fallen on hard times."

I didn't know what it was like to live such a soft life, my own education was mostly left to me to scrape together, but I knew what it was like to be sad. "You worked around that. And now you have real power."

Uncertainty rippled over her brows. "Power is a funny thing, made up of courage, and expectation, and an understanding that you belong. No one has ever offered me that sort of deep understanding. Once, when I was younger, there was a young woman who wanted, well, me." Lady Holmes laid down the puzzle pieces in her hands and stared at the distant trees.

"What happened to her?" I almost whispered.

"We wrote to each other for a time, but I couldn't stand to see myself on the page, there for anyone to stumble over. Lewis or Father. Fear of rejection, of not being proper, of showing someone my innermost self, only to find they're not interested at best or horrified at worst. That these are not womanly thoughts. That I am an unnatural woman and an unfit mother for having them. Imperfect at every turn. Is that power? Hudson, I ask you, have you ever seen me speak to another woman with this power you're referring to?" She gave me a soft look.

I shook my head sadly. "But I met you just a few days ago."

"It wouldn't matter if you'd known me since birth. Every word I've ever spoken has been on the surface of things, except those I've said to you."

I caught my breath at her admission.

"That's one trick men have played. From the outside, it appears ladies of a certain station have real power. However, the fatted calf has no say in its own slaughter. No connections means no power. When you've been taught everything you do is insignificant, it feels impossible to change anything."

The gurgling croak of a distant raven cut through the buzzing of the bees and chatter of smaller birds.

"One must forge connections, then."

"But how?" She returned to her puzzle pieces. "When unseen hands deliver the bread on your plate, you're dependent upon their mercies and alms. What is unknown is a possible threat. Above all else, you don't upset the system, because it feeds you before it feeds most others."

Sherlock burst from Musgrave Hall with something clutched in his hand, making a beeline for the rocky border of the nearby gardens. Lady Holmes watched her son, blinking. Her voice had maintained a cool detachment as she spoke, but the filmy look of her eyes spoke of soap bubbles, of tissue paper, of cauls.

I shook my head, not wanting to interrupt the clearest view of Lady Holmes I'd ever had, but unable to help myself. "That's why you were dressed as a maid. The day we met, outside the gates. What were you doing out there?"

"Luck wears different faces, Hudson, and so does freedom. I once told you I escape every chance I get. Well, that day I was escaping an unexpected marriage proposal."

"From Clarence Sterling?" I asked, horrified. "I saw him leaving that day with his father."

She nodded.

I leaned forward until she had no choice but to put aside her work and face me. "You still have the freedom to choose. Your life is still the best form of a difficult one available in society."

"Perhaps you're right. After all, it's not so bad. I have my little escapes." She handed me another completed puzzle, eyes gone the green of moss underwater. "Or perhaps such views sow division between those whose cooperation might finally win them the means to choose their own fates. Because that, my dear Hudson, is true power." The set of her shoulders pushed wide and took on new lines. "Believe me, I intend to drive a wedge into every crack I spy in the system until it lies about me, shattered."

Her words settled a bit of my rage, rekindled the day I stood outside the gates of Musgrave Hall. I stared at my hands on the smooth table, no scratches marring its surface like the one at home. So many of the world's ills lay beyond my power to fix. However, I was certain that I wanted this woman at my side while we solved what we could.

"So, what would you choose?" I asked, returning to the task of pasting.

She didn't pretend to misunderstand my question or brush it aside but rose from the table and peered at the hundreds of pieces of the puzzle arrayed around her feet. "I would choose a lifetime of days exactly like today in every respect except for one," she said, her face hidden from view. "Your presence these last few days has given me such clarity. We've had a short time for things to be as they are between us, and I wish we had more time to secure our relationship before—"

"Mother! Hudson!" Sherlock's shouts preceded his pounding feet by mere seconds.

A ripple of icy unease coursed over my skin where seconds before it had been covered in rising heat.

Huffing and red-cheeked, he skidded to a stop at our side. "Come quickly!" He grabbed his mother's arm and pointed back the way he came. "There's a dead man in the weeds, and he's wearing the right shoes."

Chapter Thirty-One

The man's feet stuck out of the long grass and wildflowers behind the garden, one shoe half covering his toes as though he'd been about to take it off.

Sickness washed over me. John's was the last body I'd seen or touched. Being this close to one now, with the sour scent of loosened bowels and blood clogging my nose, left me fighting back a scream.

I blocked Sherlock's view of the man, but he popped out from my other side.

"Do you think they meant to leave him in a patch of forget-me-nots?" Lady Holmes knelt next to the man's right arm. "It seems a trifle overdone."

I tucked Sherlock away again, only to have him squeeze out from under my arm. I gagged behind my fist and moved my arm to block Sherlock a third time, but he dropped to his knees to examine the man's feet. Damn everything. If she realized Sherlock recognized the shoes, she would want to know why, and my last secret would be revealed.

"How do you know he was left?" I asked, hoping to distract her.

She pointed at the slick of blood on the weeds behind the man's right arm. "The blood is smeared, not pooled. Also, he appears to have been shot. And since we heard no gunshots around Musgrave Hall last night, someone must have brought him here."

"And there are drag marks in front of his heels," Sherlock said. He poked the man's bare leg, and I let out a squawk of protest, my knees nearly buckling. "When Father first died, I could make white marks in the dark spots on his calves, but I can't make any in these. What does that mean?"

"Excellent observation," Lady Holmes said with the flick of a surprised eyebrow. "It means he has been dead since before midnight last night." Her eyes found mine. Midnight was not long after someone shot at us. "Can you ascertain where the drag marks lead?" she asked Sherlock.

Nose pressed almost to the ground, he scurried off. I heaved in a breath and strode forward until the rest of the man came into view, though mercifully his face was turned toward Lady Holmes.

His trousers were twisted, one leg drawn up to his knee, exposing his calf as the same sickly color as his stockings. He wore a brown jacket of wool over a once white shirt, now covered in continents of blood and soil. Gray hairs sprang from the darker ones crowning his head, a line pressed into them as though he'd worn a hat. Bugs, either curious or hungry, landed on the man or feasted where his blood coated the weeds and leaked from his lips. For a moment, my senses swarmed along with them, and a flat coppery taste washed over my tongue.

I gagged again, sour juices leaving my throat raw.

"His pockets are empty. Does that strike you as curious, Hudson?"

"I can't think of a single thing which doesn't strike me as curious about this situation. Does he look familiar?" I managed to squeeze out.

"Unfortunately, yes," Lady Holmes said. "It appears Frances was right. Tom Mudd will never talk to us now."

Her words sank through my skin and into my bones. My hands shook, fingers weaving into the bulk of my skirt. "Are you certain?"

She didn't say what we were both thinking, what this might mean for Billy. Danger. Death. Guilt. Instead, by way of an answer, Lady Holmes rose and motioned for me to take her place at the man's head.

My breaths uneven and short, I circled him. It was definitely Tom Mudd. He'd broken his nose since I'd last seen him, a detail even Billy's fine drawing hadn't caught. Other than that, he looked much as I remembered, perhaps even less like himself than in Billy's sketches. There, he'd possessed something vital, now lost.

The dead always appeared as such. Not a shell or a doll, just a little less, already splitting from the person one knew.

When John died, after his colleagues carried him home to our flat, he'd already become strange to me. Despite the reek of his excrement, his scorched clothes and hair, my first instinct was to bury myself in his shoulder and weep. Though the terrain was as familiar as my own skin, there was no longer any comfort there. By morning, I could only bring myself to hold his hand, tapping my words of grief and rage into his waxy palm. Everything seemed both harder and easier after that.

This isn't John, I repeated now. Like a refrain, like a spell, anything that might shield me. I didn't have to touch Tom's body, but I started shaking anyway. I stepped back, watching Sherlock where he scouted about thirty feet away.

"Hudson, are you quite alright?" Lady Holmes asked as she crouched near Tom's shoes.

I wasn't, but I nodded.

Luckily, she seemed to accept my assertion at face value. Unluckily, that meant her attention was free to return to the one place I didn't want it.

"These match the footprints in the Mudds' garden, but why did Sherlock call them the right shoes?" she asked, lifting an inquiring gaze to mine.

Though I disliked doing this without warning Sherlock first, I needed to face the firing squad. Perhaps I could spare him her anger if I explained things correctly. "I asked Sherlock to evaluate a footprint for me. One I found inside Billy's room just after the break-in." My voice shook, but I filled the silence with a short confession, complete except for the parts that incriminated Sherlock.

The wind picked at Lady Holmes' skirts, but she didn't even blink.

"Say something. Please," I begged while my little partner in crime crowed, waving at us triumphantly from down the path.

"I thought we were done keeping secrets?" I hated her quiet tone. The light in her eyes dimmed again. She was halfway to the island where she retreated whenever anyone drew too close to something she found painful. "But then again Lewis is currently—"

"There are marks from a handcart!" Sherlock shouted, then bent once more. "It went to the gates and back, but it came from the garden sheds!" he said before bouncing over to rejoin us. "They probably picked up a handcart because they couldn't get through our gates with …" Sherlock trailed off as he took in the ominous silence between his mother and I, Tom's feet between us. "Please, Mother, don't be angry with Hudson. It was all my fault."

I couldn't let him take the blame. "No, Sherlock—"

"It *was*. She found me at the gates waiting for the explosion I set to get the Sterlings to leave so you could escape the grounds, and she promised to bring me extra food if I let her in."

"The explosion was for me?" Lady Holmes asked, hands rising to her stomach.

He nodded. "And then, when she found me cataloging footprints in flour on the servants' stairs, she let me finish because she knew it was an important experiment. When I was sad, Hudson brought me a sweet bun and a picture with a footprint on it. It was better than the best game I've ever played, and you can't fire her for it. I won't let you." His voice quavered, but he didn't stop. "It was the first time I've felt happy since Papa and Mycroft went away. If you fire her, I'll go back to setting explosions—worse than ever." His expression grew fierce with the desperate tilt of his chin he'd inherited from his mother. "Besides, *you* haven't told her about Uncle Lewis."

My regret at lying shrank a little. After all, it had been in the service of a cause as good as Sherlock. I swallowed down something sharp, eyes suddenly hot.

Lady Holmes' eyelids fluttered, her expression returning to itself. "You performed the shoe experiment from my journals?"

He balled up his fists. "Yes."

She cleared her throat. "Then I expect you to deliver the results to me in a written report as soon as we return from Sterling Place."

He stood high on his toes. "I already wrote it up. I can go and get my notes."

"There won't be time." She shook her head, and Sherlock curled in on himself. However, Lady Holmes knelt, her hands on his shoulders. The look in her eyes was half apology, half begging to be understood. "Listen to me. You've run away again. It's so much trouble, but the remaining staff, including Hudson and I, will have to leave the house to search for you."

His demeanor had lifted minutely as she held him, but while she spoke, his spine grew straight and firm as though he'd donned armor. "How much time do you need?"

I stared between them. Had I fallen through some crack in this conversation?

"At least an hour, two would be better. Uncle Lewis will have to bide until then. Head west. Make sure someone sees you go, but that they don't see you hiding." The creak of the gates of Musgrave Hall rent the air, followed by the distinctive staccato charge of a four-in-hand carriage approaching. "Oh, and Sherlock"—she squeezed his shoulder—"be careful."

Without hesitation, he sprinted down the path and veered into the tall grass. In seconds, his dark curls peeked above the waving tops, and then Sherlock was gone.

I whirled on Lady Holmes. "What about Tom? Shouldn't we alert the police? What were you two talking about? Is that your brother arriving? Why on earth is he here?"

Lady Holmes gave me a tight grin. "The police will hinder us, a fact Tom's murderer must have been counting on by placing his body here. I understand you loathe not knowing the plan, but we don't have time. Do you trust me?"

I hadn't trusted a member of the British nobility since I climbed into a cart loaded with all our worldly goods, seven Buntings, and a broken heart, the only home I'd ever known becoming a speck on the horizon. Gone in a blink.

Belief in a system required promises to be kept, and I'd lost both after Da died, lost everything except my anger. Until I met John.

On passed notes, on summer nights, on picnics at the river, on secrets at twilight, and kisses so sweet they made my teeth ache, we built something we could trust in. Us. He helped me find good work, where I could change a little bit of the world by being a woman in a burgeoning scientific field. I loved everything about it.

Until I lost him, too. Left with nothing except my family. They saw me as someone only weakened by grief, and they wrapped their arms around me so tightly that I was stuck there, mired in tears and self-doubt. After all, what use was a telegraph clerk without a station? About as much as a wife without a husband.

In the distance, Sherlock gave a high-pitched *whoop* and a man called out to him.

"Hudson"—she reached for my hand—"do you trust me?"

I stood there, my tongue numb.

Lady Holmes had addressed each of my siblings by name, though she'd never met them before. Paid the doctor's fees for Frances. Let Sherlock keep her company in the study and aid us with our massive puzzle because I suggested it. Her arm was a cornerstone around my waist last night as we fled the town, the touch of her fingers blossomed around my ankle, and her voice held deadly conviction when she discovered the bruises Goodwin left on my arm. She was there even when what I needed most was for her to see clear to the core of my being and name what she discovered.

She fostered independence, space for my thoughts, and room for adventure, even when I was furious enough to soak her in the river. To her, I was Hudson. Investigative partner. One half of a whole. And together, I trusted there was no knot we couldn't cleave.

Her words from mere minutes ago rose up to meet me. *"Believe me, I intend to drive a wedge into every crack I spy in the system until it lies about me, shattered."*

I trusted her for the same reason I trusted myself. She'd earned it.

"Hudson?"

I would've said all of that and more, but there was no time, so instead I squeezed her hand. "Likely there is a cot waiting for me in Bedlam," I said, "but yes, I trust you."

The fond look in her eyes usurped the dangerous edge running through my veins, the whisper that I was making an enormous mistake.

"I need you to follow this path to the south and bring back a wheelbarrow from the garden shed." She grabbed my hand and squeezed. "Then wait for me here." With that, Lady Holmes strode for the front door of Musgrave Hall, her black skirts eclipsing the gravel path like a pool of London fog at night.

Chapter Thirty-Two

I avoided Tom's body and limped toward the garden shed.

"This is it, then. I'm finally going to be arrested," I muttered, the demons of my decisions already dogging my heels. "Ma will never be able to show her face in town again. The little ones will all end up at the mercy of the factories, or worse, in service. George will lose his job. Who would trust a doctor's assistant with a murderer for a sister?"

At the garden shed, a low stone building with diamond window lattices, I let myself in and surveyed the various hand tools, bags of fertilizer, and no less than three wheelbarrows.

"We'll lose the cottage," I muttered to myself as I yanked a wheelbarrow free, almost tumbling backward. "Every last Bunting out on the street, and it will be all my fault. The street if they're lucky, the poorhouse if they're not."

As I wheeled the contrivance back the way I came, I kept up my litany of catastrophes. Dire as they sounded, they were but camouflage to screen the newest dread growling in my chest. The details might not be clear, but the final results were. We weren't going to use a wheelbarrow to take the body to the police, but to move it somewhere else. Just the two of us. No, three, if one counted the body. And if the terror gripping my thoughts were any indication, that was all I counted.

No more than five feet up the path, Tom's damnable shoes stuck out of the grass like the closed eyes of some great beast. I stopped and grabbed my breath, shoving it down behind my lungs.

I hadn't been around a body since the morning after John died, just before the undertakers came. So, there was no way to know my mind would uncover the grief cloaked by my skin, the fear hiding in my muscles, and use it to cut my legs out from under me.

The gravel and flowering thyme on the path swam before my eyes, and the wheelbarrow threatened to tip. My breath broke free, spinning higher and higher until the squeal of it became a scream right behind my teeth. I dropped to my knees and hid behind the wheelbarrow, desperate to get away and yet unable to move.

Tom lay beside me, except it wasn't him. It was Da, his sweet face pale and bruised. It was John, reeking of scorched wool, skin yielding. It could be Ma, her smile lost forever. My vibrant brothers and sisters, bodies broken and souls fled. Their names tumbled over my pounding heart until I reached the most vulnerable. Oliver, still so sickly. Rosie, ever so small and dear. I sobbed into my fist, choking on my tears.

"Hudson. Hudson." Lady Holmes slipped an arm around my quivering shoulders. "Are you alright?"

I couldn't even speak. How long had I been there?

She seemed to understand, if not the cause of my panic, then at least the size of it. "Here, breathe with me."

I struggled against her. Everything in me felt too tight, too hot.

But she held fast. "You needn't fight it. I'm here for you. Whatever it is, you can trust me." She bundled my hand against her chest and held me as her warmth and rhythm sank into my fingers.

The faces of my loved ones flashed over those of the dead man once more, and I lurched to the side. "It's just like John."

"Oh, Hudson." Her grip tightened. "It isn't. It's Tom Mudd. I know you're scared, but we'll get through this. Tell me what you need."

Tom. It was only Tom. And that meant Frances, Billy, they needed our help.

I found Lady Holmes' eyes and choked in another breath. "I c-can't touch him. Don't make me touch him."

"I won't." The sound of her working thoughts hurried by like a blast of wind. "Can you stand to touch the wheelbarrow?"

Could I? My teeth found my lip and left it bloody. "Possibly," I said finally.

She pressed me to her for a second. "Turn away while I work."

I scooted around to face the sweep of fields marking the border between the lawns and the woods. The world was filled with sights divorced from sounds, my eyes and ears in disagreement with each other. There was waving grass, but the squeak of the wheelbarrow. There were trees bending in the distance, and the crack of unfurling cloth. There was one hare on the path, then another, then a low grunt.

The sounds ceased, and Lady Holmes touched my

shoulder. "All you need to do is hold the lip of the wheelbarrow and help me tip it up."

The bottom of the wheelbarrow lay tipped over with a cloth-wrapped bundle lashed to the far side. It might have been anything.

"We're going to move some grain," Lady Holmes said, reading my thoughts. "The bag will be heavy, but the job will be done. Soon. Now, on my count."

My knees shook and my numb hands fumbled it twice, but together we managed to get the wheelbarrow upright. With my eyes cast down, and a firm fist around my thoughts, I followed Lady Holmes' inky skirts toward a side door of Musgrave Hall. As she wheeled our burden, words drifted back to me. I clung to them like a drowning man who spotted a rope—with hope, not sense.

"We need to reach the back storage rooms where the trunks are kept. The servants who've returned from Sunday holiday are all out searching for Sherlock. My brother ... declined to join the search. He offered the services of his driver instead. I've stashed Lewis in the parlor with a bottle of Arthur's best whiskey, and it's unlike him to move without a cause benefitting him, so he should be out of our way."

She threw me a look over her shoulder. "My brother has decided my mourning period should be over. Arthur's illness was protracted, and so Lewis suggests I return to society, sniffing around for a second husband. I had a letter from him last week inviting me to join him for a small hunting party at Sterling Place. Considering the proposal I declined from Clarence Sterling a few days ago, right after Sherlock's little explosion, I also refused the invitation. However, since we need to get into Sterling Place, I wrote to Lewis this morning, asking him to come and collect me."

The enormity of what she'd said shocked me out of the back of my own thoughts. "Whatever happened to being done with keeping secrets?"

"Hudson, that isn't … It wasn't a secret. I should've told you earlier, but you detest Sterling Place, and I believed it would be easier if you thought you didn't have to make the choice."

"So, you just decided for me?" I wasn't angry, I was too numb to be much of anything, but whatever I was feeling, I didn't like it.

"I'm sorry. I was trying to save you." We'd reached a thick wooden door set in Musgrave Hall's sand-colored bricks. "I shouldn't have presumed."

Though I didn't appreciate her highhandedness, there was little sense in fighting about it now. "No, you shouldn't have. But it's the easiest way to get us into Sterling Place, and I refuse to let my feelings get in the way of our work. Look at what they've done to me already." I held out my quaking hands, and she clasped them.

"Thank you for trusting me. Again." Her smile was a candle in the sunlight, but even its meager warmth was a comfort as I held the door open so she could trundle our sorry bag of grain inside.

Our progress through Musgrave Hall passed in a gray cloud, my view filled with nothing except the polished floorboards. If I didn't look up, if I didn't think about it too hard, we might have been transporting laundry or astronomical equipment. Bushels of potatoes. Horse tack. Books. A particularly old dog who—

"Quick, in here," Lady Holmes hissed as she veered

through a door to our left.

We stood in a windowless room with floor-to-ceiling wooden cabinets on one wall, lit by a kerosene lamp. Several sturdy tables covered in baskets and boxes, and a collection of trunks and valises spread over the floor as though the servants had been interrupted in their packing efforts. Before I could protest at being in such close quarters with Tom's body, the trill of a cheery whistle reached us.

I turned questioning eyes to Lady Holmes. She mouthed *Lewis* and put her eye to the crack of the door. As the whistle receded, she bit her lip. "He's headed for Arthur's study. I'll pay for this later, but I don't have time to stop him. Come on, help me with this trunk."

Together, we wrestled an empty camel trunk from under the tables and lined it up with the wheelbarrow. Lady Holmes padded the bottom with spare cloth, blocks of cedar, and a handful of lavender sachets while I stood there, palms sweating, stomach roiling.

"Tip the wheelbarrow and I shall handle the rest," Lady Holmes said. She gripped the canvas wrapped around Tom's body. Before I had time to protest, she started counting. "One, two, three. Now."

I closed my eyes and heaved. There was an awful *thud* followed by a flurry of rustling and then two sharp *snicks*, as I lowered the wheelbarrow back to the ground.

"Are we bringing …" My question hung there, too awful to finish. "We're going to be arrested, aren't we?"

"No one is getting arrested. At least not today. Whoever dumped Tom on my property wanted to control where or when his body was discovered. We have to bring him with us."

My ankle throbbed after all of this activity, and my limp had grown stronger, so Lady Holmes grasped the handles of the wheelbarrow and steered it into the hallway. We retraced our steps outside, and I waited while she replaced the wheelbarrow in the garden shed. When she returned, we meant to join in the search for Sherlock, but the sound of men's voices drew us toward the front doors.

"And you brought the boy. Remarkable speed. My sister will be relieved. Good day, Constable."

"Ah, it's actually Inspector Goodwin. We met last night at Sterling Place, Lord Vernet. I happened upon the servants out looking for the boy, and he led us on a little chase, but I marshaled him home. It was your sister I came to speak with. Is she here?"

We moved past the bushes blocking our view of the front door, and the unwelcome face of Inspector Goodwin came into view, his hand clamped on Sherlock's drooping shoulder. The two of them faced a tall man, made even taller by the steps separating him from them. This must be Lewis.

Lord Vernet, I corrected myself. If I were going to interact with him, I'd better start practicing. My knees, only recently steady, wobbled again, and I pressed them together under my skirts.

From the high sloping forehead, pale blond hair, and long limbs to the sculpted cheekbones and wide green eyes, the resemblance to his sister was striking. However, where Lady Holmes favored simple black dresses, her brother wore a trim suit of beige striped trousers, sparkling dress boots, a navy-blue morning coat, and a matching silk tie. Country or city, the exceptional lines and material afforded him greater command than even the inspector's uniform. After all, the police were but saplings compared to the ancient oaks of the British aristocracy.

The bland look on Lord Vernet's face grew harder. "My sister? That won't be necessary. Goodwin, was it?"

"Inspector," Lady Holmes called as we approached. "Do you have news of Billy?"

The three males started at the sound, and Sherlock made to dash in our direction, but Lord Vernet's hand shot out and grasped his arm. A hot drum beat in my chest, the pulse echoing in my injured ankle. Beside me, Lady Holmes tensed.

"As it turns out, Billy's father had returned to the area and secured him employment at Sterling Place, where he had some connections." The inspector's jaw tightened, and he threw me a hard look. "Unfortunately, they both disappeared last night, along with two of his lordship's prize horses. Like father, like son."

Lord Vernet's eyes swung from Lady Holmes to the inspector. So like his sister's and nephew's, but where theirs were moss and shade, his reminded me of a one shilling stamp. "Do you know something of Sterling's missing horses, Sister?"

Goodwin's mustaches quivered. "Her ladyship has undertaken an investigation into a local boy's disappearance."

"How charitable," Lord Vernet said flatly.

"W-without a doubt," Inspector Goodwin stammered. "However, it proved to be nothing but a sordid little domestic matter."

This garnered a shrug from Lord Vernet. "Then that has nothing to do with my sister."

Behind us, the chatter of the returning servants drifted

on the breeze. Doors opening and closing, followed by the rattle of a carriage. In moments, the trunk hiding Tom's body would be hoisted into the air by two footmen and packed with the rest of the luggage. Under Inspector Goodwin's nose. I couldn't bear to think of it.

Unawares, the inspector tugged at his pristine cuffs. "Of course, your lordship. We had reports of suspicious happenings around the grounds of Musgrave Hall last night. And with what occurred at Sterling Place, I wanted to make sure her ladyship hadn't suffered a similar loss."

"Suspicious." Lord Vernet rolled the word across his tongue as though it were a cheap sweet.

"Witnesses saw two men traveling through town, one of them limping. They were later sighted in the countryside as well, on horseback. And we had reports of strange noises in the area around Musgrave Hall. Perhaps a gunshot, though with the storm—"

"Sister, are all of your horses accounted for?" Lord Vernet asked, his tone dangerously bored.

I half expected Lady Holmes to have Goodwin escorted from her property. To stride forward and reclaim Sherlock from Lord Vernet's grasp, make it clear that we would join him at Sterling Place at our leisure. It would have been a glorious sight to behold.

Instead, she simply said, "Of course they are. Thank you for your concern, Inspector."

"There, that settles the matter." Lord Vernet drew Sherlock toward the open front door. "You can see yourself to the gate, can't you, Goodwin?"

Lord Vernet didn't order Lady Holmes to join him inside. He didn't have to, not with Sherlock still in his grasp.

Chapter Thirty-Three

The entrance at Musgrave Hall had been designed to impress. Light poured in from double rows of six mullioned windows on either side of the door, their number and shape echoing the chimneys above. High-walled benches, gleaming parquet, velvet curtains, and sculpted molding—no matter what it must have cost to build, the price of maintenance was even higher. The backs of farmers. The knees of maids. The silence of everyone else.

Nowhere was this more evident than in Lord Vernet's grip on Sherlock's slender arm, in his words poisoning the lad's ears. "Let this be the last time I have to save you from the law. You ought to know better."

The bold tip of Sherlock's chin had lowered but not his spirit. "It was only a game, Uncle."

"I don't care what it was. You are a son of the Viscount Arthur Holmes, and should anything happen to your elder brother, one day you may hold that title yourself. What *I* care about is what *you* should care about"—Lord Vernet curled his lip and gave Sherlock a shake—"letting the police deposit you on your own doorstep like a whipped pup. Never allow such a lesser man to take advantage of you again."

Lady Holmes and I had lingered by the front door, but now she stepped forward, her expression grave. "Sherlock, Miss Johnson is waiting to have a word with you in the nursery."

His little face looked like spoiled milk, eyes swimming with tears that hadn't been there a second ago. "Yes, Mother." He slunk out from under his uncle's hand and down the nearest hallway.

Lord Vernet turned approving eyes on his sister. "I see from the boy's reaction that you've finally found a governess with a firm enough hand. Stripe his legs and bury him in lessons, that ought to keep him out of trouble while we're away. Make it clear her job is on the line if she doesn't."

Sherlock had no governess, firm or otherwise. And his clever playacting had brought the ghost of a smile to my lips. I stared at the floor, hiding it, not that Lord Vernet would notice. He'd not so much as looked at me so far.

"What the boy wants is a father. When there's no one at the helm, the crew all suffer. Thank heavens Mycroft is away at school. His headmaster is known for cracking the whip to keep everyone in line," Lord Vernet said as he pulled out his gold pocket watch. "Speaking of, we won't be keeping Sterling waiting. Be ready to depart in half an hour." He turned and headed for the parlor, whistling the same tune as earlier.

The next thirty minutes were filled with last-minute packing and double-checking, so I had no time for a private word with Lady Holmes. Instead, in the shortest of orders, our things were loaded onto a luggage wagon, and we were bundled into Lord Vernet's carriage on the road to Sterling Place.

Lady Holmes had brought an astronomical text to read as we drove, and Lord Vernet settled against the opposite seat as though he meant to take a nap. I'd been careful not to limp around him, lest Lord Vernet notice my injury. A precaution I had paid for with the return of a sharp pain in my ankle. I surreptitiously stretched it, glad the drive would take us well over an hour. Time to compose myself was vital before returning to Sterling Place. With or without a dead body, there was a growing well of dread inside me I dare not look down.

"I'm glad to see you finally packing two trunks, Sister," Lord Vernet said, shattering my moment of peace.

Beside me, Lady Holmes let her breath out steadily, but I couldn't match her calm. I pressed my shaking hands into the folds of my skirt.

"After all," Lord Vernet continued, "the blossom is no longer fresh on the vine and with two sons to consider, if you hope to interest any suitors, you'll have to work much harder than you did the first time. I hope this maid of yours is up to the task. I'd have advised choosing someone a little older and plainer. Wouldn't want your suitors drawing any comparisons."

For the first time, his light green eyes swept over me, leaving my cheeks in a cold flush.

"How do my nephews fare?" asked Lady Holmes, her tone one I recognized. Her shutters were down.

Lord Vernet waved a gloved hand as though the question

of his sons was a fly attempting to land on his nose. "I believe Lucy had a letter from them last week."

"How pleasant," Lady Holmes said.

The rattle of the carriage's wheels and the steady rhythm of the horses' hooves swept into the silence. She opened her book, and Lord Vernet stayed quiet just long enough for me to believe he meant to remain so. Without warning, he leaned forward and snatched the book from his sister's hands.

"Photoheliograph? Eclipses? For heaven's sake, Sister, don't let Clarence or Sterling see you mucking about. You and your peculiar little hobbies," he said in the same tone he'd used when he said *suitors*. As if it couldn't possibly matter. As if she'd dreamed it. As if she might have wanted to fly.

"Now tell me about your charity case, the one worth an association with a police inspector." Lord Vernet's last two words came out curdled.

Lady Holmes didn't reach for her book, didn't pause, only outlined the barest sketch of Billy's case, leaving out all mention of my part. I might have been offended if I hadn't been so busy hunkering behind the shield of anonymity she offered. And yet, my heart protested. I had lived those moments with Lady Holmes, and it was painful to hear her erase me.

It was as though there were two of her, the one riding next to me and the one sitting across from her brother. We rumbled over the bridge, and I considered rolling him out of the carriage and into the rushing water below. How on earth did she suffer through this man's mistreatment? How had she been formed in such a crucible? I was more determined than ever that Lady Holmes should see her eclipse. Even if we were still at Sterling Place in two days, as her supposed lady's maid I could invent an excuse so she could steal away.

When she finished detailing Billy's disappearance, she rounded back to the subject of Lord Sterling's missing horses, with a question as to which ones. A move so deft she must have made it on purpose, though Lord Vernet didn't seem to notice.

Past Sherrinford, around the farms and hills beyond, he spoke of horses, and he didn't stop. Not just the stolen ones, but of his own, those owned by his acquaintances, and those he hoped to buy from Lady Holmes. Mercifully, his litany covered a multitude of our sins and silences, namely the dead body jolting along with the rest of the luggage.

Our route stuck to the main road, which had changed enough in the intervening years that it wasn't until we came into sight of Sterling Place that my feelings lifted their hooves and began bucking.

Its sweeping grounds and brick walls were unchanged, however. Even the trees appeared as stable as if they'd been carved from the same marble as the lion's heads guarding the gates.

It wasn't fair.

We had lost Da and, a week later, our home. Sterling Place had no right side-stepping time and consequences like a dancer missing their partner in the reel.

We paused so the magnificent iron gates could swing open, and Lord Vernet finally stopped talking.

"Is Lord Sterling well, Brother? And Clarence?" Lady Holmes asked.

Her words caught me leaning forward, peering through

the carriage window. Aimed ostensibly at her brother, they found their true target, and I forced myself to settle against the lush cushions.

"Well, I suppose you'll learn soon enough. We've been having a bully week shooting and riding, but then ..." For the first time since I met him Lord Vernet hesitated before speaking. "Sterling has had a bit of a surprise. A family thing. A long-lost brother from the wrong side of the blanket. You know how these things go."

Lord Sterling? An illegitimate brother? The former Earl of Sterling, Lord Harold, had been little more than a wrinkled face above a pile of counterpanes by my time. Hardly rake material. I kept my face neutral as though I, too, knew how these things went.

"Of course, they're not calling him that," Lord Vernet added. "You have to be careful about such matters."

"Of course," Lady Holmes agreed.

Our carriage pulled up to the front door and stopped with the jingle of harnesses and a low word from our driver.

Lord Vernet gathered his bowler from the seat and waited for the approaching footmen to open the carriage door. "But Sterling's delighted at the prospect of reconnecting, as he has no other siblings. Andrew Dunning is the man's name. You'll meet him at dinner tonight. Most interesting chap."

CHAPTER THIRTY-FOUR

IF MUSGRAVE HALL WAS A BARRICADE, A LINE separating those with money and those without, then Sterling Place was a fortress. As beautiful as it was unassailable, it unfolded before the rolling hills surrounding our valley as though sprung from the land itself. In a way, it had. One family had held the land since the Battle of Hastings. Da told us there were the ruins of a small castle and former priory somewhere on the grounds, though he'd never seen them. Seven hundred acres could hide a lot of history.

We pulled up to the front door, flanked by a matched pair of footmen and twin towers complete with the crenelations usually reserved for castles in story books. The ruddy bricks and arched windows gave the place a forbidding air, even in fair weather like today. However, against the stark backdrop of winter or the dense fog of spring and autumn, it became as eerie as the effigy of a sleeping knight—still, but enduring.

I blinked, and the spell broke. The one woven from

picking at every unfamiliar thread visible, a story written in architectural details and held together by a history not my own. My plan had been to cobble them together into a distraction to carry me through this investigation, but it hadn't even got me through the door.

Da had been here. Every day. On the grounds, in the stables, the riding ring. He'd eaten with the other servants downstairs or performed odd jobs upstairs. His boots crunched in the pale gravel underfoot. The oil from his fingers soaked into the horse tack. His eyes knew the reflection of the approaching sunset in the western windows. This air. That tree.

They all held fragments of Da that I could never have. Slipped through my fingers and swirled away like silt from the river. This place still possessed him in a way lost to me. I wanted to drop to my knees and claw at the dirt, to rip everything down stone by stone. Never should Sterling Place know a moment's peace until I had my da back.

This was what I risked in this charade, pitting myself against the rich and powerful. Sterling Place had already cost my family a father and a home. What else might it take if I let it? My eyes and nose burned, the weight in my chest, heavier than seven hundred acres, strained against my ribs.

My resolve cracked wide open, and I teetered on the step of the carriage.

Lady Holmes paused beside me, her hand swung toward mine, magnetic, but then she pulled it back and smoothed her skirt, lips curled in a smile like a closed fist. "Do not let them see you weep, Hudson. There is no room for weakness here. There never has been. Be on your guard."

With that, she swept after her brother through the thick oak doors.

I wandered in their wake, nursing my wounded feelings and throbbing ankle. Inside the entrance hall, the past waited for me. I blinked at the gleaming pattern on the floor, against the scent of lemons in the floor polish. It might be easy for Lady Holmes to tuck her emotions away, but how could I do the same when I was faced with the ghosts of my parents at every turn? Even this floor—I'd helped Ma polish it as soon as I could hold a rag. There were four hundred stars in the parquet's pattern. I counted them once when I was five.

"Vernet! Glad to see you made it in time for dinner," a man called from the other room.

The siblings had already exited the soaring entrance hall, and I hurried after them down the long hallway to the east wing. At the door to the parlor, I hesitated. Should I accompany Lady Holmes any farther? Why hadn't she given me some instructions? Even if it hadn't been six years since they'd last seen me, I doubted the Sterlings would recognize me as their former housemaid, but just to be on the safe side, I lingered outside the door where none of them even looked my way.

The parlor ahead was large, with tall windows at the far end framing the impressive gardens and reflecting pool beyond. Generous clusters of seating were either placed to take in the views or encircle the fireplace, perfect for the audience of whoever might be holding court there.

Currently, it was a tall man with graying hair who stood outlined against the dark green marble surround. Dressed in brown hunting clothes, a bit rough at the edges, he held his back to the cheery blaze as though warming himself. Granted, I'd only seen him from the side as he left Musgrave

Hall, but he'd aged so much in the last six years that it took me a moment to recognize him as Lord Sterling.

"We had a lovely hunt this afternoon, Vernet. Clarence bagged a stag with antlers thick as a yew."

The man at the fire wasn't speaking. Instead the voice came from a set of high-backed leather armchairs beside it, two sets of men's legs sticking out toward the fireplace. I glanced between them and the man standing.

"Remember that magnificent stag Father caught when we were lads, Wallace?" the man said. "There was a painting of it somewhere."

"Sorry to have missed it, Clarence. But excellent work." Lord Vernet waved behind him. "You remember my sister."

Understanding swept over me as two men stood from the chairs and bowed toward Lady Holmes. The man at the fire wasn't Lord Sterling at all. He must be Andrew Dunning, the illegitimate brother Lord Vernet mentioned. Similar in stature and features, Lord Sterling was somewhat shorter, with deep gray hair and a blocky chin topped with elaborate mustaches. His ears stuck out in a way Mr. Dunning's did not, and his eyes were dimmer.

Clarence Sterling smiled, handsome cheeks flushed. "Of course. A pleasure to see you again so soon." He was taller than his father, with wide shoulders and a narrow waist. Also dressed in brown hunting clothes, his were tailored beautifully, his boots gleaming.

Lady Holmes dipped her head. "Indeed. And thank you, Lord Sterling. To be able to join a small party of friends is a much needed pleasure." Her mask was so complete even I couldn't see a single crack in it.

Lord Sterling took her hand. "Please, dear, call me

Wallace. The loss of Arthur was a blow to us all. When my Josephine died, it was a dark time, but you cannot live in the shadows forever. You have the boys to think of, after all."

Hearing Lord Sterling speak about grief and loss left something spiky and hot lodged in my throat, and I was more glad than ever that I'd decided to remain hidden in the hallway. This place, *this man*, they had cost me my father. I hated them all.

Lord Sterling smiled and patted Lady Holmes' hand before letting go. "Get settled after your journey. We'll see you at dinner. Clarence can tell you about his stag, and you can meet Dunning here." He clapped the other man on the shoulder. "They're both stories you have to hear to believe."

A maid collected us, and I plodded up the grand staircase behind her and Lady Holmes. I struggled to ignore my familiar surroundings, to avoid comparing them to my memories. Lady Holmes was right. Difficult as it may be, this was no time to show weakness. Seeing Lord Sterling again had brought home our precarious position. I needed to focus on hiding Tom's body and uncovering Billy's whereabouts. I had a part to play. My role. My escape.

At the door of our quarters, the iris rooms, I copied Lady Holmes' posture, squared my shoulders, and entered as though I had never laid the fires there or changed the linens.

The maid, a young woman with furiously red hair tucked under her cap, pointed out the room's amenities and our luggage stacked in the corner, then curtseyed before taking her leave.

Alone, we stood together for a beat, then both spoke at once.

"I'll begin unpacking, if you—"

"Hudson, when I said to be on your guard—"

I held up a hand. "No, you were right."

Her face pinched. "I find I cannot lay down my armor, though I might wish to. It's how I survived all these years. You need to put on your own. I couldn't stand it if they hurt you."

The room around us, with its picture box molding and soft lavender paint, all gentle curves and gleaming fixtures, seemed the mirror opposite of armor.

"I'm not sure if I have any," I said. She frowned and took a step toward me, but I turned to our luggage. "We don't have much time before the dinner bell. I'll find your dress and ... well, if you need my help, I'll be here."

Careful to open the bodiless trunk, I removed the layer of newspaper placed over the top to protect its contents, one sheet bearing a headline concerning the solar eclipse. Finally, I uncovered an evening dress of dark gray silk.

I shook out the fringe of silken flowers along its trim and hung the gown from the wardrobe. Lady Holmes, fingers flying over the buttons on her traveling dress, stepped up beside me.

My stomach somersaulted as her dress parted. I directed myself to avert my eyes but couldn't move. She stripped off the black bodice, and my eyes drank in her long arms, thin but well-muscled. When she bent to her boots, light from the windows glanced off her collar bones, setting her blonde hair afire. A thread of desire snaked through me, low. I wanted to locate each of the pins in her hair and release them one by one, keys falling from locks.

She stood, and I jerked my face away, heart hammering like a fist on a door. Lady Holmes stood before me in nothing except her cotton chemise, silk stockings, and gray striped corset.

She leaned toward her trunk, pulled a shoe bag from the top compartment, and sighed. "Green."

I gestured at the bag. "You can't wear green shoes with that dress."

"No, two days ago, when we stood in front of the shop window, you asked what my favorite color was, before all of this." She tapped the rim of the trunk. "It's green."

She had carried my words with her? What did that mean? And more importantly, what did I want it to mean? I stepped closer to her, breathing in the scent of broken rock and mint.

"Green would suit your eyes." My voice was thick with emotion. "Like growing things washed clean by the rain."

Her eyelids fluttered. "They used to be gray, like the young of the green whip snake, but they changed as I grew. *Hierophis viridiflavus*, their range extends through a wide swath of Europe ... I'm sorry, I forgot you're not fond of snakes. Only, I so rarely seem to know what to say to you. When we aren't discussing the case, that is." She placed her shoes down, picked up her gown, and slipped it over her head.

When her flushed cheeks popped out again, I stepped behind to help with the fastenings. "While I never want to hold a snake again, I'm happy to listen to you speak on them or anything else. I like talking to you, and when we're not being shot at or transporting anything horrific, I have a wonderful time in your company. Being with you makes me feel like a version of myself I forgot that I lost."

A tendril of hair escaped from her braided bun, and I moved it off her shoulders to finish tying the last ribbon on her dress. She swayed, my knuckles brushing her spine. I ran a finger over the line of bumps, delicate as pearls, and her skin rippled with gooseflesh.

"Hudson." She breathed my name. "I've never ... I've wanted to but—"

A knock came from the door, and we jumped apart. I buried my shaking hands into the clothes in the trunk, and Lady Holmes dove for the dressing table.

"Come in," she called, voice steady.

The maid who had shown us to our rooms entered with a tray of tea on a large-wheeled trolley. "Mrs. Nash thought you might like something to drink after your long ride."

"Thank you." Lady Holmes smiled at the maid in the mirror but shook her head as the maid fussed with the trolley. "Hudson will serve us. However, I will need a pot of chamomile tea before bed. I have trouble sleeping in strange places."

The maid curtseyed. "Of course, m'lady. Just ring when you've finished, and I'll be up to fetch these things."

I set out a cup and saucer as the maid left and shut the door. When she was gone, Lady Holmes surged to her feet and joined me at the trolley. My heart stuttered, and the china clinked dangerously. I opened my mouth to speak, but instead of resuming what the maid had interrupted, Lady Holmes knelt on the carpet and examined the tea trolley. She lifted one of the hinged leaves and peered underneath, testing the bottom shelf by putting her weight on it.

"Hudson, I can hear your thoughts. From the moment I

first saw you, I knew our minds ran on parallel tracks." She grinned up at me.

My heart was too full to object, so I bent to see the sturdy shelf that formed the lower level of the trolley. I regretted it instantly, as I realized exactly what she meant to do. I tipped my forehead against the edge of the cart and sighed.

"Not again."

CHAPTER THIRTY-FIVE

THE MINUTE LADY HOLMES LEFT OUR ROOMS, I realized my mistake. Since we'd arrived too late for me to eat with the rest of the servants, and since we had a body secreted in a trunk, we'd decided I should stick close to our rooms. I could question the servants once our most pressing matter had been disposed of.

Alone, however, there was no question of my staying. I'd rung for someone to fetch the tea trolley but couldn't even wait for them to arrive. Instead, I bundled it out of our rooms myself, loaded only with our tea things. I made it all the way to the end of the hall before I met with our red-headed maid.

"Oh, miss, I was on my way," she said, eyes narrowing at my offense.

"I thought I'd save you a trip since I'm heading to the kitchens for a bite to eat. Katy Hudson, by the way."

She stared at my outstretched hand, pale lips pursed, then shook it gently. "Cora McKinney. I have to stow this trolley with the others before I can take the tray down, but then I'll show you the way to the kitchens."

There was no point in hiding it. At any moment, I could meet someone who recognized me the way I did Sterling Place, right down to the bones. Lies wouldn't purchase me trust. "Actually, I worked here years ago, so I know the way. I could help with the tea things?"

"That's kind of you, miss," Cora said. "Have you worked for Lady Holmes long, then?"

"Only a few days," I admitted, letting my exhaustion bleed onto my face.

She shot me a sympathetic look. "Reminds me of things here. Bit of an uproar downstairs." I held the tea tray so she could slide the trolley into a storage closet holding three others. "We're down a houseboy, police inspectors interrogating everyone, and guests on top of that."

I clucked my tongue. "You must be run off your feet. Police inspectors?" I handed her the tray and carried the teapot so the rest would balance more easily.

"Because of the houseboy. He seemed a good lad, but then he took off with two of the master's prized horses."

At the bottom of the stairs, two housemaids, even younger than Cora, squeezed past us into the kitchen. The heat and bustle of a full dinner service hurtled over us, and I had to raise my voice to be heard. "One boy stole two horses? Did no one see anything?"

One of the maids, a dark-haired young woman, whipped her head around to stare at us, then looked away again just as quickly. However, not before I caught the stricken expression on her face.

"His da was hanging about." Cora held the door for me. "Nasty piece of work, that one. Some say Billy was taking after him. That may be, but who knows with boys. My brother would jump off the roof to impress our da."

I chuckled knowingly. "Mine taught himself to ride a horse for the same reason. The fool used the shed to climb on the poor thing's back."

Cora laughed. "Best keep an eye on that one, miss. Have a seat by the wall and I'll get you something to eat."

"Thank you, Cora. I just remembered. Lady Holmes will take a slice of cake with her chamomile tea."

She nodded and went off to fetch my meal as I sank onto the low bench by the kitchen door. The room was wide, thick with the warmth that lingered after hundreds of years of constant use. For now, the room had lulled into a restful pause, the intake of breath between dinner and night service.

As I waited, the dark-haired maid and her companion washed trays of dirty dishes then placed fresh tumblers of water and clean glasses onto new trays. Several other pairs of maids entered the kitchen to deposit dishes or on their way through to the laundry. The dark-haired maid glanced my way several times, but unlike her companions, she kept to the other side of the kitchen.

A few minutes later, the dark-haired maid grabbed a bucket of kindling and tinder, then gathered the tray of water she'd set out, clearly ready to prepare one of the bedchambers for the night. I hurried to finish my mutton and potatoes as she scurried past me without meeting my eye. As soon as she left, I deposited my dishes at the sink and followed her toward the servants' stairs.

Mrs. Nash's reign as housekeeper at Sterling Place began after my time but, judging by the pairs of maids coming and going, the house rule was still in place. Maids should enter bedrooms only with a companion. Ostensibly, the rule provided someone to vouch for you in case something went missing, but it also protected maids from the vulnerability present in entering a man's bedchambers.

This maid had flaunted the rule to avoid me.

She didn't realize I was behind her until we'd made it back to the guest wing. When the maid glanced over her shoulder, her thick brows rose almost to her cap, and she sped up. Ours was the first room along the hallway, but she carried on beyond the next suite of rooms to those at the end of the hall. I slipped past our door and put my ear to the one she'd disappeared behind.

Clanking came from inside the castle room. Named for its view of the manor house's turrets as well as the royal guests it had hosted, male guests favored it because of its proximity to the stairs leading to the smoking and game rooms below. Clarence and Lord Sterling kept rooms in the west wing of the home, so this room must have been allocated to Lord Vernet or the mysterious Andrew Dunning.

I let myself into the room. The maid had been arranging pillows but didn't gasp or startle when I entered, only closed her eyes as though she'd been expecting me.

"Hello," I said, "you look like you need saving."

Her eyes flew open. "I beg your pardon, miss?"

"In a bedroom alone? I used to work here when I was your age, and I know the rules." I put on my friendliest smile and picked up the bucket of kindling and tinder. "Here, let me help."

The maid jumped as though I'd struck her. "I couldn't. Please, Mrs. Nash will have my job."

"Nonsense," I said. "I'll help you out, then you'll help

me, and we'll be done with it. What's your name?"

The maid approached me, wringing her hands in her apron. "Elsie. Do you need something? I can nip back downstairs, miss."

"You can call me Katy. And no, I don't need anything from downstairs." I knelt at the fireplace but kept my eyes on Elsie. "What do you know about Billy Mudd?"

"Who?" she asked, voice barely a whisper. "I don't … I didn't …"

My eyes roved over her round cheeks and black locks. "You're a pretty girl. Did Billy ever sketch you?"

"You can look elsewhere for gossip," Elsie said, but her face flushed.

"I'm not looking for gossip. Billy's my cousin, and he's my brother's best friend. We're all worried sick about him. His mother, especially."

Elsie kept her eyes on the floor, her voice quiet. "Billy would hate that, miss. That's what brought us together at first, missing our mothers."

I dipped to catch her gaze. "Anything you say to me won't get back to the police. I just want to help Billy."

She twisted her apron until the material squeaked. "I don't know where he is."

I believed her, but she might still know something. "Tell me about his time here, anything out of the ordinary. It might help us save him."

She sniffed. "I can tell you Billy's not a thief. I don't care what the police say."

"Elsie, we can't—"

"No, miss. Look." She hunkered next to me, withdrew a folded sheet of paper from the pocket of her apron, and handed it over. "Can a person who draws like an angel be a bad sort?"

I'd seen dozens of Billy's sketches by now, and I could tell when he'd taken his time, when he'd been inspired, when he drew fast because he needed to capture what was in front of him before it blinked out of existence. The outdoor scene he'd created here, a likeness of Elsie half-turned to stroke the cheek of a tabby cat, left me breathless. The sunshine seeped into my skin, lily of the valley underfoot and giggles in the air when the cat inevitably flopped to the ground wriggling in delight. It wasn't a moment; it was a memory.

I blinked away tears as I returned the picture. "Any detail at all. No matter how small."

Elsie stared at the picture then folded it away. "We started at Sterling Place within a few days of each other. Billy was happy to be here, though he missed his ma and felt bad for leaving without telling her. He talked about his da, too, at least at first. His da gave him all sorts of gifts. New pencils and paper for drawing, little sweeties, postcards with outlandish animals to draw." If Elsie didn't quit wringing her hands in her apron, she was going to get a scolding for the wrinkles.

"Did you ever see his da?"

"No, but on Billy's half day off, he left the manor for a few hours and came back with a bruise on his cheek. Said he'd banged it on a doorknob, but I know what it looks like when a man's taken his fists to you."

I pressed my lips together.

She used the back of her apron to wipe a spot of dust from the floor beside her.

"Billy didn't talk about him after that. Except for once.

I found him burning the postcards and his drawings in the grate and tried to stop him. The drawings were just bits and pieces of Sterling Place, the people here, the paintings. But he wouldn't hear it. Said he wasn't about to let his da lead him into a life like his."

"What sort of life was that?"

"His da said he helped Billy get this job because he was sorry for being gone all these years, but it turned out his da had something he wanted Billy to do."

"Like what?"

Her eyes flew wide. "I don't know, miss. Only that a few days later, Billy was gone." She reached for the bucket of kindling and strips of newspaper beside me, but I shook my head.

"You finish with the bed, and I'll handle this. Then we'll leave together. And Elsie? Don't go around this house alone again. Mrs. Nash's rule is a good one."

"Yes, miss." Elsie ducked her head. "Please, you have to find Billy before his father or the police. They're both determined to drag him to jail, one way or the other."

I promised her we'd do our best, then true to my word, I laid the fire. Pieces of Elsie's story alternated with strips of wood and newspaper. That Tom had used his fists to get his way was no surprise, but what had he wanted Billy to do for him?

I struck a match, and the flame bent toward the paper like a hungry thing scenting its meal. Why would Billy burn his drawings? What use could Tom have for sketches of Sterling Place and its residents? Had he been planning a theft of some kind? After all, there were two horses missing.

Just before the match took its first bite, a flutter of paper in the dim recess at the back of the fireplace caught my eye. It wouldn't burn all the way where it was and might catch fire unexpectedly later. I shook out the match and reached past my tower of kindling. As soon as my fingers closed around the paper, my mind clicked back to another time and place.

London. Three years ago. The first time I held a telegram in my hands. John had sent me one to announce he'd secured me an interview as a telegraph clerk at the Post Office. The paper was thinner and a little rougher, with a distinctive crinkle when bent. Forever tied to the electric feeling of a new challenge, to the wonder that I could be part of a movement advancing both my own circumstances as well as other women like me.

My eyes scanned the telegrams in my hands just as greedily as I had then, but they were blank. Except not completely. The only sections filled in were where the clerk signed. Each one held a familiar signature in the upper left corner—John Hudson.

A chill swept over me. I shifted the kindling stack, but no other papers hid behind the grate. I turned to Elsie. She was stooped beside the bed, brushing a pair of men's boots.

"Whose room is this?" I asked as casually as I could.

She straightened, left boot in hand. Near the sole of the toes was a scratch a little over two inches long. A scratch I'd seen thrice before.

CHAPTER THIRTY-SIX

I SPREAD THE TELEGRAMS OUT LIKE A TREASURE MAP for Lady Holmes. She'd just returned from dinner, cheeks painted by wine and conversation. While she studied them, I explained what I'd learned from Elsie as well as what I'd seen on Andrew Dunning's shoes.

"They're blanks, but in all other respects they match the telegram Tom sent to Frances. And now the similarity of their shoes. Oh! What if it wasn't Tom who attacked Frances after all?" My mind raced so fast that I got to my feet. "The question is, were they working together? And if so, what were they after?"

She made a low noise and looked up at me. "No, my dear Hudson, the question is where did they get the same mark on their shoes? In the absence of more facts, the rest is speculation. We'll need a closer examination."

"We could get another look at Dunning's boots," I said. When her gaze pointed at the trunk in the corner, however, something nasty sank its teeth into my guts, twisting my roast mutton and potatoes into a solid mass. "You can't be serious? You are serious. I hate this. I—"

"Stop to breathe before you suffer another nervous attack. You turn the other way while I look"—she put a hand on the trunk's latch—"and I shall distract you with what I learned at dinner."

I sat on the upper corner of the bed, putting two of the four posts between us.

"As promised, Clarence recounted his adventure with the stag, though there were two things of note in his overblown tale. One: they started out later than they meant to because Mr. Dunning and Lord Sterling were still lying in after the sun rose. They may have, as they claimed, been up playing billiards as they had as boys, or they may have left the estate in pursuit of Tom Mudd."

Several snaps followed the creak of the trunk's lid.

"Either way, it's a period of time where they can only vouch for each other," I said with my hands fisted into the counterpane.

"Precisely. Now, two: Mr. Dunning takes pleasure in regaling anyone willing to listen with his childhood memories of Sterling Place."

"He lived here?"

"Supposing his story is true? Yes, when he was seven. His mother arrived in town claiming to be a widow and single mother of few means. She was eventually given employment at Sterling Place. A gentlewoman, she'd been a governess of a family friend of the Sterlings, and that's where her relationship with Lord Harold began. It's unclear whether the mother and child's connection to Lord Harold was known at the time she arrived in Sherrinford, by anyone other than Lord Harold, of course."

A rustle followed by a sharp intake of breath and a thump

came from behind me. I focused on a painting of horses in a pasture as though my life depended on it.

"Did they leave because they were found out?" I asked.

"That part of the story was insufficient. Mr. Dunning was also scant on details about what he's been doing since. A series of jobs all over the country, if he and his unusual accent are to be believed. I wish Sherlock were here to listen to it. He collects accents and can usually place them within a few miles."

I smiled at the memory of the accents he'd faked when I first met him.

"After that, Mr. Dunning made a rousing declaration of how he misses the hounds living here when he was a child. Lord Harold's favorites, a matched pair of English Pointers who ... I think it's the head of a nail."

I almost turned around but caught myself at the last moment. "A nail? Lady Holmes, are you feeling alright?"

"I was until you called me that. Coming from your lips, it sounds detestable," she said, still distracted. "The head of a nail seems like the likeliest candidate to make the scratches in the soles. I would guess Mr. Dunning and Tom repeatedly walked across the same loose floorboard. What if—"

A knock came from the door. I flew to my feet and across the room.

"Yes?" I asked through the wood, voice quivering.

"I'm here with the chamomile tea," said Cora.

"Right. Yes." I threw a desperate look over my shoulder at Lady Holmes who stood there with Tom's shoe in her hand. "Close the trunk," I whispered.

She gesticulated at Tom's legs sticking over the rim. "I can't. He slipped."

I gritted my teeth. "Put him back."

"He's stuck and won't fit without assistance. Just ..." She dropped his shoe into the trunk, stepped in front of it, and spread her skirt wide. "Answer it."

With my heart fluttering in my throat, I did as she asked. "Good evening, Cora."

"Evening, miss." She smiled at me and pushed the cart forward an inch. "If you'll back up, I'll wheel it in."

I wanted to scream. In my head, I was already howling. "Yes. Of course." My foot went back, and I froze. The tip of Tom's shoe caught my eye where it had landed behind the fold of canvas covering the body. Lady Holmes couldn't see it from her position, but if Cora took one more step, the man's shoe would be on display.

"Actually, I'll save you the trip." I grabbed the wrong end of the tea cart and dragged it forward. "I'll bring it back to storage, too. We may—"

"Hudson," Lady Holmes snapped. "Enough chatting. I'm ready to retire. And you have not even finished unpacking."

I hiked my shoulders and bit my lip, the portrait of a scolded servant. "Yes, m'lady."

Cora grimaced in sympathy and began hurrying away.

The cart knocked against the doorframe as I dragged it in, and Lady Holmes raised her voice. "Clumsy fool! You'd better not have spilled anything."

"I'm so sorry, Lady Holmes," I said as I shut the door. Once out of sight, I sagged against the panel, my chest a cauldron of relief and hysteria.

She abandoned her position at the open trunk and wheeled the cart over to block it. "Hudson, I would be elated to never hear you address me that way again."

I lifted my head from where it was slumped against the door. "As Lady Holmes? But it's your name."

"And as we discussed, it is also much more. Lady Holmes is borrowed power and false promises." She removed her jet necklace and dropped it into the case on the dressing table. "While I'm waiting for everyone else to fall asleep, I'll change into something more fit for sneaking about the halls."

At the threat of a disrobed Lady Holmes, I retreated to the far corner of the bed again, but she followed me.

"If you could release the ties, Hudson," she said and faced away.

"Alright, then." I did as she asked, careful to keep my fingers from brushing her flesh this time. "What would you prefer I call you?"

"My name. I don't believe I've heard anyone speak it with fondness since my grandmother died, just before Sherlock was born." Her voice quivered so briefly I might have imagined it. "When this is all over and we're back home at Musgrave Hall, can you not use my name?"

When this is all over. I hadn't allowed myself to think ahead yet. The wounds I carried were too fresh to bear such prodding. I had loved Da and lost him. And John, young and vital with a future full of promises we'd made to each other—that too had blinked out like a star behind the fog. My sprawling family held the tattered remains of my heart, and I would do anything to keep them safe. Anything except turn away those in need. Not just because of what Da had instilled in us, but because I knew what it meant to have my heart broken and to be the one left behind.

Evidently, so did Lady Holmes.

This afternoon, she'd asked for my trust, and I'd given it to her. But perhaps I hadn't realized the extent of what she was asking.

What would we be to each other when this was over? Society held less space for women who loved each other than they did for female investigators. Yet here we both were.

That I had come to care for Lady Holmes was impossible to ignore. I wanted to spend my days near her, to work beside her, and at the end, rest together—only to do it again upon rising. If I couldn't be a telegraph clerk any longer, at least when I was working with her, I could still make a difference in the world while caring for my family.

Trust was like grief; it never stopped asking for you to hope.

I loosened the final knot on Lady Holmes' dress and stepped away. Her nearness left me too dizzy.

She half-turned toward me, and for once, I fancied her armor was gone. "Hudson?" A whisper of strong feeling crossed her face, like a fresh blade of grass crushed under the heel of a careless boot. There and then gone again. But it was like looking in a mirror. I knew exactly what she was asking.

"Call you by your first name?" I bit my lip. "I can't. I don't—"

"It wouldn't be appropriate." She blinked, ready to withdraw again. "As your employer."

"No." I grabbed her hand and held it fast. "That is, I would, but I can't because I don't know your Christian name."

Her face, still but sculpted, drained of all expression, as

though she'd put down a mask and revealed the raw stone underneath. For a moment, I thought I'd offended her, until I heard the naked relief in her voice.

"It's Violet. Someday, when you can, call me Violet."

"That's easily done, then, Violet." As I smiled, heat wound its way from my chest to the crown of my head. Her pulse fluttered under my hand, and, unthinking, my fingers matched its tempo. I tapped out her name against her wrist. *V-i-o-l-e-t.* I added my sign-off just to make sure I could still do it in under four seconds. *K-T-B.*

She watched, lips parted. "I've seen you do that before. Tapping your fingers when you're agitated or impatient. Are you alright?"

I blushed. "It's a habit. Sometimes my thoughts and fingers can't help but speak to each other. I was spelling out your name in Morse Code."

Her smile was soft. "They zipped by. Could you do it again?"

When I ran my finger up her wrist and over her palm, she shivered. The letters dribbled out, with clear breaks between.

"You didn't …" Violet shook her head. "Last time weren't there more letters?"

"Oh, yes. My sign-off. KTB." I tapped the three letters into her palm.

"Not Hudson?"

"Most of the ladies chose an anonymous nickname of sorts because the men complained women transmitted with a choppy fist, cutting our dots short and such nonsense."

Her pale eyebrow arched. "I imagine they only made that complaint when they knew the sender was a woman."

"You imagine correctly." I smirked. "On the lines, I was *KTB*. For Katy Bunting, but also because my da said my mouth was always going like the buzzing of a bee in a flower."

Her wide eyes flicked to my lips, and I hurried on. "I liked the nickname."

"Because it reminded you of your father?"

"Yes, but I also liked what it signified. Little Katy Bee all grown up, somewhere greater than where I started, in a place I'd earned."

Violet ran her thumb over my knuckles. There was a rough patch just under her nail, and I wondered what had made it. "Should I use your nickname as well?"

"No, I don't think so." I bit my lip. "Hudson was a name I got from John, yes, but when you say it, I hear that same something more. Something I've earned."

She leaned closer, eyes locked on mine. The pull to meet her started at my toes, as though I'd jumped from a hayloft and some force still held me firm to the earth, drawing me ever closer.

A din came from the clock on the mantel as it chimed. Lady Holmes bent her neck until our foreheads pressed together. Her words tickled my lips. "It's time to be rid of this burden."

Chapter Thirty-Seven

We'd decided the less I knew about Tom's intermediate resting place, the more easily I could pretend I'd never seen it. A blessing on multiple levels.

Therefore, following the ordeal of getting Tom's corpse hidden on the lower shelf of the tea trolley and maneuvering it through our bedchamber door, I collapsed on the floor of the dressing room while Lady Holmes left to transport the body. The reek of him mingled with the scent of the lavender sachets we'd used to cover his developing odor. I should never be able to smell them again without my stomach revolting.

An army of spiders traversed the inside of my skin, my heart alternating between great leaps and fidgets. I lay with my cheek pressed into the carpet, eyes closed, until the worst of my panic subsided. Even then, I couldn't get my legs underneath me. So, I dragged myself a few feet to my own trunk and heaved open the lid to consult John's pocket watch. There, tucked on top of my things, lay two pieces of foolscap.

The first showed two women in black dresses, inked by a childish hand. One woman sat at a table with her foot on a stool, and the second held up two objects for examination. Beside them, among scattered bits of white on the grass, was a boy in short pants wearing a bright grin. He added dots of color to represent the flowerbeds and in our widow's weeds, we looked like two crows among the blooms.

The surprise of seeing the three of us depicted knocked a burst of laughter from me. What a clever, dear little thing. Sherlock had blossomed under his mother's attention, and it was lovely, but I hadn't stopped to think what I might mean to Sherlock. "*When I was sad, Hudson brought me a sweet bun and a picture with a footprint on it. It was better than the best game I've ever played, and you can't fire her for it. I won't let you.*"

Again, an ugly creature with tiny fangs nipped at my conscience, reminding me he could no more help being born rich than I could being born poor, and yet, I'd wanted to turn him away because of it. Da's words, spoken in his kind but serious voice, rippled over me. *We make ourselves useful in the world only through lightening the burdens of others.*

It wasn't in Da's nature to abandon those who needed help, and he taught the rest of us to do the same. My cheeks burned at the memory of how I'd almost failed him. I wiped my eyes and tucked the drawing back in my trunk.

The second sheet was a pieced together picture from Billy's torn sketches. When Sherlock stumbled over Tom's body, we'd abandoned our project—which felt like it must have happened years ago, surely not this afternoon? That yawning distance made me aware of just how exhausted

I was, my pulse thudding at my temples and my injured ankle.

Apparently, Sherlock had completed one more before we left and sneaked it, along with his drawing, into my things.

This sketch was a study of a hunter in a cap and Inverness coat. The tall man stood with one foot on the neck of an enormous stag, flanked by a matched set of English Pointers. A common enough pose, but instantly familiar. I'd dusted an identical painting every Monday morning for three years in the game room of Sterling Place. Just seeing it here, I smelled the sweet tang of the tobacco smoke baked into the baize of the gaming tables.

Below the sketch of hunter and hounds was the wrinkled countenance of a man's face. Lord Harold Sterling, the hunter featured beside his hounds in the painting. Not as I'd known him, as a frail fixture of his bedchambers, but with vigor still in his features—probably around the time the painting was done.

A chill swept over my limbs. Heart thumping, I lurched to my feet and hobbled into the bedchamber to examine the painting hanging next to the bed. They matched. One of the sketches we'd pieced together in the garden this afternoon showed a pasture of horses I thought was the east meadow here. But just like Lord Harold and his hounds, it was a drawing of a painting, a slice of the manor. Billy stood in this spot and risked his job by wasting his time drawing objects belonging to the Sterlings. And then someone ripped all those drawings to pieces. I reached out a finger and drew it over the frame. Ornate, but not worth stealing in a house full of finer objects.

If theft wasn't the plan, why bother sketching the close view of an older Lord Harold, a man Billy never met?

Someone knocked at the bedroom door, glazing me in fear. On the bed was a lump as though Violet lay asleep beneath a mountain of covers. It would pass muster in the dim light, but only for anyone who didn't come too close. If this was Cora, come to claim the tea trolley even though we'd told her to wait for morning, she would discover there was no trolley in the room. Could it be Lady Holmes? Why would she knock? Was she in trouble?

I set my hand on the knob and opened the door a crack. Whiskey laden breath burned my eyes and nostrils as the man standing there shouted and thumped the doorframe.

"Sister!" Lord Vernet's handsome face was flushed, his eyes half-closed.

I choked on a cough and, though it was the last thing I wanted to do, slipped into the hall and closed the door. "My lord. Is everything alright?"

He stared at me as though seeing me for the first time. "Oh, the pretty maid." His voice grew louder. "I need to speak with my sister."

Damn everything. "Lady Holmes wasn't feeling well. She's already asleep."

"I said, fetch me my *sister*." He leaned against the wall and listed to one side.

"Please, my lord." My hands wrung my apron of their own accord, and a pang of sympathy for Elsie inspired me. "Lady Holmes will have my job if I wake her."

"Might as well lose it for something useful now rather than in a few months when she can't afford to pay you any longer," he said with a thin smile.

"Sir?" I asked.

"Fine," he drawled, "I shall do the waking for you." He hammered the wall with his fist. "Sister!"

Frozen to the spot, I peered past him. Someone must have heard the yelling and would come to investigate. But who? Most of the servants had retired to their rooms by now, and the men would be downstairs in the game room. In fact, our plan hinged on it. The only one who might be up and about on this floor was Violet, and I was meant to provide her an alibi.

"Sister!" Lord Vernet shouted again, slapping his hand against the wall this time. He spun, weaving a little as he caught himself on the doorframe and glared at me. "Did you know your mistress' intentions toward Clarence, or did she keep her clever machinations to herself?"

I had no idea what he meant, but his slurred words dropped a cold stone into my chest. "Machinations, my lord?"

"Clarence asked me about her interests, her *availability*, and I came out looking like a fool. I brought her here because I thought Sterling might know someone interested in a half-withered widow like her, someone with deep pockets and hungry for the prestige of a wife with a title. A collector of sorts. But an earl's son? What does she think, she'll woo him with facts about the bloody stars? It's damn embarrassing."

Something about being in this place, in front of this man, squashed even my relentless tongue. The imbalance between us was too bare, and it cut me to the bone. What could I say to him that would make any difference? I would be safer having nothing to do with him. If he decided to have me removed from the premises, there would be no recourse. And yet, I had a job to do.

Over Lord Vernet's shoulder, one of the doors opened and Mr. Dunning peered out at us.

A flash of hope spread through my chest. I wasn't alone. "I'm so sorry, my lord. I'll let Lady Holmes know you wish to see her in the morning."

He didn't see Mr. Dunning at all, however, and went on as though I hadn't spoken. "Almost as embarrassing as this interest she's taken in Sterling's servants. That man. This boy. Whatever happened to some other bloke? No one wants to talk about a murdered groom from ages ago. Bad enough we had to sit there and entertain Sterling's bastard brother as though he's one of us."

Mr. Dunning's expression turned thunderous, and he eased into the hall, disappearing down the stairs to the game room.

"She always did have a habit of asking too many questions," Lord Vernet said, cold green eyes scraping over me.

I caught each of his words like blows. Was there even armor that could withstand an assault from outside and inside all at once?

"I'll admit," he sighed, filling the close air with another whiskey cloud, "after seeing the state of Arthur's books, it makes sense. Without an influx of cash, well, Mycroft will still have the title, but there'll be precious little else for either of her sons." His grin was like a hot coal, and he slammed a fist into the door again. "Goodnight, dear sister! You'll have to face me in the morning."

With that promise, he put his hands in his pockets and sauntered down the hall. When he reached the staircase at the far end, I stole back into our rooms, lowered myself onto the bed, and wept.

Chapter Thirty-Eight

THAT WAS THE SECOND NIGHT I SLEPT UNDER LADY Holmes' counterpane. I awoke to shouting, and fists hammering on doors. For a moment, fear wrapped long fingers around my throat, whispering it was Lord Vernet ready for another attack.

"It sounds as though they've discovered the body," Lady Holmes said from where she stood peering out the window. "I'm sure we'll have a visit from the intrepid Inspector Goodwin before breakfast."

I sat up, blinking. "Where were you last night?"

"On the way back, I had a run-in with Clarence." She curled her lip. "Fortunately, he'd been drinking, and his balance was as compromised as his manners." When I didn't smile, she crossed to the bed and sat on the other side. "What's wrong?"

"Clarence was probably drinking with Lord Vernet."

"Does it matter?"

I couldn't look at her, but I sat up straight. "Lord Vernet stopped by last night. He was angry over how you'd behaved at dinner." My eyes found her again. I needed to see how she reacted. "With Clarence."

She waved a hand. "Lewis wants to marry me off to an old industrialist to fund his love of horses the way Arthur did."

"Oh." I ran my palm back and forth over the counterpane as though it might smooth the edge off my question. "Do you have serious money troubles? Lord Vernet said—"

"I can imagine. My late husband was a man of few talents aside from squandering the fortune left to him by his father, and Lewis was happy to help him spend it. He doesn't care what happens to me or my sons, only for a friendly checkbook to cover his own debts. Lewis won't be a problem."

I nodded, still miserable. She hadn't said her brother was wrong about her lack of funds. If my job disappeared, I'd be back where I started. Worse even. Sterling Place would never hire me after this was all over. Did I mean so little to her, did she so misunderstand my position, she would let me risk myself and my family?

But then, that wasn't all she hadn't said. Her solvency, or lack thereof, was the least of my concerns.

"Lord Vernet said you'd been asking questions about my father. He used the word *murdered*." My eyes stung with the remnants of last night's tears.

A shout came from outside on the lawn, but neither of us moved.

"That's what I've been trying to tell you," Lady Holmes said.

I thumped the mattress. "You're wrong! My father was killed in an accident at the stables. A horse kicked him in the chest. Ma told me the story herself. The other grooms went to his funeral." I shook my head, staring at my knees. Da had been dead for years, but the idea I'd imagined his final moments as a lie tore something open in me. My voice shook. "Someone would have known if he was murdered."

She stepped toward me, hands out. "That's just it. People did know. There was an inquest, talk of charges—everything. But nothing came of it. Once I knew Bernard Bunting was your father, I had to do something. I've been investigating, and I have some proof, but I needed more. I needed to talk to Clarence. So last night, I—"

"Proof of what, exactly?" I asked, delicate as a last breath.

Lady Holmes looked stricken. "Hudson, your father was murdered here in the stables at Sterling Place during an attempted robbery."

She was right about so many things, but not this. It couldn't be true. I wrapped an arm around my waist, then dropped it again. I'd been shoved into a different world, one where I couldn't fit inside my own body anymore.

Lady Holmes grabbed my hand. "Hudson, breathe."

"I'm not faint. I'm livid." I yanked my hand away. "After all your talk about not keeping secrets? How could you? How long have you known?" Sitting no longer felt right, and I stood, putting the bed between us.

She stood with me but didn't approach. "You didn't want to talk about it, and I wasn't sure there was anything to talk about. Then, in Inspector Goodwin's office, when I was searching the files, I saw one with your father's name on it."

I faltered back a step. "And you didn't tell me?"

"There wasn't time! So I stole it." She crossed to her

trunk, withdrew a brown folder, and handed it to me with a grim expression. "There isn't much, but it's clear ..."

I read as fast I could, devouring the words. What she was saying, the shouts outside, and the thudding of feet in the hallway grew distant as I stared at the descriptions in the report. I drowned in them. But none of them soaked in. *Bernard Bunting, Age 48, Deceased.* Those were the few words that made sense. I pressed a shaking hand to the page, willing meaning into the symbols there.

My shock throttled my throat, and my voice came out stiff and awkward as my first telegram. "But who would shoot Da? Why?"

Lady Holmes handed me a handkerchief. "I'm so sorry, Hudson."

Da loved horses more than almost anything. He would've risked a great deal to protect them. Did he die doing so? "What will Ma say? She'll be crushed. And the others ..." I pressed a hand to my mouth to hold back a sob.

Even the raucous calls from outside stopped for a moment.

Lady Holmes stepped closer. "I'm sorry for not telling you, for what it all means. But justice isn't out of the question. I haven't discerned the answer yet. However, my brother knows more than he says. Look on the second page of the report."

When I didn't move, Lady Holmes reached for the file, but I wrenched it away. "This isn't a case!"

Hurt swept across her eyes, darkening them, there and gone again. "Of course not. Though I'd hoped to solve it for you."

"Like a birthday present? This is my father! My family!"

I beat my chest with both hands as though opening the wounds I held closed for five years. "How could you let me walk into the place where he was murdered with nothing more than a warning to keep my armor up?"

"This was already so hard for you, being in these rooms, moving the body—if your feelings got in the way of the investigation, we might fail. Your father's already beyond our help. Billy needs us."

I stumbled back as though she'd slapped me. "I know that! Why else would I be here? I've risked everything, *everything*, on this ridiculous venture of ours. If you die, your sons will have a life, a good one. But if something happens to me, who will take care of my siblings? Of Ma? And Billy? Without my income, we'll lose the cottage along with any hope of seeing my brothers and sisters get jobs with a safe future."

"Hudson ..." Lady Holmes pleaded.

"You offered me a job I believed in. You made me care for you. You asked me to trust you. And then you lied. Is that how you treat a partner, or is that how you treat a servant? What else aren't you telling me?"

Lady Holmes swallowed once. "Last night—"

A fist thundered on the door a second before Elsie burst inside. "M'lady, m'lady, come quick! In the shrubs, on the lawn"—she gasped in a breath—"it's your brother."

Chapter Thirty-Nine

As we dashed down the front stairs, Elsie spoke over her shoulder. "They're talking about moving his lordship soon, and I thought you'd want to see …" Her round eyes skated to me, and I nodded. "I heard you were asking about Billy and his father last night at dinner, m'lady. So, I thought you'd want to see his lordship before they bring him inside. Do you think this is connected?"

Lady Holmes shook her head. "Unclear. My brother is aggravating enough to provoke violence without assistance. Still, you did the right thing. Thank you, Elsie."

I glanced at her in surprise. My description of Elsie last night had been cursory at best, but it was as though Lady Holmes kept a catalog of all my words at the ready. Elsie only mumbled a quick thank-you, led us down the hall, and through a side door into the gardens. There, sticking out from under a rhododendron bush and surrounded by a half-circle of men, was Lord Vernet. He still wore his dinner clothes from last night.

As we drew closer, I scanned the bottoms of his shoes, grateful for the distraction from my own grief. No telltale scratch marred their smooth bottoms. The leather tops were pristine. If he'd been out walking long, either during the night or this morning, they ought to be covered in specks of gravel and dew.

"Lewis? Lewis!" Lady Holmes shouted. She sprinted the last few feet to where her brother lay and went to collapse at his side.

Clarence, dressed in a rumpled gray suit meant for hunting, wrapped her in his arms before she could throw herself down. "Stay, Violet. He breathes."

"Thank heavens," she cried, accepting the proffered handkerchief from a nearby gardener and pressing it to her face.

Violet. The softness in his voice echoed the careful way he held Lady Holmes. Both flayed another strip from my spirit. She might be pretending, but Clarence was not. After all, he'd proposed to her mere days ago, even if she hadn't accepted at the time. Who knows what they'd spoken of last night, what she'd been about to tell me. No doubt yet another of the secrets she was keeping from me.

I drew as close as I dared. A jagged cut over Lord Vernet's left temple crowned a large lump and bruised ring around that eye. Whether he'd been struck or hit his head as he fell, there was no likely object beside him to point to either conclusion. What had happened? For a moment, I saw again Mr. Dunning's look of rage after he overheard Lord Vernet call him a bastard.

"Dr. McNulty is on his way, as are the police," Clarence said. "We were just about to move Lewis inside."

Lady Holmes stiffened and gasped, making several of the men jump. I was too far away to note whatever she saw there, but she'd discovered some clue. "Clarence, where is your father? Is he alright? And Mr. Dunning?" she asked.

A lock of his blond waves fell onto his forehead as he leaned down to meet her eyes. "Safely abed. They were up drinking last night, swapping tales of their youth like two old sea dogs. I left them in the game room around midnight."

Midnight? That was just after Lord Vernet staggered down the hallway toward the game room stairs. What if Mr. Dunning had waited for him at the bottom and attacked him? We knew nothing of the man, his temperament, or his associates since he left Sterling Place.

Then again, if Clarence was walking the halls, he could have met Lord Vernet, who was so deep in his cups he might have said something offensive even to his close friend. Probably about Lady Holmes. Had he struck Lord Vernet in her defense? Was his meeting with Lady Holmes an attempt to give himself an alibi? Make it seem as though he were drunker than he was?

Nothing in his manner hinted he'd had any sort of encounter with Lady Holmes last night, let alone a drunken one, though the crescents under his eyes carried a deeper shadow than usual.

"You're shaking." Clarence wrapped his jacket over her shoulders. "Have Mrs. Nash make fresh tea," he ordered a houseboy on the outside of the circle of men.

"I'm just concerned for Lewis," Lady Holmes said. "Who could've done this?"

What had she said no more than a few minutes ago? *Lewis won't be a problem.* If Lady Holmes and Clarence hadn't met, but instead she had a heated argument with her brother, she might have lured him outside on the pretext of a private conversation only to decide he was best out of the way.

Lady Holmes' surprise had seemed genuine when Elsie came to fetch us, but then, so did her current distress. Yesterday, I trusted her with my freedom. Part of me still did. However, I was no longer sure which part was right. Was I just angry with her for withholding things from me or was she really a suspect?

At that moment, Lord Sterling, his tie askew, came around the corner with Inspector Goodwin in tow. The inspector's cheeks were flushed under his mustaches and sweat beaded his brow.

The men shuffled away from Lord Vernet to make room for the newcomers, and I tried to put as many of them between me and the inspector as I could.

"We were in luck. Goodwin was already on his way to discuss the missing horses, so he met our rider on the road and hurried along." Lord Sterling clapped him on the back. "What do you make of this mess? Can we move him?"

Inspector Goodwin glanced at Lady Holmes, still under Clarence's care, then bent to examine Lord Vernet and the surrounding ground. "The path is too firm to discover who else might have walked here. We can shift Lord Vernet indoors."

The men worked with a sheet of canvas and a door as a makeshift stretcher while the inspector stalked around the garden and examined the scene from different angles. When he was finished, he tugged at his cuffs and posed in full view of Lord Sterling.

"Sometime in the early morning hours, Lord Vernet

was struck with a blunt object by a left-handed person of a similar height." Everyone paused in their work to listen, and the inspector let his voice ring out. "This was not an accident. I will bring to bear every asset of Her Majesty's police force to catch the miscreant who committed such a heinous act. You can all rest assured your safety will not be compromised."

A murmur went up from those assembled, and Lord Sterling gazed at the inspector with approval.

"I don't speculate ahead of facts," he continued, "but it's well known Tom Mudd and his son Billy Mudd are left-handed. And they are still at large."

I scoffed inwardly. Billy was absolutely not left-handed and was nowhere close to Lord Vernet's height.

Goodwin gave the servants around Lord Vernet a hard stare. "We should take care to lock all—"

"My lord, my lord!" A balding man barreled around the corner of the mansion, wide cheeks ablaze. "There's another," he wheezed. "There's a body in the hedges outside the library." He pointed to the rear of the house, then plopped on a nearby bench. "It's Tom Mudd."

Chapter Forty

Inspector Goodwin's expression bounced between surprise, horror, and rage like the flash of a fish underwater. The shocked silence of the crowd broke into questioning murmurs. As four men carried Lord Vernet inside, the rest of us trailed after Inspector Goodwin to the rear of the manor, eager as ducklings. There, Tom's lower half sprawled across the path, his head mercifully hidden by the box hedge, one arm pointing in the air as though he were accusing the men peering down at him.

Lord Sterling frowned at the body and shook his head, jowls shuddering, while Inspector Goodwin spoke. Judging by the speed of his lips and the scarlet of his cheeks, he was doing his best to see light from the hole he'd dug with his self-important little speech about Lord Vernet's attacker.

Clarence spoke into Lady Holmes' ear and gestured for her to join me where I stood under an arbor wrapped in faded vines. When she reached me, I scanned from the second-floor windows to the ground in equal parts awe and horror.

"You dropped him out of the window?" I whispered.

The reek of Clarence's cigarettes wafted from the jacket she still wore. "It was the most convenient manner of getting him outside."

I stared at my feet. She hadn't said *unaided*, but the word echoed loud in the silence between us. Perhaps I should've insisted on helping her. She'd assumed the bulk of the risk, and together, we might have achieved more with the placement of the body.

"However, it still took a great deal of effort. I'm sure Billy couldn't have moved his father's body," Lady Holmes said.

"Replace *couldn't* with *wouldn't* and we're in agreement." I shook my head. "Coming here feels like a mistake. We're farther from answers than we've ever been."

Her thin face flushed. "Hudson, about last night. Clarence proposed again. He feels—"

"What did you see on the ground? Around Lord Vernet?" I blurted out. Clarence could choke on his feelings for all I cared.

She sighed. "A footprint bearing a deep slash across the left toes. We know it wasn't Tom, but Mr. Dunning's boots bear the same mark."

"I saw Mr. Dunning last night, outside his room," I said.

A houseboy sprinted around the corner, announcing the arrival of Dr. McNulty.

"So, there's a pocket of time where Dunning and Sterling weren't together, and it may not have been the only one. They both had opportunity." Lady Holmes hummed. "What if Sterling had a run-in with Lewis and hit him in defense of his brother or his son?"

I met her eyes, heart tumbling. "People will do anything to keep their family safe."

When she spoke, her voice sounded threadbare. "Sterling made it clear at dinner last night he considers Mr. Dunning family."

"Do you believe him?"

We'd fallen back into a pattern, examining the case and each other like a spiraling waltz. Dizziness swept over me.

Lady Holmes spoke as though delivering a verdict. "A long-lost brother returns? A petty thief ensures his son's employment? That son completes drawings of the estate, its collections, and inhabitants? Afterwards, they disappear with a pair of horses, only for Tom to show up murdered the next day? Hudson, I can hear your thoughts on this matter as clearly as if they were my own."

"You know, that's the first time you've made that claim and it actually turned out to be true." Her smile, its hidden warmth, threatened to undo me. My throat grew tight, and I blinked furiously. "Even if Dunning is who he claims to be, your brother's insult could still have provoked him, and if he isn't, then perhaps Lord Vernet discovered his true intent. If Dunning felt threatened ..."

"Almost time to play the concerned sister again," Lady Holmes said as Clarence peeled off from the group and approached us. "Hudson, what you said earlier, I never meant to put you in danger. While we are apart, promise me you'll be careful."

Before I could refuse, she joined Clarence on the path. They were well matched in height and coloring with the bearing of a lord and lady striding across their seven hundred acres. The thought crumbled to ashes on my tongue. I couldn't stand it any longer.

However, as I started to make my way inside, Inspector Goodwin stopped me.

"I didn't expect to find my fiancée here." He glowered at me as though I were a rambunctious pup. "Come with me."

There were few things I wanted less, but could see no good way out of it, so I followed him back to the withered arbor where I'd stood with Lady Holmes.

As I turned to him, my ankle protested, and I stumbled forward. He caught me with both hands. "Are you hurt?"

I blushed. "I stepped wrong running down the stairs on our way to see to Lord Vernet."

He gestured for me to take a seat on a nearby stone bench and wedged himself onto the seat beside me. Both too close and too large, I itched to move away, but I refused to let him know he unsettled me.

"Why are you out here?" he asked.

If he was going to ask stupid questions, he was going to get stupid answers. "Attending Lady Holmes."

"This isn't the place for a lady."

I wasn't sure he was talking about Lady Holmes anymore, but I ignored his insinuation. "Her brother was injured."

"I meant this entire situation." Goodwin watched the men milling around the perimeter he'd set up surrounding Tom's body.

"We came to Sterling Place on Lord Vernet's invitation."

Goodwin tipped his head. "Even though Lady Holmes hasn't finished her mourning period yet?"

"That's not my decision." She could defend her own actions.

The inspector looked thoughtful, scratching at the long whiskers on either side of his face. He removed his cap, placed it on his knee, and moved his hand closer to mine. "Katy, I'll admit it looks bad to have my fiancée wrapped up in this, but if you're out of your depth, I can help you."

I hated myself while I considered it. Goodwin was well placed to protect me and my family, and if I married him, I could expect a safe life so long as I toed the line. I would do anything for my family, but not until I was out of other options. "Reggie, when was the last time you saw my father?"

For a moment I was worried he would hurt me again, but he only narrowed his eyes. "When was the last time you saw Tom Mudd?"

"I didn't even know he was in the area until one of the servants here mentioned it." However, Goodwin had known for weeks. "Did no one tell you?"

Gratifying red patches colored his cheeks. A policeman really ought to know how to lie better. "Judging by the condition of the body and its positioning, someone moved it here." His voice grew stern. "Anything you're not telling me?"

"That depends. Do you know anything you're not telling me about my father's death?"

No matter what came next, I didn't regret speaking. None of this was fair. Da shot and Sterling Place still standing, his murderer roaming free. Ma, Goodwin, Lady Holmes—everyone parceling out information to me like scraps of food to a child at the poorhouse, as though that information didn't already belong to me. I tipped my chin up to Goodwin's open-mouthed stare, daring him to deny what I'd seen with my own eyes just that morning—his name in the file, his hands all over my father's case.

Instead, he shook his head. "It must break your mother's heart to see your mind twisted with grief, making a spectacle of yourself. Why would you do this to her? Dredge all that up again for nothing?" He jammed his helmet back on. "Keep your head down, Katy, and get a different job. Or better yet, find a husband who can support you as he should. Not cart you off to a strange city and make you earn your keep."

I thrust to my feet, eyes straight ahead. "John was worth a thousand of you, and you've always known it. Men like you scrabble for every scrap of borrowed power you can find until all you have are masters. Goodbye, Reggie. If you wish to speak with me further, you can do so through my employer."

Chapter Forty-One

INSIDE, STERLING PLACE HAD GROWN QUIET. However, this silence held no peace. It was the skillful waiting of an animal about to pounce.

One thing was clear: Lady Holmes and I should make our escape before Sterling Place caught us by the tail. I wasn't sure what we still were—partners, more, or nothing at all—but she was the closest thing I had to an ally. I needed to find her.

The few staff inside headed toward the dining room. I turned to follow, but Mr. Dunning exited from Lord Sterling's study. I expected Lord Sterling to come out as well, but Mr. Dunning simply hurried away toward the dining room. Puzzled, I followed suit.

Lord Sterling met him at the threshold. "Come in and have some breakfast. Can't face this mess on an empty stomach."

"Why all the fuss this morning?" Dunning asked.

"Remember the horse thief I told you about?"

I would swear Mr. Dunning's hands twitched before he

thrust them into his pockets. "Yes, of course."

"The man's body showed up on the grounds this morning. And Vernet had a bit of an accident or something," Lord Sterling said.

The men's voices faded as Mr. Dunning closed the dining room door behind him.

A squeak came from down the hall. I peered into the shadows there, where a black gown and cap over dark curls were just visible.

"Elsie?" I whispered.

She waved me forward. "Miss, it's so exciting." With a finger to her lips, she clasped my hand and drew me down a side corridor.

Was this about Billy? Had she remembered something else he'd said, some clue to—

Lady Holmes. My entire body vibrated as I froze in place, staring at her wrapped in Clarence's embrace. My feet fixed in place like tree roots. I stood in the east wing of Sterling Place for moments that felt like days. I might have stared across a sunbeam for eons, watching Clarence's blond head as it bent so he could embrace Lady Holmes. Her arms, still clad in his jacket, snaked around his broad back. Clarence. Lady Holmes. I only needed a lightning flash to understand what I saw, but I still couldn't make sense of it. Anyone would wish to kiss her full lips, but she wasn't supposed to kiss them back. That was my—

I turned and ran.

Hounds at my heels, I didn't stop until a jolt in my ankle brought me up short. I was near the side door I'd come through minutes ago. Back when I hadn't known Sterling Place was about to steal something else from me. Where was I going? Where *could* I go?

Not outside with the men and the police. Not downstairs as a servant. Not in the dining room as a guest. Not even upstairs in the private space where Lady Holmes had laid down her armor long enough to be Violet.

At least, so I had believed.

Now, I knew the truth. This place and everything it stood for would take everything I loved until I had nothing left. I should run away and cower like a hare in the grass, hoping its sharp eyes and teeth would pass me over this time.

No one expected the hare to fight back. Surprise was the only advantage left to me. I would leverage it to pry this place apart, along with all its secrets, until it released everything it stole. Da, Billy, my memories, and my heart.

At the gleaming door of Lord Sterling's study, I let myself inside. I'd dusted here often as a housemaid, so I could bypass the walls crammed with potted plants, family portraits, and polished brass, heading instead for the expansive desk hulking across from the windows.

Newspapers, a small pile of outgoing mail, and an unfinished letter cluttered its surface. The letter was a short note addressed to Lord Sterling's London solicitors referencing a recent change to his will. Unfortunately, it didn't describe the change.

Despite the mess, something felt out of place. Three fountain pens, a box filled with stationery, a few sheets of blotting paper, paper-wrapped lemon drops, *The Eustace Diamonds* by Trollope, a dirty cup and saucer, and a full ashtray. Nothing unusual.

Then it struck me; the blotting paper was blank. Crisp and new, without even a test stroke. Lord Sterling was halfway through his letter, and there were four more he'd already finished and addressed. He would've blotted the page at least once. A servant might have tidied away a full sheet of blotting paper, but if someone cleaned the desk, they would've emptied the ashtray and removed the dirty china. Then again, what purpose could used blotting paper serve? Unless someone wanted to find out what Lord Sterling had written. Or to hide it.

I tugged at the desk drawers. The first three on the left side were locked, as well as the top two on the right. However, the bottom right drawer slid open.

There, sitting on top of a row of file folders, was a telegram. I let out a gasp, breath stolen. This one also displayed John's forged signature.

```
Andrew Dunning legitimate seventh earl of
Sterling STOP £7,000 to keep your secret
STOP Think of your family STOP Telegram
to follow with instructions STOP
```

I sank to my knees beside the drawer. Andrew Dunning legitimate? That tinder would set Sterling Place ablaze. Had Dunning just snuck in here and left this telegram? But if so, how were they forging John's name? He and Tom bore the same wear mark on their shoes. They could've been working together, perhaps double-crossed each other.

The rumble of men's voices came from outside the study door. I shoved the drawer closed, stuffed myself into the knee gap under the desk, and dragged my skirts in after me, the blackmail telegram in hand.

A second later the door swung open, and the shoes of

two men appeared in the crack between desk and floor.

Lord Sterling's deep voice made the walls of the desk vibrate. "What am I paying you for then, eh?"

"This is nothing but a wrinkle. I just need a little more time," Inspector Goodwin said.

"It's nearly as bad as what happened with that groom years ago. But you handled that for me, so I'm trusting you to handle this as well." Lord Sterling huffed. "With my upcoming nomination, this isn't a good time. Any sign of the boy?"

My thoughts were as thick as old treacle. Were they talking about Da? Did Lord Sterling kill him? And had Reggie covered it up?

"Hiding in the hills is the likeliest, though he could've hopped a train. If he gave up the horses—"

"That's your department, Goodwin. Figure it out. Now, I've been in touch with my solicitors about the estate. Nothing's finished yet, but I plan to see Dunning has what he needs. It's not too late to do right by him."

"It is, as you said, a precarious time, and I have more avenues to investigate in his background—"

"Careful, you're speaking about my brother." Lord Sterling's tone held all his authority. "I knew from the moment I read his letter. Why, the things he remembers, how we've fallen back in with each other—we might as well be boys again. He spent his life unaware of the circumstances of his birth, but I never forgot him. I was only five when he left, and I've always wanted to seek him out."

If that's what Lord Sterling truly thought, then he must not have seen the telegram yet. I held my breath, heart racing.

"My lord, I know he presented you with what appeared

to be letters from your father to his mother, but they might be skilled forgeries," Goodwin said.

"Do you think me a child?" Lord Sterling's tone sharpened. "Complete whatever investigations you want. I recognize my father's handwriting. I hear his voice in those letters and the truth in Andrew's words. I'll not let my brother suffer under your mistrust or my political aspirations."

If the inspector knew about Mr. Dunning's forged telegram blanks, the scratch on his shoes, the rage I'd glimpsed on his face when Lord Vernet disparaged him, he never would have agreed. And if he didn't know about those things, what else was he missing?

As though Lord Sterling read my thoughts, he asked, "What's happening with Vernet? Do you think this Mudd fellow hit him?"

"Judging by the condition of the body, Mudd's been dead for over a day."

"Hmm, could Vernet have tripped and fallen, then? He was drunk as the devil last night."

"Is that what you want me to say, my lord? I could take measurements and announce I was mistaken in my earlier assessment."

My skin buzzed as though I'd touched the wrong wire. Reggie Goodwin was a power-hungry little toad, but was he so in Lord Sterling's pockets that the truth had become immaterial?

"No, after what everyone heard you say, it's probably best to poke around. Could've been Mudd's son, though. Seems a likely fit."

"You may be proven correct, sir. I recovered evidence from Mudd's pockets, several forged telegram blanks matching a fraudulent telegram he sent weeks ago."

My stomach dropped like a stone down a well. Lady Holmes had searched Tom's pockets, and they'd been empty. Did someone put telegrams on the body between last night and this morning? Did they match the one I was holding? Or was Goodwin lying? He could claim to have found the crown jewels in Tom's pockets and no one would be able to prove him wrong.

"How do you know they're forged?" Lord Sterling asked.

A cold and certain dread crept over me.

"The signature is that of a deceased clerk. We've known for some time to be on the lookout for it. In fact, we'll be putting our hands on the forger shortly."

"The way able-bodied men cheat the system rather than work for a day's wages. It's a drain on society. That's rather good. I should write that down," Lord Sterling said as he approached the desk.

My heart pounded so hard it seemed to echo off the walls of the desk all around me.

The door clicked open, and Lord Sterling stopped. "Violet? Clarence? Everything alright with Vernet?"

"He hasn't awoken yet, but Dr. McNulty is hopeful," Clarence said. "However, there's something I believe all of you need to hear."

The dark swath of Lady Holmes' skirts brushed the neat cuffs of Clarence's slacks, and I tried to banish the glimpse I'd had of the two of them entangled.

"Last night, I ran into Vernet wandering near the end of this hallway. He was muttering something about having proof, but he was so drunk at the time, I didn't pay it any mind," Clarence said apologetically. "I thought he was referring to drinking more alcohol, and I tried to encourage him to retire. He brushed me aside, saying he needed to leave someone a message so he could pay his debts. I don't know what he meant, but in light of this morning's discovery, I thought it best to … well, I thought it might be connected. He likes to bet on horses, and perhaps he fell in with an unsavory crowd?"

I bit my lip. Every muscle screaming at me to run. Lord Vernet must have been referring to the forged telegram. The one clutched in my hands.

"I'm stricken that my brother might be involved in any of this," Lady Holmes said. "However, if Lewis was near this room, he might have used the writing supplies in here for this message. Lord Sterling, may we examine your desk?"

Chapter Forty-Two

FOR THE LAST SIX MONTHS, I THOUGHT MY MOURNING clothes had made me invisible. But I'd been wrong. Instead, I was cipher and balefire for those I'd encountered, a conspicuous vessel forced to receive their pity, their shared experience, even their avoidance. Not invisible, but ignored. Everyone had seen me and my pain, but they'd chosen to look the other way. If only that would happen now.

I hunched under the desk while four pairs of feet approached, circling the meager walls guarding me from my doom.

"I was working here yesterday evening, so things are a mess," Lord Sterling said. The whisper of shuffling papers and the clink of china came from above. "Odd, my blotting sheet's blank, but I didn't change it."

"You're sure you used it, Father?" Clarence asked.

"Yes, because I left Simmons in town and was going to have to change the damn thing myself."

"If Lord Vernet wrote something here and used the blotting sheet, he might've removed both at the same time,"

Goodwin suggested.

On my right, Lady Holmes bent to the floor, so close I could've touched her. "There's nothing in the wastebasket. Is anything missing from your desk?"

If I slid the telegram under the bottom of the desk, she could pretend to have found it on the floor and create some way for me to escape. Before I could, the chair beside me scraped backward over the rug.

"My memory's not what it used to be, but perhaps if I sit in my usual position, anything odd will jump out at me," Lord Sterling said as he came into full view. In the space of several eons, we locked eyes. His weathered face took on an almost comical note of surprise, all shifting eyebrows and forehead trenches. "Who are you?" he asked.

I opened my mouth, but nothing came out. Footsteps thundered across the floor as everyone sprang to see. Goodwin frowned and Clarence seemed confused, but a fiery look flared in Lady Holmes' eyes before the shutters clamped down.

"Get out of there and explain yourself at once," Lord Sterling said.

My hands shook so hard the ransom note rattled as if in a strong breeze. "I didn't mean to intrude." I unwound myself and threw a wild look at Lady Holmes, but her expression remained blank.

Clarence ripped the paper from my hands, his handsome face crumpling as he read. "What the devil is this?"

"Isn't she your maid, Lady Holmes?" Inspector Goodwin asked, and I glared at him.

Lady Holmes examined the paper in Clarence's hands. "I hired Hudson last week. As you well know, Inspector."

Hope bounded in my chest like a fish breaking the surface of the water. "Lady Holmes can vouch for me. This is all a misunderstanding—" I tried to go on, but she spoke over me, and the others acted as though I hadn't spoken at all.

"Of course, I thought she was a woman of good character based on your recommendation; however I see now we were both misled." She took a step closer to Clarence. "I dismiss her from my employ, effective immediately."

My soaring hopes crashed so hard it jarred my teeth.

Inspector Goodwin spared me one sorrowful glance, then turned to Lord Sterling. "Do you wish to press charges, my lord?"

He started a little. "Charges? On what grounds?"

"This woman is a known associate of Billy Mudd. She's also the forgery suspect I spoke to you about just now. Her late husband's signature is on the other forged telegrams as well as this one trying to blackmail you. Consistent with an eyewitness statement, she bears the same ankle injury as a suspect seen with Tom Mudd shortly before his death. She and Lord Vernet were also seen arguing last night, and I wouldn't be surprised if she was the one who struck him. We need to take her into custody immediately."

"God, what an awful morning it's been." Lord Sterling waved at the inspector. "Do whatever you think's best."

Panic washed over me in a brutal wave, and I gripped the edge of the desk. Each breath came painfully short, my corset cutting into my ribs. Goodwin put a large hand over my shoulder and marched me out of the study. My last glimpse was of Lady Holmes once again locked in Clarence's embrace.

I didn't look up again.

Head down while Mrs. Nash searched me and my clothing. Head down while I was loaded into a wagon for the long drive back to town. Head down while Inspector Goodwin wrapped my arm in an iron grip, digging into the bruises he'd left. The ones Lady Holmes had vowed to avenge. The list of her betrayals grew ever longer.

It wasn't until the inspector led me into the police station that I returned to the world. The ghost of Lady Holmes and my former self met me at every point. Only two days ago, I'd walked through the back door of the station with Lady Holmes, hope clutched to my chest again. We had held true power in our hands for once, determining our own destinies based on our desires—for truth, for justice, for each other.

Without a word, Goodwin led me to the last cell, past four other empty ones, as though the passageway were an oubliette and I was to be forgotten.

"I did warn you, Katy," he said just before the barred door clanged shut behind me.

I winced at the scrape of the key in the lock.

Thanks to the newness of the building and Mrs. Wakefield's labor, the cell was passably clean. The only dirty thing was me.

My knees buckled, and I sank onto the thin cot.

When I first stood outside the gates of Musgrave Hall, I thought Lady Holmes was a fool. Stupid enough to hire a housekeeper who fell for a telegram fraud scheme. But I'd fallen for a scheme of even bigger proportions. One where Lady Holmes betrayed me, on purpose.

Could I blame her? If her money troubles were as severe as Lewis described, how could she sacrifice a marriage offer from Clarence Sterling? If it meant protecting my family, I might've done the same.

Except I hadn't.

Inspector Goodwin made his own offer clear this morning, and I turned him down like the naive fool I was. Blinded by affection and the promise of hope, I let myself borrow some of Lady Holmes' seeming invincibility. She'd warned me the power wasn't hers, could never be hers. Not to own and certainly not to give.

Minutes dragged themselves past my cell. Inside, time passed with its teeth and claws bared. My thoughts spiraled into the hours, dark as the long shadows creeping up the sides of the jail as the sun sank below the horizon. At some point, the door of my cell clanged, and a meal was thrust inside. Too exhausted to weep or pull the short blanket over me, I curled around my broken heart and shivered as my past hunted me.

Those I loved, dead before their time. Every future I tried to build, smashed. I'd twisted on the end of this rope for too long, wishing for someone to come and save me. But here I was waiting again, alone in a small dark room. Just as I'd been that endless night, keeping vigil beside John's body. Sometimes I wondered if I never really left that room. If I'd borne witness to not only his destruction but mine as well.

I'd already lost so much. How could I survive the rawness of it? Forcing me to cut away pieces of myself until there was nothing left.

When Lady Holmes and I became partners, I allowed myself the luxury of hope. That I could provide for my family, teach my siblings a trade and make sure they grew hale and well. Keep Ma from working until her bones ached, save Billy, and have a job where I made a difference. That I might love again. Most recently, that I could win justice for Da. Success, happiness, fulfillment—they hinged on that dirtiest of all ideas. Nothing could bring one lower than hope.

I dared to believe again, and I lost everything.

I had failed us all.

Silence and darkness filled the room as night swept in.

Chapter Forty-Three

THE RATTLE OF THE CELL DOOR YANKED ME FROM an uneasy sleep.

"You won't be sleeping at the crown's expense tonight. You're free to go, Mrs. Hudson."

Assuming the voice was yet another phantom of my fevered mind, I didn't move.

A hand clamped onto my shoulder. "Did you not hear me? You're free to go."

I stared up into the youthful face of Constable Marks. My tongue refused to move, and he thrust a stale cup of water into my hands. After a deep drink, I stood and cleared my throat. "Why am I being released?"

It felt wrong to question what I'd wished for so desperately, but I needed to make sure it wasn't a cruel joke.

He shook his head. "Your patron convinced Lord Sterling and the inspector that you were innocent."

Lady Holmes? Perhaps she had Clarence free me as an engagement present.

The constable led me to the door of the station. "Now,

you behave, Mrs. Hudson, and we won't see you here again."

He shut the door behind me as I stood on the steps, blinking against the rain falling through the chilly morning air. It was so beautiful out here, I could have swallowed Sherrinford whole. I wanted to sprint for home. However, hunger set my legs trembling. Determined not to hope, I forced myself to walk, my thoughts as numb as my feelings.

Within minutes, I reached our gate and for the first time since my arrest, I let out a terrified sob. I clamped a hand to my mouth, lest anyone else hear, and allowed myself a few minutes of silent tears.

Before I quite finished, Oliver opened the door, shouting, "Ma, Ma! Katy's here!"

Moisture rolled down my hair and dress, and I must have looked a fright after two days without changing my clothes or washing myself, but Oliver ran down the path and threw his thin arms around my waist, holding me like iron. Seconds later, another tiny body slammed into me, then another. Rosie and Louise started talking at the same time, and when Elizabeth joined them in the scrum it nearly toppled us all over.

"Thank the Lord," Ma said, from the doorway. "Get in here, all of you."

Once I was inside, and after I'd been embraced and kissed at least several dozen times, Ma plopped me on the sofa next to Frances with blankets, food, and something hot to drink. Then she sent the children to play in the girls' room.

"Your trunk arrived yesterday without a word of where you were," Ma said. With purple smudges under her eyes and deep lines around her mouth, she didn't look in any better shape than me.

Frances grasped my hand. "What happened, Katy?"

I couldn't look at Frances while I told her about Tom and how Billy was the main suspect in his death. But in fits and starts, I unraveled the story. Our discoveries, the betrayal, my failure—everything except my feelings and the truth about Da.

When I stopped to drain my cup, Ma frowned and poured me more tea, but Frances patted my hand. "So my Billy's still out there. He might be fine." Her voice quavered.

"I'm so sorry. I failed you. I failed everyone." Despair curdled in my throat.

"Katy, you put your heart and soul into this investigation," Ma said. "You barely made it back to us."

"You don't understand. There's more. I ... I lost my one and only chance to get justice for Da. He didn't die in an accident at the stables. Someone at Sterling Place shot him."

I thrust to my feet and flung myself down at my trunk tucked into the corner of the room. "Look, I can prove it. I have Da's case file." As I flipped open the locks, I braced myself for their disbelief, their disappointment, but they only watched me sadly. Inside, each of the doors on the compartments John had built me were shut tight, and my things were folded and packed as though someone had removed each item then taken great care in organizing them. On top of it all lay the slim volume of *The Victoria Regia,* just as I had last placed it.

But the file was gone. Lady Holmes wouldn't even let me have this one thing.

I sat back on my heels. "I don't understand. She must have taken it."

My voice broke, and Ma gathered me up from the floor, leading me back to the sofa.

Frances cleared her throat and stared at the side of Ma's face. "Tell her," she said, voice sharp as a needle.

I sniffed. "Tell me what?"

Ma pressed her lips together. "I know. I've always known about Da. Remember, they brought his body back to us, and Frances helped me get him ready. We saw the bullet wound. We knew what killed him."

Of course. Ma and Frances dealt with Da's body, and I'd been grateful for their sacrifice all these years. Why hadn't I seen the truth?

I couldn't feel my hands. "And the police?"

Frances just shook her head and Ma shrugged. "The police don't work for people like us. They came around to the house, but it was to offer us a bribe from Lord Sterling. To pay for our silence."

"You took it?" The sorrow in my voice softened the accusation.

"Of course she did." Frances put a hand on Ma's shoulder. "I would've done the same."

Ma covered Frances' hand. "That money paid for the down payment on this cottage, for food before we found work, for your wedding." A lance of guilt pierced my stomach. "So, you see, Katy, you didn't fail your father any more than I did. He would've wanted me to take the money, to see you kids safe with a good home. It's all either of us ever wanted."

I wiped the fresh tears from my cheeks, and Ma wrapped me in a fierce hug. "I didn't hope for justice—it wouldn't bring your father back. The best I could hope for was to survive it."

There was that awful word again, hope. Ma rubbed my back while I cried as though I'd lost Da anew, and I allowed myself to melt into her familiar shape.

"There, there, Katy Bee. Shhh … you've had a time of it. I love you so much, and we're bursting with pride for you. We all are. Now, why don't you go wash your face at the pump, and I'll scoot the kids out of the bedroom so you can have a nap," Ma said and handed me a handkerchief from her apron.

I plodded through the kitchen, wiping my face. Outside, the rain had turned to mist, and it cooled my overheated cheeks. My heart had grown too swollen to fit inside the paltry cage of my chest. Ma and Frances hadn't been disappointed in me. They'd loved me enough to carry the terrible burden of this knowledge all these years, and to share their guilt with me so I needn't be alone anymore.

The familiar squeak of the pump came from around the corner, and I pushed my soggy hair from my forehead. I didn't relish seeing any of our neighbors right now, but when I rounded the fence, I stood face to face with the freckled cheeks of my brother Ralph.

He had his foot propped on the low wall around the pump, pant leg pulled up to his knee, washing his leg with a bucket of water. When he saw me, he dropped it down and put his foot on the ground, but not before I'd spied the angry red skin peppering his leg.

"You're back," he said.

"Why aren't you at work?"

"What? Oh, all the guests left the inn to travel farther on, trying to find fair weather to see the eclipse today. So no business." His smile didn't quite land.

I pushed away the thought of Lady Holmes and Clarence ensconced in a train carriage, headed to find the sun, and focused on Ralph. "What happened to your leg?" I asked, my tiredness replaced by an anxious thrumming in my fingertips.

"Nothing. Anyway, Ma needed some water." He reached for the bucket, but as he bent, I dove for his pants cuff. I yanked the material up and locked my hand around his ankle. He screamed and thrashed, knocking the bucket over. I didn't let go even as the water soaked the hem of my skirts.

"Ow! Blazes, Katy! What are you doing?"

One of the blisters on his skin popped, and the warm liquid oozed over my hand. "Why do you have the same rash as Eddie Beale? What've you been up to, Ralph Bunting?"

He tried to dance away but I held fast. "Ow, ow, let go and I'll tell you!"

I grabbed his wrist, only then releasing his leg. "Have you been sneaking out together? What are you up to?"

A pinched look overtook his face, so like Da's, and I read the truth there. Clues and details rose from the churning morass of my thoughts to form one solid picture. A sketch Billy made of the three of them—Billy, Eddie, and Ralph fishing together at the river. Something they'd done often after school, but now each worked and they never had the time. In that sketch, they hadn't been school children, though. They had the stature and serious faces of young men.

"Damn everything. You know where Billy is, don't you? You've known this whole time! You've been hiding him since he left Sterling Place."

When he didn't answer me, I gave his arm a shake and

hissed. "I spent last night in jail over this."

Shock arched his eyes and lips into circles. "Katy, you can't tell anyone. You have to promise—"

"I'll do no such thing. Billy's in grave danger. Remember what Da used to say? We don't stand around. We help." I stared into Ralph's dark brown eyes, willing him not to fight me on something, just once. Maybe I'd messed everything up, lost my partner, missed the most obvious of clues, failed to get justice for Da, but I could still do one thing. I could save Billy. I just needed Ralph to trust me.

After a long moment, the tension went out of his arm.

I dropped his wrist and started back through our yard. "Let's go tell Ma and Frances where we're headed. You lead the way, and I'll tell you why Billy will be as good as dead if someone else finds him first."

CHAPTER FORTY-FOUR

THE RAIN FOLLOWED RALPH AND ME THROUGH THE town. As we veered onto the river path, it pecked at the oil cloth of our umbrellas and dimpled the surface of the water. It stirred up the scent of decaying plants and earth under our feet. My ankle complained at the long walk but lying overnight in the cell had forced me to rest, and it was mostly healed.

Ralph shook his head, his damp brown locks skating over his forehead. "She let you go to jail? For something you didn't do?"

Feelings choked my throat so that I could only nod.

"The stinking coward." Ralph's deep scowl was a salve to my hurt feelings.

I hadn't told him about Da's murder. I couldn't. For the same reasons Ma didn't—love, not wanting to see the hurt on his face. However, my reasons also aligned with those of Lady Holmes—so I could depend on Ralph and better find Billy.

"When did John tell you about this barn?" I asked.

"The Christmas right after you got married. When John's

cousin sold their family farm to Mr. Beale, and John told us how he used to play with his cousins in an old barn there, near the river. One day last summer, when the fish weren't biting, me and Eddie and Billy wandered down that way until we found it." Ralph helped me cross the stile marking the boundary between the Beale property and the old Hudson farm. "Off by itself behind some trees, we set it up as a den. The only problem was Mr. Beale wanted to expand the fields, so Eddie did what he had to."

I snorted. "Meaning he ripped out the marrow seedlings on the opposite side of the farm to keep his da busy."

Ralph grinned. "Eddie's a crack at sneaking about. Not like me and Billy. Alfie caught us on our way there a few times, even saw me bringing food and stuff to Billy a couple of days ago. But he's a decent sort. Didn't mention it."

Alfie was far too comfortable keeping my brother's secrets from me. I'd have to have a long talk with him about it for the future.

"Still paid a price though." Ralph gestured at his ankles. "There're patches of wild parsnips around the farm, and in the dark they're hard to miss. You don't even know you've got any on you till the sun hits the spots and they bubble up all nasty like." Ralph winced.

"There's a cream ..."

A line of trees and scrub bushes materialized out of the mist, the dim outline of a building just beyond. It was a small old barn, listing to one side, weathered boards mottled with green and gray lichen.

Ralph put his hands to his lips and gave the call of a wood pigeon. It brought gooseflesh to my arms, as though he might raise more than just Billy from the moldering boards.

He frowned. "He's not answering." Before I could hold him back, Ralph took off toward the barn.

"Wait!" I called, voice muffled by the fog.

I hoisted my leaden skirts and ran after him. They snagged on some thorns as I waded through the bushes, and Ralph made it to the building ahead of me, disappearing inside. I found him just beyond the door and opened my mouth to scold him for being reckless, but my words cut out as though someone had shut off my battery.

The bottom level of the barn was a single room, and it was darker in here with only one window. In the center, crates and boards served as a makeshift table, littered with a pail, a crust of bread, and a cracked pitcher. Though relatively clean, the damp lingered, stinking of rotten fish and river mud. A blanket over a pile of straw huddled in the driest corner. Above it, tucked into the grooves of the old boards or hanging from the rusty nails, were sketches covering the far wall.

I stumbled closer in the dim light, open-mouthed. Elsie, her big eyes crinkled in laughter. Then Lord Sterling, jowls shadowed like an old hunting dog. Inspector Goodwin straightening his cuffs, Mrs. Nash looking stern, the entrance hall at Sterling Place. There were Clarence, Andrew Dunning, and Tom—his face stretched in rage in one drawing and horror in another. All the characters marched across the wall, the events of the past few weeks in pictures, clear as if I'd been there.

Billy was in none of them and all of them at once. These were through his eyes, his memories. I felt his delight, his worry, his fear. Frances looked down from the largest piece of paper, stuck onto a nail right beside the bedding where

Billy could comfort himself with his mother's smile as he fell asleep. My heart cracked and I rubbed at the pain there.

"I'm so sorry, Billy," I murmured.

Ralph poked around the room. "I don't understand. All his stuff's here. Maybe he's upstairs."

"How do you get up there?"

"There's a ladder attached to the wall outside," Ralph said before turning and dashing back the way we'd come in.

I didn't like to try my ankle and rain-laden skirts against a rickety ladder, so I didn't follow. His footsteps faded, leaving me with the oppressive quiet. The rain had lightened, falling in uneven drops like someone spelling out a faltering message in Morse Code.

There was little else of Billy in this room, and I soon returned to the wall of sketches. Eddie and Ralph must have pilfered paper and pencils for Billy to use because one drawing shared a page with an advertisement for seeds and several others were receipts from The Four Hounds. A corner of paper extended beyond the others, and there, tucked behind it was a small sketch I'd missed the first time.

My finger shook as I moved the covering page aside and stared at the gruesome scene before me. Tom Mudd, dead, sprawled across rough wooden boards. Had Billy seen his father's body? His murder?

The sheet of foolscap next to my hand was covered in a close-up of Andrew Dunning's face wearing a jovial smile. The paper fluttered as though blown by an errant breeze through one of the building's many cracks. I snatched my hand back. There was no wind.

I ripped the page away. Behind was a narrow split and through it, the unmistakable eyes of Billy Mudd.

CHAPTER FORTY-FIVE

FROM THE MOMENT I SAW FRANCES OUTSIDE THE police station, I'd burned, needing to find Billy. Ahead of Lady Holmes, ahead of whoever pursued him, ahead of my own demons for once—I'd finally found him.

"Billy"—I wedged my fingers into the gap and pried the board away—"it's only us. We're here to save you. You're safe now."

He spilled out of the narrow space, face dirty and thin, clouded with anger. "They'll kill me! Just like they killed my da and yours."

The walls of the small room were too close. My chest clenched. "Who?" I whispered, faint as the rain outside.

The door creaked open. "He's in here, Ralph," I said, unable to look away.

"Well, I'll be damned," a man said from behind me. "Goodwin was right. He said if we let you out of jail, you'd lead us right to the boy."

Billy shrank against the wall, but I spun, putting myself between him and Clarence Sterling.

"Run, Billy," I whispered, but Clarence heard me.

He raised his arm and pointed a long-barreled pistol at us. "No one's going anywhere."

"What are you doing here?" I asked, hoping to stall Clarence long enough to give Ralph a chance to run for help, assuming Clarence hadn't already hurt him.

"Oh, Billy understands, don't you, boy?" Clarence smiled knowingly.

He didn't move, but his breath quickened.

I tried to shield him with my broad skirts. "What does Lord Sterling want with Billy?"

"That old simpleton?" Clarence's handsome face clouded. "He invited Dunning to come and stay with us, swallowing that huckster's story like a worm on a hook. Goodwin and I've been running around the countryside, up at all hours, trying to save my father from himself."

Clarence did look exhausted, the fine lines around his eyes deepening the shadows there.

I shook my head, trying to clear it. Not Lord Sterling? Clarence and Goodwin? As I slid the men into the holes in the case, everything shifted. Pieces of the investigation popped across my vision, lightning over distant hills, a thief's lantern, the snap of a match into flame.

"It was you. You wrote the forged telegram. You killed Tom and moved his body to Musgrave Hall," I said, willing him to hold my gaze, to ignore Billy.

Clarence shrugged. "I take credit for the first two, but the third was all Goodwin's ingenuity. The things he said after the body showed up back at Sterling Place, well, it's not for the ears of a lady. When Goodwin gets here, he'll be glad to dispose of you two and see the end of this, truly. His nerves are shot."

A whisper of movement came from outside just as the rain started up again. Ralph couldn't be back with help so soon. Unless he never left. A jolt of fear coursed through my veins. Something tapped on the barn wall behind me, then again, this time shorter. Followed by a repeat of the first. As taut as I was with fear, the familiar even pace caught another part of my mind. One that worked without my thinking.

KTB STOP Wait five min then run for door STOP Trust me STOP LH

Lady Holmes was here? My heart and brain coiled, ready to explode. It might have been nothing but my own imaginings. And even if it wasn't, five minutes was an eternity to spin a story for Clarence. I thought I understood how it all fitted together; still, I wasn't Lady Holmes, so I wasn't sure. But I didn't have to be right. Guesses took time, and so long as Clarence thought he had the upper hand, he might still give me what I needed.

Through all my racing thoughts, no matter how I flogged it back, hope sprang forward like a horse too long in the stable.

"Dispose of us?" I said, unable to keep my voice from shaking. "You mean arrest us?" The light in the spare room seemed to dim.

"Perhaps." Clarence sniffed. "Goodwin's cleaned up more than one mess for me. He's a practical man. Knows the value of a pound in the right hand or a word in the right ear. It was his idea to steal Father's horses and blame it on Tom and Billy. Gave us a reason to shoot at them. So, who knows? Maybe he'll claim you two shot each other over the loot. Dishonor among thieves."

"The way you shot Tom, you mean?"

Clarence grinned like an open grave. "You've been talking to the boy. Listen, Tom showed up claiming he possessed a marriage certificate between Dunning's mother and my grandfather, one that predated my grandparents' marriage." The tip of his gun sagged. "If my father was illegitimate, we would lose everything. And over what? A dead man who couldn't keep his lust in check? A greedy, lying thief? I couldn't risk it. My debts are … well, let's just say they're deep."

I raised my hands, palms out. "I don't think Dunning is legitimate. He's a forger Tom worked with. Those telegram blanks were all fake. He probably faked any marriage certificate as well, if it really exists."

Clarence shook his head, and the pistol dipped even lower. "He possessed all sorts of real memories about my family and the estate."

I nodded slowly as though figuring things out and not preserving precious seconds. "Tom fed him details about Sterling Place that Tom remembered from when he was employed there. Dogs' names, the way the rooms were decorated, who worked there, what the older family members were like. He used Billy to get information, too, used his drawings to tutor Dunning and make him a convincing fake. Even used him to steal old letters of your grandfather's." I was casting guesses like they were seeds, but I would feed Clarence every detail if it meant another moment of life.

"Billy was an unwilling participant. He thought he was working, making money for his family, that his father was back in his life, that he cared about him for once. When he found out Tom used him, he burned the drawings and ripped up the ones at his home. Right, Billy?"

The lad jerked as though I'd stung him. "Yes, I did. When I wouldn't give him any more drawings, Da hit me and said he didn't need a useless son like me anyway. He knew I had more drawings at home, though, just not where. I'd hidden them under the boards so Ma wouldn't ask any questions. Da and Mr. Dunning were planning to go and look for them, but I got there first and ripped them up." The satisfaction in his voice was so clear he must not know they'd taken out their anger on Frances as well as the rest of his artwork when they broke in.

Clarence frowned as his arm lowered halfway. "So, there's no real evidence left?"

"No," I said as calmly as I could manage. "Tom's gone now. You can let us go. Your fortunes are safe."

The churring song of a nightingale came from outside.

"I wondered where Dunning was getting all his information. He was the real thing, or he was an excellent con man. Either way, he couldn't be allowed to stay." Clarence rolled his shoulders and lifted the gun, fixing his aim on me. "But you're wrong, I can't just let you go. I won't face the threat of blackmail a third time."

My heartbeat clunked before starting up again. The edges of Clarence went fuzzy, and I squinted to see him better. "Third?"

"Oh, that. Some years ago, one of Father's grooms caught me liberating horses from the family stables to cover my debts. I'm afraid he was rather insistent, tried to rip the reins out of my hands—as if I didn't practically own the beasts. Had to shoot the poor fellow to get him to give up." He took a step forward as though he too were having trouble seeing in the gloom.

I clenched my fists and tasted revenge. This man had killed Da.

"Goodwin covered it up for me, but Lewis witnessed the entire thing and came to me with a nasty little deal to keep quiet. I couldn't stand it one more second, so when he showed up at my bedroom the other night, drunk and insulting, demanding more money, I taught him the high cost of crossing me." Clarence set his jaw. "That's what I do with people who are in my way."

I swallowed, forcing myself not to react. Clarence murdered Da. Lord Vernet and Goodwin, they'd known the most painful secret of my entire life and treated it like it was nothing more than a business deal. Hate rippled under my skin like a wild animal in a sack. I wanted to tear Clarence's cheeks to shreds. But if I did that, he would win.

Even if we survived, it would be his word weighed against mine, and the scales were broken in his favor. Anger clouded my vision, and I could barely see. I forced myself to speak. "That's why you courted Lady Holmes. If she married you, then you'd have leverage over her brother."

Clarence snorted. "I say, that would've been clever, but no. You see, I too am a practical man. My late mother was a very rich woman. Unfortunately, she wrote her will so that her money is tied up in a trust until I marry. No solicitor I've visited has been able to break it. Debts have a way of growing, and Violet is a suitable match. Not perfect on paper, below my station, but she'll do."

It was still morning, but the door behind him had become a rectangle of weak gray light as the eclipse progressed, my hope fading alongside the sun behind the shadow of the moon. Violet had better hurry.

I scrabbled through my thoughts for something else to say. Anything that would distract a few moments longer. "That's a sorry reason to marry someone. When she finds out, I can't imagine she would—"

"It doesn't matter what a maid can or cannot imagine. I have Dunning to deal with, and I can't waste more time waiting for Goodwin to arrive. He'll just have to take care of the mess when he gets here." Clarence gestured at us with the pistol. "I'd advise you to turn around for this part, but I doubt the good inspector could explain how you both managed to shoot each other in the back. Perhaps you should just close your eyes."

I kept them wide open.

He shrugged and aimed his pistol at my chest.

The outline of a tall person in a slouched hat filled the doorway. I reached out to grasp Billy by the hand, tugging him closer. He squeezed until my knuckles creaked, but I couldn't see him in the gloom.

The silhouette leaped from the doorway onto Clarence's back with the *clang* of metal on wood. The two went down in a dark tangle, slamming into the crate that held the pitcher. It clattered to the floor.

"Run!" I shouted and dragged Billy to the door.

He didn't need any further encouragement, but broke free from my grasp and sprinted ahead. Within moments he faded into the faltering morning light, disappearing into the strange twilight around us. I hefted my skirts and took off after him.

A few seconds later, the unmistakable crack of a gunshot ripped through the fog.

I whirled, teeth clenched against pain that didn't come.

Where had Billy gone? Where was Ralph?

Clarence staggered from the door of the barn and shouted. He swung from side to side as though searching for something. I froze.

It was so dark.

In my black dress, unless I moved, he wouldn't see me against the inky outlines of the trees ahead. His eyes skipped over me, then circled back again like a blow to the chest. My ears rang. I couldn't hear the pounding of my heart, only how each beat flooded me with fear. He stumbled forward, and his arm whipped back and forth, first taking aim at me, then away, then back once again.

Before I had time to duck, a second gunshot cracked open the world. The bullet zipped by my cheek. I dove into the grass as a third gunshot echoed through the river valley. Clarence gave a muffled roar, as I peered through the weeds. He dropped to his knees and collapsed to the ground writhing.

I stood and inched through the grass back toward the barn, knees shaking. Should I grab Clarence's pistol? What if he was faking his injury?

A dark shape peeled itself away from the barn and stooped to pick something up.

"Ralph!" I rushed to him. His face was pale as death, but he held two guns steady in his hands.

"Lady Holmes gave me her revolver, but I didn't think … Katy, I shot him." Ralph looked sick.

Clarence scuffled against the earth, where a strip of blood so dark it was almost black marred the grass. Out of the mist, Billy reappeared, taking it all in with wary eyes.

"Guard Clarence." I clutched Ralph's arm. "Billy, go and

get help. The police and a doctor!"

Then I dove back into the barn. Enough light had returned that I could make out the still form on the floor. I flung myself down at Violet's side.

She was dressed in slacks and a jacket again, long hair tucked under a slouched cap, but I would recognize her anywhere.

"Hudson. You're supposed to be in jail," she said, her jaw set as though speaking caused her pain.

My hands fluttered to where she grasped her shoulder, blood staining her fingers scarlet. "What have you done?"

She grimaced, her breathing shallow. "Saved you from a fate worse than becoming a biddable wife."

I grabbed the blanket from the pile of straw and spread it over her. "Shh, don't talk. I sent Billy for the doctor and the authorities. Not that it'll help us if Goodwin shows up."

"Goodwin's in the custody of Scotland Yard. That slowed them down a little, but they should be here in no more than eight minutes."

I scowled, jaw open. "How on earth ...?"

"Ninety minutes for you to find Billy, seven minutes to talk to Clarence, and one minute to wrench the gun from his grasp." She bit her lip and closed her eyes for a long moment. "I miscalculated that last item, though not catastrophically. I couldn't have lived with myself if you'd been hurt."

I squeezed her shaking hand and leaned close to give her as much of my meager warmth as I could. "Well, if you die before I can be properly angry with you for sending me to jail, I shall quit."

"That's my Hudson, still so dramatic." She closed her eyes.

I panicked and chafed her cheek. "Violet! Violet, open your eyes."

She sighed but opened them again. "As your employer, I want you to know I'm listening to your concerns."

Tears burned my eyes and dropped onto the blanket like spilled ink. "I don't know how you did it, but thank you," I whispered, "for saving us. And not just today. Even when I would've gladly tossed you in the river, you challenged me and shocked me out of my grief. You made me grasp for more, Violet. I couldn't have done it without you."

Her bloody fingers intertwined with mine where they pressed at her shoulder. "You would have. When we first met, you stared at Musgrave Hall like you wanted to burn it down. And—"

"I wasn't, I didn't." She had to know I didn't feel that way about her, not anymore.

"No, you did, Hudson. I recognized the look. I've seen it in the mirror often enough." Violet hissed and took an unsteady breath. "I've longed to take the place apart stone by stone and stick by stick. Return it to the earth in a riot of fire and freedom. Throw open the doors and let nature undertake its inexorable work."

Our eyes caught each other's, never wavering. Something clicked into place in my chest, and a deep well of understanding overflowed, washing over my skin.

"I didn't even know your name," she said, "but I couldn't stand the idea of never seeing you again. What burned in you, the same burns in me. I needed to let you know. We are the same, you and I."

The world paused. The old barn, the sounds of birds repeating their dawn chorus as the eclipse faded and the world found its light once again, they all grew distant. I leaned down and pressed my forehead to hers. Together, we tilted our heads until our lips locked in place.

It wasn't hunger. The feeling lay somewhere beyond, satisfying a need even deeper and more painful. The nectar of it tasted all the sweeter because I had starved for so long. Because I had thought I would never taste its like again. Because, in truth, I had never eaten this deeply, had never drunk my fill.

The honey of it was dark and complex, but this time, I hoped I wouldn't let it slip from my fingers.

Epilogue

THE SHERRINFORD GRAVEYARD EXTENDED BEYOND the town. From the back of our church and down an uneven slope toward the forest to the north, it grew a little longer each year. Since it was a Sunday afternoon, families picnicked near the final resting places of their loved ones. The sounds of children playing among the motley collection of headstones drifted to where I sat on a stone bench, staring at the Holmes family plot.

Tucked under towering trees along the eastern edge and surrounded by a wrought-iron fence, the marble monuments and ornate mausoleum dominated the space much the way Musgrave Hall anchored Sherrinford and the surrounding countryside.

I frowned at the headstone in front of me, then at the basket by my feet, and leaned down to reach for the last item.

"You won't eat the seedcake or the sweet buns, but will you at least try one of the currant scones?" I unwrapped the small bundle.

Violet, her face still more pale than I liked, eyed the golden-brown pastries with a measured look. "My dear Hudson, always trying to tempt me."

Even though we were alone, my cheeks flushed. "I beg your pardon?"

"Biscuits, scones, a bit of cake. I never touch them, but they appear next to my teacup like a genie from a lamp. Why?"

What could I say? That I dreaded the pinched lines of her cheeks? That seeing the bones under her skin left me picturing her resting beside her husband in the family crypt? That everyone deserved a little sweetness? But we'd barely seen each other these last few weeks as she burned with fever, let alone made any declarations about what we meant to each other. I almost lost her once. Too much rode on my answer, and the words stumbled on my tongue.

"I thought you might be hungry." I handed her a scone and watched with satisfaction as she took one bite and then another.

Ma and Frances sat on a blanket at the end of the row where Da was buried, chatting with Elizabeth, Billy, Ralph, Georgie, and his sweetheart, Amelia. They'd already come over to give their thanks to Violet, cluck at her arm wrapped in a sling, and wish her a speedy recovery. Then they'd scooped up Sherlock, and it wasn't long before he and my siblings were fast friends.

"Will Mycroft be home soon?" I asked.

"Yes, for the summer." She frowned. "Sherlock will be delighted."

"And you?"

The church bell tolled the hour, its final tone echoing across the hills.

"I'm not sure. We used to be close, but he hasn't been the same since his father's death. Things were strained between us before he left."

"Grief is a strange monster." My eyes wandered to Da's squat headstone. "Mycroft will work through it."

We ate our scones together in silence, watching Sherlock play pirates with Oliver, Louise, and Rosie across the graveyard. Oliver's pale cheeks flooded with healthful color for once, his breathing clear as he ran. The new medicine from Dr. McNulty was working wonders.

"Usually, our thoughts run on similar tracks, Hudson, but you haven't asked about the plan for our future."

I bit my lip. "I wasn't sure we had a plan."

"I'm not dead, so you can't quit." She leaned into my shoulder for a moment, but I didn't smile. "Is this about Lewis' dire predictions as to the Holmes fortune?"

"You never denied them."

She waved a hand. "I may have been young and naive when I married Arthur, but I wasn't blind. He ran through money so quickly I knew I needed to secure my own. The London Stock Exchange is a much more secure investment than racehorses."

Delight spread from my chest until my fingertips tingled. "On that topic, has your brother recovered from his injuries?"

Violet brushed a crumb from her soft gray skirt. "He's now equal to the tasks of berating his sons, ordering about his wife, and demanding I abandon my useless study of astronomy and marry his elderly banker who recently became a widower."

I laughed indignantly. "You used an eclipse to save my

life! Please don't give up your useless astronomy." My smile faded. "I'm so sorry you had to miss viewing your once-in-a-lifetime eclipse."

"Total solar eclipses happen approximately every eighteen months and are easy to predict. It was you I never saw coming." Her wide green eyes tipped toward emerald, and I thrilled to see it. "Speaking of near misses, Dunning was spotted in London, but Scotland Yard failed to apprehend him."

"The case against Clarence can proceed without him, though?"

"I have every assurance it is. Since Dunning disappeared, Lewis' testimony is crucial. Although we still have the seized correspondence between Goodwin and Clarence, as well as Goodwin's secret case notes." She tilted her face to the sun filtering through the sprouting leaves above. "It was thoughtful of him to so thoroughly catalog his sins."

"Is that how you got Scotland Yard to run all the way to Sherrinford on short notice?" I asked.

I'd written in somewhat oblique terms of our adventures to Eleanor and Samuel, but once the news hit the papers, they'd demanded a full accounting. Their correspondence had once again kept me company during a dark time, while Violet convalesced.

"No, actually. Remember Arthur's ambitious cousin, Sergeant Forrester? I sent him a series of increasingly strident telegrams demanding that if he didn't arrive by the next morning, he would not only be responsible for several deaths but would also lose his chance to make at least two high-profile arrests." Violet adjusted the top of her sling to ease the pressure on her neck. "He would like to apprehend

Mr. Dunning in connection with a forgery ring in London. The good sergeant has collected all of the practice forged telegrams, birth, and marriage certificates from Tom's rooms in Eastbourne where he and Mr. Dunning had been preparing for their blackmail scheme. He even located the loose floorboard that scratched the bottoms of their shoes. It's quite a tidy case. I hear he's to be made an inspector."

I smiled. "So, he's in your debt?"

She pressed her lips together. "I doubt he'll think of it like that."

"Well, it'll be a novelty to have a police officer who's not trying to frame me for murder."

Violet stared at the Holmes family monument then settled her unnerving gaze back on my face. "You may just ask me about it, Hudson."

Part of me wanted to feign ignorance over her meaning, but the other part was too curious. "You kissed him!" I said, more angrily than I planned.

"Of course I did. We'd already exhausted the topics of firearms and horses. If he was going to tell me anything useful, I needed to move on to kissing." She sniffed. "Seventy-eight seconds of detached boredom bought me enough trust that he revealed his plan to frame you as well as Lewis, from which I also gleaned Lewis had been blackmailing him about your father's murder."

The idea was still so new I couldn't help but wear the pain on my face.

"I'm sorry I excluded you from that side of the investigation," Violet said, the hand of her uninjured arm opening and closing on the bench where it rested next to mine.

Our skirts offered cover as I locked our fingers together.

"I understand why you kept it from me. You don't have to apologize."

"Perhaps, but it's much easier to break things than it is to put them back together. I didn't want to leave my regret unsaid between us."

The wind sighed through the trees, gathering up the chatter of our families as though it were all one sound, without sense but rich with meaning.

"Do you ever think about all the things that are said that no one hears? Whispered prayers or curses. Farewells," I said, my finger tapping out a quick message on the bench beside me. "Sometimes, if the lines had failed or your equipment malfunctioned, you'd send an entire telegram before you realized no one was listening. Just *dits* and *dahs* wandering off who knows where." Inside me, the tender house that had sheltered my grief put out the last lamp in its windows as I slowly shut the door. "I suppose it's better than the things you never get to say to those you love."

With a laugh, Sherlock leaped from the bench he'd clambered onto, makeshift sword held aloft. The twins chased him toward the trees.

"Much like it's easier to forget than it is to remember," Violet murmured. "Dr. McNulty says the infection is almost cleared, you know. If you want to go and visit John's grave, I promise to be here when you return."

"I can't."

Her eyebrows lifted.

"Since he died in an accident at work, the Post Office offered to pay for the interment. I couldn't afford to bring him home, so I accepted the spot in the Brompton Catacombs."

"Oh, Hudson." Violet frowned at the Holmes family mausoleum about ten yards away.

"You're lucky," I said.

"Pardon me?"

"You can visit Arthur anytime you like."

A long silence dropped between us.

"Sorry," I said, "I shouldn't have brought it up."

She squeezed my hand. "Is it terrible this is the first time I've visited Arthur's grave since his funeral?"

A cluster of purple flowers, violets, grew on the ground beside the bench. I bent to pick one and tucked it into her hand. "I've never known you to do something you didn't deem necessary."

She rolled the delicate stem between her fingers, and the sweet scent lifted into the air.

"Arthur married me for the same reason he bought his horses: because Lewis told him to. I should've refused, but I was too young to know better. He was amused by me, my eccentricities and interests. Like a fine mare that demands only this or that comb or who has a favorite corner of the paddock. He humored me. He housed me. My quirks and desires were tolerated so long as I showed well and bred soundly."

I snorted, but she shook her head, eyes serious. "Before I met you, the thought of coming here reminded me I was destined to die alone. In my husband's fine house, surrounded by my husband's fine things, I would leave no mark on the world except for a set of heirs wearing my husband's face."

"Lady Violet Vernet Holmes? Leave no mark upon the world?" I dipped my head to catch her pained gaze. "Why,

I heard she was the one who drove a wedge into every crack in the system until it lay about her, shattered."

Oliver took a bad spill over a low headstone, and I held my breath. However, Sherlock dropped his wooden sword and knelt beside him, then helped him to his feet. The two of them chased after Louise, their childish laughter caught by the weathered marble and limestone monuments for a moment before it finally found its way free.

Violet smiled and stroked my knuckles with her thumb. "Perhaps. However, she didn't do it alone."

Lady Holmes and Hudson will return in

A MOST REMARKABLE FORGERY

Coming May 2027

Acknowledgements

WRITING THIS BOOK WAS BOTH A STRUGGLE AS well as a joy, and I was lucky to have a fabulous group of people with me along the way. Thank you to the wonderful team at Azantian Literary and especially my incomparable agent, Mara Hollander, whose dedication, enthusiasm, and creativity never fail to inspire me. I'll take a break at some point, I promise. Truly, every writer should be so lucky as to find such a champion for their work.

Enormous thanks to my editors, Peyton Stableford, Anouska Levy, and Tania Doney, as well as the many other talented team members at Head of Zeus and Bloomsbury for their insights, hard work, and expertise. Thank you for giving this story a home and seeing that it arrived with its hair combed and boots shined.

To Bethany Hensel whose clever feedback on the opening pages sharpened the voice and the setting in such fun ways. To the Pitched to Published Writers and the Corning Writers Group for being supportive and welcoming communities for writers of all levels.

Writing is famously a lonely pursuit, but writing friends are the best workaround for that. Thank you to my precious Soup Club and the Raccoon Den. You're brilliant. I love you all. Never change, unless it's to get even weirder.

My beta readers approached the heavy lifting like absolute champs. Anna, Christy, Dawn, Jerry, Michelle, and my dad—thank you for encouraging me, listening to me plot and whine and dream. You were so kind when you pointed out my many errors and so generous in your support that it brought only more joy to the process.

Readers in general are just amazing! Thank *you* for taking a chance on this book. I hope you stick around for more.

To my intrepid alpha readers (aka: my family), thank you for handling the story gently when it was a baby and only capable of sustaining praise. In addition, thank you to my mom and dad, my husband, and to my kids for their patience, encouragement, and unflagging support. You're the best, and I probably still owe you donuts.

And finally, thank you to my delightful husband for generously allowing me to credit both him and his vasectomy in the dedication of this book. Without both of them, this book truly wouldn't exist. I'd like to say I'll never tell anyone the full lore, but I will tell absolutely anyone. Just ask. If you've made it this far into the acknowledgments, you deserve a fun story.

About the Author

MATTEA ORR holds a Master's in English Literature from Binghamton University. Her most recent short stories appear in the anthologies *Transcendent* from Transmundane Press, *Toil & Trouble Literary Magazine*, and *Witch House Magazine*. She lives in upstate New York with her partner, three children, and any number of cats, where the natural landscape and lore inspire her writing.